A JESAL THRILLER

by
Larry A. Winters

Copyright © 2013 by Larry A. Winters

All rights reserved. No part of this book may be reproduced or transmitted in any form or by any means, electronic or mechanical, without the written permission of the author.

This book is a work of fiction. Names, characters, places and incidents are either products of the author's imagination or used fictitiously. Any resemblance to actual events, locales, or persons, living or dead, is entirely coincidental.

for Joan

1.

After a six-hour drive, Woody got his first good look at the death house. He climbed out of his car and stretched his cramped limbs. The stench from the complex stole much of the sweetness from the crisp October air. *No surprise there.* Like other prisons, SCI Greene exuded an almost palpable stink, something like sweat and old bowling shoes. A bus—carrying either prisoners or their visitors—rumbled off the highway behind him and paused at the perimeter fences he'd just passed through. *Time to get moving.*

He carried only what he needed—a counterfeit driver's license, a forged letter from the Philadelphia Legal Aid Society, and Gil Goldhammer's retainer letter.

Inside the main building, he quickly identified the lobby officer, a middle-aged man with a face that looked like it had been carved out of rock. A nameplate identified him as Officer John Rice. Rigid posture and a spotless, perfectly pressed uniform gave Rice a military air which, Woody knew, would not be unusual in this place. Rice had likely served in one of the armed forces—most of the personnel here had. SCI Greene was the most secure facility in the Pennsylvania correctional system, the home of Pennsylvania's most brutal criminals, including over a hundred men on death row.

Behind Lobby Officer Rice, a laminated poster detailed the prison's visitation policy. Woody scanned the rules, pausing at the list of individuals prohibited from visiting inmates:

- Former inmates of any correctional system;
- Any person who is currently under parole or probation supervision;
- Any current inmate in pre-release status;
- Any DOC employee;
- Any former DOC employee;
- Any currently active volunteer for the DOC;
- Any current or former contract employee; or
- Any victim of the inmate.

Although one of these described Woody, none described the person identified on Woody's counterfeit driver's license, which he handed to Rice.

"I'm here to see Frank Ramsey."

Rice glanced at the driver's license, then studied Woody. It had occurred to Woody that one of the COs here might recognize him. While he was almost certain he'd never met Officer Rice, the man's scrutiny twisted a sliver of fear in his stomach. He reminded himself of the changes in his appearance: He was three years older now. His figure, once bulging with steroid-fed muscle, was now slim, unremarkable underneath his clothing. He wore his hair cropped close to his head, and he'd grown a goatee. He touched that patch of facial hair now and the bristles reassured him. He would not be recognized.

Rice opened a file on his desk. "I don't see your name on Ramsey's visitor list, Mr. Butler."

BURNOUT

"I work for Mr. Ramsey's attorney." Woody reached into the inside pocket of his leather jacket—Rice tensed at the motion—and withdrew the forged letter. Under the letterhead of the Philadelphia Legal Aid Society, a few sentences written in the name of Ramsey's *pro bono* appellate lawyer identified Donald W. Butler as his paralegal. The document looked real, and Rice didn't question it. He stamped Woody's hand with invisible ink.

"Ramsey's Custody Level 5. Are you familiar with the rules?"

"Yes."

Rice looked like he might recite them anyway, but a noisy group bustled into the lobby. The passengers from the bus, probably relatives and loved ones from Philly or some other city distant from this remote southwest corner of the state. Rice turned his attention to them and waved Woody toward a metal detector.

Woody passed through the metal detector. He tried to ignore the numerous eyes—human and electronic—that he knew were tracking his every move. This place held murderers, rapists, and every other manner of violent offender, and it was appropriately locked down. After only five or six steps, he faced two more guards.

"You the guy visiting the Family Man?" the younger of the two guards said.

"His name is Ramsey." Woody didn't need to feign offense at the guard's use of Ramsey's nickname. It genuinely pissed him off. The media's idiotic practice of naming serial killers as if they were superheroes was bad enough. A correctional officer should know better than to buy into the bullshit.

"What are you carrying?" the other guard said. Like Rice, he had a military bearing. A frosty white crewcut and flat cheeks made his head look like a cube, and a shallow scar running from the corner of his mouth to his chin suggested he'd seen some combat, either in a foreign country or the concrete and steel battlefield of SCI Greene. Or maybe he'd just tripped at the playground when he was a kid. A tag on his uniform identified him as CO Earl Gunn.

Woody held up Gil Goldhammer's retainer letter, the only document on him that was real. "Legal document," he said. "I need Ramsey's signature."

"Let me see it," Gunn said.

Woody tightened his grip on the paper. "Sorry, Officer. Attorney-client privilege."

"Doesn't matter. I need to check it for contraband." He yanked it from Woody's hand, flipped through the three-page letter as if a chisel or a machine gun might fall out. When he handed it back to Woody, the paper was bent and marred by a smudged thumb print. "Here ya go."

Woody forced a polite smile. "My client is going to need a pen."

Gunn sighed, turned to the other officer. "Get me a flex pen." *Flex pen* was prison-lingo for the special pen consisting of a small ballpoint ink refill set in a four-inch cylinder of soft rubber tubing, a pen even the most homicidal or suicidal inmate would find unworkable as a weapon.

The younger guard handed the flex pen to Gunn, who handed it to Woody. "Get a few extra autographs, you can sell them on Ebay for fifty bucks a pop."

Woody thought this might be true. Frank Ramsey's crimes and trial had been front-page news. He had no doubt that hundreds—maybe thousands—of people would bid for his signature.

"That's not what I'm here for."

Gunn's condescending smile faltered. "Do I know you from somewhere?"

He didn't like the way the CO was staring at him. There were cameras on him as well, and the last thing he wanted was for Gunn, curious, to show his picture to his friends. "I've been in some newspaper photos, in connection with Mr. Ramsey's appeal."

This was a lie. Woody had no connection to Frank Ramsey's appeal, which had been handled—and lost—by a neophyte Legal Aid attorney.

"That must be it." Gunn nodded and Woody's lungs exhaled a quiet breath of relief.

He passed through a series of doors that were locked and unlocked by remote guard posts. The *thunks* of the locks brought back unpleasant memories, but he had little time to dwell on them.

Inmates in the general population enjoyed the luxury of meeting their visitors in the relaxed setting of the visiting room. Food and drinks were available, and the inmates were allowed limited physical contact with their visitors. They could sit side-by-side with their loved ones, embrace when meeting and departing.

Ramsey was not a member of the general population. He was in the RHU—Restricted Housing Unit—separated from the rest of the prison, and accessible only by interior walkways. Ramsey spent twenty-three hours of every day alone in his cell in G Block, one of the sections of the RHU reserved for convicts sentenced to die by lethal injection.

Woody met Frank Ramsey in a small, secure room with two guards posted outside the door. No physical contact was permitted in here, and that was fine with Woody—he hadn't come for a hug. A metal table, stained and sticky with patches of some substance he chose not to contemplate, separated him from the inmate.

Ramsey regarded him with a prisoner's stare, a guarded look accentuated by the dark hollows around his eyes. His face had lost some of the fullness and the ruddiness it possessed in the video clips that played on TV whenever a fresh bit of news emerged about him, but even so, prison had failed to diminish him the way it did most men.

He wore a blue "visiting" jumpsuit, which he had likely changed into moments before entering the room. In SCI Greene, there was a jumpsuit for every occasion. Cocoa-brown for the general population, white for the kitchen workers, gray for inmates on work detail outside the prison perimeter, orange for the workers inside. Inmates classified at Custody Level 5, like Ramsey, wore gray-and-white stripes like a kid's Halloween costume. But all inmates were required to change into blue "visiting" jumpsuits before meeting people from the outside. The better for guards to identify who was supposed to be where—and who was not.

The ragged specimen that clung to Ramsey's body didn't look very clean. It had probably been worn by at least a couple of other inmates today, maybe more. As long as it had been washed once in the past month, it would be considered clean by the standards of prison hygiene. On Ramsey, the thing looked too small. He'd retained his impressive physique. Woody half-expected the material to split down the center of his chest if he shifted his shoulders.

A pair of handcuffs reflected the dim overhead light like

cheap jewelry. They bit deep into the flesh of Ramsey's wrists, where the skin was red and pocked with scabs and sores. Woody wondered how many hours of the day Frank endured those shackles. He probably wore them constantly, even showered in them. Kill enough people, and even seasoned prison guards will prefer not to take chances.

Seconds passed like minutes. Ramsey spoke first. "You're not my attorney."

"No." Not taking his eyes from the man, Woody placed the retainer letter and the flex pen on the desk. "My name is Donald Butler. You can call me Woody."

Ramsey nodded. "I'd shake your hand, Woody, but I'm not in the mood for a beating today." He nodded at the guards watching them through reinforced windows in the door. "No offense."

"Trust me, I have no desire to shake your hand, Mr. Ramsey."

The insult didn't faze him. After over a year in the RHU, it would take more than casual cruelty to ruffle him. He said, "Call me Frank."

"Are you familiar with a lawyer by the name of Gil Goldhammer?"

Ramsey shook his head. "He the one sent you?"

Woody had prepared for this meeting, but staring into the man's eyes was getting to him more than he'd anticipated. He felt a sudden urge to flee, to grab Goldhammer's letter and the tiny prison pen, and bolt.

He clasped his hands together, concentrated on the contrast between the smooth, soft texture of the skin between his knuckles and the hardness of the bony joints, a relaxation ritual he'd taught himself.

He breathed.

"Something wrong, Woody?"

"Gil Goldhammer is one of the best criminal defense attorneys in the country. He's defended celebrities, politicians. Maybe you read about Jorge Bonilla, the Florida businessman accused of importing cocaine from Colombia?"

Ramsey shook his head. "I don't get much news in here. Warden turned down my request for an iPad."

"Gil got him acquitted six months ago." He pushed the letter and the pen closer to Ramsey. "This is a retainer letter. Sign it and Gil will become your counsel of record."

"If I could afford the best lawyer in the country, do you think I'd be represented by a girl just graduated from law school last May?"

"You don't need to worry about that. The financial arrangements have already been worked out."

Instead of grabbing the flex pen, scrawling his signature, and thanking Woody on his hands and knees—which is what a sane man in Ramsey's position would have done—the killer burst into laughter.

"Maybe you haven't noticed, Woody, but a jury's already convicted me. My first lawyer, from the public defender's office, petitioned the trial judge to reconsider the verdict, but—big surprise—he denied it. Then I got a new lawyer, from the Legal Aid Society. She's the one just recently passed the bar. She wrote up my appeal and argued it, but—again, big surprise—the Superior Court affirmed. Few weeks ago, she came by here to give me the happy news that the Pennsylvania Supreme Court has refused to hear my case. So you see,

Woody, unless this lawyer pal of yours is butt-buddies with the governor himself, I'm fucked."

Woody regulated his breathing, concentrated on the tactile stimuli of his hands. The urge to run had receded, but now he was seeing himself smashing Ramsey's face against the filthy surface of the table, shattering his nose, knocking out a tooth—and that was worse. There were guards outside the door. There were walls and locks all around him, razor wire around that, guard towers, assault rifles. He was inside the highest security section of a maximum security prison and this was abso-fucking-lutely *not* the place to lose control.

He thought of his brother. Don't let him down. Don't you dare let him down this time, Woody.

Ramsey was staring at him. His angry laughter had subsided, and with it the only spark of life he'd shown since entering the room. He looked hollow again, hopeless.

Good.

"I'm not a lawyer," Woody said. "Gil has assured me that you are not out of options. He's going to get you out of here."

"I'm sorry if I don't sound grateful to you. But when you're in here long enough, you get careful about your feelings. Especially hope. Hope's a treacherous feeling in here."

Woody thought of his brother again. Hope was in short supply in many quarters.

Ramsey picked up the flex pen, and flipped to the final page of the retainer letter without reading a word of it. The chain connecting his wrists jingled merrily as he signed his name.

"You know what Mumia Abu-Jamal called this place?" Ramsey said. "A bright, shiny hell."

"Here's some advice," Woody said, not looking at him. "You want to get out of here with your heart still beating, find someone to quote besides a convicted cop killer." He took the letter, folded it, returned it to the inside pocket of his leather jacket, and stood up.

"Hey." Ramsey was watching him intently. "Why are you doing this? What's in it for you?"

Nothing comes without a price—a typical criminal's assumption, natural when your worldview includes neither mercy nor kindness, where friendship and love are myths.

But hey, in this case it was accurate.

Woody offered him a half-smile. "You'll find out soon enough."

2.

A familiar bell *tinked* as Jessie shoved open the stiff door to Quick Mart and shouldered her way inside. The owner, Alish, didn't even glance up from his Armenian newspaper to acknowledge her, even though she'd been coming here every weekday morning for years. *Morning to you, too.* She moved through the narrow aisle toward the back of the store, half on autopilot at 6:00 AM, drawn by the smell of coffee.

Alish's convenience store didn't have the selection of a Wawa—or the fresh air and elbow room, for that matter—but it did have a couple key things going for it. First, it was really close to work. Only a couple of steps from the Philadelphia District Attorney's Office, where her coffee would still be hot when she settled behind her desk. And second, that coffee. The smell was fully in her head now, tingling in her nose and on her tongue, as the grimy carafes came into view beyond the racks of Doritos and Tastykakes. The best coffee in Philly.

She was filling her travel mug when she saw the kid out of the corner of her eye. He wore jeans and a sweatshirt with the hood up, a few flakes of snow still melting in the black material. He held a magazine in his right hand, but his left hand picked four-packs of Duracell batteries from the rack and slipped them into the wide front pocket of the hoodie. He was good, but not good enough to get away with it here. She shook her head. Let him learn his lesson the hard way. She had a ton of work waiting for her down the street.

But something about the kid—maybe the youthful face shadowed by the hood—made her think of Kristen Dillard. Rationally, she knew this stranger had nothing to do with the fragile, orphaned crime victim recovering at Philadelphia Center for Inclusive Treatment, but sometimes rationality lost out to instinct—especially before any coffee hit her brain. She sighed and stepped beside him. "I wouldn't do that if I were you."

He whirled on her with narrowed eyes. "Do what?"

She tilted her travel mug at his sweatshirt pocket. "That."

He rolled his eyes, turning away. "Yeah, why don't you mind your own business?"

"I'm an assistant district attorney. This is my business. Not that I prosecute shoplifters anymore, or juveniles. But I did enough of that when I was starting out. And you'd be surprised how many of my cases involved this store."

He chewed his lip. "What are you talking about?"

She gestured at the security camera bolted to the wall near the ceiling, dusty and enmeshed in cobwebs. "That thing works, believe it or not. And the old man's been watching you for the last five minutes. He looks like he's reading, but Alish has eyes in his forehead. Probably already called the police."

"Bullshit."

"And he will press charges. He always does. He loves going to court."

The kid seemed to hesitate, then his left hand began to unload his pocket. He didn't thank her for the advice, or even say goodbye, before strolling out of the store. The bell jangled and he was gone.

She walked to the front of the store, put her mug on the counter, and pulled her wallet from her bag. Alish, gazing longingly at the door after the would-be battery thief, said, "Why you gotta ruin all my fun?"

"Give me a free coffee and I'll let you have the next one."

He snorted and gave her something close to a smile. "What is it you lawyers say? I'll take that under advisement."

She was pulling two dollars from her wallet when her phone vibrated. She passed the money to Alish and answered the call. The person on the other end of the line, one of her contacts at the courthouse, started telling her about a recently filed petition. Her face must have betrayed what she was hearing, because the old Armenian left her money on the counter and looked at her worriedly.

"Everything okay, Jessie?"

She shook her head. "No. Not at all."

The first things Jessie noticed when she barged into her boss's office twenty minutes later were the protein shake in place of his usual bacon-egg-and-cheese sandwich and a pair of running shoes in the corner. Otherwise, the office of the head of the Philadelphia District Attorney's Homicide Unit looked the same as ever—cramped, lightless, and overflowing with paper. She had to gently push a stack of documents aside with her foot just to edge into the room.

"Hard to believe it's only November," Warren said, and she heard the complaint in his voice as he watched snowflakes slant past his window. He leaned back in his swivel chair, springs creaking loudly under his weight, and shook his head. "So much for my plan to start jogging during lunch."

"Sounds similar to the plan you had three months ago, before you realized it was too hot."

He took a sip from his protein shake and made a face. "How can I fail with a cheerleader like you in my corner? But I'm guessing you didn't stop by to talk about physical fitness."

"You know why I'm here," Jessie said.

"Yes." He glanced down. Piles of documents covered every inch of his desk. The man seemed to have a compulsion to print hard copies of everything—even e-mails. She couldn't have said what the surface of his desk looked like, as she'd never seen it. But even among a sea of similar documents, she spotted Ramsey's Post Conviction Relief Act petition before he lifted it from the top of a stack beside his keyboard.

The corner was stapled, but she didn't see any fold. "You didn't read it yet?" she said.

His face looked sallow, puffy, but her three years in the Homicide Unit had taught her that these were his natural features. "Do you know how many PCRA petitions cross my desk in a—"

"This one isn't typical."

Warren sighed. "Because it's for our infamous Family Man? Come on, Jessie. How many times has Ramsey tried to appeal his conviction? And failed? There's nothing to appeal. No holes in your case. Relax. The Appeals Unit will knock this one down and Ramsey will march one step closer to his lethal injection." He let the petition drop back on its pile and turned to his monitor. *End of discussion*, apparently.

"I'm not sure it's going to be that simple." She squared

her shoulders. "I think I should handle the response, just to be sure."

He barked a laugh, and took another slurp of his protein shake. "Post-trial chores are the responsibility of the Appeals Unit, you know that."

"I can do a better job."

"No shit. But it's not your job. You need to convict the next murderer, not dwell on past cases. It's not like you have a lot of free time." He turned to look at the oversized dry erase calendar on the wall behind his desk, where her name appeared over and over again. "And besides, the newbies need to practice on something."

Was that supposed to make her feel better? She bit her lip, remembering her own rise from the Appeals Unit through the Juvenile Unit, to the Felony Waiver Unit, to the Trials Division, and, finally, to Homicide. Thinking of her skill level as a fresh-faced law school grad only made her more uncomfortable trusting Ramsey's petition to a rookie.

"You know this is personal for me," she said.

He looked up sharply. "Oh, I'm not likely to forget."

Heat rushed to her cheeks, but she forced herself to maintain eye contact. "I'm not talking about Detective Leary."

Leary had been a mistake, a one-night thing, and if she could go back in time and undo the adrenaline- and alcohol-fueled sex they'd had in Leary's car in the alley behind the Thirsty Giraffe Pub where half the police department and DA's office had celebrated the end of the Ramsey trial, she wouldn't hesitate. She'd certainly knock out the legal blogger who'd managed to take a fuzzy phone pic and post it on his (mercifully low-traffic) website. The best sex she'd ever had, and the dumbest.

"An affair with the lead detective." Warren stabbed a finger at the petition. "I hope that's not in here."

"It's not. And I'm talking about Kristen Dillard."

"I know." He spread his hands, and for a brief moment he actually looked sympathetic. "Look, I know you got close with the girl. You're not the first prosecutor to form a bond like that. It's a hazard of the job. But there's nothing I can do. This is protocol. Standard operating procedure."

"Not if you convince the DA to make an exception."

That elicited another laugh. "You think this is Rivera's first rodeo? The fact that Ramsey got a lot of press is not going to scare him into assigning a top homicide prosecutor to handle a Hail Mary PCRA petition."

Top homicide prosecutor? She liked the sound of that, but wasn't about to let Warren flatter away her valid concerns. "Some Hail Marys win the game. Read the petition. You can't trust a rookie to deal with this. Did you even look at the signature at the end?"

He flipped to it now. Made a face.

"Yeah," Jessie said. "Gil Goldhammer. He's not a lawyer we can afford to underestimate, right? And besides that, there might be some merit in his argument."

Warren's eyebrows came together. "I thought it was an ineffective assistance of counsel claim. The PCRA judge will toss this after a ten minute hearing. Who represented Ramsey at trial, anyway? I can't remember. Wasn't it someone from the public defender?"

"Yes. Jack Ackerman."

"Ackerman. That sounds familiar." She watched his eyes shift out of focus as he started to put the pieces together. "Oh

Christ."

"Right. The crazy guy. Call Rivera."

She knew she was getting through. Warren was a politician at heart. He must know they had a situation here, one an elected official like District Attorney Jesus Rivera could not ignore. Ramsey had a shot at wriggling out of his conviction because he had been represented at his trial by a lawyer who'd subsequently resigned because of some sort of nervous breakdown. If Ramsey overturned his conviction, every newspaper, blog, radio talk show, and TV broadcast would opine about what went wrong within the city's venerable district attorney's office.

Warren turned to his PC, moved his mouse. "Looks like the Appeals Unit already assigned petition."

"To whom?"

"Elliot Williams." Warren's face colored briefly, and she knew he was referring to his nephew. Jessie had never met the kid, but the rumor mill had not been kind.

"He's pretty new, isn't he?" she said, straining for a diplomatic tone.

Warren tapped a finger to his lower lip, thinking.

"And with him being your nephew and all, if he screws up, wouldn't that reflect on you?"

He held up a hand. "All right, I get it. Maybe, considering your personal investment in this case, a small exception can be made here. The matter will remain with the Appeals Unit, but you'll assist Elliot. I'm sure he would appreciate the help of someone with your experience."

"That's not what I asked for."

"No, but it's what I'm giving you. I'll brief Rivera after

you and Elliot have had a chance to review the file."

She took a breath, willed herself to remain calm. "This is not a mentoring opportunity, Warren. It's an emergency. You must see that."

"It's a PCRA petition. Not a homicide prosecution. I can justify your involvement as a support function based on your knowledge of the trial, but that's as far as I'm willing to push."

"Fine." She had more to say, but bit off the words. Warren wasn't going to budge—she could see that much in the set of his jaw and the hardness in his gaze. Her only option was to do this his way. Not ideal, but not terrible, either—it would get her close to the pleadings, into the courtroom. Even in a support position, she could make a difference. She owed Kristen that much. "I'll keep you posted," she said, and turned to leave.

"You're welcome," Warren said to her back.

3.

Jessie still kept her copy of the Dillard file in a cabinet in her office, although there wasn't much need. For months after the trial, she had seen the pages every time she closed her eyes. Even now, she could recite the facts from memory.

The bodies were found upstairs in the master bedroom. The police had found no broken windows at the crime scene, no signs of forced entry, leading them to conclude that the killer had gained access to the house simply by knocking on the door—a theory later confirmed by the prosecution's eyewitness. The burglar alarm had never been set. The Dillard family had gathered around the TV to watch sitcoms. They had probably planned to engage the alarm before going up to bed a few hours later.

Why had they answered the door? It was a question that still haunted her.

The lead homicide detective on the case, Mark Leary, believed the family was herded upstairs at knife point. Bob Dillard, the father, a forty-three-year-old biochemist, had defensive wounds on his hands and legs, suggesting he had put up a fight. In the master bedroom, his hands were bound behind his back, as were those of his wife and daughter.

According to the medical examiner's report, Bob Dillard had been killed first. His body was found on the floor to the left of his king-size bed. A weapon with a blade at least eight inches in length and slightly less than an inch in width had inflicted seventeen stab wounds to his chest.

His wife Erin was found with a pair of balled-up panties in her mouth. Her attacker had torn them from her body with such force that the thin cotton had bruised her left hip. Her attacker raped her but left no trace evidence. A lubricant common to several brands of condom was the only foreign substance recovered. Like her husband, she was stabbed to death. Eleven stab wounds were found in her chest and upper abdomen, one of which had severed the major artery from her heart.

Their daughter Kristen had been raped and then stabbed three times in the chest, once in the back, and once in the neck.

She was bleeding when the police arrived, and still, barely, alive.

Months later, trembling on the witness stand, she had pointed her finger at Frank Ramsey and positively identified him as the man who had murdered her family and attempted to murder her.

She found Elliot Williams in one of the Appeals Unit's conference rooms. He was sitting at an oval conference table, his back to the door, hunched over a legal pad and some printed pages. He barely looked up to acknowledge her when she stepped into the room and closed the door.

"I'm Jessie Black." She placed her thick file folder on the table in front of him, but she didn't sit down. She crossed her arms over her chest. This was their first meeting, and she wanted to establish a chain of command. This might be his case, but he needed to understand that she would be running the show.

After a moment, he leaned forward and peered up at her. "I know. I got your e-mail."

The room had no windows, and the florescent bulbs humming from the ceiling seemed to tint his face yellow. He was short like his uncle, but unlike Warren, he had a full head of hair. Judging by the severity with which he'd raked it back and plastered it in place, she guessed the chestnut mane was unruly if left to its own devices. Even Elliot's liberally-applied gel failed to contain three wayward strands that stuck out from the top of his head like spears. His hair was the only energetic part of him. The rest slumped in his chair.

"Listen," he said, "I appreciate that you want to help me—I'm grateful—but I know what I'm doing. I don't need a coach."

She took the seat beside him and opened her folder, arranging its contents on the table in front of them. Everything from the initial police reports to the Pennsylvania Supreme Court's denial of *allocatur*. The color photographs and the muddy, photocopied reports and transcripts formed a grim mosaic.

"I'm not here to be your coach, Elliot. I'm here to defeat Ramsey's petition."

"Is that right?"

She sighed. "Working together wasn't my idea, either, but this is how Warren wants this matter handled. Look at the bright side. You might learn something."

"Uh-huh." He turned his attention to the photographs

and documents arrayed in front of him. The color photo of Erin Dillard's stab wounds made him cringe, and he pushed the photo beneath the medical examiner's report that she'd placed beside it. "You might get a kick out of dwelling on gruesome details, but I have everything I need right here." He patted the print-outs on the table. "Standard forms for defeating an ineffective assistance of counsel claim."

"You think all you need is forms?"

"No. I've also been researching case law on the subject. It's damn hard to prove ineffective assistance of counsel. You basically have to show that the lawyer did something so crazy that no competent lawyer would have done it." She must have flinched, because he said, "What?"

"You used the word 'crazy.'"

"So?"

"You don't even know who Jack Ackerman is, do you?"

"He's the guy who represented Frank Ramsey at trial. A lawyer from the public defender's office."

"Let me give you some advice, Elliot. Not as a coach, of course, since you don't need one of those, but as a colleague. Here in the DA's office, finding the right form, and researching the law, these are the smallest, least important parts of our job. The most important part—the crucial part—is knowing the facts. All of them. Inside and out. You're shocked by these photos, almost like you've never seen them before. You don't know who Jack Ackerman is. Have you even reviewed the petition?"

Elliot's smile was gone. He watched her, his eyes locked on hers.

She went on, "This petition isn't based on anything Jack

did or didn't do during Ramsey's trial. That's what it *should* be about, in a perfect legal world, but the Pennsylvania criminal justice system is far from perfect. What this petition, and the evidentiary hearing that will come with it, are actually going to focus on is the nervous breakdown suffered by Jack Ackerman two weeks after Ramsey's trial."

"Ramsey's lawyer had a breakdown?"

"Gil Goldhammer is going to ask the judge how he can allow a death sentence to stand when the convicted man was represented by a lawyer who may well have been mentally unstable at the time of the trial. You've heard of the insanity defense? Well, this is the my-lawyer-is-insane defense."

"That's a new one." Elliot appeared to think it over.

"We need to prove that Jack was sane—that he was effective—when he represented Ramsey."

"How are we going to do that?" Elliot said.

"To start with, I'm going to find and talk to Jack. You're going to stay here and continue your legal research."

"I thought you said researching the law was one of the least important parts of the job."

Jessie nodded. "I did."

4.

When she saw him waiting for her on a snow-dusted bench in Rittenhouse Square, the ankle of one leg crossed over the knee of the other, his arms stretched out behind him along the back of the bench, head tilted back to gaze at the gray sky, she almost didn't recognize him. Was this the same Jack Ackerman whose posture was never short of ramrod-straight, whose suits were always immaculately pressed, whose hair looked as sculpted as a Ken doll's?

She reminded herself that it had been over a year since Jack had stepped foot in a courtroom. She would probably be a lot more relaxed, too. If she was being completely honest with herself, just being outside was lifting her mood, despite the nasty surprise of Ramsey's petition. The chilly breeze against her cheeks, and the icy flakes that touched her eyelashes, felt good. A typical day for Jessie did not involve much exposure to nature. Aside from quick dashes between the District Attorney's office and the courtrooms of the Criminal Justice Center three blocks away, she lived her life inside cramped workplaces and cold hallways and stuffy courtrooms. She'd grown accustomed to the smell of paper, dust, and the nervous sweat of witnesses and criminals. In contrast, the simple scent of the wind was almost a shock to her nostrils. Being a prosecutor did not afford many opportunities to stroll up and down the lanes of a picturesque park like Rittenhouse. Jack was probably feeling similar.

Then he spotted her, and the dimple in his right cheek drew inward and his teeth shined in a smile. That stopped her in her tracks. She'd never seen him smile, unless you counted the tight, pained grimace she sometimes glimpsed when she beat him in court. And now he was beaming. It made him look like a different person.

The weather couldn't explain that. She couldn't imagine that anything could. How could he look so content, so *at peace with the world*, when she'd just informed him less than an hour ago that a serial killer's chance at a retrial hinged on a world-famous defense attorney demonstrating that he was nuts?

Maybe because he *is* nuts?

She pushed the thought out of her mind and tugged her coat tighter, stepping carefully to avoid patches of ice. His smile widened as she approached, and she noticed something else. He was handsome. *Really handsome.* She'd never noticed before.

He rose to greet her and she extended her hand, but instead of shaking it he embraced her, pulling her against his chest. His *well-defined chest.* It was a quick hug, only seconds, her face close to the snow dotted sleeve of his black pea coat. But it was so unexpected she froze for a moment, then patted his back. He didn't seem to notice her awkwardness. He released her and gestured toward the bench.

He said, "I see you brought your work with you."

"Well, yeah. That's why we're meeting, isn't it?" She propped her briefcase on the bench between them. Before she could sit down, he produced a handkerchief and wiped a thin layer of water from the bench. When she sat, she could feel the icy wood through her skirt, but she was dry. "Thanks." He was still smiling at her and she couldn't resist smiling back. "It's good to see you, Jack."

He laughed. "I never thought I'd hear you say that."

Neither had she. In their days as adversaries they had not been friends. Far from it. He'd been her enemy then, plain and simple. The idea seemed silly out here in the park. They were both lawyers, professionals, doing their jobs. But in the courtroom, it had not seemed that way. The man had been relentless, a Harvard-educated machine who never consented to an extension of time or any other favor without extracting something in return, who employed his seemingly photographic memory of case law to embarrass her whenever she made the slightest mistake, and whose words had a maddening ability to sway jurors to his cause with an almost gravitational pull. That all of his genius was in the service of helping one murderer or another escape punishment only made it worse. She'd always seen him as the bad guy, not to mention a bit of an asshole.

And as far as she had known, the feeling was mutual. Whether victorious or defeated at the end of a trial, he never lingered for post-trial small talk the way friendlier defense attorneys did. He treated her with the barest level of courtesy required by the rules of civility governing their profession.

And yet today, with his hair mussed and his collar unbuttoned and his face smiling, he looked positively elated to see her.

He cleared his throat. "So, let's not beat around the bush. You want to know if I'm sane." She suddenly felt abashed. After years of arguing with him before countless judges and jurors, walking with him down the same corridors, riding elevators, negotiating, she had not once even considered calling him after hearing about the breakdown he'd suffered. And now that she had called, what was her reason? To discuss a case. *Maybe I'm the asshole.*

"I don't know if you're sane, but you sure seem … different. You look younger, healthier—"

He laughed. "The hospital had an excellent gym."

"I'm being serious."

Some of the sparkle faded from his eyes. "I don't need to tell you how it is, when work becomes your whole life, what that can do to you."

No, he didn't have to tell her. She knew all too well. Her job was never absent from her mind, with its victims and witnesses, dates and deadlines, and right now the thought of Frank Ramsey was casting a shadow over the pretty day. She said, "Gil Goldhammer is going to try to make you out to be a lunatic. I need to prove him wrong."

"You're going to fight for my honor."

She saw the irony. A prosecutor defending a defense attorney. Wonders never ceased. "Actually, I'm only assisting. Elliot Williams from the Appeals Unit will be addressing the court on behalf of the Commonwealth. So, technically, *he's* fighting for your honor."

"Much less romantic."

She peered at him. Had Jack Ackerman just made a joke? "Wasn't my first choice either."

"Elliot Williams. I'm not familiar with the name."

"Warren Williams's nephew."

That seemed to take him by surprise. "Warren has a

family? Huh." He rubbed his chin in mock contemplation. "Scary thought."

"Tell me about it." She was surprised by the ease of their banter. She couldn't completely let down her guard—not with this guy—but she felt herself leaning closer to him on the bench.

"He's probably hoping some of what you've got will pass to the kid through osmosis," Jack said.

"Now you're trying to flatter me?"

"No, I'm just trying to say what I've always felt. That I respect you. That you're a damn good lawyer." Now she was the one smiling. Maybe he was trying to flatter her, but maybe not. Maybe the time had come when they could both look past the sides they'd chosen in their war. She respected him, too, and couldn't deny his talent.

That Frank Ramsey would accuse him of ineffectiveness—and that Gil Goldhammer, an officer of the court, would endorse that argument in finely-drafted legal prose—was not just desperate. It was despicable.

Unless, of course, it was true.

Again, she pushed away the thought. Ineffective? She'd been in that courtroom with him during Ramsey's trial, fought him tooth and nail. Jack had been effective, almost effective enough to win. Thankfully, she'd been more so.

She hesitated for a moment, then touched his arm. "I'm glad to see you looking good."

"Worried you were going to find a madman frothing at the mouth?"

"I didn't know what I'd find."

He nodded. "Fair enough."

BURNOUT

"And I am—I mean, Elliot and I are—going to fight for you."

"Why don't we start with dinner tonight? Without Elliot."

Had he just asked her out? For a second, her stomach fluttered and she felt like a sixteen-year-old girl with a crush. But just as suddenly, the breeze felt cold, the bench hard, and she was back in reality. Anything other than a strictly professional relationship would put Ramsey's conviction at risk—not to mention her career. The incident with Detective Leary had been bad enough, but at least she could blame that misstep on alcohol. "Are you crazy?"

"Depends who you ask."

"This isn't a joke. We can meet in a DA conference room with Elliot."

He sat back against the bench and mulled her words. "Much less appealing than what I had in mind."

She smoothed her skirt. "That's the way it needs to be."

He turned his head, his gaze directed out at the park. A breeze ruffled his hair. "You know, it occurs to me that my psychiatrist's testimony might be useful to you. Of course, that information is privileged, so you can't call him to the stand."

"You can waive the privilege," she said.

"The Jessie Black I know," he said, his dimple reappearing as if by magic, "is tough, but willing to entertain reasonable offers."

"Going on a date with you while participating in Ramsey's hearing is not a reasonable offer."

He raised a hand. "Who said anything about a date? Call

it diligence. We'll discuss the Ramsey trial over a good meal. That's all."

She chewed her lip. The fact was that although she did not necessarily need Jack's cooperation, or that of his psychiatrist, in order to beat Ramsey's petition, having both would certainly increase her chances. And what was the big deal about one dinner? Colleagues ate together all the time. And what better way to get a sense of whether his new personality signaled a healthy change or a psychic break than observing him in a social environment? She could control this situation. *Would* control it.

"Fine," she said. "Does eight o'clock work for you?"

When his eyes brightened, she felt suddenly uneasy about her decision. But there was no turning back now.

5.

On the hospital bed, Woody's brother looked like a skeleton. "It's not that big a deal," he was saying. Sunlight from the window cast shadows on the white sheets that accentuated the sharp boniness of his limbs. In his right hand, he held a clear plastic oxygen mask.

Michael had woken the previous night, fighting his own body for breath. If his live-in nurse, Natalie, hadn't heard him and called for an ambulance, he'd be dead.

In Woody's hand was a prescription written by Michael's doctor for a BIPAP machine. According to Michael, it was a gray box about the size of a toaster oven, attached by a tube to a face mask. Every time he slept, he would fit a mask over his nose and mouth, and the machine would counteract the effects of his disease on his chest's ability to expand.

One more addition to Michael's bedroom. Once furnished with expensive antiques, it now resembled the supply room of a nursing home.

Here at the hospital, Woody squeezed his brother's bony shoulder. He wanted to say something, but words wouldn't come. Words had never been Woody's strong suit. Natalie smiled her encouragement from the corner.

Finally, Woody said, "You're getting worse, aren't you?"

Michael laughed, and pain flashed across his face as the muscles in his torso protested. "That's what having a progressive neurodegenerative disease is all about."

"The doctors say he can go home in a few hours," Natalie said. She stepped out of the corner with a cautious smile. A slender, pretty brunette, she wore glasses and kept her hair up in a neat bun. Not Woody's type at all, yet he caught himself glancing at the rise of her chest under her white, collared blouse.

Christ, even with your brother dying in the same room. Maybe there was something wrong with him.

"Woody."

Michael's rasping voice snapped him from these thoughts. He leaned closer to his brother's stubbly cheek. As children, they'd been inseparable, and Woody was shocked now to find that even in this hospital that stunk of antiseptic solutions and medical equipment, the smell of his big brother remained startlingly unchanged. Maybe his mind was playing tricks on him, substituting memory for reality because reality had become too depressing, too desperate. But he could swear that when he leaned close to his brother, the faint odors of the past were real—freshly cut lawn, well-oiled baseball gloves. He backed away from the bed, almost frightened by the pull of happier times.

The days spent breaking in baseball gloves were long gone. Age seemed to rob most siblings of the intimacy fostered by the limitations of childhood, but in his case, he believed the distance that had formed between Michael and him had been worse than most. And he knew it had been his fault, not Michael's. Michael's superior intellect, his 4.0 GPA and perfect SAT scores, had driven him to college and graduate school, then to wealth and prestige. Meanwhile, Woody's inability to get even average grades in high school had led him to drop out and leave home. Too intimidated or embarrassed—or maybe just too resentful of his brother's abilities—Woody had dropped out of Michael's life without even saying goodbye.

When Michael's first symptoms had struck—when he'd begun tripping on flat surfaces, fumbling with pens, dropping cell phones and forks and TV remotes until his klutziness became a running joke among his friends—Woody had been hundreds of miles away, haunting the corridors of the state prison in Huntington.

By the time Woody returned to Philadelphia, Michael had sold his business. His speech had begun to slur like a stroke victim's.

The day they reunited, Michael could barely close his arms around Woody in a hug. The effort with which he had tried had brought to Woody's eyes his first tears in at least a decade. Michael had a nurse living in his house with him. He couldn't drink a glass of water without struggling to swallow. His arms and legs had shrunk to sticks and he motored around in a powered wheelchair.

It was an irony even a high school dropout like Woody could grasp—the varsity baseball player felled by a disease named for a baseball player. Lou Gehrig's Disease. Amyotrophic lateral sclerosis. ALS. Incurable, a plague afflicting over thirty-thousand people in the United States, with eight-thousand new cases diagnosed every year.

On that first day together after twenty years—their reunion day—the two of them had sat at Michael's kitchen table. Woody in a chair and Michael in a wheelchair. Woody drinking Bud and Michael struggling to sip water. Michael had told him everything, described the whole ordeal. He confided that, at first, he had refused to believe the diagnosis. Refused, as if the power of denial could reverse the disease's effects on his body. It took a series of muscle and nerve biopsies, a spinal tap, and several MRIs to convince him.

He wasn't going to wake up one day and be all better. This disease was going to cripple him, muscle by muscle, tissue by tissue, until he was dead.

"When I realized I had nothing to lose," he'd told Woody, "the money no longer mattered. It's like they say—you can't take it with you. So I started to talk to people. Doctors. Scientists."

He'd lured researchers away from their professorships and corporate posts. Sent lobbyists to Washington. Built a state-of-the-art biomedical research facility from the ground up.

He'd built the Rushford Foundation.

Now, once again snapping Woody from his thoughts to the present, Michael said, "How's our project?"

"Goldhammer filed a petition today." Woody didn't want to speak Ramsey's name in front of Natalie, unsure how much his brother's private nurse knew. If she recognized the name—and who in Philadelphia wouldn't?—she might not understand. Right now she cared for Michael with a diligence bordering on obsession. Woody didn't dare say anything that might darken her opinion.

Besides, Michael's mind was as sharp as ever. ALS was harmless to its victim's intelligence. The body atrophied, but the intellect was immune. It was either a blessing or the cruelest of curses. It left the mind with no body to carry out its will.

Fortunately, Michael had Woody's body.

"Did you go to see him?" Michael said.

Woody nodded.

"And?"

"He's evil." Woody would never speak so silly a word in any other context, but here it was the only one that fit. Woody had spent eleven years of his life in the company of killers, gangbangers, child molesters. He knew bad guys, and even so, all the newspaper articles he had read—sensational as they had been—had failed to capture Ramsey's horrible essence, the mechanical brutality that brooded behind those eyes. Facing Ramsey across a scarred metal table in the Restricted Housing Unit of SCI Greene, Woody had recognized the terrible blackness of the inmate's pupils, like a couple of tar pits in his face. Ramsey had eyes that would watch, steady and disinterested, as his hand plunged a knife into flesh, ripped it free, then plunged it in again. Chopping an artery, hacking a rib, impaling a lung.

"Once he's free," Woody said, "he'll do it again."

Michael nodded, wincing with the effort this gesture required. "Shame. But necessary."

"I hope you're right."

Michael's fingers closed on Woody's sleeve and tugged him closer. "You're the only one I trust."

"Just stay alive. Everything's going to be okay."

Michael's eyes met his, sick and trembling in their deep sockets; Woody didn't dare look away. Almost too quietly to be heard, Michael said, "Even if I die, don't stop."

"You're not going to—"

"Even if I do!"

Gently, Woody pried his brother's fingers from his wrist and backed away from the hospital bed. The exertion of their meeting had taken its toll; Michael's eyelids were drooping. He groped for the oxygen mask, pulled it over his face. Through the clear plastic, Woody could see his eyelids flutter, then close.

Woody lifted his leather jacket from the back of the visitor's chair, and slung his arms into the sleeves, preparing to leave.

"Everyone should be lucky enough to have a brother like you," Natalie said. There was not a trace of irony in her voice.

Woody walked to the door. "Thanks."

She approached him, took the nearly-forgotten sheet of paper from his hand. The prescription for the BIPAP machine. "I'll handle this." She folded the prescription once, placed it on the table next to an empty bedpan. "I know you're busy."

"Yeah. The project I'm working on, it's about to heat up."

6.

Jessie felt some of her concern fade when Jack called to suggest Monk's Café. Monk's was famous for its huge selection of Belgian beers and award-winning hamburgers, but was hardly a romantic destination. Casual, crowded, and reasonably priced, it was a place where she could discuss the case over a sandwich, and, even if he insisted on picking up the tab, keep within the bounds of professional conduct.

She should have known better.

He buzzed her apartment at exactly eight o'clock. He had a taxi waiting at the curb. He held the door while she climbed inside the car, then slid in beside her on the squeaky vinyl seat.

His first words once they pulled away from the curb were, "You look beautiful."

"Jack—"

"Just take a compliment from an old friend."

They both knew they had never been friends, and she wasn't seeking compliments tonight, but she sighed and said, "Thanks."

"I like the boots. Hot."

"Don't push it." She watched Center City scroll past the windows. "Just so we're absolutely clear, I'm here to strategize about your testimony at the PCRA hearing."

"Not because you find me irresistibly charming."

"Correct."

He grimaced, clutched his chest. "You wound me."

"That's why blackmail is a bad way to get a date."

"Well, I tried internet dating first."

"What happened?"

"I couldn't find your profile."

She turned away from him, struggled to keep from rolling her eyes. "I was born with a low tolerance for corniness, Jack. You're going to have to tone it down or risk making me laugh at you."

"Actually, I was going for the laugh."

They sat in silence. Strangely, it didn't feel awkward. She felt her shoulders relax into the seat and watched the familiar scenery outside the cab. Five minutes later they arrived. The neon sign in the window made her smile.

"This place hasn't changed since I used to come here back in law school."

"You went to Penn Law, right?"

She nodded. "Seems like a long time ago."

"Couldn't have been too long ago. You're what, twenty-five?"

"Funny." She was thirty-two, and felt every year of it.

Jack paid the driver and they climbed out of the cab. The breeze whipped her hair around her face. Jack jogged ahead of her, yanked the bar's door open.

"Thanks."

She stepped past him into the warmth of the restaurant.

BURNOUT

The front bar was packed with people. The aroma of beer and the din of conversation were almost overwhelming. She pushed through the crowd to a podium where she gave her name to a man dressed in black. Asking for a table for two felt strange, and she realized how long it had been since she'd gone out to dinner with anyone. What had Jack said? *I don't need to tell you how it is, when work becomes your whole life, what that can do to you.*

Leaning against the wall of Monk's front bar, looking at Jack and straining to hear his voice over the clamor of the other patrons, she tried not to think about his bright blue eyes or his sensual mouth. She needed to remember her purpose here. It didn't matter that he was handsome and apparently into her. Only that he was sane—and that she would be able to prove it to the judge at Ramsey's evidentiary hearing.

"You want a drink?" He had to yell to be heard over the noise.

She almost said no out of reflex, then thought better of it and peered over Jack's shoulder at the beers on tap. One wouldn't hurt. "What do you recommend?" She had to lean close to him to be heard.

Rather than back away, he leaned in even closer. "Well, I was going to get a Lucifer—" He laughed when she raised an eyebrow. "No defense attorney jokes, please."

"Never crossed my mind. I guess I'll try one, too."

She still found Monk's atmosphere safely non-romantic, but the back room, where they were seated, had a cozy, old-world ambiance that was seductive in its own right.

After they ordered, she said, "You're still practicing law?"

"Only part time. Estate planning, mostly. Wills. It's not as challenging as criminal law—at least, not in the same way—but it's less stressful."

"You should have joined the DA's office. You might have found prosecuting murderers less nerve-racking than helping them." The words were out of her mouth before she could stop them—maybe the beer was affecting her judgment. "Sorry, that was an obnoxious thing to say."

But he didn't look insulted. In fact, his open face suggested that he wanted her to continue. "I always thought prosecuting would be more stressful than defending," he said. "Doesn't it ever bother you—the possibility that you might be responsible for sending an innocent person to prison?"

"The vast majority of them are guilty."

"But some aren't."

A warning bell sounded in her mind. "Please tell me we're not talking about Ramsey." She looked around for their waitress.

"Isn't that why we're here? To talk about his trial?"

"Your effectiveness at his trial. Not his guilt or innocence."

"All I'm saying is that sometimes the system makes a mistake."

"Maybe that's true in some cases. Not in his."

"And the others don't bother you?"

"We have to make some sacrifices if we want to live in a safe society."

"You mean sacrifice the poor for the safety of the rich?"

Her cheeks flushed, and not because of the beer she'd consumed. "My father's a factory worker. I wasn't exactly born in the lap of luxury. And believe me, the poor are victimized by crime a lot more frequently than the rich."

Jack raised his hands, palms out. "Hey, I'm sorry. I was just talking."

The waitress arrived and they ordered their food. She hoped the break in their conversation would give them a chance to move on to less sensitive subjects, but Jack looked ready to launch back in.

She cut him off before he could speak, "Let's talk about something else."

"I didn't mean to piss you off, with the rich and poor comment."

"You didn't piss me off."

"Look, I'm not good at this, okay?" He sighed, unfolded his napkin and spread it on his lap. "When I was with the Defenders Association, all I did was work, night and day. I'm trying to.... I don't know. I guess I don't remember what it's like to have a conversation that isn't a debate."

She remembered what he'd been like, all too well. And she understood what he was feeling now, because she felt it herself. Having a conversation, being a normal person—it didn't come as easy as it used to. Her profession had changed her, and she wasn't sure she liked the changes. "I suppose I can relate," she said. She took a sip of water.

He shrugged. "I'm getting better at it. Just takes practice."

"Is that what this is? Practice?"

He reared back with a mortified expression. "This? No! I've always had a thing for you."

"Come on." She laughed.

"I'm serious. I found you attractive long before I went bonkers."

She laughed again. "What did you like most? My rudeness toward you or my refusal to negotiate with any of your clients?"

"You negotiated when appropriate. But you always had a good reason, and a full grasp of the facts and the law. Facing off against you was never boring, that's for sure."

"You're a pretty good lawyer yourself," she said.

"Yeah, but your legs are nicer."

"You definitely need to work on the corniness, though."

He shrugged. "It's my new style."

"So what happened? Really?"

His smile faltered, then fell away completely. He rubbed his chin. "That's the question, isn't it? I don't really have an answer. One day I was zealously defending my clients, the next I was playing a Cindy Lauper song for the jury while I danced around the courtroom to *Girls Just Want to Have Fun*. It seemed like a good idea at the time."

"How could that possibly seem like a good idea?"

A fraction of his smile returned, bringing the dimple with it. She leaned forward. "Actually, I was impeaching one of the prosecution's witnesses. This eighty-year-old woman claimed she heard my client berating his girlfriend—the victim—in the apartment next door to hers a few days before she was killed. But other neighbors testified that my client was blasting his stereo at the time of the incident—a fact corroborated by two police officers who responded to a noise complaint. My idea was to recreate the scene for the jury and demonstrate that, given the volume of the music, it was unlikely that the old lady could have heard an argument between my client and the victim."

"And the dancing?"

"Indicates there was something going on besides brilliant lawyering. My psychiatrist thinks—well, I'm sure he can give you a more satisfying explanation than I can. I'll give him a call tomorrow morning and encourage him to be forthcoming with you." He fished a business card out of his pocket and passed it across the table. She read it in the light from the candle on their table. *Joseph Brandywine, M.D., Medical Director, Wooded Hill Hospital.*

"But we agree that you were competent when you represented Ramsey at trial?"

"You were there."

She put the card down. "I certainly hope you'll give a better answer than that if I put you on the stand."

He rocked his chair back, the legs creaking. "You want to hear what I'd say on the stand? I'll tell you."

She watched him skeptically. "Okay, go ahead."

"Ramsey's innocent. He didn't kill Bob and Erin Dillard. He didn't rape and stab Kristen Dillard."

"That's still not what I want to hear, Jack."

"You think Ramsey is the Family Man because the Dillard murders fit the serial killer's profile. But the police were unable to link Ramsey to any of the killer's other victims. Ramsey was prosecuted for only *one* of the Family Man's attacks."

"That's the great thing about the death penalty. One successful prosecution is all you need."

He held up a finger. "Hear me out. The Family Man

always takes a souvenir from his victims. When he killed the Anderson family, he took Donna Anderson's bracelet. When he killed the Millers, he took Paul Miller's coat."

"And when he attacked the Dillards, he took Bob Dillard's briefcase," Jessie said. She heard the edge in her own voice. He was making her angry.

"Yes," Jack said. "But the police found none of those items in Frank Ramsey's home."

"Many serial killers hide their trophies. We never found his. What we did find was an eyewitness."

"One eyewitness. A traumatized girl."

Jessie stopped. Her hands had balled into tight fists beneath the table. She force herself to unclench them. "What are you doing, Jack?"

"I'm confiding something to you. Frank Ramsey's not the first accused murderer that I've represented, okay? I used to deal with these guys every day. But when Ramsey told me his story, I believed him. Frank Ramsey is innocent."

"Jack, we need to be absolutely clear about something." She leaned toward him. "Elliot Williams is calling you to the stand at the PCRA hearing, and when he does, you are going to tell the judge the truth about your sanity during Ramsey's trial. Ramsey's guilt is not the issue here. Your effectiveness as his lawyer is the issue. Please tell me I can count on your honesty."

"Yeah," he said, looking slightly hurt. "Of course, Jessie. You can trust me."

The waitress delivered their meals and she watched him tuck into a giant cheeseburger. Her own burger sat untouched for a moment as she studied him.

BURNOUT

As a general rule, she'd found that people who announced their trustworthiness tended to be the least trustworthy. But with Jack, general rules didn't necessarily apply. She wasn't sure what to believe. Maybe that was what bothered her the most.

7.

The next morning, Jessie turned her Honda Accord onto the winding drive of Wooded Hill Hospital, the private institution to which Jack Ackerman had voluntarily committed himself. Loose gravel crunched under the tires as the car approached an ornate, wrought-iron gate blocking entrance to the property.

"So this is what a mental asylum looks like." Elliot craned his neck to get a better view. The wonder in her boss's nephew's eyes reminded her just how green he was.

Despite herself, she smiled. "Not what you expected?"

"I don't know. I was imagining towers, lightning, hunchbacks. This looks like the library at my college."

It wasn't exactly what Jessie had expected either. She'd only seen one other mental hospital, the state institution where Kristen Dillard continued to suffer from the nightmare of Ramsey's invasion. There, the walls surrounding the grounds served to keep the inmates locked inside. She had a feeling that Wooded Hill's gate served the opposite function. To keep unwanted visitors—such as a couple of nosy lawyers—out.

She pulled up to the guard's booth and rolled down her window. A balding, middle-aged man leaned toward the car.

BURNOUT

He smiled affably as she explained that she and Elliot had an appointment with Dr. Joseph Brandywine, then made them wait in the car while he stepped back inside his booth and made a phone call. A moment later, she heard a hum of motors. The gate began to open.

"The practice of psychiatry's come a long way since the days of hunchbacks," she said to Elliot once they were moving again. "They don't lobotomize people anymore, either. At least not at places like this."

The lane wound past acres of lawn frosted with snow. The hospital's main building sat on the hill's crest, no doubt affording the resident patients soothing green vistas in the warmer months. In a small visitors' parking lot, she parked the car and she and Elliot got out.

"I heard celebrities check into this place," Elliot said. He leaned toward the car to fix the knot of his tie and check his hair in the window's reflection.

"If that's why you're preening, don't bother. I doubt we'll run into any pop stars or heiresses today."

He stood up straight, cheeks red. "I just want to make a good impression."

Jessie nodded. "Good." She had been around long enough to know that impressions mattered, and not just inside the courtroom. She'd worn one of her more expensive, conservative suits for this trip. It never hurt to remind a potential witness that he wasn't simply talking to a lawyer, but to a prosecutor. Especially when a show of authority might be necessary. "But don't be surprised if this doesn't go smoothly. You can fix your hair all you want. Doctors have a tendency to be recalcitrant witnesses. Doctor-patient privilege and all that." She started walking toward the building, Elliot one step behind her.

"Not this guy, though, right? I thought Ackerman said he was going to tell Brandywine to help us."

She remembered her dinner with Jack and doubt gnawed at her stomach. "He also said Ramsey is innocent. I'm not sure what's going on in his head."

Elliot caught up, stopped in front of her. "Hold on. What are you saying? You don't know if Brandywine's going to cooperate?"

"He sounded strange when I called him to make an appointment."

"Define *strange*."

"Just let me do the talking in there."

Dr. Brandywine's office managed to be simultaneously large and cozy. On one side of the room, a desk stood in front of a bank of windows commanding a view of the grounds. On the other side of the room, leather-upholstered furniture had been arranged in a semi-circle near a fireplace. It was to this side of the room that Brandywine steered them, urging them to sit on a leather sofa. Elliot dropped into the thick cushions with a deep sigh.

"If you don't mind, Doctor, I'd prefer to talk over there." She gestured toward the wooden chairs facing his desk. Elliot glanced up at her, clearly reluctant to pull himself off of the cushions. But she wanted to manage the tone of this meeting, make sure Brandywine understood that this was a conference between professionals.

Brandywine shrugged. "Certainly."

The doctor had an athletic build and moved with a grace

that seemed incongruous with his creased face and steel-gray hair. He stepped behind his desk and sat down, regarding his visitors with disconcerting intensity.

"So. You're from the District Attorney's office."

"That's right," Elliot said, taking the wooden chair next to Jessie. From his frown, she inferred that the leather sofa had been more comfortable.

"As I explained on the phone," Jessie said, "we'd like to ask you some questions about a former patient here. Jack Ackerman."

"We prefer to call them *clients*, as opposed to patients. And you need to understand, before we go any further, that the confidentiality of our records is taken very seriously here. In fact, our discretion is the reason many of our clients choose us over other facilities. To the extent I can answer your questions without impinging on Mr. Ackerman's privacy, I intend to do so, but no more."

"Wait a second." Elliot leaned forward. "Mr. Ackerman didn't call to give you his permission to cooperate with us?"

"He did call. However, I would prefer to protect the hospital's interests as well as his. If I understand correctly, this matter involves the Frank Ramsey murder trial that received so much media coverage last year. My concern is that the court proceeding will draw a lot of publicity. If the hospital's name appears in the news, other potential clients may be discouraged from trusting us."

"That's not our problem," Elliot said. "You—"

Jessie shot him a glance that shut him up. She softened her voice. "Let me explain something to you, Dr. Brandywine. Ramsey is represented by Gil Goldhammer, one of the best defense attorneys in the country. Goldhammer's argument is that Ramsey is entitled to a new trial because Jack Ackerman, his lawyer at his original trial, was nuts. Jack's commitment here—whether or not it was voluntary—is evidence that supports his argument, so you can bet he's going to bring it up as often as possible. In court. In interviews with the press. And I promise you, he's not going to call your patients *clients*. It's to his client's benefit to describe Wooded Hill Hospital as a madhouse."

Brandywine swallowed. "I see."

"There's no reason we shouldn't help each other, Doctor. I need to prove that Jack was sane during Ramsey's trial. You need an opportunity to set the record straight about Wooded Hill and its clientele."

The psychiatrist sighed. "I suppose there would be little harm in discussing Mr. Ackerman's stay here. What do you want to know?"

"Is it true that Jack suffered a nervous breakdown?"

"Well, 'nervous breakdown' is not a clinical term, by which I mean it has no psychiatric definition. The general public uses the term as a kind of shorthand to describe a variety of mental illnesses that generally involve some sort of emotional collapse. Clinical depression, anxiety, post-traumatic stress, all of these could fall under the umbrella. But simply using the term 'nervous breakdown'—that's very imprecise."

"How would you describe Jack's problem?" Jessie said.

"I believe Mr. Ackerman suffered from a condition known as brief reactive psychosis. It most commonly affects people between the ages of twenty and forty and can have a variety of causes. Chronic and unresolved grief, work stress, guilt, any major life change can trigger the condition. Mr.

Ackerman's case was fairly mild. Symptoms can include delusions, hallucinations, impaired speech. Mr. Ackerman's presented only disorganized behavior."

She managed to maintain a neutral expression as the doctor lectured on. *Psychosis?* Maybe she would have been better off respecting the hospital's confidentiality policy after all. She risked a glance at Elliot. He looked as stricken as she felt.

"What caused the ... behavior in Jack's case?" Jessie said.

"In his case, I believe the condition was precipitated by work-related stress. Not uncommon in your field."

Elliot turned to Jessie with a sardonic smile. "That's comforting."

She kept her focus on Brandywine. "How did you treat him?"

"Well, typically I would prescribe an antipsychotic medication for a client with his condition, but because Mr. Ackerman's symptoms were mild I decided to try psychotherapy first. Mr. Ackerman responded well. As you know, he checked himself out of the hospital after six months of treatment."

"So he was cured?" Elliot said, perking up.

Brandywine shifted in his chair. "The word is inappropriate in this context. I helped him to cope with the stress that initially triggered his condition."

Jessie leaned forward. "In your opinion, was Jack suffering from the condition at the time of Frank Ramsey's trial?"

"To answer that question I would have to interview Mr. Ackerman about the trial. Perhaps if I could examine the trial transcript, that might also help. But it will be difficult to form an opinion with any certainty. You're talking about the past, about a time prior to my first meeting with him." He looked at them apologetically.

Jessie nodded and thanked him for his time.

Outside, Jessie couldn't help noticing Elliot's stunned expression. He seemed to stagger back to the car. She laughed. "What's your problem? I thought that went well, considering."

He jolted out of his trance and snapped his gaze in her direction. "Considering? You warned me he might be recalcitrant. I wish you'd been right."

She opened her car door. "Would you rather have heard Brandywine's diagnosis for the first time in the courtroom, in front of the judge? Now we have foreknowledge. We can prepare. That's invaluable."

She slid behind the wheel. Elliot joined her, fumbling with a pair of sunglasses. She twisted her key and the engine roared. Once they were moving, he said, "We could lose this thing."

The gates of Wooded Hill Hospital flashed past on either side of the car, and they left the place behind. "I'm glad to see you're starting to see the stakes."

8.

After their meeting with Dr. Brandywine, Jessie and Elliot spent the next several days in deep preparation mode, poring over the trial transcript, reading media accounts of the trial, calling psychiatrists and psychologists, and rehearsing. When the hearing date arrived, and the elevator doors finally opened on the third floor of the Criminal Justice Center, Elliot looked surprised to find the corridor empty.

"Expecting the paparazzi?" Jessie said.

"I thought the hearing would draw *some* attention."

His reaction did not surprise her. When a case consumed your life, it was easy to assume that the rest of the world—or, at least, Philadelphia—would care as much about it as you did. The truth was, that was rarely the case. "I'm sure there will be a few reporters in the courtroom."

She stepped out of the elevator. He followed her. "I don't get it," he said. "Ramsey's trial was big news."

"Most reporters know this type of hearing is routine. It'll be big news if we lose today."

"What if we win?"

"Didn't your uncle teach you anything? If there's one thing Warren's always been right about, it's that the only news deemed worthy of publication is bad news."

Their footsteps echoed as they followed the diamond-patterned floor. Empty benches extended from the walls on either side, bathed in harsh light from a window at the end of the hall. Jessie had seen countless witnesses and victims squirm on those stone benches, awaiting justice. Justice that—no matter how confident she might feel about a given case—she could never guarantee.

Justice was not guaranteed at today's hearing, either. She knew that Jack had provided Ramsey with stellar legal counsel, and Ramsey knew it, too. But that wouldn't stop Goldhammer from leveraging Jack's breakdown to secure for Ramsey a retrial, one that would drain the court's resources and expose Ramsey's only living victim, Kristen Dillard, to another series of painful court appearances.

Not to mention the possibility that—given a second chance at hoodwinking a jury—Ramsey might well get away with murder this time.

Elliot would do all of the talking today, while she sat silently at his side, passing him the occasional note. She still believed that this approach was a mistake—this hearing was too critical to trust to a beginner—but it was Warren's call. All she could do was help where she could, and hope for the best.

Columns flanked the dark wooden door of Judge Spatt's courtroom. Before she could open it, Elliot reached for her arm, stopping her.

Jessie looked at him. "Nervous?"

"Yeah." He took a deep breath.

"Good. I am, too. The day you're not is the day you lose."

"Don't worry. If nervousness is what you want, I've got it covered." He laughed uneasily.

"You're prepared, too. That's what matters." She opened the courtroom door. Elliot followed her inside.

A handful of seats in the gallery were occupied—not a packed house, by any means, but a bigger audience than your run of the mill hearing. The court crier and the judge's staff moved about in their section of the room to the right of the vacant judge's bench, rustling papers and preparing for the judge. They acknowledged Jessie with friendly nods.

"Do you know everyone?" Jessie whispered.

"I don't know anyone."

Jessie chewed her lip. He really was a rookie. "Come on." She took his arm and guided him to the chubby, grandmotherly woman setting up a stenography machine. "This is Edna Lindauer, Judge Spatt's court reporter. Edna, this is my associate, Elliot Williams."

Before Edna could respond, the door opened and Gil Goldhammer swept into the courtroom surrounded by assistants and helpers. Even if Jessie hadn't recognized his face from the numerous cable talk shows that offered him screen time, she would have identified him by his manner alone. Despite the fact that he wasn't much to look at—short and stout, with a face as puffy as a marshmallow and almost as pale—he strutted to the defense table like a celebrity walking a red carpet. His entourage followed, claiming the first two rows of the gallery on his side of the aisle.

Jessie summoned a professional smile as she approached him. From the corner of her eye, she saw Elliot following her.

Goldhammer's cologne, as musky and pungent as a sweaty horse, filled her mouth and nose the moment she stepped within a foot of him. As politely as she could, she coughed into her left hand. She extended her right hand in greeting. He shook it, then Elliot's, with a dry grip.

"Gil Goldhammer." He announced his own name in the clipped staccato of a TV homicide cop. In her years as a prosecutor, Jessie had met many real-life homicide cops, none of whom spoke that way.

"I'm Jessica Black. This is Elliot Williams."

At least six inches shorter than her, Goldhammer had to look up to make eye contact. She was surprised they could even see each other through the cloud of his musk. "Beautiful courthouse," he said.

"Is this your first visit to Philadelphia?" she said.

"It is. I've wanted to come here for a long time, but the opportunity hasn't presented itself until now."

Translation: The Philly mob families were loyal clients of their high-priced attorneys. Goldhammer, even with his nationwide reputation, had not been able to break in. Yet. "Rescuing Ramsey from death row might help you attract more Philly business." She tried to keep the edge off her voice, didn't quite succeed.

"There are certain people who might notice."

"Is that how you've justified foregoing your usual fees, by writing this case off as an advertisement to the Philadelphia underworld?"

His marshmallow face wrinkled, folds in his skin almost swallowing his eyes. "I don't ever forego my fees, Ms. Black. I'm ideologically opposed to *pro bono*."

"You're being paid? By whom?"

He chuckled. Jessie could not seem to summon a polite

chuckle of her own. The veneer of their professional banter splintered. "I assume you've appeared before Judge Spatt before?" he said, changing the subject.

From another lawyer, this question might have signaled a nervous probe for information about the extent of her home court advantage. But Goldhammer wasn't probing. He was taunting.

Usually, the same judge was assigned to a PCRA petition that oversaw the original trial. But in this case, Judge Alfred Kapron, the judge at Ramsey's trial, had retired seven months ago, which was why they were in Judge Spatt's courtroom instead.

And Judge Martin Spatt was the last person in Philadelphia she would have chosen for this hearing. On the surface, he was unremarkable—a black man in his sixties, slim, average height, with gray hair. Below the surface was another story entirely. A long time ago, he must have been a practicing lawyer himself, but apparently that was not a part of his life he recalled fondly. Now he hated lawyers, regarding them as vermin daily invading his otherwise pleasant courtroom. Jessie had seen him take both prosecutors and defense attorneys apart, piece by piece, savoring their dismemberment as if he could taste the blood.

Judge Kapron would have denied Ramsey's petition after a token hearing. He had observed for himself Jack's more-than-competent representation of Ramsey at trial. But Judge Spatt, with no evidence but the transcript and the testimony of witnesses, might easily decide that Jack was a nut-job and that a new trial was warranted. Hell, the idea of a mentally disturbed defense attorney would probably fill him with glee.

Goldhammer conveyed his full awareness of this situation

in the twinkle of his eye.

"No, I haven't appeared before Judge Spatt before," Elliot said, even though Goldhammer's question had been directed at her. "This will be my first time."

Goldhammer's gaze shifted to Elliot. The grin that slashed across his doughy face reminded Jessie of bullies she'd faced in elementary school. Mercifully, their conversation was interrupted when two sheriff's deputies brought Frank Ramsey into the courtroom.

Handcuffed, dressed in an orange jumpsuit, Ramsey's eyes scanned the room as if he were looking for someone. Jessie knew he had no family. The few friends he'd once had abandoned him as soon as they'd learned what a monster he was. When he didn't find whatever person he was looking for, he turned his eyes to the defense table. Still standing in the aisle, Jessie blocked Ramsey's route to his chair.

His eyes met hers.

He'd lost some weight in prison, but his muscular body—honed by twenty years of professional firefighting—remained imposing. The deputies handled him carefully, hands close to their holstered guns. They followed closely as he made his way toward her. She noticed his awkward shamble before she realized his ankles had been shackled in addition to his wrists.

He got close enough to breathe in her face before the deputies grabbed his arms and yanked him to a halt. Unlike his lawyer, Ramsey didn't have to look up to make eye contact with her. In heels, she was about his height. His eyes bore into hers.

Elliot gulped, but Jessie wasn't about to let this creep intimidate her. She met his stare.

BURNOUT

She could see the muscles in his arms flexing under the coarse jumpsuit material, fury coming off of him in waves. She was sure there was nothing he wanted more than to make her his next victim, stab her with the sharpest knife he could get his hands on. As a prosecutor, she'd made few friends in the criminal ranks, but sexual predators like Ramsey—men whose hatred of women stemmed from fear and insecurity—hated her the most. The feeling was mutual.

Goldhammer nudged her out of his client's way as politely as he could, then took Ramsey's arm. "Why don't you sit down, Frank, make yourself comfortable?"

Ramsey held her stare a moment longer, then broke it. Chains jingling, he took his seat at the defense table with as much grace as his hand and ankle cuffs allowed.

Jessie took her seat at the prosecution's table. She settled into the familiar wooden chair, placed her briefcase on the table, opened it. She arranged her papers in front of her—a pile of tabbed cases, a highlighted copy of the trial transcript, witness notes. A clean legal pad and a pen.

Elliot joined her. He looked dazed as he unpacked the dog-eared, food-stained, ink-smeared contents of his own briefcase. This evidence of his days of preparation should have allowed her to relax. To breathe easy. Take a back seat, as Warren had instructed. But it didn't.

The fact was, her blood was up. With Ramsey sitting mere feet away from her, there was no way she could relax. She wouldn't be able to relax until she heard Judge Spatt tell the bastard that his petition was denied, until she watched Gil Goldhammer get back on his private jet and fly the hell out of her city. Even then, she wouldn't completely drop her guard. Not until the needle slipped into Ramsey's skin, the plunger pushing poison into his vein.

Morbid? Maybe. But after what he'd done to Kristen and all his other victims, it's what he deserved.

The courtroom door opened behind her. She glanced over her shoulder in time to see Jack Ackerman slip inside. She noted his expensive suit and breathed a sigh of relief. As much as she hated to admit it, a part of her had feared he'd show up in a gorilla costume or a tutu, or not show up at all.

She nodded at him and he gave her a warm smile before taking a seat in the gallery. Whatever his feelings might be about Ramsey's guilt or innocence, he'd apparently decided to put it behind him. Good.

"Jack's here," she whispered to Elliot.

He nodded, apparently too nervous to turn around.

A moment later, Judge Spatt strode into the courtroom and everyone jumped to their feet.

9.

Not surprisingly, Goldhammer's first witness was Dr. Joseph Brandywine. The psychiatrist looked significantly less at ease on the witness stand than he had in his comfortable office at Wooded Hill, especially when Goldhammer began to question him about every detail of his career, including his education, the various journals in which he'd published, the practices to which he'd belonged and every position he'd held.

The dents and pits in Judge Spatt's craggy face seemed to deepen as he watched the celebrity lawyer. "Mr. Goldhammer, I don't believe the Commonwealth disputes Dr. Brandywine's expertise." He turned his gaze to the prosecution's table, waited a moment, then released a long, exasperated sigh. "Well?"

Jessie nudged Elliot and he shot up from his chair. "Your Honor, the Commonwealth is willing to stipulate to Dr. Brandywine's expertise in the field of psychiatry."

"Good," he said, as if speaking to a child. "That just about makes my day. Mr. Goldhammer, if you wouldn't mind skipping past the BS...."

"Certainly, Your Honor." Goldhammer cleared his throat, checked some notes on his table, then approached the witness. "Doctor, you testified that you are currently a medical director at a hospital, correct?"

"Yes. At Wooded Hill Hospital."

"And what kind of hospital is Wooded Hill? Do they treat heart problems, chronic pain, cancer?"

"It's a psychiatric hospital."

"Ah." Goldhammer nodded as if this information were a great revelation. "So what types of afflictions do the patients there suffer from?"

"Mental and emotional conditions."

Goldhammer turned to Jessie and Elliot with a baleful look. Jessie ignored him and hoped Elliot was smart enough to do the same. On her legal pad, she took notes she doubted would ever be of use to her. The act of writing helped her to maintain a poker face in front of the judge.

"Are you familiar with a man named Jack Ackerman, Doctor?"

"Mr. Ackerman was a client of the Hospital."

"A client? I'm sorry, how is that different than a patient?"

Brandywine hesitated, his face pained. "I suppose it's just a matter of semantics."

"I'm not sure I understand. Would it be accurate to say that Mr. Ackerman was a patient at Wooded Hill Hospital?"

"Yes."

"When was this?"

Brandywine thought for a moment, then said, "He began his stay at the beginning of July of last year. He stayed until New Year's Day of this year."

"In what capacity did you know Mr. Ackerman?"

"I was his therapist."

"During that time, how often did you interact with Mr. Ackerman?"

Jessie flipped to a clean sheet and wrote a message, then showed it to Elliot. It said: *Doc didn't see trial. Emphasize on cross.* Elliot nodded.

"Four, sometimes five days a week, for hour-long sessions."

"Would you say that you got to know him reasonably well?"

"I'd like to think so, yes." The doctor leaned back, getting more comfortable. "Wooded Hill prides itself on the relationships it forges between its doctors and clients."

"I'm sure it's wonderful." Goldhammer let his condescending tone hang in the air for a moment, then said, "By clients you mean patients, of course. Mental patients."

Brandywine squirmed again.

"In your expert opinion, Doctor, based on your six months of interaction with Mr. Ackerman, what mental disease does Mr. Ackerman suffer from?"

Jessie whispered, "Object."

Elliot turned to her with a quizzical expression and she elbowed him hard in the arm. He jumped from his chair, fumbled with the pen in his hand. "Uh, Your Honor, I object to this line of questioning."

Spatt looked at Elliot and a tight grin cracked his face. Jessie held her breath. The old bastard smelled fresh blood.

"Mr. Ackerman's, um, mental condition during the time he was at the hospital is irrelevant. The Ramsey trial took place in June of last year. That's a month before the witness met Mr. Ackerman."

Spatt's hatchet-face turned to Goldhammer. His white eyebrows rose.

Goldhammer spread his arms in a gesture of reasonableness. "Your Honor, I believe Dr. Brandywine's testimony will demonstrate that Mr. Ackerman's work life prior to his commitment at the hospital, including Ramsey's trial, is what precipitated his need to be in the hospital. For that reason, the opinions formed by Dr. Brandywine during Mr. Ackerman's treatment will shed light on the issue of whether Mr. Ackerman's mental instability already existed at the time of the trial."

Judge Spatt returned his gaze to Elliot. "Your objection is overruled, Mr. Williams. In future, try not to waste the court's time with meritless objections."

On the legal pad, Jessie wrote: *Ignore him. He's an A-hole.* Then quickly scribbled ink over it until it was unreadable.

Brandywine shifted in his chair. "What was the question?"

Judge Spatt looked at Edna and asked the court reporter to read it back.

Edna read, "In your expert opinion, based on your six months of interaction with Mr. Ackerman, what mental disease does Mr. Ackerman suffer from?"

Goldhammer waited for the answer he already knew.

"In my opinion, Mr. Ackerman was suffering from a condition known as brief reactive psychosis."

In the quiet courtroom, Jessie heard the distinct sound of Judge Spatt's sharp intake of breath.

"Now, Dr. Brandywine, would a case of brief reactive psychosis be conducive to good lawyering?"

"Probably not."

Goldhammer smiled, inviting the judge to smile along with him. Spatt declined, but his body language—neck thrust forward, face pensive—suggested to Jessie that the testimony was achieving its desired effect.

"Why?"

"Well." Brandywine looked to Jessie as if she could rescue him from this inquisition. Instead of returning his stare, she concentrated on the legal pad in front of her, adding a couple more lines over her crossed-out appraisal of Judge Spatt. "For one thing, the condition might make concentration difficult."

"What about hallucinations, delusions?"

"Those symptoms have also been associated with the condition, yes."

"Wow. Poor concentration, hallucinations, delusions. Sounds pretty serious to me." Goldhammer looked at the judge, then back to the doctor. "Would those symptoms necessarily be apparent in a trial transcript?"

"Not necessarily."

"I didn't think so. No further questions."

It was now the Commonwealth's turn. Jessie wrote: *Good luck.*

Elliot rose for the first cross-examination of his career. His chest faced the judge and the witness, but for a moment his eyes refused to leave his own legal pad, where he had organized his copious notes with bullet points. When he managed to wrench himself free of this crutch and approach the witness stand, Jessie released her pent-up breath, but under the table, her fingers were crossed so tightly they ached. Brandywine's testimony had made an impact on Judge Spatt. Elliot needed to undermine it. Fast.

"Um, Dr. Brandywine—how are you this morning, by the way? Are you thirsty? Would you like a glass of water?"

Oh Christ.

Jessie snuck a peek across the aisle. Goldhammer was smiling like a wolf, but Ramsey watched calmly, his expression neutral. No surprise there. Ramsey had maintained a sober aspect throughout his trial and appellate proceedings. The only time Jessie had ever seen a smile on his face was in a photograph taken a few weeks before his arrest, in which he'd posed with three friends from the fire department.

"I'm fine." Brandywine smiled awkwardly. "Thank you."

"Okay then." Elliot forced an awkward smile of his own. "You told the Court that it is your opinion that Jack Ackerman suffered from a condition you called brief reactive psychosis."

"That's right."

Elliot glanced at Jessie, then turned to the witness stand and said, "Dr. Brandywine, did you have occasion to observe any part of Frank Ramsey's trial?"

"No. I read about it in the papers, of course—"

"Right. But you didn't see it yourself?"

"No."

"In fact, you never saw Jack Ackerman before you met him at Wooded Hill Hospital, a month after the trial had ended?"

"That's correct."

"So you can't tell us for sure, one way or the other, if Jack

Ackerman suffered from his condition during Frank Ramsey's trial?"

Brandywine thought about the question, then shook his head. "No."

"For all you know, he was fine during the trial?"

"Well." Again Brandywine took a moment to think about what he was being asked. "I believe that work-related stress—"

"A yes or no answer, please."

Jessie smiled, glad to see her nervousness had been mostly unfounded. Elliot was doing well.

"Yes," Brandywine conceded. "It's possible Mr. Ackerman was fine during the trial."

Judge Spatt leaned back in his chair, apparently expecting Elliot to end his cross-examination. He'd done as much as he could to neutralize Brandywine's testimony. One of the key cross-examination skills was knowing when to stop.

But Elliot didn't.

"Since it's your opinion that Jack Ackerman might have suffered from the condition at the time of the trial, let's explore that."

The judge looked annoyed, then interested. He leaned forward again. Jessie recognized the glint in his eye—he expected Elliot to stumble and he was looking forward to it. Goldhammer stopped taking notes and studied Elliot with interest. Jessie considered standing up, interjecting, but then thought better of it. This was Elliot's case. She was only here to assist. Besides, maybe he knew what he was doing.

"Would brief reactive psychosis *necessarily* impair a person's ability to practice law?" Elliot asked.

"Not necessarily, no."

"A lawyer with that condition *could* put on a competent, even a zealous defense?"

"I don't think so."

"And—" Elliot faltered. Watching his face, she could almost read his thoughts. He'd made a classic cross-examination mistake, and he knew it. He'd given the witness an opening to offer more testimony for the other side. "You mean ... are you telling me that you can't imagine a situation in which a lawyer suffering from brief reactive psychosis could successfully represent a client?"

Jessie willed him to shut up. Cut their losses. Sit the hell down.

Brandywine's eyes looked past Elliot, past Jessie, and into the gallery. She didn't need to turn to know exactly where his gaze was directed. The only person sitting back there who Dr. Brandywine would look at was Jack Ackerman.

When she saw the apology expressed in the doctor's eyes, she knew their case was about to be sunk. "Brief reactive psychosis is a very serious condition," Brandywine said. "I know I wouldn't want to be represented by a lawyer suffering from it."

"That, that's not what I asked." Elliot sputtered, sounding as if he were barely able to get the words past his lips. "That—"

Jessie could take no more. She stood up, drawing the attention of the judge, Goldhammer, Ramsey, everyone. "Your Honor, the Commonwealth has no more questions for this witness."

Elliot wheeled around to face her, but said nothing.

BURNOUT

"Oh, Ms. Black, I didn't notice you there." Judge Spatt leered at her. "You're Mr. Williams's babysitter, I presume?" He turned to the mortified young prosecutor and added, "Looks like it's bedtime for you, counselor."

Elliot looked from the judge to Jessie, unable to respond. Ignoring him, Judge Spatt asked Goldhammer if he'd like to redirect.

"Yes, your Honor." Goldhammer rose, stepped past Elliot. "Dr. Brandywine, what is the clinical definition of brief reactive psychosis?"

"A sudden display of psychotic behavior, prompted by a stressful event."

"A sudden display of psychotic behavior." Goldhammer spread his hands. "In that case, I agree with you, Doctor. I wouldn't want to be represented by a lawyer suffering from that either."

10.

Before Goldhammer could call his next witness, a door at the back of the courtroom opened and a man entered. He strode down the aisle to the bar separating the lawyers from the gallery and leaned over it, careful to keep out of reach of Ramsey. He was young—a paralegal fresh out of college, Jessie guessed—and moved with a frat boy's swagger. Goldhammer twisted in his seat to exchange whispers with him.

"You have a lot of nerve." Elliot, still fuming, apparently hadn't noticed the newcomer. The flush in his cheeks had not dissipated since he'd taken his seat after being chided by the judge.

"I understand you're upset." She turned away, strained to hear the conversation across the aisle. She picked up a few words, but out of context, they meant nothing.

"You understand?" Elliot's voice, though barely louder than a whisper, obliterated the words between Goldhammer and his underling. "That's all you're going to say?"

"Being mocked in open court isn't fun, but it happens, especially in Judge Spatt's courtroom. If I invited it by speaking for you, I apologize. You were floundering. I had to act and I didn't see another way."

"I wasn't floundering. If you had allowed me to finish—"

"You would only have caused more damage to our case." She saw his blush deepen and realized she was making things worse. She had never been good in situations like this. She was not a mentor. She was a loner, and had been for as long as she could remember. "Look, Elliot, I'm sure you're going to be a great lawyer someday—"

"Someday?" His voice began to rise. In addition to destroying any chance she had to eavesdrop on Goldhammer, it risked drawing Judge Spatt's attention—never a good thing.

"Please lower your voice."

"I graduated from law school, you know. I passed the bar. I'm not a kid."

She turned in her chair. "Look, Elliot, even the best lawyers sometimes step in their own traps during cross. When that happens, all you can do is back off. No matter how many times you asked, Brandywine wasn't going to give you an answer you wanted."

His jaw set. "We'll never know."

She glanced back at Goldhammer. The paralegal had taken a seat in the gallery. The defense attorney rose to address the judge.

Spatt regarded him with a mixture of skepticism and disgust. "Something troubling you, Counselor?"

"Your Honor, there's been a new development in the case. We request the Court's permission to call a witness who was not identified in our petition."

Jessie was on her feet in an instant, realizing too late that she'd once again usurped Elliot's role. She felt his glare at the edge of her vision but ignored it, focusing all of her attention on Goldhammer and Spatt. "That's not fair. The Commonwealth was given zero notice of this witness."

"Fair?" Goldhammer smirked. He stepped out from behind his table, approaching the judge with outstretched hands. "My client is facing death because of the ineffective representation of a mentally unbalanced lawyer, and Ms. Black is complaining about the fairness of an unexpected witness?"

"Your Honor, Mr. Goldhammer is clearly attempting to blur the issues."

Judge Spatt's eyes narrowed. "Ms. Black, in my experience, when lawyers tell me how clear something is, it's usually as murky as a fouled toilet bowl."

She tried not to allow that image to form in her mind. "But—"

Spatt leaned forward. "You know what's *clear*, Ms. Black? What's clear is that allowing this witness is within my discretion. The rules of evidence at a hearing are not as strict as those at a trial."

"I agree, Your Honor, but—"

"You agree? Good. Call your witness, Mr. Goldhammer."

"Thank you, Your Honor." Goldhammer watched the judge warily, apparently not confident that Spatt wouldn't lash out at him next. When no further invective issued from the bench, he said, "Petitioner calls Mr. Seth Caylor to the stand."

The door at the side of the courtroom—the one through which Ramsey had been escorted—opened. A sheriff's deputy brought another jumpsuit-clad man into the room.

"Who's he?" Caught up in events, Elliot had momentarily forgotten his anger. He stared at the new arrival with open bewilderment.

Jessie scanned the gallery until she found Jack. The expression on his face was grim.

"Shit."

"What?" Elliot said. "Who is he?"

"Guessing by Jack's reaction, someone we don't want up there."

The deputy seated Caylor on the witness stand. As he was sworn in, Jessie wracked her brain for a strategy. The best she could conceive was to beg Judge Spatt to give them the afternoon to prepare. Somehow, she doubted he would grant the request.

Goldhammer strutted closer to the witness stand. "Mr. Caylor, what do you do for a living?"

Caylor stared at the lawyer as if he'd lost his mind. "I'm in prison."

"Oh. How long have you been there?"

"Almost eighteen months now."

"You received a trial, I assume."

Caylor shrugged. "Nah, I pleaded guilty. Made a deal with the DA."

"Really? To what offense did you plead?"

Caylor looked confused.

"What was your crime?" Goldhammer said.

"Felony murder."

"What's that?"

Judge Spatt grunted. "I think everyone here is familiar

with the concept, Mr. Goldhammer. If you want to teach criminal law, do it in a law school."

"I apologize, Your Honor." Goldhammer returned his attention to Caylor. "Why don't you just tell us what happened? Why were you arrested?"

Caylor cast a wary glance at Jessie and Elliot, as if they might hear his story and prosecute him a second time.

"It's all right," Goldhammer said. "No one's on trial here, Mr. Caylor."

Tell that to Jack Ackerman.

"We robbed a bar. Me and two other guys. One of them, Bobby, had a shotgun. He wasn't supposed to use it. The plan was to walk in, wave the shotgun around, make the bartender empty the register. But one of the guys drinking at the bar, this big black guy, tried to knock the shotgun out of Bobby's hand. The shotgun went off, killed the guy. We all three of us got arrested for his murder."

Goldhammer nodded slowly. "Did you have any criminal record prior to this incident?" He rubbed his chin as if he were evaluating all of the facts of the case, preparing a defense.

Jessie stood up, knowing as she did so that it would be hopeless to try to justify her behavior as falling within the supporting role she'd been assigned, but what was the point of holding back now? *In for a penny, or whatever the phrase was.* "Your Honor, how is this relevant?"

"Objection sustained. Mr. Goldhammer, you're making me regret my earlier decision about this witness."

Goldhammer retracted the question, asked another. "After the police arrested you, Mr. Caylor, what happened?"

"I demanded a lawyer."

"Smart man." Goldhammer smiled, but his witness seemed to miss the joke. "And a lawyer was appointed to you?"

"Yeah."

"Do you remember the name of that lawyer?"

"That's him in the back."

Goldhammer turned to follow the path of Caylor's pointing finger. "Let the record reflect that the witness has pointed to Jack Ackerman."

Jessie stood again. "Your Honor, relevancy."

The judge nodded, his wrinkled face looking grim. He turned directly to the witness and Caylor's face paled. "Mr. Caylor, can you tell me the approximate date Mr. Ackerman was appointed as your counsel?"

"Sure. It was in May of last year."

"A month before the Ramsey trial," Spatt said, turning his attention back to Jessie. "Sounds to me like this witness may have something relevant to say."

"If he's in prison, he's obviously biased against Mr. Ackerman—"

"An excellent topic for you to explore on cross."

"Yes, Your Honor." Reluctantly, she sat down.

"Were you happy with the job Mr. Ackerman did for you?" Goldhammer asked Caylor.

"No. He sucked."

Jessie was tempted to glance over her shoulder to see how Jack was taking this, but didn't dare. Already her thoughts were fast-forwarding to the end of Caylor's direct examination. They would need to establish bias to impeach his testimony, then drag a few of Jack's satisfied customers to the stand to sing his praises.

"I'm hardly convinced," Spatt said, "that this witness is qualified to evaluate the performance of his lawyer."

"My intention is to elicit his impressions so that the Court can draw its own conclusions," Goldhammer said. "Mr. Caylor, tell us about your experience with Mr. Ackerman."

"First time he met with me, he already had a deal from the DA's office. Told me I should take it. I tried to explain to him that I didn't kill anybody, that Bobby was the one holding the shotgun and he probably only shot the black guy by accident, but the lawyer, he don't care. He tells me it's a good deal, I should take it."

"Objection," Jessie said. "Hearsay."

"Don't tell us what was said," Goldhammer told the witness. "Just describe the nature of your conversations."

"The nature?"

"Did Mr. Ackerman suggest possible trial strategies, defenses, anything like that?"

Jessie stood up. "Objection. Leading the witness."

"You can't have it both ways, Ms. Black," Spatt said. "Mr. Caylor, answer the question."

"No, we didn't talk about defenses."

"Did Mr. Ackerman behave normally?"

"Objection." Jessie half-rose from her seat, but Judge Spatt shook his head, stopping her.

"No," Caylor said. "He acted weird. Like he was on drugs or crazy."

"What do you mean?"

"His eyes were bloodshot and he kept looking around, like I wasn't interesting enough for him. And he was shaking a little, his hands. Wasn't acting like any lawyer I ever saw."

"Did he exhibit any other strange behavior?"

"That's all I remember."

"Thank you. No further questions."

Spatt didn't bother to conceal the smirk on his face as Elliot approached the witness. To his credit, Elliot ignored the judge.

"Um, hello, Mr. Caylor."

Caylor's lip curled.

"You testified that Mr. Ackerman was acting—you said—weird. You said he had bloodshot eyes, he was shaking—"

"I know what I said."

"You never saw a person with bloodshot eyes that wasn't on drugs or crazy?"

Caylor shrugged.

"Yes or no."

"Of course I have."

"How about the shaking. You've never seen a person with shaky hands who wasn't on drugs or crazy?"

Caylor gnawed his lip and cast his gaze away from Elliot. "I guess some people's hands shake that are normal otherwise."

"And you said Mr. Ackerman kept looking around. Only people on drugs, or crazy people, look around?"

Now Caylor met Elliot's gaze. There was a defiant gleam in his eyes. "It was the combination of all three, the way he was."

"That's not what I asked."

"He didn't seem all there. I didn't get the feeling he was in the right frame of mind to be my lawyer. He—"

"Mr. Caylor, I didn't ask—"

"Well you're trying to twist my words. You're taking apart everything I said. Trying to make me sound stupid. I know a person can have bloodshot eyes and not be a fucking crackhead, okay? I'm saying—"

"Mr. Caylor—" Judge Spatt raised his gavel, but didn't bring it down. Jessie, by rising from her chair, must have caught his eye. Before she knew what she was doing, she found herself standing beside Elliot in front of the witness stand. "What's this?" Spatt said. "You gonna tag-team the witness?"

Jessie looked into Elliot's shocked face. Quietly, she said, "Sit down."

"Your Honor." Goldhammer was out of his chair, looking incredulous. "What is this?"

"I'm wondering the same thing," Elliot said with a huff.

Jessie ignored him. To the judge, she said, "I'd like to ask the witness some questions."

"This is completely improper," Goldhammer said.

"You said the rules weren't as strict at a hearing," she reminded Spatt.

"The rules of evidence," Goldhammer said. "Not the rules of procedure."

"I can't believe this," Elliot said to no one in particular.

"Please." Jessie held the judge's stare. "I'll be brief."

Spatt sighed, nodded. "Fine. Go ahead."

She watched Elliot return to his seat and wondered, for a moment, what kind of mess she was getting herself into. Then the more pressing task of impeaching Caylor descended on her, demanding the entirety of her attention.

"Mr. Caylor, do you understand why this hearing is being held?" she said.

Goldhammer objected. "Beyond the scope of direct."

"Overruled," Spatt said. "Answer her."

"You're trying to decide if Ackerman's a nutjob."

"Do you understand what happens if the Court decides that he is?"

Caylor shrugged. "Frank Ramsey gets a new trial."

"Why?"

"Because he's entitled to a lawyer that isn't nuts?"

"But, by that reasoning, wouldn't *you* receive a new trial as well?"

Caylor avoided her eyes. "Never occurred to me."

"Of course it didn't. Do you understand the elements of felony murder?"

"If your accomplice kills someone, you're automatically guilty, too."

Jessie nodded. "Did your accomplice kill someone?"

Caylor rolled his eyes. "I already told you he did."

"And Mr. Ackerman advised you to plead guilty."

"He acted weird."

She turned her back on him before he could continue. On her way back to her seat, she said, "I have no further questions, Your Honor."

Judge Spatt grimaced. "Let's take a fifteen minute recess."

11.

She led Elliot to a witness preparation room adjacent to the courtroom, hoping to use the precious recess to plan their next move. But the moment she closed the door and shut them inside the tiny space, he whirled on her. "What the hell were you doing in there?"

She glanced at the door. "Lower your voice. The walls are thin."

"Oh, thanks for the tip. I wouldn't want to embarrass myself."

"I told you, I'm sorry I took over—"

"You did it numerous times."

"Two or three times. I'm sorry."

"Oh, I can tell. You're drowning in remorse." He started to pace the room, a frustrated tiger in a cage. His hair had broken its gelled bonds; strands of it extended in disarray. His suit, too, looked more rumpled than it had an hour before. She watched him with a mixture of sympathy and annoyance. She'd wounded his pride in order to save their case. She understood how he felt, but didn't have time to soothe his hurt feelings just because he couldn't see the bigger picture.

The fifteen minute recess was a gift, a chance for them to

catch their breath and strategize before Goldhammer launched his next volley. Elliot was wasting the opportunity.

Elliot stopped pacing. "I want your word that you'll stay out of my way for the rest of the hearing."

She thought about it. She knew she should be appreciative—he was offering her a second chance, rather than running to his uncle. And for the most part, she thought she could live with staying in her seat for the remainder of the hearing. Unless Goldhammer planned another surprise, only two witnesses remained to cross-examine. One was a psychiatrist specializing in psychoses. Jessie and Elliot had prepared arguments for precluding his testimony, and she believed Elliot could persuade Judge Spatt to do so on the basis that another psychiatrist's testimony would be cumulative after Brandywine's. But the other witness was Ramsey. The monster had chosen not to testify at his trial—a wise move—but at this hearing he had little choice. He was the only person truly in a position to testify convincingly about Jack's behavior at the time of his trial. Jessie had taken over the cross-examination of Caylor as a measure of last resort. Could she really promise she wouldn't do the same thing during Ramsey's testimony, if she thought staying quiet would result in his conviction being overturned?

"I want your word," Elliot repeated.

"No."

He gaped at her. "What do you mean?"

"Listen to me, Elliot. If you thought Brandywine and Caylor were difficult witnesses to cross-examine, Ramsey will be a thousand times worse. He's a sociopath. He doesn't have normal emotions. He can't be manipulated or trapped like you learned in school. I've spent years cross-examining people like him. If we're going to win, I should be the one who does it."

Elliot stared at the table, moving his finger along gouges and chips in the wood, where legions of lawyers and witnesses had left evidence of their use of this room. "So you're just going to commandeer my case?" he said. "Just like that?"

"Why do you have to think of it that way? This is *our* case. We're working together."

He sneered at her. "Yeah, it sure feels that way."

A knock on the door cut off their exchange. When the door opened, Jessie half-expected to see Goldhammer's gloating smile, but Jack Ackerman stuck his head in instead. "Am I interrupting? Sounded like you guys were having a heated debate."

"That's one way to describe it," she said.

Elliot stood up. "I was just leaving." He elbowed past Jack and slammed the door behind him. For a moment, Jack watched the door vibrate in its frame, a comical expression on his face. Then he took Elliot's seat at the table. "Way to inspire loyalty in your troops, Sarge."

"Don't start."

Jack laughed. "Maybe you should have given him more of a chance to prove himself. Everyone starts somewhere."

"This hearing is too important to be a learning exercise."

"I disagree. The tough cases are the best learning exercises. He might have risen to the occasion, if you'd given him a little more room."

"Or he might have irrevocably destroyed your career."

Jack shrugged. "Or that."

She smiled. How he could be in such a lighthearted mood after hearing two witnesses describe his mental problems was a mystery. But she was grateful. After Elliot's anger, Jack's humor was a relief.

"Caylor was lying," Jack said. "About the bloodshot eyes, the shaky hands. I never had any of those symptoms." His face was serious now, as if it were important to him that she know this information. "And you know there was nothing strange about seeking a plea bargain. Not with an open-and-shut felony murder charge. It took me two grueling days to negotiate Caylor's plea bargain. Believe me, there was nothing ineffective about my work."

"Who was the prosecutor?"

"Andrew Meyer. I'm sure he would testify—"

She nodded. "I'll give him a call if we need to. Since Caylor was a surprise witness, Spatt should allow us to add a new rebuttal witness. But honestly, I'm hoping your testimony this afternoon will be enough. We've still got a few minutes. You want to go over the questions again?"

Jack sat back in his chair and smiled.

"What?" she said.

"I don't know. *This*. You and me working together. I never thought it would happen. It's fun."

"That's not the word I would use." She sighed, but felt a smile tug at her mouth a moment later. "It is nice to be on the same side for once, though." She looked at her watch. "Recess is over. Back to work."

12.

Back in the courtroom, there was no trace of Elliot.

"I guess he really took off," Jack said after surveying the courtroom.

"Looks that way."

"Warren's not going to be happy."

Jessie tried not to imagine the inevitable confrontation in her boss's office. "Probably not."

She watched Jack walk to his seat in the gallery, then headed toward hers up front. Goldhammer and Ramsey were already seated across the aisle. As she approached, Goldhammer rose to meet her.

"Where's your partner?" His smile was all teeth.

"He's been called back to the office on another matter."

"What a shame. He seemed perfect for this case. Ineffective lawyering obviously being his specialty."

If he had expected her to laugh at the joke, he was disappointed. Ramsey, sitting within earshot, did not laugh either. He looked away from his lawyer as if he were embarrassed to be associated with him.

"I don't know where you were admitted to the bar, Mr.

Goldhammer, but in Pennsylvania, we practice something called professional courtesy."

He grinned at her. "From what I've seen, that's not exactly *your* forte either."

"My forte is putting murderers in prison." She glanced at Ramsey, caught his eye. "And keeping them there."

"Yes, I know," Goldhammer said. "Your reputation is very intimidating." His mocking tone caused her to grind her teeth, but she didn't break eye contact. Backing down from a man like Goldhammer would only make him bolder. "I'm looking forward to Mr. Ramsey's new trial. It will give me a chance to put you in your place, show the locals there's nothing to be afraid of."

"Ramsey's already had his trial. He isn't getting another one."

"I'm sure that's what you think."

Jessie took her seat, fuming. This day was getting worse and worse.

Judge Spatt stared at Goldhammer, incredulous. "You want to put *another* headshrinker on the stand? Doctor Gin-and-tonic wasn't enough?"

"Dr. Brandywine testified in his capacity as Mr. Ackerman's therapist, Your Honor. Dr. Putnam will assist the Court in understanding the complexities of Mr. Ackerman's condition."

Jessie shook her head and was relieved to see her own frustration reflected in the judge's weary gaze. "Your Honor," she said, "Dr. Brandywine testified as to both his firsthand knowledge of Mr. Ackerman *and* as an expert. Further expert testimony relating to the same psychiatric concepts would be merely cumulative."

"I agree. I'm granting the Commonwealth's motion to preclude Dr. Putnam's testimony."

Finally, something had gone according to plan. She wished Elliot had been here to see it. Goldhammer pouted, but managed to thank the judge anyway. "In that case, Your Honor, I'd like to call my final witness, Frank Ramsey."

Every prosecutor hopes that the defendant will forsake his right to remain silent and risk the witness stand. Frank Ramsey, under counsel of Jack Ackerman, had been too smart to testify at his trial, but at this PCRA hearing, where the issue was not Ramsey's guilt or innocence but the effectiveness of his trial lawyer, Goldhammer had decided that Ramsey's testimony was necessary. Jessie planned to show him the error of his ways.

The bailiff escorted Ramsey to the witnesses stand and helped him into the chair. If Ramsey was embarrassed by his shambling walk and jingling chains, he didn't show it. He sat with his spine straight, acknowledged the judge with a nod, and faced Goldhammer.

"Tell us about your court appointed defense attorney, Jack Ackerman," Goldhammer said.

"Well, I'm not surprised to hear he had psych problems. Explains a lot."

"What do you mean?" Goldhammer prompted.

Ramsey turned a maddeningly neutral expression toward the gallery, where Jack sat watching the testimony. "The decisions he made were irrational and unreasonable. When I tried to discuss why I thought his strategies were flawed, he refused to listen."

Jessie wrote the words on her legal pad: *Irrational. Unreasonable. Refused to listen.* Goldhammer had studied the Pennsylvania case law on ineffective assistance of counsel and had coached his client well.

"Can you remember any concrete examples?" Goldhammer said.

"There was a witness, a sixteen-year-old girl." Hearing Ramsey speak of Kristen Dillard—the girl he'd raped, stabbed, orphaned, and attempted to kill—made Jessie grind her teeth. "She claimed to be a victim and an eyewitness," Ramsey continued. She failed to pick me out of a photo array, but then she picked me in a lineup. I told Ackerman she had to be either lying or mistaken. Because I was innocent. I told Ackerman he needed to drill her with questions. Find the inconsistencies and contradictions. They had to be there. But Ackerman refused. I think it was part of his nervous breakdown—"

"Objection, Your Honor," Jessie said, barely able to keep her tone civil. "The witness is not a psychiatrist. In fact, the witness is not even a high school graduate—"

Spatt leveled at her one of his warning stares. "Sustained."

"Without speculating about Mr. Ackerman's mental condition," Goldhammer said, "tell us what happened."

"He barely questioned her," Ramsey said. "It's like he was sick of attacking witnesses, like he'd done it so many times as a public defender that he was burnt out—"

"Objection."

"Sustained."

"Mr. Ramsey," Goldhammer said, "do you think Mr. Ackerman's refusal to aggressively cross-examine Kristen Dillard resulted in your losing the trial?"

"I know it did. The jury found me guilty based on her testimony. She was either lying or confused—I don't know. Because of Ackerman, the jury never doubted a word she said."

Jessie could not even muster a polite smile for the man on the witness stand. He regarded her with a neutral mask—the face of a sociopath, if she'd ever seen one.

"Did Mr. Ackerman explain to you his rationale for not, as you put it, *drilling* Kristen Dillard on cross?"

Goldhammer bounced up from his seat. "Objection. Ms. Black is mischaracterizing my client's testimony. She's taking that word out of context."

"Your Honor, I apologize. I wouldn't want to make the witness sound bad."

Behind her, she heard Goldhammer mutter something.

"All I know," Ramsey said, "is she told the jury she was one-hundred percent sure I was the man who did all those things to her and her family. She was either lying or she made a mistake."

"I see. What, exactly, were the things she said you did?"

"Objection," Goldhammer said. "We all know what crimes Mr. Ramsey was convicted of. They're not relevant here."

Spatt turned to Jessie, raised his eyebrows.

"They're relevant to demonstrate the reasonableness of

Mr. Ackerman's legal tactics, Your Honor."

That seemed to satisfy him. "Objection overruled. Mr. Ramsey, answer the question."

"She said I raped her mother. Stabbed her mother and father to death. Raped her. Stabbed her. Left her for dead. None of it is true."

"It must have been heartbreaking, hearing a sixteen-year-old girl describe those things happening to her," Jessie said.

Ramsey shrugged. "You were there."

"So, to rephrase my first question, did Mr. Ackerman explain to you his rationale for not aggressively challenging Kristen Dillard's story on cross?"

"He thought it would turn the jury against me."

"Did he explain why?"

"Objection," Goldhammer said. "Hearsay."

Jessie looked at the judge. "The statement is not being offered as evidence of its truth, only as evidence that Mr. Ackerman was acting in a reasonable manner."

"Overruled. Answer."

"He said the jurors would see him attacking the girl and they would see it as me attacking her. He said they would look at it as another violation."

She held his stare for a moment. "I'm finished with this witness." She turned, started walking back to her seat.

"Wait."

Ramsey's voice, a flat monotone, froze her in place.

Spatt said, "Mr. Ramsey, please refrain from speaking unless you're asked a question."

Jessie turned around, faced the man.

"What would you have done, if you'd been my lawyer?" Ramsey said.

"Mr. Ramsey—" Spatt's cheeks tinted red.

Ramsey ignored him. His stare was fixed on Jessie. "Would you have let her off easy, just in case the jury felt bad for her?"

"Mr. Ramsey," Spatt said, his voice louder now, "you do not ask the questions here."

"Well?" Ramsey said.

"It's not a choice I'll ever have to make," Jessie said. "Because I don't represent murderers."

Ramsey's eyes flared. "That's not an answer!"

The bailiff stood up. Ramsey immediately took the hint, shut his mouth, and folded his hands in front of him. The bailiff sat down again. Ramsey looked up at the judge and said, "I'm sorry, Your Honor."

But he'd shown his true self. For ten precious seconds, his mask had slipped. Hopefully that would be enough.

13.

Although Jessie had seen Jack Ackerman in various courtrooms throughout her career, the sight of him on the witness stand unnerved her. She recognized his Armani suit—one of many in which he'd once dressed to impress jurors—and he regarded the judge with the same confident demeanor he'd often employed with great effect in front of juries. But there were no jurors here today, and the only witness was himself. Under the cold appraisal of Judge Spatt, the former star of the public defender's office looked as fragile as his former clients, stripped of the authority accorded lawyers in a courtroom, authority he'd once wielded with such relentlessness. Yet he looked relaxed, even happy.

"Hey, Jess."

The warning glare with which she returned his greeting wiped the smile off his face. He might find humor in the novelty of his inverted circumstances, but she did not.

"Mr. Ackerman, did you represent Frank Ramsey at his murder trial?"

He leaned forward slightly, the smile returning to his face as if he just couldn't help himself. "Yes ma'am."

Judge Spatt looked from Jack to her, then back again. No

doubt sensing an in-joke from which he'd been excluded, his eyes narrowed with displeasure.

Jessie soldiered on as if there were nothing strange about Jack's answers. "How would you describe your performance at the trial?"

"Exemplary. I definitely should have won."

She could hear Goldhammer frantically taking notes behind her and wondered what he'd made of Jack's flippant tone. If she was lucky, he'd missed it. But she didn't think Goldhammer missed much.

"Why didn't you win?"

"It happens." Jack shrugged. "Juries are unpredictable. There's no such thing as a sure victory. Especially against a skilled prosecutor."

With his sanity and professional aptitude on trial, was he actually *flirting* with her again?

"Would you briefly describe your strategy for representing Mr. Ramsey?"

"From the beginning, Mr. Ramsey refused to entertain any deals, period. And even if he had been amenable, the prosecutor didn't offer any." He winked at her. "So there was no way to avoid a full trial."

"What was your strategy for the trial?"

"In my opinion, the prosecution's case was weak. No offense. The police had not found any physical evidence linking Mr. Ramsey to the crime—no semen, no blood, none of those little flakes of skin, no hairs. They couldn't even locate the murder weapon. The prosecution's whole case was based on the testimony of one eyewitness. My strategy was to emphasize the lack of physical evidence."

"What about the eyewitness?"

"Her name was Kristen Dillard. She was one of the victims of Ramsey's alleged crime. She was sixteen, had clearly been brutalized by someone, and was an incredibly sympathetic witness."

"What was your strategy for dealing with her?"

"In my experience, when you have a victim-witness who is very sympathetic, it's best to handle her with kid gloves or not at all. If you cross-examine her too belligerently, you risk alienating the jury and coming off as a bully. I asked Miss Dillard a few questions to establish that, for much of the incident, her back was to the assailant. I also established that she initially failed to identify Ramsey, when the police showed her his picture in a photo array. That was as far as I dared to go."

"Mr. Ackerman, what happened to you in July of last year?"

"I burned out, I think. I had a breakdown. But that happened weeks after the Ramsey trial was over."

"During the Ramsey trial, you weren't burned out?"

"No."

"You provided effective assistance of counsel?"

"Absolutely."

"Thank you. I have no further—"

"Hold on," Judge Spatt said. "I have some."

Jessie held her breath. It was not uncommon, especially at a hearing or a bench trial, for a judge to ask his own questions of a witness. But with Judge Spatt, even common actions threatened to undermine her case. As she watched him gather his thoughts, her legs suddenly felt tired, her feet uncomfortable in her heels. She had been on her feet—or poised to pop up for an objection—since morning. Now she would have to stand mute in the middle of the courtroom as the judge grilled her witness.

Spatt's eyebrows, stark white against his dark complexion, twitched as he leaned toward the witness stand. Jack did not flinch from him, but he didn't wear his usual smile either. His eyes regarded the judge with caution.

"Mr. Ackerman, you're a criminal defense attorney, is that right?"

"Well, I used to be. Now I practice trust and estate law, mostly drafting wills—"

"Yes, but when you defended crooks for a living, did you ever find it necessary to attack the credibility of their victims?"

"It's a tactic every defense attorney uses at some point."

"That's not what I asked you."

"Sometimes I found it necessary, Your Honor. Yes."

"But not in Mr. Ramsey's case? Where there was no evidence except for the victim's word?"

Jack leaned toward the judge. His face shifted to an expression Jessie recognized from the not-so-distant past—his lawyer face. "Attacking an already-devastated victim is a tactic almost certain to backfire."

"Aren't most victims devastated, Mr. Ackerman?"

"Most? I don't know—"

"Aren't most of them sympathetic?"

"I'm not sure you can quantify—"

"I'm not asking you to quantify. I'm asking a simple question."

"Your Honor," Jessie said, "I object to your badgering of the witness."

Spatt ignored her, his attention locked on Jack. "A simple question, Mr. Ackerman. Lawyer to lawyer."

By some miracle, Jack retained his composure. "Many crime victims are sympathetic witnesses."

"What was special about Kristen Dillard?"

Jack opened his mouth, closed it, shook his head. "It was just a feeling I had."

"I see." Spatt looked at Goldhammer. "Do you want to cross this witness, Mr. Goldhammer?"

"Uh, no, that won't be necessary, Your Honor," Goldhammer said, half-rising. "I think you covered all the bases."

"Good," Spatt said. "Because I've made my decision. I'm not a psychiatrist, but Mr. Ackerman's mental issues appear to me to be too serious, and too close in time to Mr. Ramsey's trial, to ignore. I am granting Mr. Ramsey's petition. His guilty verdict is hereby vacated and he will have a new trial."

Spatt slammed his gavel, and left the room before anyone could speak.

14.

Jessie went directly to the DA's office from the courthouse, part of her hoping she would be fast enough to deliver the bad news to Warren first, in person. The rest of her was already resigned to the likelihood that he'd heard everything already, and that he'd only heard one side of the story. He was on the phone when she arrived at his office breathless from her hurried walk through the brisk November air. He waved her inside as he continued talking. Judging by his side of the conversation—which was characterized by obsequiousness as opposed to his typically condescending tone—he must be on the line with a superior.

As the head of the Homicide Unit, Warren didn't have many superiors.

Warren hung up, looked at her. "Word of advice—if you're going to steal a colleague's case, make sure you win it."

Shit.

She offered what she hoped was an appropriately self-deprecating nod. "Was that District Attorney Rivera?"

Warren ran his hand through his sparse hair. "I'm getting it from two directions. Rivera's terrified that Goldhammer is going to turn Ramsey's retrial into some kind of indictment of the DA's office. And Rasch is bitching at me because you screwed over Elliot."

Holly Rasch, the head of the Appeals Unit. Jessie cringed. Up until this point, she and Holly had been on good terms. Women were a minority in the DA's office and Holly had acted as an informal mentor during Jessie's first few months at the office. Her stomach twisted at the thought of Holly taking today's events as a betrayal of their friendship. "I'll talk to her."

"Rasch is the least of your problems right now. Or do I need to remind you that stabbing your boss's nephew in the back is not generally considered a good career move?"

The knot in her stomach tightened. "What are you saying?"

He uncapped a marker. The smell filled the small office, made her dizzy. "I'm taking you off the Zuhdi double homicide." He found her name on the big dry erase calendar on the wall behind his desk and slashed it with black ink. "And the DeSena killing." Another slash. "In fact, I'm clearing your calendar." More slashes, one following another.

"What does that mean? You're firing me? What did Elliot tell you? I think you should hear my side of the story. After all these years working together—"

"Relax, Jessie. I'm not firing you. But you're going to need to focus all of your attention on Ramsey. We have a potential disaster here, and Rivera wants to make sure it's prevented. You put Ramsey away once. You can do it again."

She closed her eyes for a moment as the tension drained from her body. "Thank you."

When she opened her eyes, he was staring at her. "Don't thank me. Get a conviction for me."

She nodded. "I didn't win Ramsey's trial because of Jack's mental condition. I won it because of Kristen Dillard. There's no jury that wouldn't convict the bastard based on her testimony."

Warren leaned back, his chair squeaking. "Don't be so sure. Gil Goldhammer's read the trial transcript. Trust me, he's memorized Kristen Dillard's testimony. He has surprises in store for us. Don't doubt it. He isn't paid a thousand dollars an hour for nothing."

She remembered her earlier conversation with the celebrity lawyer. "Who's paying him? Ramsey has no money. No family or friends."

"You know how it is with death penalty cases, the philanthropists crawl out of the woodwork. Maybe some anti-death penalty faction?" Warren shrugged. "Who knows."

"The information might be useful."

"What are you saying? You want to put someone on it?"

"Not someone from our office."

His face looked puzzled for a moment, then cleared with understanding. "Leary? Are you kidding? What's the deal? You still have a thing for him? Hoping for a return trip to the backseat of his car?"

It had been the front seat, not that it was any of Warren's business. "I don't have a 'thing' for Mark Leary," she bit out. "He was the lead detective on the Ramsey case. It makes sense to get his help again now."

"Detective Leary has fresh homicides to work. Scumbags don't wait in line to kill people, you know. They don't put their murders on hold while we resolve last year's crimes. Leary—"

Jessie knew the power Warren wielded with the police. "If you make a call, Captain Henderson will reassign Leary to the Ramsey case without a moment's hesitation."

"We don't need a homicide detective wasting time working a case he closed over a year ago. If you miss him, send him flowers."

Miss him? She'd barely thought about him, especially since the new and improved Jack Ackerman had entered her life. Not that she was going to mention *that* to Warren.

"Leary knows the case. He can help us anticipate Goldhammer's traps. You just said Goldhammer has surprises in store for us."

He wagged a finger at her. "Jessie, what have I told you about throwing my own words back in my face?"

"I can't help it. They're so intelligent, so perceptive, so—"

"The answer is no," he said, cutting her off. "I am not going to ask the Philly PD to re-open a case in which we already have an eyewitness who can identify the murderer. If you can't win with that evidence, you don't deserve to work here."

"I understand." The threat was tacit but unmistakable. Her career was on the line.

15.

Woody slipped out of the courtroom gallery immediately after the judge ruled in Ramsey's favor. After watching the hearing from the back of the room, careful to avoid giving any indication that he knew any of the participants, he had driven straight to Goldhammer's hotel.

The doorman looked him up and down before grudgingly opening the door. Woody resisted the urge to inform the idiot that the massive Christmas bonus he'd probably receive next month would be coming out of Woody's—or, more accurately, Woody's brother's—pocket. In addition to booking a massive temporary office space that spanned almost an entire floor of the hotel, complete with office equipment, cubicle dividers, high-speed Internet access, and God only knew what other necessities, Goldhammer had also helped himself to a luxurious personal suite with a view of the city. Woody rode the elevator to the suite now, his irritation growing with each floor the elevator pinged past.

One of the blowhard's minions greeted him at the suite door holding a flute of champagne. "Gil's just changing out of his suit. He said to give you this and tell you he'll be right with you."

"No thanks."

Woody knocked aside the man's hand, spilling champagne onto the carpet and knocking the grin off his face, then brushed past him into the suite. Woody had dealt with plenty of lawyers just like Goldhammer during his years as a corrections officer. People like Goldhammer, Ackerman—even the prosecutor, Jessica Black—were all the same. Arrogant, self-important, and soft, they thought they were more critical than the cops and the prison guards and the other real servants of the justice system, who they barely deigned to acknowledge.

Well, Woody had never let lawyers boss him around at SCI Huntington, and he sure as hell wasn't going to take any bullshit from Goldhammer.

"I'll talk to him now."

"He said he'll be right out." Woody barged past him. The man trailed him through the suite. "Would you prefer a beer?" The main room swarmed with Goldhammer's underlings, most of whom appeared to be drinking. Did any of these assholes realize that the real trial hadn't started yet? Woody flung open the door to Goldhammer's bedroom and slammed it behind him in the minion's face.

Goldhammer sat at the room's desk, wearing nothing but a silk robe and a stretched-out pair of jockeys. His pricey suit lay in a heap on the bedspread. Woody found it impossible to ignore all the pale flesh on display. Oblivious to his own immodesty, Goldhammer peered at his laptop screen through a pair of reading glasses and made no effort to cover himself. "It's polite to knock before entering a room." He didn't bother to look up.

"It's also polite not to spend your client's money on a celebration before you actually win."

"Frank Ramsey is my client, not you." He swiveled from the computer and met Woody's gaze. "And we did have a victory today. We secured Ramsey a new trial."

"You still need to win it."

Goldhammer chuckled. "No honest lawyer can guarantee success."

Woody walked past him and sat on the edge of the bed. "So tell me how a *dishonest* lawyer would."

Goldhammer smirked. Woody had never met a lawyer who didn't relish hypotheticals.

"A trial's nothing but a war of minds. A criminal trial pits a defense lawyer's mind against a prosecutor's. Now, suppose a dishonest lawyer somehow gained access to his adversary's thoughts? That kind of advantage would virtually guarantee success."

Woody began to slide off the sagging mattress edge. He pushed his shoes against the carpet, thrust himself further back onto the puffy bedspread.

"I wouldn't touch that." Goldhammer pointed at the bedspread as if lice might swarm out of it onto Woody's hands. Never mind that Goldhammer was practically naked on a hotel room chair.

People who were put off by hotel linen had always amused Woody. They should work for a few years at a state prison. The experience would quickly put their idea of basic hygiene in the proper perspective.

"You're telling me you want to be able to read Jessica Black's mind?"

Goldhammer laughed, put up his hands defensively. "All I said was a dishonest lawyer might benefit from ... well, insider knowledge."

"You mean like a mole."

Goldhammer returned his attention to the computer screen. "Mr. Butler, the hotel is charging you a hefty fee for my use of this internet connection." He pressed a pudgy finger to the laptop's touchpad, moved it, clicked a button, typed. "You should let me finish this e-mail."

"Do you treat all your clients this rudely?"

As quickly as he'd lost Goldhammer's attention, he got it back. The lawyer dropped his hands from the computer and turned to look at him.

"I already told you, Frank Ramsey is my client. That's something you need to understand if this relationship is going to be effective."

"I retained you."

"You pay my fees, but Ramsey is my client. Mull it over. If you can't accept the situation, we need to terminate our relationship."

"Give me a break." Woody got up from his perch, walked to the door. He could hear Goldhammer's fingers back on the keyboard, clicking away. "You want to know what our relationship is, *Gil?*"

Goldhammer squinted at him.

"You do what I say, or I shoot you in the fucking head. Mull *that* over."

Before the lawyer could form a response, Woody grabbed the doorknob and left.

16.

It was raining and cold on Thanksgiving. Jessie drove to the Philadelphia Center for Inclusive Treatment to take Kristen Dillard out for the day. She parked her Accord in the lot, cut the engine, and remained in the car for a moment, staring past the rain-smeared windshield at the foreboding tower. It was hard not to draw comparisons with the picturesque grounds of Wooded Hill Hospital. The contrast couldn't be more stark. The unfairness of it riled her. Unlike Jack Ackerman's nebulous "nervous breakdown," Kristen's symptoms were all too clear—acute depression, night terrors, suicidal tendencies. Yet Jack had recovered in an idyllic hideaway, with the constant attention of the best therapists money could buy, while Kristen stared at gray walls and ate meals that a high school cafeteria would refuse to serve. High school cafeterias had to answer to parents. Kristen no longer had parents, or any family.

That's why you're here, she reminded herself.

After a deep breath, she exited the car, opened her umbrella, and headed for the entrance.

She was surprised to find Kristen in the waiting room. The girl rushed forward and embraced Jessie in a hug strong enough to stifle her breath. The nurse waiting with her smiled and touched Jessie's arm. "I think it's so great what you're doing. Kristen's been talking about it all week."

"How are you?" Jessie said.

Kristen's smile did not falter, but in her eyes Jessie saw the sadness that never seemed to leave her, even for a moment. "It's kind of sad with the holidays coming."

"I know."

"I used to give my mom a hard time, tell her I thought her turkey was too dry." Tears welled in her eyes, and she shook her head. "I'd sure like to eat some of her turkey now."

"I know."

Jessie signed the necessary forms, thanked the nurse, and took Kristen's hand. Outside, they didn't bother with the umbrella, instead running for the car like a couple of kids.

Jessie's father lived in a small house in Cherry Hill, New Jersey. He hugged Jessie and then Kristen, treating the girl like family even though he'd never met her. He even managed not to stare at the scar on her neck, reddish, jagged evidence of the knife Ramsey had plunged there.

They ate a simple dinner together. Not like the elaborate Thanksgiving feasts of her childhood when her mother had still lived here, and probably not like the holidays Kristen remembered. But they did have turkey, cranberry sauce, mashed potatoes, and stuffing. And it was good.

After Jessie helped her father clear the dishes, she excused herself and took Kristen into the family room to make sure she was holding up.

"Everything okay?" Jessie asked.

"Yeah. I'm having fun. Your dad's nice."

"Thanks."

"Thank you. For having me."

"Every year," Jessie said. "For as long as you want to come. You're welcome."

Jessie moved toward the doorway, but Kristen touched her arm, stopping her. "The doctors tried to hide it from me, but I heard Ramsey's name on the news. He had some kind of appeal?"

Jessie chewed her lip. Telling Kristen about Ramsey's victory at the PCRA hearing, and what it meant, was inevitable. She had hoped to postpone the conversation until after Thanksgiving. But now that Kristen had brought up the subject, there was no avoiding it. As much as her instincts urged her to protect the girl, Jessie refused to be dishonest with her.

"Not an appeal. A petition under the Post-Conviction Relief Act. We don't need to talk about it tonight, Kristen—"

"I want to. Please."

"Okay. Close the door."

Kristen shut the door, damping the sounds of her father washing dishes and leaving them alone with the patter of the rain against the windowpanes. They sat on the scratchy cushions of an old floral-print sofa.

"Frank Ramsey has been granted a new trial."

Kristen shook her head. "What does that mean? The jury found him guilty. I was there. They gave him a death sentence."

"I know." Since the moment Judge Spatt had granted Ramsey's petition, Jessie had been dreading this moment. She had spent hours playing this scene in her mind, over and over, trying to imagine how she could possibly tell Kristen what had happened. And now that the moment was here, she still had no idea what to say. She decided to speak plainly. She owed Kristen that much. "He filed a petition and it was granted. He's going to have a new trial. The old verdict doesn't matter any more. He's presumed innocent until I prove him guilty again."

"But—" Kristen's eyes blinked rapidly as she grappled with the concept. "You mean I have to do it all over again? I have to testify again about what he did to me?"

Jessie nodded. A lump had formed in her throat and she was afraid that if she spoke, her voice would betray her. She knew that Kristen needed to believe that Jessie was in control, that she could fix this. Otherwise, Kristen might not be able to summon the courage to take the stand again, face the judge and jury again, face *Ramsey* again. And without Kristen's testimony, Jessie could not win.

Jessie hugged her, pressed her face to the girl's shoulder. She could feel Kristen's tears soak into her sweater. When the lump in her throat dissipated, she said, "The system isn't perfect. But Ramsey won't escape justice. I promise you that. Do you understand?"

Without moving her face from Jessie's shoulder, Kristen nodded her head.

"You ready to go back to the dining room? I'm pretty sure my dad mentioned a pie."

"My mom used to make amazing pumpkin pie."

Jessie rocked her gently. "So did mine."

17.

Weeks passed, and before Jessie knew it, Christmas was only days away. She sat in her shoebox-sized workspace in the DA's office, eyes on her window and the clear blue sky outside, and tried to summon some holiday spirit.

Even with her door closed, she could hear Christmas music jingling from someone's radio down the hall. She had stepped out of the elevator this morning to find a potted evergreen, placed there by Ron McGowan as a joke. He'd decorated it with the mug shots of murderers convicted over the past twelve months, added some tinsel, and completed the effect with a banner reading *Naughty Tree*. Another colleague, Evan Geroff, had shown up in a Santa suit.

Of her fellow prosecutors, only Warren seemed to share her lack of interest in the imminent holiday. He had left her a message scrawled on a yellow Post-It note that he'd stuck to a document in her inbox. It said, *I told you Goldhammer would have a surprise in store for us. This is it.* His handwriting was decidedly non-jolly.

She peeled off the sticky and tossed it. The document was an expert witness report. Jessie started reading. By the time she finished, she was livid. She gripped the report tightly and headed for Warren's office.

"She's infamous," Warren said when she stepped into his office an hour later, expert report in hand. His own copy sat on one of the piles of paper on his desk. "Do a search on Westlaw for cases where the prosecution's argument depends on eyewitness evidence. Katherine Moscow's name pops up nine times out of ten."

"I've heard of her," Jessie said. And after a Google search, she knew even more about the woman. A research psychologist and memory expert, Kate Moscow had made news by testifying at criminal trials all over the country, and it was rumored that she had taken a more behind-the-scenes role in dozens more. Her testimony, backed by impressive experimental data, had persuaded juries to acquit murderers and rapists despite confident eyewitness identifications. The *Review of General Psychology* had listed her as one of the twenty-first century's Top 100 psychologists. She held a professorship at New York University's prestigious psychology department. She had been described as a defender of the wrongfully accused, and as a champion of evil, depending on your point of view.

"I can't let this woman near Kristen Dillard," Jessie said. "The damage she could do.... I don't want to think about it."

"The damage she could do to Kristen Dillard, or to our case?"

"Both."

In the hallway behind her, a woman broke into song. Jessie had not thought it possible to slur *Fa-la-la-la-la*, but if anyone could do it, it was an overworked employee of the Philadelphia DA's Office.

Warren closed his eyes. "Would you mind shutting the

door?"

Jessie kicked it shut with her heel, but the thin door did little to mute the sounds of merriment.

"At least the law is on our side," Warren said. "Pennsylvania courts have consistently refused to allow this kind of expert testimony. Maybe you can get her excluded."

"If there's one lawyer that might convince a judge to let Dr. Moscow testify, it's Goldhammer."

Warren nodded. "That's what worries me. This type of evidence is gaining acceptance in other jurisdictions. If Goldhammer convinces the judge to allow Kate Moscow's testimony in Ramsey's case, the floodgates will open and we'll find ourselves facing a memory expert in every trial involving eyewitness testimony. Can you imagine?"

"Judge Spatt's not easily impressed."

"By lawyers, no." Warren turned to some other documents on his desk. "But he loves scientists. His son is a biochemist who's served as an expert witness in six pharmaceutical patent cases. Last year, Spatt admitted expert testimony on an issue relating to DNA analysis."

"This isn't hard science, though. It's psychology. And it's testimony about the credibility of a witness, which is the province of the jury. I can make Spatt see that."

Warren shrugged. "Good."

"I'll file a motion *in limine*."

"Good," he said again. But the way he pinched his lower lip between his thumb and forefinger and looked down at his papers did not convey a lot of confidence. "One more thing."

"What?"

"You remember a few weeks ago, after you lost the

PCRA hearing, when you suggested that getting Mark Leary involved might be helpful?"

She stiffened, but nodded. "You were pretty clear about your feelings on that plan."

He waved her words away and thrust a finger toward the expert witness report in her hand. "That was before Moscow. It's a different ballgame now. Get him involved."

18.

This doesn't need to be awkward, she told herself. But of course it would be. Every encounter she'd had with Detective Mark Leary since *that encounter* had been awkward as hell.

Arriving at Philadelphia Police Headquarters, Jessie was further dismayed to discover that Christmas cheer had also infected this building. Didn't anybody work anymore? She ducked tinsel and fake snow, slipped past a cardboard Santa wearing a badge that identified him as Sergeant Kringle, and headed for Homicide. Police Headquarters—dubbed the Roundhouse because of its distinctive, curving architecture—had become familiar territory to her years ago. It took her mere minutes to navigate to the office of the homicide division.

There she found the cramped collection of desks, chairs, filing cabinets, and computer equipment surprisingly unused. Most of the detectives had abandoned their desks in order to hunch over a table on which an assortment of plastic pieces had been carefully arranged.

"New case?" She approached the table, figuring she might as well lend her help to the investigation.

One of the detectives, Nick Jameson, turned and put an

arm over her shoulder. He drew her close to the table. "Thank God you're here, Black. This one's got us all stumped."

She peered at the plastic pieces. Their shapes seemed random, illogical. "What are these? Where are they from?"

Another detective, Robin Scerbak, passed her a large sheet of paper with some sort of schematic printed on it. "Death Station Command Center."

"What?"

"From Wal-Mart," Nick Jameson said. "Toy aisle."

Chuckles and snickers rose from the circle of cops.

"It's for my son," Robin Scerbak said. "Need to be a fucking brain surgeon to put the thing together."

Jameson said, "Can you help us, Black? You're our only hope."

Jessie knocked his arm off of her shoulder. "Don't you guys have work to do?"

"Relax, Black, it's Christmas," Jameson said.

"I'd love to help," she said, "but I'm a little pressed for time."

As if on cue, Mark Leary appeared at her side. "Hi, Jessie. Captain Henderson said you'd be stopping by."

"Sorry to ruin your holidays," she said. Aware that she was avoiding eye contact, she silently cursed herself and forced her gaze upward—only to find him carefully studying his shoes.

And this is why you don't have casual, drunken sex with your coworkers.

"Let's go outside," he suggested.

BURNOUT

* * *

She told herself again, *this doesn't need to be awkward.* She pulled her coat tighter around her. The sky was clear blue and she could feel the warmth of sunlight on her face, but she still felt a deep chill. She could taste winter in the air.

Leary had not bothered to grab a coat or scarf on their way out of the Roundhouse. The temperature did not seem to bother him. She shifted her weight, watched cars pass on the street. Now that the distraction of the Jameson and Scerbak comedy routine was behind them, silence descended.

She cleared her throat. "I guess by now you've heard that Frank Ramsey was granted a new trial."

Leary nodded. "Captain Henderson said the DA's office asked for help bolstering the evidence."

"Makes sense," she said, as if it hadn't been her idea. "You were the lead detective."

"It's a case I'm not likely to forget." He finally looked at her. There was a rueful note in his voice, but not a sarcastic one. Had they reached the stage where they could shake their heads and laugh at what they'd done? Peering closely at him, she didn't see any resentment in his expression, but she knew he could be difficult to read. Did he still bear a grudge for her refusal to take things any further? He had wanted to. He had called her three times after their encounter, and had hung up on her in anger after the third rejection.

The wind gusted, and she tucked her chin into her coat. "Ramsey's lawyer is going to try to discredit Kristen Dillard's testimony," she said. "He's planning to have an expert named Katherine Moscow testify about the fallibility of eyewitness identifications. She'll talk about the photo array you showed Kristen, argue that the photos influenced her later identification at the lineup—"

"That's ridiculous," Leary said.

"Dr. Moscow gave similar testimony in seven other recent cases. In each of them, the jury acquitted."

"So you want me to investigate Dr. Moscow?"

Jessie shook her head. "I can do that. I want you to find more evidence against Ramsey. Something physical. Something that will corroborate Kristen's testimony."

"Like what? Ramsey was too careful. He left no prints, no blood, no semen."

"Find something."

"You know the only reason we got him was because Kristen survived."

She knew that all too well. Ramsey was a serial killer, but she couldn't prosecute him for the other families he'd raped and killed because he'd left no evidence behind. Absolutely nothing linking the killings to him. His one mistake—the only one he'd ever made, as far as she knew—was stabbing Kristen, but not making sure she was dead.

"The killings stopped after his arrest," Leary said. "Can you use that?"

"I want something concrete."

"I'll try. Maybe we should get together later, go over all the old evidence again."

Was there a note of hopefulness in his voice? She couldn't tell. He was doing his job, probably, and nothing more. She silently prayed that was the case. Surely he understood by now that what had happened had been a mistake.

"I can't today," she said.

BURNOUT

She saw color bloom in his cheeks but pretended not to notice. Forced herself to maintain eye contact.

"When you have some time in your schedule, I mean," he said. "We'll go through the file. See if maybe we missed something the first time."

"Yeah." She nodded. "Definitely."

They stood together, the street noise the only break from the silence. After a moment, he said, "How have you been? You know, overall?"

"I've been good. How about you?"

"Holding up."

"Good," she said. "That's good to hear."

He nodded. Put his hands in his pockets. "Good."

Nope. Not awkward at all.

19.

Still thinking about Leary as she walked the final steps to her apartment building, she almost jumped when she found Jack Ackerman waiting by the door. He leaned against the brick wall, his hands in the pockets of a long black coat, a hat pulled down over his ears.

"Happy holidays," he said.

"What are you doing here?"

He came away from the wall. "Wow. We haven't seen each other in weeks. Gotta say, I was expecting a warmer welcome."

The truth was, her heart was fluttering. With the PCRA hearing over, she had thought he might disappear from her life, but here he was, smiling, looking at her with those blue eyes. But she didn't want to encourage him, not when there was no way she could allow anything to happen between them. She forced herself to frown. "It's late, Jack."

He stepped closer. "Jessie, something's been bothering me. About the Ramsey case. I'm very concerned."

"Okay, so call me at my office."

"Judge Spatt granted Ramsey a new trial because of my breakdown. So what I'm concerned about is, does that mean I don't get another date with you?"

She sighed. Did he really think an endless stream of corny jokes was the best way to get her attention? "We never had a first date, Jack."

He gazed into her eyes and she felt another flutter in her stomach. "That's not alleviating my concern," he said.

"How long have you been waiting here?"

He shrugged. "Not long. Maybe an hour."

"An *hour*?"

"It's no big deal. I have a lot of free time now."

"It's freezing out here."

"Does that mean you're inviting me in?"

She hesitated for a moment, tempted. But she knew better. She needed to end this, and she needed to end it now. No mixed messages. "Jack, it's no more appropriate for us to get involved now than it would have been during the PCRA hearing."

"Not true. My role in the Ramsey case is over. He has a new trial now, and a new defense attorney."

"You know none of that changes the attorney-client privilege between you. The law—"

He waved his hand as if the law was of no consequence. "You know I would never disclose anything confidential."

The door to her apartment building was mere feet away. All it would take was a step or two, and she would be past Jack, inside the warmth of her building, and safely on her way to bed. So what was she doing standing outside in the cold, arguing the same points over and over?

"It's the appearance of impropriety that concerns me,"

she said, as much to herself as to him. "I can't take any chances with this trial."

A gust of wind whipped down the street. She turned her face into the collar of her coat, cringing at the icy slap to her cheek. From the corner of her eye she saw Jack pull at the bottom of his hat.

The wind faded, and he said, "So we can't even be friends?"

"It seems pretty clear you want to be more than friends."

"I'm a lawyer. I know how to settle." He extended a hand. "Friends?"

She knew how to settle also, and she never took the first deal offered. "Professional acquaintances would be better," she said.

He gritted his teeth. "Ouch."

"Take it or leave it," she said.

Part of her hoped he would refuse, but he grasped her hand. Even through his glove, his grip was firm—not the macho death-grip some men employed to telegraph their masculinity, but strong and confident and warm. They shook, then she watched his hand slide into his pocket. She wondered what kind of deal she'd just made.

"Now that we've reached an understanding," he said, goofy smile undercutting the seriousness of his tone, "what can two professional acquaintances do to get out of the cold, a few nights before Christmas?"

"You're not going to dress up as Santa Claus or chase me around with mistletoe, I hope."

"No. I'm Jewish."

"I guess it's safe, then."

"If you want, I could chase you with a menorah. Or a dreidel? But I was thinking we could take a walk."

She laughed, her breath visible in front of her face. "It's been a long day, and I'm tired."

"One of the things I learned during my stay at the nuthouse was that sometimes the best thing you can do for your body and your mind is to just take a walk. The cold won't bother you so much once we get moving. Why not give it a try?"

"Believe it or not, I have walked before. It's not some new thing I need to try—"

"Once around the block. Then I'll leave you alone. I promise."

It would be so easy to say no. Just shake her head, tell him goodnight, and walk through that door into her building.

"Once around the block," she said, "but that's all."

Of course he was right. Once they started out, the air felt less chilly and her body seemed to gain renewed energy. Soon she was noticing the snow-dusted buildings, the holiday-decorated windows, even a few stars shining above the towers of the city. She had forgotten how beautiful Philadelphia could look in the wintry darkness.

"Did you always know you wanted to be a prosecutor?" Jack said. "I mean, was that why you went to law school?"

"Hell no." She shook her head, smiling as she remembered her younger self. "I thought I was going to be a big-shot corporate lawyer, working on huge deals and raking in the bucks."

"Really? What changed your mind?"

"The state paid off a chunk of my student loan debt in return for a commitment to work for the government."

He laughed. "Come on, you expect me to believe that's why you became a prosecutor?"

"Penn Law ain't cheap."

"Jessie—"

"Okay, the truth is I had a really inspiring Criminal Law professor. Christine Keller. I worshiped the woman. She got me interested initially, and then I worked a summer for the DA's office, and after that, working for some big law firm didn't seem appealing anymore."

Jack nodded, looking satisfied. "Criminal law isn't for everyone, but I think, for a certain type of person, it draws them. I knew back in college, when I volunteered for various justice projects. I applied for law school because I wanted to be a defender."

She watched his face as they walked. Even in the shadow of his coat collar, she thought she saw sorrow pass across his expression. She hesitated, then said, "Do you miss it?"

"Yes. Badly. But.... It wasn't healthy for me."

"I'm sorry."

Jack matched his pace to hers, so close that his shoulder touched her every few steps. She doubted the contact was innocent, but she didn't tell him to stop. What harm could there be in a few bumps, when they were both bundled in heavy coats?

"Drafting people's wills isn't bad," he said. "Once business picks up, it should keep me relatively busy. And I'll have time to pursue my hobbies."

"You have hobbies?"

He shrugged and his shoulder nudged her again. "I'll come up with some. Knitting, maybe? Go-kart racing?"

"I'm serious."

"Maybe I'll teach. Inspire some students of my own? Assuming any law school would have me, after my infamous episode."

"Don't dwell on that. It happened to you, but it doesn't have to define you." They stopped at the edge of Chestnut Street where it arced over the Schuylkill River, and Jessie looked down at the dark water. A few plates of ice drifted on a slow-moving current.

"Big plans for the holidays?" Jack said.

"I'll probably spend Christmas with my dad."

Without warning, he leaned forward and kissed her. His lips felt cold at first, but quickly warmed against hers. She jerked away, shoved him, and backed up a step.

"*What the hell, Jack?* I thought I was clear."

"I'm sorry." He rubbed a gloved hand over his face. "It just felt right. I wasn't thinking."

"This is why we can't be friends, or even *professional acquaintances*, Jack. Because you want more than that."

"And you don't?" His eyes flashed.

"I *can't*. Don't you understand that? I can't." She turned away from him, and started walking.

"Where are you going?" he called after her.

"Home. And you should go home, too."

20.

Woody had never cared much for Christmas. His parents had not instilled in him the religious convictions that he had observed in many of his coworkers at SCI Huntington. To them, Jesus was real, a God that was present everywhere, even in a close-security prison. To Woody, Jesus was nothing but a stained-glass-window decoration and—when worn around the neck of a busty woman—a titillating fashion accessory. That half the world celebrated the birthday of some guy who lived over two-thousand years ago—and only to the age of thirty-three—had always struck Woody as pretty fucking ridiculous.

"What are you thinking about, baby?"

He blinked, finished his lukewarm coffee. Amber sat on the carpeted floor beside him. Morning sunlight filtered through the ornaments hanging from her Christmas tree, tinting her long blonde hair red, green, and white. He had been asking her to stop calling him that for six months, but at least it was moderately less cringe-worthy than *sweetheart* or *honey*.

He shrugged and put his empty mug on the carpet by his hip. "Jesus."

She laughed—not the idiot giggle she used at the club but

her real laugh. "You're thinking about Jesus?"

"It is Christmas, remember?"

"Sure, but—" She crawled over to him, nuzzled her face into his neck, and any irritation over her pet names for him evaporated. He found her even sexier in her striped pajama pants and plain white tank-top than he did when she wore the thongs, push-ups, thigh-highs, and platforms that comprised her professional wardrobe. Her breasts, swelling beneath the cotton tank, crushed against his bare chest. "I've never seen your pious side before," she said into his ear.

She slid a hand past the waistband of his boxers. He grabbed her wrist, stopped her.

"Are you going to open your present?" he said.

Only two gifts waited in the shadow of the tree. His gift for her and hers for him. He hadn't known what to get her, had almost resorted to a teddy bear before his brother pointed out the bracelet in a jewelry catalog. Michael, always smarter, even now.

She began to kiss his chest.

"I'm serious," he said. "Open it."

Her lip curled. He recognized the sly grin from her performances. She turned and reached for the small box under the tree. Her tank-top lifted as she stretched, revealing the tattoo on her lower back.

She sat Indian-style beside him, the box in her hands. "Is there something you want to say while I open it?"

"Not really."

She peeled away the wrapping paper and opened the box. When she looked inside, her grin slipped into a look of disappointment. "Oh."

"Put it on."

She lifted the bracelet out of the box. But before she could work the clasp to close it around her wrist, her body hitched and she started to cry.

"What the hell, Amber? It's returnable."

"It's not that. I just thought—"

She didn't need to finish the sentence. "What are you, nuts?" He reached for the edge of the chair behind him and pulled himself to a standing position. Her blonde head bobbed as she cried. "You thought I was going to propose to you?" Shaking his head, he walked to the kitchenette and refilled his coffee mug.

She followed him. "Woody—"

"You really think I'm going to marry a girl who spreads her legs for tips?" With his free hand, he snatched the bracelet from her. "You don't like this, I'll take it back."

"Don't, I like it."

He turned his back on her, stared at the sink. He knew the real reason for his anger had nothing to do with her marriage fantasies. It was that by crying she'd changed the mood of the morning and made things more difficult than he'd planned. Now when he pitched his idea she would take it as an insult instead of seeing it as a fun game. She would be wounded. She would refuse. And then he'd have to threaten her.

He sighed.

"What is it, Woody? Why are you mad?"

Without makeup caked all over her face, she looked twice as beautiful as she did at the club, but he would never tell her that now. He'd already managed to put all kinds of wrong ideas in her head. God only knew what kinds of scenarios she'd imagined. The two of them raising a family? Amber nursing their infant with one of her implant-gorged breasts?

His eyes looked past her and found the other present under the tree. "What did you get me?"

A sad smile brightened her face. She pushed a sheet of blonde hair away from her eyes, turned, and skipped to the tree. He watched her ass move under the pajama bottoms and tried to convince himself that the morning could still proceed according to plan. She was a free spirit, uninhibited, adventurous.

The words no longer rang true. Amber had exposed her all too conventional heart and now he could see her only as what she was. Fragile, vulnerable. *Damn her.*

She returned with his present, a flat rectangle wrapped in red tissue paper. He tore away the paper. "A book?"

"Look at it."

It was a beginner's guide to chess. He opened it, flipped through the pages. "Michael loves chess." His brother had mastered the game at a young age, though in high school he'd preferred varsity sports.

"I thought you could teach yourself the game and then, when you visit him, the two of you could play."

He put the book on the kitchen counter. "Thank you."

"Can I have the bracelet? I'm sorry I cried. It was silly of me. Sometimes I get stupid around the holidays."

He gave it back to her. This time, she put it on without bursting into tears. She held up her wrist so the white gold links reflected the kitchen light. "It's pretty."

She kissed him, wrapped her arms around his waist. *Now*

or never.

"Amber, there's something I want you to do for me."

She looked into his eyes. "What?"

With her face so close to his, and her cheeks still damp with tears, he couldn't tell her. He gestured toward the other room. "Let's talk on the couch."

After he'd made his request, she threw one of the couch pillows at his head. Years working at a prison had honed his reflexes. He deflected the missile with his right forearm and it went spinning into the Christmas tree, where it knocked ornaments and pine needles to the floor.

"You asshole!"

"Calm down, Amber."

"I'm not a whore!"

All he'd asked her to do was turn on her charm and seduce a guy—something she did three nights a week with countless slobbering strangers anyway. As he'd feared, she took it as an insult to her character.

"A whore fucks for money," he said. "I'm not offering you any."

"Like that makes a difference. I don't even know the guy."

"You'll like him." Woody highly doubted the truth of this assertion, but he plunged forward anyway. There was no other option now but to bull his way through. "He's a lawyer, a very smart guy."

"How can you ask me to do this? Don't you care about me at all?"

BURNOUT

"Yeah I care about you." He leaned toward her lips but she flinched away from him until her back pressed against the armrest of the couch. "Damn it, Amber, I wouldn't ask you to do this if I didn't think you were tough enough."

She threw another pillow at him. "Is that what you think about me? I'm tough?" She was crying again, the tears making her cheeks shine.

"The trial won't last more than a month, two at the most. I'm not asking for that much."

"Fuck you." She jumped off the couch. He pursued her slowly to the apartment's door, trying to gauge how real her resistance was. Either she was serious or she was trying to act virtuous, make him think of her as marriage material. A girl he'd watched grind on strangers' laps for thirty dollars a dance.

She yanked the door open. A gust of cold air from the hallway made her nipples harden against the material of her tank-top, but if she saw him looking, she didn't care. "Get out."

"Amber." He crossed his arms over his own chest. "Don't make a big thing out of this."

"A big thing?" She gaped at him. "Get the fuck out of my home, you dick."

"Close the door, will you?"

"Are you deaf? Get the fuck—"

He grabbed her by the throat and shoved her back into the apartment. Slammed the door. Threw the deadbolt. Amber sprawled near the tree and stared up at him. Her mouth hung open. She rubbed her neck.

"Get out." Her voice squeaked.

Woody squatted a foot from where she lay. "His name is

Elliot Williams. There's a bar in Olde City where he likes to go with his friends on Friday nights. That's where you'll meet him, make him think you were turned on by his eyes or whatever. He won't be able to resist you."

"I told you I won't."

"You will, Amber, and I'll tell you why. Because if you don't, I'm going to drop by Heartbreakers the next few nights and hand out cards with your real name, address, and phone number printed on them."

She looked like she wanted to spit at him, but all she did was tremble.

"I bet you have a lot of fans who would love to know where you live. Some might show up here at random hours with flowers and chocolate hearts. And you know what? I bet there are some others who would just rape you instead, beat the living shit out of you and fuck that pussy and ass you've been waving in their faces night after night."

"Please, Woody—"

"Elliot Williams. Friday night. The bar is called Dean's."

She nodded. From the look in her eyes, he knew he'd never get to fuck her again. But that was okay. He had a more important use for her now.

His knees popped as he rose. He felt her eyes track him as he walked to the kitchenette, but she didn't move. He took his Christmas gift from the counter and walked to the bedroom, where he quickly dressed. Back in the other room, she'd moved to the couch, where she lay curled in a fetal position. She was sobbing into the only pillow left on the couch, the only one she hadn't hurtled at him earlier.

On his way to the door, he stopped by the couch.

BURNOUT

"Thanks for the chess book." She didn't look up from the pillow. He could see the wet fabric near her eyes. "It was a thoughtful gift." Her back shuddered and she pressed her face harder against the pillow. "Merry Christmas," he said. "I'll be in touch."

21.

As Christmas passed, then New Year's, Frank Ramsey was never far from Jessie's thoughts. She found herself flipping through her old files late at night—her research notes from the first trial, court transcripts, police reports, photographs. During the day, she researched the defense's expert witness. She found everything she could on Dr. Katherine Moscow, but even after reading the psychologist's papers and interviews and the transcripts of her testimony at other trials, Jessie still felt unprepared for the pre-trial hearing that was quickly approaching. There was only so much you could learn from papers and books. You didn't need to be a homicide cop like Leary to know that nothing beat hands-on investigation. The pre-trial hearing at which Spatt would hear Jessie's arguments for precluding Moscow's testimony was only days away. She needed to be as persuasive as possible.

She Googled Moscow's colleagues at NYU and started making phone calls, posing as a writer researching background information for an article. The first few yielded nothing but canned responses, carefully worded and no more informative than the web pages she'd already read. But her third call, to another psychology professor named Stamer, had been more interesting. In a tight, quiet voice—*professional jealousy?*—he had said, "If you want an honest look at Kate's work, you should talk to Monica Chan."

"Who is she?" Jessie leaned forward, her fingers tightening around her pen. "Can you give me her number."

"I would suggest you visit her in person, if you want the good stuff. She used to be one of Kate's graduate students."

"Used to be?"

But Stamer would tell her nothing more.

Later that day, trapped in gridlock, Jessie's Accord was boxed in on all sides. Traffic into Manhattan was backed up. She could see the tunnel ahead but was powerless to maneuver closer to it. She didn't know how people commuted every day from New Jersey into New York without exploding with road rage, but, observing people in neighboring cars apparently talking to themselves, she figured cellular technology had probably played a part.

Jessie merged with her neighbors into the tunnel's mouth and followed the tiled passageway beneath the Hudson River. When her car emerged from the other end of the tunnel, she reached for her printed directions to the NYU building where Stamer had told her to look for Monica Chan.

Jessie stepped into the hushed silence of a dimly lit lab. Across the room, an Asian girl stood hunched over a counter. She appeared to be sniffing a petri dish. "Excuse me? Monica?"

The girl—dressed for the cold weather in jeans and a baggy sweater, over which she wore a lab coat—looked up from the dish. She had pulled her fine black hair back in a ponytail. "Do I know you?"

"Professor Stamer told me you were one of Katherine Moscow's graduate students."

"I used to be."

Jessie shook the girl's hand. "My name is Jessica. I'm doing some research about Dr. Moscow."

A sardonic smile spread across the girl's features, and she put a hand on her hip. "Stamer hates Kate's guts. If he sent you, you can't be good news for her."

On instinct, based on Monica's words and body language, Jessie decided to be honest. "I'm a prosecutor with the Philadelphia District Attorney's Office. Dr. Moscow is scheduled to testify as an expert witness for the defense at an upcoming trial. Why does Stamer hate her? Professional jealousy?"

Monica snorted. "She turned him down when he asked her on a date. Guys are always coming on to Kate. You know she was in beauty pageants when she was a teenager?"

"I didn't know that."

"Stamer never forgave her for rejecting him."

"I did sense some anger." Jessie recalled the tight, quiet voice on the phone. But she did not want to get sidetracked into talking about Stamer. "What are you working on?" she said, indicating the petri dish. "It looked like you were smelling something."

"I'm researching the link between scent and memory. Did you know that odors are the strongest memory triggers experienced by humans?"

Jessie had read a few articles about the subject, but she shook her head, hoping to keep the girl talking. "I didn't know that."

BURNOUT

It worked. Monica's eyes lit up and she leaned forward with the petri dish. "Smell this." Feeling slightly silly, Jessie sniffed. The strong odor of leather filled her nostrils.

Monica watched her closely. "What are you thinking about?"

"My first boyfriend," Jessie said. It was true. "He had a leather jacket he loved. Wore it every day. He always smelled like this."

Monica took the dish back from her, fitted a cap over it, and placed it near a spiral notebook on the table. "You probably already know everything I could tell you about Kate. I mean, do a Google search and you'll find hundreds of articles about her."

"You didn't get along?"

Monica looked at her a little more guardedly. "Did Dr. Stamer tell you that?"

"No. Just a guess."

"Kate doesn't like people who question her methods."

"Her methods?"

"Research methods. In the last few years, she's conducted some unorthodox experiments."

"Give me an example."

"You know that she testifies in court as an expert witness. Well, apparently, a few years ago another expert challenged her. He said that her conclusions about eyewitness identifications were faulty because they were based on experimental data gathered in an artificial environment that was too different from a real occurrence of violence."

Jessie smiled and held up a hand. "You're going to have to slow down. They don't teach us about this stuff at law school. What do you mean by faulty?"

"I'll give you an example. Kate used to base a lot of her theories on an experiment she called 'the enthusiastic questioner.' In that experiment, she gathered volunteers from the campus and put them in a classroom where she lectured to them. Meanwhile, behind her, a guy would enter the room, empty the garbage can, and leave. Then she split up the volunteers and her graduate students questioned them individually. They showed each of the volunteers a sheet containing six photographs. One was of the man who had emptied the garbage can. The volunteers were asked to identify him.

"She called the experiment 'the enthusiastic questioner' because its purpose was to gauge the influence of the questioner's demeanor on the volunteer. So, for example, if the volunteer pointed to the wrong photo, the questioner, sounding disappointed and impatient, would respond with a question like, 'Are you sure? Do you want to take a little more time to think about it?' If the volunteer pointed to the correct photo and said something like, 'This might be the guy, but I'm not sure,' the questioner would become excited and say, 'You recognize that man as the man who emptied the garbage? Would you say that you're confident about that identification?' And so on until the volunteer positively identified the correct man.

"The problem, according to the other expert, was that the experiment involved college kids looking to make some extra spending money. Kids with no emotional investment in the experiment. So when Kate returned from that trial, she decided to construct a more realistic experiment."

"You disagreed with that idea?"

Monica leaned a hip against the lab counter and flicked a strand of hair away from her cheek. "Not in concept, but what Kate came up with.... A volunteer, believing he was participating in a survey about study habits, arrives at the designated building. Before he can enter, two paid actors run around the side of the building. One punches the other. A few seconds later, campus security arrives and takes both actors away. The volunteer is then taken inside the building and questioned by a security officer."

"But the security officer is really one of Dr. Moscow's graduate students?"

"Right. But at that point, the volunteer doesn't even know the experiment started. I refused to participate. I told her that I didn't think it was ethical to deceive the volunteers to that extent. I proposed that we modify the experiment. That was the end of my relationship with Kate Moscow."

"What were the results of the new experiment?"

"They corresponded almost perfectly with the enthusiastic questioner experiment. So she proved that she was right. No surprise there. If you talk to all the people who work with her, you'll see they all agree on two things about Kate Moscow. One, she's a total bitch. And two, she's a genius. She's brilliant. She's always right."

The snow began to fall as Jessie trekked back to her car. The trip to New York had been enlightening, and might help her raise some doubts about Moscow if she made it to the trial, but it would not be particularly helpful at the pretrial hearing.

At least Jessie had formed a pretty clear picture of the woman. Beautiful, brilliant, and ruthless, a tenured femme fatale. Even the people who disliked her could not help but speak of her in reverent tones.

If Kate Moscow made it to the stand, she would be a hell of a tough nut to crack.

22.

Elliot hadn't missed a Friday night gathering at Dean's in years, even though he had long ago stopped thinking they were fun. They were his only hope of crawling out of the purgatory that was the Philly DA's office. Wasting money on overpriced drinks while listening to his law school friends boast about their year-end bonuses—some of which exceeded Elliot's entire salary—was hardly something he looked forward to. But these former classmates worked at the best firms in Philadelphia. If he maintained these tenuous, inebriated connections, while simultaneously racking up trial experience, in a few years he might be able to transition to a six-figure salary in the litigation department of a respectable firm, and leave his government job behind. So, once again, he forced himself to throw on a nice sweater and head out into the snow.

He caught a taxi on Chestnut and headed for the Olde City section of Philadelphia, where college students and young professionals milled along the sidewalks, and trendy bars like Dean's were lined up side-by-side. Elliot paid the driver and got out of the cab, then hurried through the falling flurries to the entrance to Dean's.

The heat of too many people and the smell of beer assaulted him the moment he stepped through the door. He pushed through the crowd, headed directly to the stairs and climbed them to the second floor. It was generally less crowded up here. He spotted his friends at a table near the windows. Jason McKinney, who'd been rich before landing his big firm job, waved him over with a half-finished martini.

"Happy New Year, Elliot."

"You, too." He forced a smile as he shrugged out of his coat. His hair—which had always been a bitch to control, ever since middle school—had soaked up the snowflakes outside and now dripped icy water down the back of his shirt collar. A barmaid materialized at his side and he ordered a vodka tonic. He turned to Linda Pierce, who looked as beautiful as ever in a cashmere sweater. "Did you enjoy the holiday?"

"I loved it. Sean and I spent Christmas in Rome."

"Sounds great."

"It was. We visited all the ancient sites. Of course, I've seen them before, but I was too young to appreciate them then."

Elliot tried not to think about his own depressing Christmas and New Year's with his parents at the Williams household, where the closest thing to Roman history was his father's DVD of *Spartacus*.

"Bust any bad guys lately?" Jason McKinney said. He pulled the toothpick from his martini and sucked an olive into his mouth with a grin.

"I'm still working in the Appeals Unit. But I've had a few good experiences arguing before the appellate judges." He didn't mention the fiasco in Judge Spatt's courtroom, where Jessie Black had made a fool of him.

"I did a criminal appeal *pro bono*," Jason McKinney said.

BURNOUT

"It was an interesting break from my other work. I wouldn't want to do it full-time though." He shuddered.

"So," Chris Murphy said, studying McKinney over the rim of his wine glass, "did you get your bonus?"

Elliot settled in and waited, longingly, for his drink.

An hour later, buzzed but not even close to drunk enough to tolerate his friends' banter, Elliot excused himself and shouldered his way through the thickening crowd to the men's room. Before he reached the door, a woman stepped in front of him and blocked his path.

He murmured an apology and attempted to sidle past her. She put her hand on his arm. That stopped him.

Hitting on women at bars—women who typically arrived in intimidating groups and never regarded his presence with anything but boredom—was an activity he'd dismissed as futile years ago. His surrender to hopelessness had become so complete that he barely noticed women now when he went out. He had trained himself not to see them. So when this stunning blonde touched her crimson fingernails to his sweater sleeve, he assumed she was about to push him out of her way.

But she didn't.

"I hope you don't mind my eavesdropping. I thought I heard you say you work for the DA's office." As it was every Friday night, Dean's was crowded and loud. The girl leaned closer to him to make herself heard. With difficulty, Elliot restrained himself from peeking down her plunging neckline. "I think that's really exciting. My name is Amber."

He swallowed. Took her hand. "Elliot."

"Is it really like on TV?"

"No, it's not as exciting in real life. Trust me."

"What's it like in real life?"

He realized with dream-like unbelief that she was guiding him toward the wall, that she wanted to have an actual conversation with him. Looking at her eyes, her lips, her perfect white teeth, he could barely concentrate on her words. She didn't seem to mind. She smiled at his blurted responses as if he were reciting poetry to her.

Was she drunk? High? She looked and sounded sober. His mind sought a rational explanation, but found none.

"Let's grab those seats." A man and a woman had vacated two stools at a small table in the corner. Before anyone else could take their seats, Amber skipped toward the table and claimed them. He hurried after her.

When she pulled herself up onto one of the stools, her skirt rose three inches up her thigh. Elliot's heart jumped into his throat and nearly strangled him.

He sat down across from her. "Do you— Can I buy you a drink?"

She leaned forward. She had the most magnificent cleavage he had ever seen outside of a dirty magazine. "A Cosmopolitan would be nice."

Hours later, his friends had gone home—Jason McKinney favoring him with a wink and a thumbs-up that Amber thankfully could not see—and the second floor of Dean's was practically deserted. He had no desire to leave— he was having the best time of his life. With Amber as his enthusiastic audience, he had recalled all the glories of his career at the DA's office, and had found that he didn't even have to embellish them much to make them interesting. Amber hung on his every word, probed him with questions, and—best of all—touched his hand or his thigh when he made her laugh.

Now they sat, drinks empty, ignoring the stares of the busboy wiping down the other tables. It was time to leave. Elliot had grown quiet as he debated the best way to ask for Amber's phone number.

"Where do you live?" she said.

He told her.

She smiled. "Maybe we could go back there, have some coffee?"

"Uh ... yeah, definitely. We ... *definitely*."

23.

Judge Spatt's chambers were dark and moody, like him. Jessie and Goldhammer sat in leather chairs facing the judge's massive cherry wood desk. There were no windows, and the walls were bare except for a few dusty photographs and ancient-looking diplomas.

Spatt regarded them with an irritated grimace. If the deep creases in his face reflected his current mood, then maybe he had already begun to regret his decision to grant Frank Ramsey a new trial. *Good.* This was only a pre-trial hearing. If the judge was exasperated now, he'd be yanking his hair out by the time a jury was impaneled, and with luck, some of that frustration would be directed at the defendant.

This morning, Goldhammer bore the brunt of it. The judge's withering gaze settled on him.

"Let me get this straight, Mr. Goldhammer. You're asking me to ignore the clear holdings of the Pennsylvania Supreme Court and—like some kind of rogue judge—invent my own law instead, just so you can make a woman who's been raped, stabbed, and left for dead look like a chump?"

Goldhammer swallowed. "I'd like to remind Your Honor of some words of wisdom spoken during the PCRA hearing. I believe Your Honor told Ms. Black that when a lawyer uses the word 'clear,' the reality is usually anything but."

The judge absorbed his own words and brooded.

"The law covering the admissibility of this type of evidence is not clear," Goldhammer said. "It is self-contradictory, illogical, outdated—"

"Your Honor," Jessie said, "in *Commonwealth v. Simmons*, the Pennsylvania Supreme Court held—" She shuffled through the Westlaw printouts in her lap until she found the highlighted paragraph she was looking for, then read it to the judge: "Appellant's expert would have testified generally about the reliability of eyewitness identification. Such testimony would have given an unwarranted appearance of authority as to the subject of credibility, a subject which an ordinary juror can assess. Moreover, appellant was free to and did attack the witnesses' credibility and point out inconsistencies of all the eyewitnesses at trial through cross-examination and in his closing argument. Thus, the trial court properly excluded appellant's proposed expert testimony." She returned the decision to its place in her folder. "That sounds pretty clear to me. Allowing Dr. Moscow to testify would be directly opposite to the law of this jurisdiction."

Goldhammer was shaking his head. "No, Your Honor."

"No?" Spatt's bushy eyebrows jumped to his forehead.

"Dr. Moscow does not intend to testify about things the jurors already know. As I detailed in my brief and as she states in the attached affidavit, Dr. Moscow intends to offer testimony regarding specific problems with eyewitness identifications and memory. She intends to instruct the jury on subjects such as unconscious transfer, weapon focus, exposure duration, overestimation of time, and the relationship between confidence and accuracy. Subjects which are not—to use the language of *Simmons*—the kind that an ordinary juror can assess without the guidance of expert testimony."

"That argument has been rejected by Pennsylvania courts," Jessie said.

Goldhammer's marshmallow face softened further. "Your Honor, the Commonwealth's entire case against Mr. Ramsey rests on one eyewitness identification. Dr. Moscow intends to introduce data that supports arguments that might otherwise strike the jury as contrary to common sense. A ruling that precludes that testimony would prevent Mr. Ramsey from putting on an effective defense."

"Your Honor," Jessie said, "the jury is certainly capable of deciding for itself whether or not Kristen Dillard's testimony is credible."

"I agree," Goldhammer said. "Dr. Moscow does not intend to encroach on the traditional role of the jury. But Dr. Moscow's testimony, carefully limited to a discussion of the factors that can affect identifications and memory, will aid the jurors in deciding the ultimate issues of fact."

Judge Spatt leaned back in his chair. She could hear movement outside his chambers, but in here it was silent as a tomb. Finally, the judge cleared his throat. "Mr. Goldhammer, just about every court in Pennsylvania that's considered this issue has refused to allow expert testimony on these subjects. I've done a careful reading of the briefs and of the relevant cases."

Goldhammer pursed his lips in frustration. Jessie exhaled her pent-up breath. The tension drained from her neck, her shoulders.

"But I've determined that all those cases are bunk."

Jessie looked up. Her chest tightened as she realized that Spatt had made this decision before the courthouse had even opened its doors. This whole conference had been nothing but a cat-and-mouse game, a bit of entertainment for the judge as he made the lawyers squirm.

"These cases are based on obsolete principles," the judge continued, "and backed by an insipid reasoning all too typical of my supposedly distinguished brethren. My guess is that law clerks wrote them, idiots who spent more time playing video games than paying attention to the narrowing interstice between science and justice. I'm not persuaded."

Jessie could barely speak. "Your Honor— You'll be reversed on appeal."

"I'm trembling in my robe." He sighed theatrically. "Ms. Black, your motion to exclude the testimony of Dr. Katherine Moscow is denied."

The judge stood. Goldhammer popped up quickly, and Jessie followed suit. This conference was over. Jessie waited until they were in the hallway before she allowed herself to consider the consequences of this latest setback. With Kate Moscow in the trial, she would need more evidence incriminating Ramsey, evidence that would corroborate Kristen's identification and render Moscow's pseudo-science irrelevant. And she would need it soon.

24.

The campus of the Rushford Foundation sprawled across twenty acres of land in West Conshohocken, fifteen minutes outside of Philly. Mark Leary experienced a sense of *déjà vu* as he strolled across the concrete-paved courtyard, his shoes crunching a thin blanket of icy snow. When he'd first visited the state-of-the-art biomedical research facility during his investigation of the Dillard killings over a year ago, he'd thought the place looked like something out of a science fiction movie. This time, knowing what to expect, it just looked like a more sophisticated version of the police department lab. He could see Dr. Randolph Tiano waiting in the lobby of the main building, watching him through floor-to-ceiling windows. Leary waved. Tiano waved back.

Leary had first interviewed Tiano, one of the researchers who had worked closely with Kristen Dillard's father, over a year ago. That meeting had pretty much been a dead end in his investigation. Other than a bunch of notes about the work Tiano and his colleagues did studying a disease called amyotrophic lateral sclerosis—Lou Gehrig's Disease—he hadn't learned much, and certainly nothing relevant to the rapes and murders at the Dillard house. As far as Leary could tell, Ramsey had selected the Dillards at random, and he did not expect to learn anything today that would change his assessment. Still, he had promised Jessie he would look into everything again, just in case.

Tiano shook his hand in the warm lobby. The man looked reserved, almost glum.

"Welcome back, Detective." He led Leary down one of the corridors connecting the main building's various offices and labs. "I read in the paper about Frank Ramsey's new trial. The legal system in this country is absurd if you ask me."

"No argument here." In Leary's experience, the 9-mm semi-automatic nestled in his shoulder holster was significantly more reliable than a legal brief, no matter how expertly wielded.

Tiano took an abrupt right turn. They entered a different office than the one Leary remembered. Tiano offered Leary a seat, then he closed the door and walked around an expansive oak desk to sit and face him. Bookshelves built into two of the walls held thick medical treatises, while a third wall displayed Tiano's impressive array of diplomas, certifications, and awards. Behind the desk, plush drapes hung on either side of a huge window overlooking a man-made lake, where a thin layer of snow stretched over the frozen water, pure white and unmolested.

"They upgraded you," Leary said, looking around.

"Yes." Tiano slipped a card from a silver holder and passed it across the desk to Leary. "New business cards, too."

"Director," Leary read. "Congratulations."

Tiano shrugged. "Ed Urlyapov resigned three months ago. Couldn't take the pressure anymore. Lucky me, I got his job."

Leary nodded. "Lucky you."

"I can't remember the last time I had a weekend off."

"Sounds stressful. Is something big happening? A breakthrough?"

Tiano snorted. "Michael Rushford's dying, that's what's happening. He built this place expecting a miracle, and we haven't been able to deliver. Now he's cracking the whip."

Leary recalled that the Foundation had been established and funded by Michael Rushford, a successful Philadelphia-area businessman stricken with the disease. "I'm sure the death of Bob Dillard set you back," he said, guiding the conversation from pleasantries to the matter at hand.

"I told you, Bob was one of the smartest guys here. When he died...." Tiano threw up his hands. "The Foundation never recovered."

"I know I asked you this question during our first interview, Dr. Tiano, but is there any chance that Bob met Frank Ramsey prior to the attack on his family?"

"I don't see how their paths could have crossed. Bob was a scientist, and a workaholic."

"Ramsey was a fireman. Were there any fires at the facility, any emergency that would have resulted in a call to the fire department?"

Tiano shook his head.

"How about human test subjects? Could Ramsey have participated in some kind of clinical experiment?"

Again, Tiano shook his head. "None of our studies has progressed beyond animal testing."

"What kind of work was Bob doing? Don't take this the wrong way, but did he have access to any drugs that he might

BURNOUT

have been selling for their street value?"

Tiano laughed. "Bob? A drug dealer? If you didn't have something interesting to tell him about progressive neurodegenerative disease, Bob wouldn't spare you a hello in the hallway. He certainly wouldn't have spared the time necessary to conduct a criminal enterprise."

Leary did not bother taking notes. He had heard all of this before. For the sake of diligence, he said, "What was Bob researching at the time of his murder?"

"He was working mostly with C1-esterase inhibitors and clioquinol, and he had a growing interest in the possibilities presented by embryonic stem cells."

Leary was about to move on when the reference to stem cells caught him off guard. He did not recall anyone mentioning stem cell research before. "Isn't that kind of stem cell research illegal in the U.S.?"

"Yes," Tiano said, shifting in his chair, "but studies in China have demonstrated that human embryonic stem cells can become motor neurons. A very exciting development. ALS operates by attacking motor neurons in the brain and spinal cord. If stem cells can replace those motor neurons and form the appropriate connections, it's possible that they could improve muscle function and possibly alter the onset and progression of the disease. Bob was reading everything about it that he could get his hands on."

"What if he was doing more than reading?"

"I don't follow."

"You said he took his work home with him. Is it possible he worked with embryonic stem cells at home?"

Tiano's chair squeaked as he shifted his weight. "Are you

suggesting that the attack on Bob's family was somehow related to stem cell research?"

Leary kept his expression neutral. He did not believe for a second that the Dillard murders had anything to do with stem cells, but the detective in him couldn't let this line of questioning drop, not after observing Tiano's nervous body language. "We are following every lead," he said.

"But that's just silly, isn't it? Frank Ramsey is a serial killer, not an anti-stem cell activist. Unless ... you're no longer sure Ramsey did it?"

"I'm sure."

"Then why ask these questions?"

"The motive for one crime is often found in a different crime. A drug deal motivates a burglary to steal the money or the drugs or both. A rape motivates the murder of the rapist by the victim's husband or brother. I agree that even if Bob Dillard was involved in illegal stem cell research, it's probably not related to his murder. But I'd prefer to know all of the facts so I can come to my own conclusion."

Tiano ran his fingers through his thinning hair. "Well, I can assure you that the Foundation has never stepped beyond the bounds of the law."

"I appreciate that, but you still haven't answered my question."

Tiano leaned forward, lowered his voice. "Michael Rushford is a very wealthy man. He's also very desperate. Is it possible that he helped Bob set up some kind of secondary laboratory somewhere to secretly study the use of stem cells in the treatment of ALS? Sure. Anything is possible. Does that answer your question?"

Leary nodded slowly. His instinct was that this hypothetical was as close to a confession as he was going to get from Tiano, and for a detail that was most likely irrelevant to his case, it was enough. "Yes. Thank you."

"I think you should leave now. If you want to continue this conversation, then I'm going to have to invite the Foundation's attorneys to participate."

Leary laughed. "And here I was under the impression that you shared my low opinion of lawyers." He stood up and fixed his jacket. "Relax, Dr. Tiano. I'm not investigating the Foundation."

Tiano's posture remained tense. "I have an appointment in a few minutes, Detective Leary. If you have any other questions, you have my number."

"And you have mine." Leary handed Tiano a business card with his cell phone number written on the back.

Tiano opened the door and they headed into the hallway. He escorted Leary to the building's exit and opened the door. A cold breeze swept in from the parking lot. "Good luck with your investigation," Tiano said. "Bob and I weren't friends exactly."

"Workaholics can be difficult to get close to." Leary thought of Jessie Black.

"Exactly. But I liked and respected him."

Leary braced himself for the cold. "Thanks for your help."

25.

Motion practice and pretrial hearings led to three straight days of jury selection. Arriving at home, Jessie could feel exhaustion dragging at every fiber of her being, and the actual trial had not even started yet. When she found the man waiting in front of the door to her apartment building, dressed in a long coat over jeans and a sweater, a suspiciously large duffel bag resting on the icy steps near his ankle, she was almost too weary to be surprised.

"Jack," she said.

"How did jury selection go?"

Jessie stopped and stared at him. "Haven't we done this already? You surprise me at my apartment, I tell you there can't be anything between us, and you go home? Do we really need to do it again?"

"This time it's going to be slightly different," he said. "I surprise you at your apartment, as a friend. An *ashamed, apologetic* friend, who knows he fucked up last time, and wants to make it right. The part about me going home still happens, but first we have a nice time. As friends."

She looked at the duffel bag, doubtful. "Really? Because it looks like you're planning a sleepover."

A grin broke across his face and he lifted the duffel bag and shook it. She heard metal objects clang inside. "Pots and pans."

She fished her key from the pocket of her coat. "You brought a bag of kitchenware to my apartment?" Still smiling, he stepped out of her way as she fit the key in the lock. His mood was as infectious as it always seemed to be, and soon she was smiling with him. She looked down at his bag and wrinkled her nose in mock distaste. "Pots and pans—they make sort of a sexist gift, don't you think?"

Jack laughed. "I'm not *giving* them to you. They cost me a fortune at Williams-Sonoma."

Heat from the entryway greeted them when she opened the door. The surprise of Jack's appearance was wearing off, and in its place, her exhaustion was returning. After spending a whole morning and afternoon in court questioning strangers and arguing with Goldhammer and Judge Spatt, she had been looking forward to collapsing in front of the TV. But if Jack had really come to atone for his previous romantic ambush and be her friend, she couldn't just turn him away. Did he even have any other friends?

He stepped across the threshold after her, waited patiently with his heavy bag as she checked her mail slot.

"There's food in here, too," he said, hefting the bag. "Marinara sauce, cheese, chicken cutlets, some other stuff. The eggs I kept here." He opened his coat, revealed a carton of six eggs protruding from the inside pocket. "For safe keeping."

"I'm surprised you're not wearing a top hat concealing a chocolate cake."

"Damn. I forgot about dessert."

She led him past the stairwell and unlocked the door of her first-floor, one-bedroom apartment. "If I had known you were stopping by, I might have cleaned up."

"Really?"

She opened the door. "No, not likely."

Inside, he found the small kitchen area and began unpacking his bag. She leaned against the wall and watched. "If you had called me, I would have told you that I do, in fact, have my own pots and pans."

He arranged the contents of the bag on the counter between her stove and fridge. "But then it wouldn't have been a surprise."

"Congratulations. I'm thoroughly surprised. Now why don't you tell me what you're doing."

"Remember what I said about finding some hobbies?" He turned and smiled at her. "Cooking seemed like a cool skill to pick up."

"And what will you be cooking, exactly?"

"Chicken *parmigiana*." The word rolled off his tongue in a ridiculous attempt at an Italian accent. For emphasis, he thumped a box of pasta on the counter. "With a side of spaghetti."

She opened a cabinet under the sink and pulled out an apron—a gift her sister-in-law had given her years ago that she'd never used—and handed it to him. "Here, put this on. You don't want to ruin such a nice sweater."

"Thanks."

"I'll be right back."

She retreated to her bedroom and locked the door. She kicked off her heels and sat on the edge of the bed for a moment—tried to organize her thoughts—then changed out of her suit. She wasn't sure what the appropriate attire was for a surprise home-cooked dinner from a friend, and a quick scan of her closet didn't give her many ideas. In the end, she chose to emulate Jack. She pulled on a pair of jeans and a sweater.

Be careful.

Getting involved with Jack was stupid. She knew that, which was why she'd resisted his advances the last time he'd surprised her at her door. If she got involved with him, and word got out, the appearance of impropriety would be enough to torpedo the Ramsey case. And she didn't even want to think about what Kristen Dillard's reaction would be, learning that she'd been romancing the man who'd cross-examined her at Ramsey's first trial.

So why was she so glad to see him?

She couldn't deny that part of her had missed him. Missed him and missed that kiss. There was something between them. She couldn't ignore it. But she couldn't welcome it either, could she? Not with so much at stake.

But she'd given so much of herself to her work. Did she really have to give this, too?

Yes. Yes, I do.

Back in the kitchen, she said, "When did you start taking cooking classes?"

"I didn't."

"So where did you learn to make chicken parm?"

He flourished a folded sheet of printer paper. "The Internet."

"You've never tried the recipe before?"

"Nope. Never cooked anything more complicated than a

grilled cheese sandwich." He lifted a pan, examined the Teflon surface, then filled it with marinara sauce and placed it on a burner.

"You're joking."

"Oh, and I almost forgot." He reached into the duffel bag and pulled out a long cardboard box. Inside was a bottle of white wine. "Better put this in the fridge, let it start to chill."

Her conscience would not permit her to leave him here to prepare their dinner while she watched TV, so she hung around the kitchen and watched. It wasn't easy. Jack managed to splash raw egg on her wall, get bread crumbs in his hair, even drop a slice of provolone cheese between the refrigerator and the wall—all the while apologizing profusely, mopping up his messes as best he could with one hand while cooking with the other.

She lifted his marinara-stained recipe from the counter and searched in vain for an indication of source. "Who wrote this? A famous chef?"

Jack shrugged. "Some lady. She posted a bunch of recipes to her Web site." He yanked a handful of paper towels from the roll, squirted anti-bacterial soap and water on it, and attempted to clean the raw chicken juices he'd left on her cutting board. "So tell me about jury selection. Did it go smoothly?"

She sighed and leaned against the wall. Her day in court had seemed endless, and she'd spent most of it on her feet. Her back throbbed. It was nice to have someone to come home to and talk about it with. "You mean aside from being forced to inhale Gil Goldhammer's industrial-strength cologne? I guess it went as well as expected."

BURNOUT

"What's that mean?" He wiped his hands on the apron.

"Goldhammer did his best to load the jury with unmarried, working-class men. A construction worker, a tow-truck driver, a painter. I guess he figures they'll identify with a fireman. I don't know. In a case like this, I'm not convinced you can predict the makeup of the ideal jury."

"What types did you favor?"

"Parents. I figured the idea of a man who butchers families in their homes would strike a chord with them. Also young women. I'm hoping they identify with Kristen when she tells her story."

"I wonder if Frank will testify this time?"

Jack's use of Ramsey's first name irked her. "Let's not talk about the case. I don't want to start arguing, spoil the evening with a fight."

"You're right. Better to spoil it with really bad Italian food."

She laughed. "Uh-oh."

Jack used a spatula to transfer the chicken parmigiana cutlets from the pan to two plates. The breadcrumbs had blackened and the cheese looked watery.

"Maybe it will taste better than it looks," she said.

The wine, at least, was delicious. But because Jack's chicken parmigiana tasted like burnt shoe leather, they made do with the spaghetti and a bag of Chex Mix for dinner. Jessie didn't mind. Before long they were both tipsy and laughing.

"To the law." Jack raised his wineglass and clinked it against hers. "A noble institution."

"For someone burnt out on law, you sure seem to love

talking about it."

"Well, it's the only thing we have in common."

Maybe it was the wine buzzing in her head, but his words stung. After their walk, she had thought they had a lot in common. "Come on, Jack. That's not the only thing."

He sipped his wine. "You're right. For one thing, we're both very committed people. You're committed to your work, and I was committed to a mental hospital."

"Hilarious."

"And we're both very good-looking. Don't forget that."

"That's key," she said, taking a long sip from her own glass.

"Right."

She shook the bag of Chex Mix and said, "You done?"

"Yeah. I guess we should clean up." He gathered their plates and stood. At the same time, she made a decision. There was something here, something real between them, and ignoring it would be a mistake. She wasn't willing to make that mistake.

Before he could walk to the kitchen, she stood, pulled him closer to her, and kissed him. His eyebrows arched in surprise, but then she felt his smile as he returned the kiss. It was as good as their kiss over the Schuylkill River. *Better.* She pressed her lips against his, then flicked her tongue against his teeth, into the warmth of his mouth. He dropped the plates and they clattered on the table. His arms wrapped around her.

"I'm ... confused," he said.

"Just go with it." She pulled back for air, feeling a giddy smile on her face.

He said, "If this is the wine—"

"It's not the wine."

"What about the appearance of impropriety?" he said.

She looked up into his eyes. "We're going to need to be careful. Discreet. At least until Ramsey's trial is over."

"I can be discreet," he said.

"Good."

"And careful."

"Yes."

"You know, I'd be lying if I said I wasn't hoping something like this would happen. I picked cooking because it's a *romantic* hobby."

"Did Dr. Brandywine tell you that?"

He laughed and shook his head. "My own brilliant idea. I just wanted to kiss you again."

"Are you satisfied?"

He grinned. "Not remotely."

26.

The next morning at work, Jessie tried without much success to keep the stupid smile off her face. It wasn't the sex—she'd never been the type of woman who believed a roll in the hay imparted some mythical glow—but it had been a long time since she'd woken up with a man beside her, a long time since she'd begun her morning with a kiss, and she was feeling happy. Even the e-mails that greeted her when she logged in to her computer—e-mails that promised tedious meetings, assignments she had no time for, and repeated requests from Warren for progress reports on the Ramsey trial—could not dispel her mood.

Elliot Williams's appearance in her doorway, however, did the trick.

This was the first time she'd seen him since he'd stormed out of Ramsey's PCRA hearing. She braced herself for a confrontation. "Hi, Elliot."

"Do you have a minute?" Surprisingly, he sounded chipper.

"Sure." She pointed to the second chair in her office.

He sat down. "I've been thinking a lot about what happened at Ramsey's hearing. About how you took over."

BURNOUT

"I told you. I was only doing what I felt was necessary to prevent Ramsey from succeeding. I'm sorry it didn't work out the way either of us wanted it to."

He dismissed her apology with a wave. "You did the right thing. I was too inexperienced, didn't know what I was doing. I didn't realize that at the time, but looking back on it now, I do."

"Okay." She wasn't sure where this conversation was heading, but her skeptical mind predicted that he would soon be requesting a favor.

"I think there's a lot you could teach me."

"You'll learn everything yourself. That's how it works. Start in Appeals or Municipal Court, then things get a little more interesting in the Juvenile Unit, and then in the Felony-Waiver Unit, you'll really hone your skills. By the time you reach the Trial Division, you'll know your way around the CJC and you'll be a pro at dealing with cops, witnesses, judges, everyone. Trust me."

"I know that's the way the office is set up, but I was hoping that, informally, you could be a kind of mentor for me."

Stalling for time, she looked at her computer monitor. She really had nothing against the kid, but the Ramsey trial was going to be hard enough without adding mentoring to her list of challenges. Not to mention having a top-secret relationship with Jack. "I've got a lot on my plate right now, Elliot."

"I know."

"I mean, maybe we can have lunch together once in awhile and I'll give you some pointers, but...." She let her voice trail away, hoping he would take the hint.

"Have you started working on your opening statement yet? For Ramsey?"

She had planned to polish it this morning before appearing in court on other matters. She turned to her computer and loaded what she had done the day before. "I have a rough draft. Needs some more work." And then she would have to memorize it—juries always responded better to speeches that were spoken instead of read.

Elliot craned his neck to see the screen. "Would you mind printing a copy for me? I've never had the chance to study an opening statement before. And then we can talk about it over lunch one day. You know, to kick off the mentoring?"

Right now, the only kicking she wanted to do was kick him out of her office so she could get back to work. But he looked so eager and sincere, she couldn't bring herself to say that. Besides, good intentions or not, she had embarrassed him during the hearing. Giving him a little attention now could only be good karma, not to mention ingratiating to her boss.

"I guess that would be alright." She hit the print button. "Just be careful with the document. I wouldn't want anyone else to see it."

He smiled. "Who would I show it to?"

"If you discover any great wisdom in it, make sure you tell me so I don't revise that part."

"You got it."

She stared at him—his smiling face, his relaxed manner. "You seem ... different," she said.

"Really?"

BURNOUT

She nodded. "Less tense. More—I don't know—friendly."

He laughed. "I was thinking the same thing about you." He stretched his arms and yawned, then stood up, walked to the printer in the hallway, and returned with the document. "All right, I'll tell you the truth," he said. "I met a girl. I guess it's changed my outlook. I was kind of depressed before. Now I feel good about things. I know, I'm a walking cliché, right?"

But he looked pretty happy to be one.

"Good for you, Elliot. Balancing professional responsibilities with a personal life isn't easy. Maybe you should be my mentor instead of the other way around."

"You're not involved with anyone?"

She felt an unpleasant churn in her stomach, whether from shame, guilt, or both, she didn't know. "I guess I'm still looking for the right man," she said.

"I hope you know him when he shows up." He tapped the document in his hand. "Thanks. I really appreciate this."

27.

For a man who had created a successful business and then sold it for millions of dollars, Michael Rushford's house was comparatively modest—a four bedroom colonial in the upscale Philly suburb of Chestnut Hill. As Rushford's nurse led him toward the staircase, Leary noticed some antique furniture in the hall—Leary's mother was an admirer of antiques, and he recognized them when he saw them—but these pieces appeared to be Rushford's only indulgence. The lion's share of Rushford's money had gone either to his medical bills or the Foundation.

Rushford's private nurse—an attractive, petite brunette named Natalie Baron—led Leary up a curving stairwell to the second floor. She treaded silently and Leary found himself trying to do the same. The house was so quiet that he could hear the hum of machinery above them.

"Mr. Rushford has a lot of trouble sleeping." Natalie tilted toward him on the stairs to whisper close to his ear. "But I told him you were coming and he said it would be okay to wake him."

"I appreciate it," Leary said with a nod. It was generous of the dying man to agree to meet with him, especially to discuss a murder investigation that had supposedly closed over a year ago.

"Mr. Rushford was very fond of Dr. Dillard and wants to help you in any way he can."

Leary remembered Rushford saying something similar during his first investigation, although to Leary's ear, he had not sounded particularly sincere. At the time, Leary had wondered if Rushford could even have identified Bob Dillard by sight. But he smiled at the nurse and said, "I remember."

"Oh yes, I forgot you've met Mr. Rushford once before." She touched his arm, halting his ascent. "Just so you're prepared, his condition is significantly worse."

"I'm sorry to hear that," he said. The bedroom door was open. Inside, an array of medical equipment surrounded a king-size bed. Michael Rushford lay stretched out above the sheet. His limbs looked painfully scrawny and feeble. An oxygen mask was fixed to his face.

Natalie walked to the side of the bed and put her hand on Rushford's shoulder. He woke instantly, opened his eyes and looked at her. She removed the oxygen mask, placed it on the machine it was connected to, and switched off the machine. Then she arranged the pillows against the headboard and helped Rushford lift himself into a sitting position. Leary watched all of this from the doorway, feeling like an intruder in a private moment.

Rushford's eyes wavered from the nurse to Leary. "Come in, please." His voice, although it rattled out of his throat and barely carried across the room, had retained a cadence of authority. For a brief moment, Leary could imagine the wasted man—whose pajamas seemed to cover only bones—commanding a boardroom full of executives.

Leary approached the bed, extended his hand.

Rushford's grip was weak, but he shook it. "Welcome, Detective Leary."

Natalie placed a wooden, high-backed chair close to the bed—it was another antique, Leary thought, possibly from the Edwardian period, and he felt almost guilty sitting on it. She retreated to the door, but instead of leaving them, sat in a chair beside the doorway and folded her hands in her lap.

"Mr. Rushford, I'd like to ask you some questions about Bob Dillard."

"It was a tragedy, what happened to Bob and his family." Rushford's voice was barely more than a breath. Leary had to lean forward to hear him.

"Yes, it—" Leary stopped, watched Rushford's face. In his years as a homicide detective, Leary had earned a reputation for his skill in the interrogation room. He had a knack for seeing past people's disguises. Now, he had the sudden intuition that Rushford was wearing one. Just as he had during his initial investigation, Leary sensed insincerity. "It was a brutal crime."

Rushford nodded. "How can I help?"

"I'm trying to learn as much as I can about Bob Dillard."

"If you talked to people at the Foundation, you know he was a workaholic." Rushford smiled as if at a fond memory. "He was very dedicated to his research. Unfortunately, his dedication cost the Foundation millions of dollars and years of lost time."

"What do you mean?"

"He had a habit of taking his work home with him. His mind was always on his research and he liked to have his notebooks at hand. After his murder, Bob's briefcase couldn't be located."

"The Family Man always takes a souvenir," Leary said, remembering. It had been one of the holes in his case, a point that Ramsey's lawyer Jack Ackerman had hammered at the jury over and over again. Leary had searched every location Ramsey had an attachment to—his house, the firehouse, his childhood home—but had found none of the personal items that had been taken from the scenes of his crimes. Including Bob Dillard's briefcase.

"Bob's lab notebooks must have been in that briefcase, because they were not in his lab or in his house," Rushford said. "Now, all that knowledge, all that progress, is lost."

"Didn't Dr. Dillard keep backup files, copies, some record of his work?"

"He was supposed to. But Bob had a mind that ran on a single track. Everything else, he let slip."

Leary studied the man's face. His words sounded like bullshit—what kind of scientist doesn't back up his notes?—but Rushford spoke with such genuine regret, it was hard to believe he was lying. "You said these were handwritten notebooks? He didn't transcribe his work into digital form? That doesn't make sense, unless he worked completely alone, with no interaction or aid—"

"He preferred to work alone. Only a handful of high-ranking people at the Foundation even knew what he was doing."

"Okay. But what about the Foundation's computers? Wouldn't he need to enter the data to run scenarios or build theories?"

Rushford shook his head. "I don't know."

"But you knew what he was working on, right?"

Rushford studied him, his expression turning wary. "Yes."

"I heard somewhere that human embryonic stem cells could be the key to treating ALS," Leary said, holding the man's gaze.

"Somewhere?" Rushford grimaced. "I'll have to remind Dr. Tiano of the dangers of wild speculation."

"You must be familiar with the studies done in China."

"I'm familiar with them. Unfortunately, such experiments have been outlawed in our country by narrow-minded religious zealots."

"That must be very frustrating for you."

"Yes, it is."

Leary leaned back in his chair as he imagined a secret lab—separate from the Foundation but funded by Rushford—where Dillard might have conducted his research. Rushford certainly had enough money. And might a man like Bob Dillard keep his notes handwritten and in one place, if he were performing that type of research? Research that could have saved lives, but that also could have put him and his patron in prison, and the Foundation out of business? It was a crazy idea. *Wild speculation*, to borrow Rushford's phrase. But what if it was true? How close might Dillard have been to a breakthrough that might have extended—or even saved—Rushford's life?

"Are you investigating me, Detective?"

The raspy voice broke Leary from his reverie. He looked at Rushford's wasted body and shook his head. "No, I'm just trying to see the whole picture."

BURNOUT

"You're trying to make order out of chaos. I have that tendency as well." The man smiled weakly. "It doesn't work here. Believe me, I've tried. The Dillard murders were a random act of violence, completely unrelated to Bob Dillard's work. And the loss of that work is...." Rushford's voice choked off. "It's tragic." His gaze wandered to the doorway, where Natalie sat patiently staring into space. "Detective, my disease makes prolonged conversation difficult. My lungs don't work like they should. I apologize, but I need to rest."

"Can we continue this conversation later?"

"I think I've told you everything I know."

Leary nodded and rose from the antique chair. Across the room, Natalie also stood up. She was going to escort him out of the house, and he doubted he'd receive a second invitation. That was all right. His audience with Michael Rushford had been brief. But it had not been fruitless.

28.

Amber lay on Elliot's bed. The first week with him had been rough, sucking his cock and pretending to get off when he fucked her. But his apartment was beginning to seem less alien, and she felt comfortable enough to lay in a natural position, stomach on the bedspread, bare feet swinging in the air, and not worry about whether or not she looked seductive enough.

She read the rough draft of Jessie Black's opening statement, and was surprised by how easy it was to understand. When Woody had suggested she try to get her hands on some documents prepared for the upcoming trial, she had been afraid they would contain impenetrable legalese.

"Wow. This is really well written."

Elliot snorted. "You think so?"

"You don't?" She pushed a sheet of blonde hair behind her shoulder and looked at him. She wasn't the only one to become more comfortable—Elliot had, too. When she'd first met him at Dean's, he'd been tolerable. Cute in a dorky, shy way she found endearing. But after getting used to the idea of having her around, he'd morphed into a strutting, arrogant, overbearing asshole. He reminded her of her stepfather, a boastful loser whose fatal heart attack she'd cheered.

He paced in front of the bed, holding forth like he was one of the O.J. lawyers or something. "It's a little overly dramatic, don't you think? If I was on the jury I think I'd bust out laughing."

Amber didn't see any humor in the account of the Dillard family's last night together—she couldn't imagine experiencing anything so terrible—but Elliot had been through college and law school, so she supposed he knew what he was talking about. "It's kind of overdone, I guess."

"Kind of?" He laughed.

She didn't like the way his eyes started to roam her body. The last thing she wanted was to have to fuck him again. "I bet you could write a better one," she said.

He stopped pacing, dropped into a chair in a corner of the studio apartment. "I told you, it's not my case. I worked on the PCRA hearing, but now that Ramsey's getting a new trial, it goes straight to the Homicide Unit."

"To Jessie Black."

"Right."

She made herself perk up as if a new idea had just occurred to her. "But she stole the case from you, right? Can't you steal it back?"

He smiled, shook his head as if at a child. "It's not that simple."

"But it would be so cool to watch you in court." She showed him her best princess pout, the one she used whenever a patron at the club hesitated about buying a thirty dollar lap dance.

"I might be able to force my way into the case. I'd have

to go to my uncle, convince him to force Jessie to let me assist her. If I could make him feel guilty about how she screwed me over the first time...." Elliot thought about it, then shook his head. "But Warren won't feel guilty. I know him."

"Might as well try, right?"

He got up from the chair and climbed onto the bed with her. Inwardly she groaned. Something she'd said or done had accidentally turned him on, and now she'd have to pay the price. He cupped her cheek and turned her face to his, closed in for the kiss. His other hand squeezed her ass, then her left breast.

"Elliot, I'm not in the mood."

He kissed her one more time before giving her room to breathe. "Why? Is something wrong?"

"No. I just don't feel like it." *And never do.* Not with him. Woody had been a different story. With Woody, she'd always been in the mood. But she had loved him. And had thought that he loved her. *What a joke.*

"Do you have a headache?" Elliot rolled off the bed and headed for the kitchen area of the small apartment. "I have Excedrin."

"I'm fine. I was just ... into our conversation. I want to hear more about the Ramsey case."

Elliot turned from the kitchen cabinet, his swagger returning. If there was one thing he liked almost as much as fucking her, it was talking about himself. And unlike fucking, he could talk for hours.

Amber wasn't sure which was harder to endure.

29.

Unlike the PCRA hearing, which had attracted little media attention, Judge Spatt's courtroom was packed on the first day of Ramsey's new trial. Reporters from newspapers, television stations, radio, and Internet news sites filled the benches of the gallery and spilled out into the hallway, where they milled about impatiently, descending like vultures on anyone who looked like interview fodder. Jessie, who would be considered excellent interview fodder, kept her head down when she walked past them, ignored the questions launched in her direction, and made it to the prosecution table unscathed.

Goldhammer and Ramsey were already seated at the defense table. Goldhammer turned and nodded to her as she unpacked her bag, his puffy face exuding cocky self-assurance. Ramsey, his neutral expression already fixed in place, didn't acknowledge her.

She sat down. In spite of all of her preparation, her heart raced. The courtroom triggered an adrenaline rush in her body. This morning, as always, she was thankful for it. Soon the jury would file in and the trial—one of the most important of her career—would start. She needed every advantage she could get.

* * *

She began her opening statement to the jury, as always, by introducing herself as an assistant District Attorney with the Philadelphia District Attorney's Office, and thanking them for their important contribution to the criminal justice system. The jurors watched her from their seats—twelve of them, plus two alternates, an audience of fourteen.

Emphasizing her position of authority and role as the lawyer representing the state—while by implication reminding the jury that the defense attorney, a man not affiliated with the government, served only the accused—had been shown to foster additional trust in jurors.

As she had told Jack, she did not believe the outcome of this trial would be determined by the makeup of the jury. Factors like race, age, and sex would not play significant roles. Nevertheless, she had studied the jurors' questionnaires the night before in an attempt to identify those who might be problems. She had come up with three. Trent Slaney, a white, unmarried, fifty-two-year-old construction worker whose answers suggested a distrust of cops, lawyers, and the government. Malcolm Clonts, a black, married, thirty-year-old middle school janitor with ties to a militant church that condemned the white middle class. And Jenna Gottlieb, a white, single, twenty-year-old nursing student whom Jessie had noticed glancing in Ramsey's direction, her gaze a little too admiring for Jessie's comfort.

Jessie made repeated eye contact with each of these problem jurors. The attempt at forced intimacy might seem obvious to an impartial observer, but in practice, it usually worked. Jurors did not like being silent spectators; they wanted to feel like real, integral participants in the trial. Even the most cynical of them—like Slaney, who had indicated on his questionnaire that he believed most cops lied in order to

BURNOUT

convict accused criminals—would bask in her attention without questioning its sincerity. As the enormously profitable industry of jury consulting demonstrated, human nature was remarkably consistent and predictable.

She did not neglect the other nine jurors or the two alternates, however. During her opening statement, she met the eyes of every one of them at least once, gratified if they leaned forward as if physically pulled closer by her words. She kept her arms at her sides, paced as little as possible, smiled when appropriate and scowled when necessary. The opening statement was her first real opportunity to influence the jury. A good prosecutor took full advantage.

"The road ahead is not going to be easy," she said. "You have been selected to serve as jurors in a trial involving multiple stabbings, rapes, murders and attempted murder. You are going to see crime scene photographs that may haunt your nightmares for years to come. You are going to hear heart-wrenching testimony from one of the defendant's victims. And you are going to be faced, eventually, with deciding the fate of the man you see sitting at the defense table. A sociopath with a mind like a reptile's—no conscience, no mercy.

"When police officers responded to a neighbor's report of loud noises next door, they found nothing suspicious outside. The Dillard's home looked secure and serene. No broken windows. No busted locks. They rang the doorbell and knocked, but received no response. They might have returned to the station had one of them not noticed, through the partly closed drapes, a dark red stain on the stairway carpet inside.

"The lead detective assigned to the case, Mark Leary, will explain to you that the condition of the doors and windows lead to his conclusion that Mr. Ramsey gained access to the house simply by knocking on the door.

"The Dillards had been sitting together in their family room, watching sitcoms. Why did they answer the door? I can't answer that question. I suppose Robert Dillard, although a brilliant scientist, lacked street smarts. He did not believe the person at his door might be a vicious predator. He did not believe that a man he'd never met—Frank Ramsey—had come to his house with the sole purpose of torturing and killing his family."

She paused, let the jurors imagine the scenario. She knew that most if not all of them watched TV alone or with their families, that most if not all of them had experienced the unexpected ring of the doorbell. Maybe they had opened their doors to discover only a cookie-peddling Girl Scout or a Jehovah's Witness.

She noticed with satisfaction that several jurors turned to regard Ramsey with angry, frightened stares.

Time to move on.

"After exploring the first floor of the house, police found bodies upstairs in the master bedroom. Detective Leary will tell you that he believes Mr. Ramsey drove the family up there at knife point. Robert Dillard, a forty-three-year-old biochemist known to his friends and family as Bob, was found with gashes on his hands and legs. Defensive wounds. A deputy medical examiner will testify that these wounds indicate that Bob Dillard tried to fight. He tried to defend his family. But Mr. Ramsey, a professional firefighter, easily overpowered him. Eventually, Mr. Ramsey forced Bob Dillard's hands behind his back—breaking his left wrist in the process—and bound them with the electrical cord of the alarm clock on the table next to the bed. Police found Bob Dillard's wife, Erin Dillard, also with hands bound behind her back, hers with a phone cord. Their sixteen-year-old daughter Kristen's hands had been tied with a cord torn from the base of a reading lamp. As photographs will show, the cord on Kristen's wrists was tied so tightly that it sliced through her skin.

"The deputy medical examiner will explain to you that Bob Dillard was killed first. Police found his body on the floor, near his bed, where the carpet was soaked with blood. There were seventeen stab wounds in his chest. The deputy medical examiner will testify that the weapon used to inflict these wounds had a blade at least eight inches long and one inch wide."

She demonstrated with her hands, first holding them up about eight inches apart, then measuring an inch with her thumb and index finger. The gestures had the same effect on this jury as it had on Ramsey's first jury, driving home the sheer size of the weapon. They gasped, muttered, cursed. One woman brought her hands to her face and wiped her eyes. Jessie omitted a detail that Goldhammer would no doubt harp upon, when his turn came—the murder weapon had never been found.

"Police found Erin Dillard with her own panties stuffed in her mouth as a gag. The deputy medical examiner will testify that Mr. Ramsey tore them off of her so hard he left a bruise on her hip. Mr. Ramsey then raped Erin Dillard in front of her terrified daughter."

But he had been careful to leave no trace evidence. The only foreign substance recovered from her vagina had been a lubricant common to several brands of condoms. Goldhammer would emphasize this fact as well—the evidence made clear that *someone* had raped Erin Dillard, but not that his client had done it. She silently forced herself not to dwell on the weaknesses in her case. She could not afford to project anything but total confidence.

"Erin Dillard was stabbed to death, just like her husband. Eleven stab wounds to her chest and upper abdomen. One, the deputy medical examiner will tell you, severed the major artery from her heart. But what most horrified police at the scene was Bob and Erin's daughter.

"Kristen Dillard—now seventeen years old, but only sixteen on the night of Mr. Ramsey's attack—is going to testify at this trial. You are going to see her bravely take the witness stand. She will tell you in her own words what happened that night. She will tell you that she watched Mr. Ramsey stab her father to death and then rape and stab her mother. And she will tell you what Mr. Ramsey did next. That he raped her, then stabbed her. Three times in the chest. Once in the back. And once in the neck.

"But Mr. Ramsey made a mistake. Assuming that Kristen Dillard was dead, he took off his ski mask for a breath of fresh air before leaving the scene of his crime. And Kristen Dillard—still very much alive—saw his face. And she managed to cling to life until emergency personnel called by the police rushed her to a hospital for treatment. And later, recovering from her multiple wounds, she identified Mr. Ramsey in a lineup."

Every juror stared at her, rapt, unblinking. If ordered by the judge to reach a decision right now, Jessie had no doubt that every one of them would find Ramsey guilty as charged.

Of course, a real trial wasn't that easy. The defense had its opportunity to speak, too. And the goal of every defense attorney worth his retainer was to sow seeds of doubt—plant them witness by witness, embed them within objections, emphasize them in opening and closing statements—until, in the jury's confused minds, the factual foundations of the prosecution's version of events had been eroded, making a judgment of guilt beyond a reasonable doubt impossible.

"Ladies and gentlemen of the jury, in addition to hearing from me, you are going to hear a lot from Mr. Ramsey's lawyer. You may have heard of him. Mr. Goldhammer is a bit of a celebrity, famous for defending accused gangsters and drug dealers and murderers." She inclined her body toward Goldhammer, who was staring studiously at his notes. "He's spent as much time in cable news studios as he has in courtrooms, and he's a very good speaker. He is going to tell you there is not enough evidence here to convict Mr. Ramsey for the crimes I just described. He is also going to introduce you to a witness—he will tell you she is a very respected psychologist—who will try to convince you that eyewitness identifications are worthless. I urge you to compare her theories with your own experiences, with your own common sense, and decide for yourselves whether Kristen Dillard's testimony is reliable."

When the jurors' dirty looks settled on Goldhammer, Jessie had to struggle to prevent herself from grinning. Hopefully she'd just sown some seeds of doubt of her own.

"Ladies and gentlemen of the jury, you are here to study the facts of a gruesome and horrifying crime. I apologize in advance for putting you through this, but our American system of justice guarantees every criminal, no matter how heinous his crimes, the right to be judged by a jury of his peers. I have faith that you will reach the correct decision in this case. That you will find Frank Ramsey guilty beyond a reasonable doubt."

She returned to her seat, pleased with her opening

statement and its effect on the jury. Judge Spatt, who had not made a sound during her speech, turned to address the jury.

"You will now hear from Mr. Goldhammer, who represents the defendant. I remind you, once again, that you are to judge this case only on the evidence. What the lawyers say—no matter how convincing it might sound—is not evidence." He glared at Jessie, then leveled a warning stare at Goldhammer. "Go ahead, Counselor."

As Goldhammer rose from his chair, two people hurried past the bar of the court and took the two empty seats next to Jessie at the prosecution's table. Elliot and Warren.

She picked up her pen, turned to a fresh page on her legal pad, and wrote: *What's wrong?*

Warren took the pad. On the line underneath her question, he wrote: *New development. Elliot is second-chair.*

She stared at him. Warren stared back. Between them, Elliot shifted uncomfortably in the hard wooden chair.

Jessie wrote: *Why?*

Before he could respond, Elliot took the pad and added his own comment: *I won't get in your way. I just want to learn.*

No.

Goldhammer had already begun his address to the jury. Jessie turned away from Warren and Elliot to focus on him. "Ms. Black spun you a terrifying tale, but she miscast the villain," he was saying. "Frank Ramsey did not enter the Dillard household and terrorize that family. Frank Ramsey has no history of violence, no criminal record. You want to know who he was before he was wrongfully accused of this crime? I'll tell you. He was a fireman. He *protected* houses. He *rescued* people. He's a hero, not a villain.

BURNOUT

"Ms. Black told you to trust your own common sense. I agree. And your common sense will tell you that the prosecution does not have enough evidence to prove beyond a reasonable doubt that Mr. Ramsey committed the crimes of which he is accused."

Warren took the pad. *This is not a debate. My Homicide Unit, my decision.*

Jessie nodded, trying not to let them distract her. "Were Frank Ramsey's fingerprints found at the house?" Goldhammer asked the jury. "The police will admit to you that they were not. Were his fingerprints found on the murder weapon? No, nor was the murder weapon itself ever found, even when the police searched Frank Ramsey's house and vehicle. But most importantly, how about this eyewitness Ms. Black told you about?"

In front of the jury box, Goldhammer spread his arms theatrically. "Did Kristen Dillard see Frank Ramsey's face while he was allegedly raping and stabbing her? The prosecutor just admitted to you that she did not. Could not. Because the man who assaulted Kristen Dillard was wearing a ski mask. Ms. Dillard herself will admit that the only glimpse she got of her attacker's face occurred *after* he had finished raping and stabbing her. As he was turning away from her. When he was walking out of the room. When she was bleeding and on the verge of losing consciousness. *That's* when she claims he took off his mask. *That's* when she claims—for a matter of seconds—to have seen the face of my client. Now, I ask you, does that sound like a solid eyewitness identification? Does that satisfy your common sense? Is that enough evidence to condemn Frank Ramsey to multiple murder convictions?"

I can help, Elliot wrote.

She quickly scrawled, Why don't you start by listening and taking notes?

"I beseech you to remember your duty in this trial—your duty to hold the prosecution to the high standard that our country demands. If the prosecution cannot prove its case beyond a reasonable doubt, then you must—must, as a matter of law—find Frank Ramsey not guilty."

Goldhammer, chest puffed with satisfaction, strutted back to his seat at the defense table. Judge Spatt aimed a suspicious eye at the prosecution table, where the lawyers must have appeared to him to be multiplying. With a withering stare and a dry tone, he said, "Why wasn't I invited to the party?"

Warren jumped up. "Your Honor, I apologize for the intrusion. A decision was made at the last moment that Elliot Williams would act as second-chair for the Commonwealth. I wanted to get him here in time to listen to Mr. Goldhammer's statement."

Spatt smirked. "Didn't look to me like he was listening."

Jessie, feeling the scrutinizing eyes of the jurors shift in her direction, pasted a pleasant expression on her face that she hoped projected a dull, business-as-usual impression, even though what was happening was anything but.

"Always a pleasure to see you in my courtroom, Warren." Even with a total absence of sarcasm in his voice, Spatt managed to launch his words like poisoned arrows from the bench. "It's a pity your administrative responsibilities afford you so little time to try actual cases. In fact, when was the last case you tried?"

Warren's cheeks reddened. "A few years ago, Judge."

"Yes, at least." Turning to the jury, he said, "Mr. Elliot Williams, another lawyer from the District Attorney's office, will be assisting Ms. Black during the trial."

Elliot stood up, gave the jury a smile and—Jessie clenched her teeth—waved at them. Across the aisle, Goldhammer could not suppress a chuckle.

Warren patted Jessie's shoulder—a gesture of encouragement or apology, she didn't know—and fled from the courtroom.

"May we continue?" Spatt drawled.

Jessie breathed slowly, and deeply, and rose from her chair with a smile. "Yes, Your Honor."

30.

Michael Rushford had told Leary that only the top people at the Rushford Foundation had known about the briefcase—and the important materials inside—that had been lost because of Bob Dillard's murder. It took Leary a day and a half to track down the topmost person he could think of: Eduard Urlyapov, the former director of the Rushford Foundation who, according to Randy Tiano, had retired due to stress.

According to the one-page bio Leary had printed off the Foundation's Web site during his first investigation of the Dillard murders, Urlyapov was a biochemist who had studied at Moscow State University and later at the Shemykin Institute of Bioorganic Chemistry in Pushchino, Russia. At the time that Rushford recruited him to run the Foundation, Urlyapov had been in London researching the engineering of non-viral transporters for specific targeting to motor and sensory neurons.

What any of that meant, Leary had no idea. During his initial investigation, he'd only skimmed the scientific language. Now, even after doing some research, the words still conveyed no meaning to him.

Tiano had told him that Urlyapov retired three months ago. With some more digging, Leary learned that after leaving his post at the Foundation, Urlyapov had made plans to leave the United States. Making phone calls from his desk at the Roundhouse, Leary discovered the rental of a flat in London, the purchase of airline tickets, and preliminary negotiations for the sale of Urlyapov's house in Bala Cynwyd. But Urlyapov had never left. Sixty-seven years old, he had suffered a stroke that put him in the hospital about a week ago. He was still there, convalescing.

Leary decided to visit.

Liver spots dotted Urlyapov's head, bald except for a few white strands on the top. He had the appearance of a large man who had suffered a sudden loss of weight, his loose, pale skin hanging in flaps from his arms and neck. When he saw Leary in his doorway, he struggled to a sitting position. His teeth were brown and spaced too far apart; his breath whistled between them.

It seemed that this investigation was taking Leary from one deathbed to the next.

"Dr. Urlyapov?"

"You're pronouncing it wrong," the old man corrected. His rasping voice and Russian accent forced Leary to lean forward and struggle to understand. Urlyapov sighed. "Just call me Ed."

Leary smiled. "Okay, Ed. My name is Mark Leary. I'm a homicide detective with the Philadelphia Police Department. We spoke briefly about two years ago."

"Yes. I remember. A phone call."

"I was investigating the murder of Dr. Robert Dillard."

"Bob, yes. And I told you everything I know."

Leary scraped a plastic chair over the linoleum floor and sat down close to the bed. "Are you sure? We didn't talk for long. According to my notes, our conversation lasted about five minutes. You passed me off to Dr. Tiano."

"He was closer to Bob than I was."

"Is there anything you might have forgotten to tell me? Something about the nature of Bob Dillard's work?"

A shadow seemed to pass over Urlyapov's face, although the sun outside the grimy hospital window had not moved. His eyelids fluttered. "Show me your badge."

Leary, startled, did as the old man asked. Urlyapov twisted on his side to squint at Leary's identification in a ray of sunlight. "I can't tell if this is real." Urlyapov's eyes moved from the ID to the gun peeking out from Leary's jacket. "Did Rushford send you? Make it quick."

"Make what quick?" Leary took back his ID, and saw that Urlyapov's gaze remained fixed on his gun. "You think Michael Rushford would send someone here to kill you?" Was the old man suffering from delusions or paranoia? Suddenly tempted to examine the old man's medical chart, Leary refrained. Instead, he closed his jacket over his holster and made eye-contact with the man. Trying to impart steadiness. Trust. If Urlyapov was impaired by some mental condition, he'd find out soon enough.

But if he wasn't....

"Ed, why do you think Rushford wants to hurt you?"

"I've tried to get out of this hospital so many times. Knew this day would come. Easy target."

"Did you leave the Foundation because you feared for your life?"

"Of course. Michael had Bob killed. Only a matter of time before me."

"You believe that Michael Rushford is responsible for Bob Dillard's murder?" The accusation made no sense. Why would Rushford murder a man who was working night and day to save his life? The urge to check the medical chart tugged at Leary again. Urlyapov was paranoid—what other explanation could there be?

Urlyapov coughed. "Bob's research threatened the whole Foundation. Illegal."

"Because it involved stem cells?"

Urlyapov nodded.

"But that research was Rushford's best chance at finding a treatment," Leary said, "maybe a cure. The intruder in Bob Dillard's house attacked the whole family. He raped Dillard's wife and daughter. Stabbed them savagely. Those actions indicate a crime of passion or the acting out of a psychotic fantasy, not a murder for hire."

"In Russia, KGB often disguised political assassinations. Same way."

Now they were talking about the KGB?

"No fingerprints," Urlyapov continued. "No weapon."

Leary felt his skepticism weaken. Urlyapov had a point. The absence of physical evidence *was* more consistent with a professional hit than with the actions of a psychopath. But the Dillards were only the last of a series of rape-murders committed by the so-called Family Man, and physical evidence had been found at none of the other scenes either. No killer-for-hire, no matter how intent on covering his tracks, would risk additional violent crimes solely to create the illusion of a serial killer. The chance of being surprised in the act or otherwise caught outweighed any benefit that killing the other families might bring.

Leary shook his head. "Ed, you're letting your fears get the best of you. How long have you been at this hospital?" He already knew the answer—almost a week. "If someone wanted you dead, you would be dead by now."

Urlyapov's hand brushed at Leary's arm. Leary recoiled automatically from his touch—skin as brittle as paper. "Maybe they have other uses for me," he said.

"What do you mean?"

The old man fell silent. His watery gaze shifted to the window. "Detective, if I'm found dead in here, remember this talk."

Leary nodded. He didn't think he could forget this conversation even if he wanted to. The old Russian was obviously paranoid—perhaps he'd had some personal experience with the KGB of which he'd ominously spoken—and despite his better judgment, some of Urlyapov's fear was transferring to Leary, spooking him.

"I should be going," Leary said. "Thanks for talking to me."

Urlyapov only nodded.

In the hallway, Leary found the nearest nurse's station and showed the woman behind it his ID. "I have some questions about the patient in room 401."

"Dr. Urlyapov?" The nurse—a large black woman—pronounced her patient's name in flawless Russian. "He's doing well, considering his age and the severity of the stroke."

"What about his psychological problems? His paranoia?"

His questions met a puzzled expression. "Dr. Urlyapov? He's sharp as a tack."

Leary felt a burst of heat bloom in his stomach. "Are you sure?"

The nurse nodded vigorously. In the next moment, her eyes shifted from Leary to a man approaching the counter. The man said, "Could you point me toward 401?"

The nurse's eyes shot back to Leary, who shook his head as imperceptibly as he could—*don't involve me.*

There was nothing outwardly unusual about the man—he was tall and broad-shouldered, with a short haircut and a neatly trimmed goatee—but something about him sent warning bells ringing in Leary's mind. Maybe it was the timing—seeing this man appear immediately after listening to Urlyapov voice his suspicions about Rushford. Or maybe it was the way the man asked for Urlyapov's room without trying to pronounce his name, like a friend or a family member would. But mostly it was because, just standing next to him at the nurse's station, Leary sensed tightly coiled energy and something else. *Malevolence.*

The nurse pointed down the hall. "That way."

"Thanks."

Leary waited ten seconds, then turned and followed the man toward Urlyapov's room. Walking, he reached under his jacket and flicked off the safety on his 9-mm. Just in case.

He stopped inches from the open doorway. Purely by luck, a glass cabinet door reflected a view of the bed. Without exposing himself, Leary watched the reflection. The man took Leary's place in the chair he had dragged close to the bed. Rather than attack Urlyapov—as Leary half-expected him to do—the man took Urlyapov's hand in his own and patted it in a familiar way. The old man leaned forward. Although Leary could not read his facial expression in the glass, his body language did not suggest fright.

Leary exhaled his pent-up breath. Touched his gun and switched the safety back on. The old man's conspiracy theories had infected him. Now he was the one acting paranoid.

Still, the nurse had assured him that Urlyapov's mental state was fine. He could not ignore the information the man had given him.

He could no longer consider Frank Ramsey his only suspect.

31.

The next morning, Jessie woke up in her bed, Jack beside her. He was smiling, and in one hand, he held a key. "Good morning."

"What's that?"

"What does it look like?" He pressed it into her hand. "I was hoping to give this to you over breakfast, but I've never been good at delayed satisfaction."

She looked at his naked body, on top of the covers, and remembered the previous night. "Yeah, I noticed." She looked at the key, then at him.

"I'd really like to take our relationship to the next level," he said.

"What level is that?"

"You know—exclusivity."

"You think I'm dating other people?" She laughed, then abruptly stopped laughing. "Have *you* been dating other people?"

"No. I was taught to always aim for the top. If you reject me, I'll work my way down."

"Well, thanks."

He cleared his throat with theatrical volume. "Can I have something in return?"

"I'll have to visit a locksmith." In truth, she intended to postpone that trip. She didn't like the idea of anyone—even Jack—having a key to her home.

"I was talking about a kiss."

"Oh." She kissed him, then glanced past his face at the clock on the nightstand. "I'm going to be late for court."

"I'll take a ride with you," he said.

In the lobby of the CJC, lawyers, witnesses, cops, and reporters milled in long lines to the metal detectors. Through the windows, the day looked gray and dreary.

Jessie turned to Jack. "I'll see you later?"

"Definitely. Good luck in there."

He leaned toward her and puckered his lips.

She flinched. "Jack, that's not funny." She felt the burn of anger as she quickly looked around, assessing the situation. "What's wrong with you? You could cost me my job."

He pouted and leaned closer. "Just a quick—"

Jessie heard a gasp and yanked her face away from his. Kristen Dillard stood with one of her minders from the institution. Kristen gaped at them, then turned and ran.

"Shit."

The woman accompanying Kristen looked too startled to respond. Jessie closed the gap between them, leaving Jack behind. "What is Kristen doing here? She's not testifying today."

"She asked to come. Dr. Schafer thought allowing her to

observe the trial would have therapeutic benefits."

"Witnesses aren't permitted to watch the trial before they testify."

"Oh. I didn't realize."

"Wait here."

Jessie caught up with Kristen at the guard desk. She stopped the girl before she could walk away. "Kristen, wait. Let's talk."

"Talk? I saw you with him. You were practically kissing."

Tears brimmed in the seventeen-year-old's eyes, and the sight stung Jessie more than she'd realized it would. What had she been thinking, letting Jack come here with her today? "He doesn't represent Ramsey anymore. He's not even a defense attorney now." The words sounded false as they tumbled from her lips. Jack had represented Ramsey at his first trial, and had been responsible—even if only indirectly—for the success of Ramsey's PCRA petition. In Kristen's eyes, Jack was the enemy. And Jessie must be something even worse—a betrayer.

"Don't you remember what he told the jury?" the girl said. "He said Ramsey was innocent. *He said I must have made a mistake.*"

"I know," Jessie said. "And I can't imagine what it felt like for you to hear that. I'm so sorry."

Kristen shook her head, disgusted. "Fuck you. I'm never coming to this place again. *I hate it here.*"

"Kristen, I can't convict Ramsey without you. You know that."

"What's the difference? He'll just find another way to get

out of it anyway."

People were turning to stare at them. Jack, mercifully, had disappeared. "That's not true," Jessie said. "He'll have exhausted his remedies."

"He won't be able to appeal if he loses this trial?"

Jessie exhaled through clenched teeth. Defending the criminal justice system to a crime victim was almost as difficult as defending defense attorneys. "If he loses this trial, he is entitled to appeal—"

"I can't believe this! It never ends!"

Kristen turned, fled through the glass doors. It angered Jessie that the girl had been allowed to come here, but the anger she felt toward the hospital staff paled next to the guilt she felt at having been caught with Jack.

What were you thinking?

Jessie pursued her outside. A light drizzle fell from the clouds, spattering the sidewalk with icy rain. Jessie caught up with her under the dripping awning of a deli, took her by the arms, forced her to meet her gaze.

"We're a team, Kristen. I would never betray you."

People seated at a table inside had turned to stare at them through the deli's fogged window.

Real professional. If only Warren could see her now.

Kristen looked at her shoes. Drops of rain had collected in her hair. She hugged herself. After a moment, she looked up, meeting Jessie's gaze with red-rimmed eyes. "I don't want to testify. I'm scared."

"They want you to be scared. Don't be. You beat Ramsey last time. You'll beat him this time, too." But the girl had good reason to be scared, Jessie knew. If Kristen had found *Jack's* cross-examination trying, the one-two punch of Goldhammer's cross and Kate Moscow's testimony would drop her to her knees. Jessie would do everything she could to protect the girl, short of keeping her off the stand. Without her testimony, Ramsey would walk.

"How can I trust you anymore?" Kristen said.

According to her doctors, the ordeal Ramsey had put her through had rendered trust an almost alien emotion for Kristen. That she had ever trusted Jessie at all had been a minor miracle. To think Jessie may have lost something so precious now made her want to cry herself.

She didn't. She maintained eye contact with the girl, held her trembling look with the stern stare of an adult. "You *know* you can trust me, Kristen. I'm the same person I've always been."

She did not release her pent-up breath until Kristen, staring at a soaked cement square of the sidewalk beyond the cover of the awning, nodded her head.

When Kristen raised her eyes, she focused on something beyond Jessie and gasped. Jessie spun. She half-expected to find Ramsey standing behind her with a knife, but it was only Elliot, holding an umbrella.

"What's going on?" he said.

32.

Woody braced himself before opening the door to Goldhammer's war room. He hated the massive temporary office space, and not just because the hotel provided it at an exorbitant cost. The space was like a cubicle-partitioned maze, loaded with desks and chairs, high-end PCs, and other equipment. Keyboards clicked, voices spoke into phones, copiers and printers whined as they spat out page after page. Freeing killers was big business, and it sickened Woody to be a part of it.

He found Goldhammer at a long table in the back of the suite. The cubicle walls provided some privacy, but did nothing to block the din. Sitting in a chair beside his, poring over a document with him, was the Ice Princess.

That was Woody's name for her anyway, since he picked her up from the train station and she treated him like a chauffeur. Katherine Moscow, the quack psychologist from New York.

She was leaning forward over the document. Her blonde hair—silky and natural, unlike Amber's crinkly dye job—had been pulled back and secured in a neat spiral at the back of her head. She wore a dark blue suit over a white blouse. A few rings and a watch that looked more like a bracelet than a timepiece complemented her soft hands and slender white fingers. Goldhammer, hunched beside her, looked troll-like in her presence.

Woody cleared his throat, and the lawyer's head popped up. "I don't know how you can hear yourself think in this hellhole," Woody said.

"The bustle helps focus my concentration." Goldhammer's mouth crinkled in distaste. "If you don't mind, we're kind of busy."

Woody stepped closer and looked at the document. "What's that?"

"The transcript from Ramsey's first trial. We're taking a closer look at Kristen Dillard's testimony. Kate is helping me prepare to cross-examine her."

For the first time since he'd entered their little work area, Moscow looked up from the document. Her eyes—a light, icy shade of blue—seemed to pierce through his skull and catalog the folds of his brain. He wondered if her background in psychology gave her the power to perceive his secrets, or just the ability to cast an illusion of having that power. Whatever, he didn't like the bitch.

He focused his attention on Goldhammer. "What about Leary, the detective?"

"He won't be a problem." Beyond the cubicle walls, keyboards continued to click. "Did you come for a reason, or were you just in the neighborhood?"

"I don't need a reason."

"Great. Well, I guess I'll see you later." Goldhammer picked up the trial transcript, pointed at a line near the top of the page. The Ice Princess leaned closer to scrutinize it.

Dismissed, Woody shook his head and turned to leave. Then he stopped himself. "Dr. Moscow?"

The Ice Princess looked up and he met her cold stare one more time. She didn't blink, but the corner of her lips tugged up in a half-smile. "Yes?"

"Jessica Black drove to Manhattan, talked to some of your colleagues and students about you. I thought you might want to know."

Her ambivalent expression did not change. "She's not the first prosecutor to check up on me."

"If there's anything you don't want her to find, you better let me know now."

"I have no dark secrets, if that's what you're implying."

Goldhammer waved a hand without looking up. "Kate's a pro. You don't need to worry about her."

"I don't need any help," Moscow said. "I've done some investigating of my own. Believe me, I'm not intimidated by Jessica Black."

Woody was surprised to find himself insulted by her tone. There was no reason that her dismissal of his enemy should offend him, but it did. "She's won a lot of murder trials. And not all of them had eyewitnesses."

Unimpressed, Moscow continued to stare at him, her half-smile maddening in its superiority. "To your untrained eye, Miss Black may seem like a threat. But I see her for what she is—conflicted and emotionally compromised, a troubled woman in need of therapy."

Goldhammer looked from Moscow to Woody, giddy with her analysis. "You see? Everything's going great."

"All I see is a couple of arrogant assholes."

The lawyer recoiled from his words, but the psychologist only stared at him. "Maybe Jessica Black's not the only one who needs therapy," she said.

"Where I come from, you don't brag until *after* you've won," Woody said.

"And where is that?"

Goldhammer ruffled the pages in front of him and cleared his throat. "Woody is kind of enigmatic about his origins. He's a true man of mystery." He looked at Woody, and this time his gaze took on a hard edge. "We really have a lot of work to do. I would be happy to discuss the case with you later, at your convenience."

"You're so accommodating." Woody smiled at Goldhammer, then tipped his head to the Ice Princess. "See you around, Doc."

33.

Prepping Kristen for trial would have been difficult enough if the girl hadn't caught her with Jack. Now it was almost impossible. Sitting together in the dark conference room, it was a challenge to get Kristen to look at her, much less take her advice.

Jessie usually liked to video record her witnesses during prep, to give them the chance to see how their testimony looked from the outside. The process helped to eliminate mumbling, fidgeting, and other nervous tics that might negatively impact the jury's impressions. She followed the same procedure today, but with more reluctance. On the screen, Kristen recited the details of her attack with a blank expression. The decades-old TV-VCR combo in the Homicide Unit's conference room was never kind. Faces on the screen always seemed enlarged, distorted, and overly pixilated. At least the TV's speakers were decent—cadence and tone were critical—but now all they did was emphasize the monotone voice with which Kristen had uttered every sentence. She looked as if she wasn't even listening to her own words.

"You sound too unemotional," Jessie said.

Kristen did not turn to look at her. She continued to

watch herself. The light from the TV screen glowed on her pale face. "Maybe I should kiss the defense attorney. Would that be emotional?"

Jessie gritted her teeth. "This is serious. You can't hold back when you testify for the jury. You need to put yourself back in the moment—as hard as that will be—and drag the jury there with you."

"Like you care."

"It's not enough for them to hear about it," Jessie continued. "They need to experience it through you."

"I get it," the girl snapped.

"Good."

Still refusing to turn, Kristen spoke toward her own image on the screen. "I'll tell them what happened. That's all I can do."

Jessie stopped the video. She decided to do something she had never done before. She ejected the tape and inserted a different, older one. She pressed *play*.

"What's this?"

"This is a tape we made when we were preparing for your testimony in Ramsey's first trial."

For a few seconds, snow buzzed on the screen. Then the noise ceased and a conference room appeared. A blurry head in the foreground focused to reveal a younger-looking Kristen. Her hair was in disarray, tangled and knotted. She wore no makeup. Tears slicked her face below bloodshot eyes. Her mouth hung slightly open, saliva pooled at the corners. The scar on her neck looked more red and puffy than it did today.

"I don't want to watch this."

Jessie did not stop the tape. On the screen, the younger

Kristen shifted in her seat. A voice—Jessie recognized it as her own—spoke comforting words in a soothing tone, but the girl did not relax. Staring past the lens at the woman talking to her, she opened her mouth but could not speak.

"Please." Illuminated by the TV, Kristen's stony expression shifted in concert with the one on the screen. Her mouth trembled, and tears welled in her eyes. "I don't want to watch this, Jessie."

Jessie's protective instinct overwhelmed her, and she paused the tape. The image froze. Kristen's face flickered on the TV screen.

"If you bury your emotions, we'll lose."

Finally, Kristen turned to face her. "I'm not burying anything. You want me to pretend to cry?"

"If you relive the experience in your mind, you won't have to pretend."

Kristen flinched as if Jessie had slapped her.

"Kristen, the jury is going to scrutinize you." She stopped short of warning Kristen about Kate Moscow's testimony. That testimony would come after Kristen's, and if Kristen did not know about it, it would not hurt her. It might hurt the case, but it would not hurt her. "Even though it might not be fair, the jury is going to equate misery with sincerity. When it comes to victims, they always do."

Kristen glanced at the screen. "Believe me, I'm just as miserable now as I ever was. It doesn't fade."

Jessie shut off the TV and turned up the lights. She loaded the tape back into the video camera, framed Kristen in the viewfinder. "Are you ready to try this again?"

"Do I have a choice?"

BURNOUT

Before Jessie could begin recording, someone knocked on the conference room door. The door opened and Warren stepped inside. "Excuse me," he said. "I need to borrow Ms. Black." He offered Kristen an apologetic smile, and gestured for Jessie to join him in the hallway.

Jessie stepped out of the room and closed the conference room door, but did not let go of the doorknob. "What's up? I'm in the middle of preparing a witness."

Warren's face pinched with barely-controlled anger. "Let's go to my office."

"What's going on?"

"We need to talk."

"Now? About what?"

She followed him down the hallway to his tiny office. This time, he closed the door but did not sit down. Standing with him in the small space made her feel claustrophobic. "Are you having some kind of relationship with Jack Ackerman?"

"What?" In surprise, she stepped away from him. Her back struck the door, rattling it in its frame. The knob dug into her hip.

"Elliot overheard an argument you had with Kristen Dillard."

"He eavesdropped on me?"

"Are you romantically involved with Jack Ackerman? Yes or no?"

"That was a personal conversation. He had no business—"

"Jessie." Warren's face darkened. "You are. Jesus. I can't believe this. What a fucking mess."

"I'm sorry. It just kind of happened. I tried to keep it secret."

He looked angry enough to take a swing at her, but instead he pounded his desk. Papers scattered. "Are you nuts now, too? Is Ackerman's craziness contagious? Do you know how improper this is? Dating a lawyer for the other side?"

"He's no longer involved in the case."

"It's a massive conflict of interest. Lawyers have been disbarred over less."

"You're blowing it out of proportion. I've been seeing Jack socially. That's all. He hasn't been helping me with the case. We've barely talked about the case at all. He hasn't violated any obligations to Ramsey."

"No? Is that what you'll tell me next year, when Ramsey gets a *third* trial?"

The idea struck her speechless.

"Thank God Elliot's second-chair," Warren said.

"What?"

"He's up-to-speed on most of the research, knows the facts, and he's been present during the trial. The jury's familiar with his face." Jessie knew better than to interrupt. She had seen Warren rant like this before. "He can take over. True, he doesn't have enough experience to handle a murder trial on his own, but we can guide him from the sidelines."

"The sidelines? What are you saying? Warren, this is my case."

Warren shook his head. "Not anymore."

34.

Surrounded by reporters and other spectators, Jessie waited for Goldhammer to realize she was no longer seated at the prosecution table. Sure enough, when no one joined Elliot after ten minutes, the defense attorney twisted around in his chair and scanned the courtroom. He located her in the third row of pew-like benches in the gallery. His face bunched with confusion. Then the bastard smiled.

Sheriff's deputies brought Ramsey into the courtroom and escorted him to his chair next to Goldhammer. A moment later, Judge Spatt entered from his chambers and took his place at the bench. The jury filed in last.

"Someone want to tell me something?" the judge said.

Elliot rose. "Your Honor, I will be handling the remainder of the trial for the prosecution."

"News to me."

"Well, uh, we tried to contact you, but your clerk said you were unavailable—"

"I was."

Elliot shifted his weight from one leg to the other, waiting for the judge to continue. Spatt made no further comment—he became engrossed in some documents, flipped pages, marked them with a pen—and after a moment Elliot sat down.

"Okay," Spatt said. "Call your next witness, Mr. Williams."

Elliot called Kristen Dillard to the stand.

Kristen's eyes found Jessie's as the girl was guided to the witness stand and sworn in. The previous day, when Jessie had told her that Elliot would be taking over the case, any anger Kristen had harbored toward Jessie had disappeared. She had demanded that Jessie be the person who interview her on the stand. It had taken over an hour for Jessie and Warren to calm the girl down and assure her that she would be in good hands with Elliot.

Please, God, let that be true.

As Kristen began her testimony, Jessie was relieved to see that her preparation with Kristen—despite being cut short—had paid off. When she told her story to the jury, the girl's voice was confident but not robotic. She described the pleasant evening of TV watching that had preceded the nightmare, recalled the doorbell chime that had drawn her father to the front door. Instead of looking through the peephole, she said, her absent-minded scientist father must have simply opened the door.

"I guess his attention was still focused on the TV show. He was probably listening to it from the entryway so he wouldn't miss any of the story."

Kristen and her mother, seated on the couch, had heard a loud *bang* and *thump*—the door being thrust open and slamming against her father's chest—and had run to the entryway. There, a tall, broad-shouldered man in a black ski mask stood in their house.

Jessie watched the jurors react to that image. One woman's mouth dropped open. The face of the man next to her paled. Even the three jurors Jessie had identified as potential holdouts—Trent Slaney, the skeptical construction worker, Malcolm Clonts, the anti-middle class janitor, and Jenna Gottlieb, the love-struck nursing student—leaned forward in their chairs, their faces transformed by empathy for the victims.

Good job, Kristen. Keep going.

Kristen's voice thickened as she described the serrated knife in the intruder's hand. He had already stabbed her father once, and her brain seemed to go numb as she watched her father's blood well from a wound in his chest that he tried to cover with his hand. The man in the mask twisted the deadbolt behind him and ordered the family upstairs.

"I know this is hard for you, Kristen, but can you tell us what happened upstairs?" Elliot's voice was gentle. His sympathetic tone seemed genuine.

Kristen described her fear as Ramsey herded her and her parents into the master bedroom. Her voice broke. Tears ran down her cheeks. She recounted the murder of her father, then the rape and murder of her mother.

"What happened next?"

"He threw me on the bed. He yanked my pants down and turned me on my stomach. He—" She brought her hands to her face and cried.

Judge Spatt's jaw clenched as he watched her from the bench. "Maybe we should take a break."

"No, I'm okay." She sniffed, wiped her eyes. "He raped me. Then he ... he—" Sobs hitched from her body in painful jerks. "He stabbed me. Over and over."

Elliot waited for her to regain some of her composure. Jessie's eyes moved to Goldhammer, who sat silently, his body as still as a statue.

"Kristen, what happened next?"

Assuming that all of his victims had died of their multiple stab wounds, the intruder had walked away from the bed, stretched, and pulled off his ski mask. Then he had left the room. A minute later, Kristen had heard the back door open and close downstairs.

"When the man removed his ski mask, did you see his face?"

Kristen nodded. "I saw him."

"Is the man who raped you and murdered your family here in this courtroom today?"

"Yes." She pointed at the defense table. Although her vantage point in the gallery prevented Jessie from seeing Ramsey's face, experience told her that the man stared forward, his expression blank. "That's him. Frank Ramsey."

"And you identified him to the police?"

"I identified him in a lineup at the police station."

"Were you confident then that Frank Ramsey was the man who had attacked your family?"

"Yes."

"Are you equally confident now?"

"Yes."

Kristen's trepidation was apparent in her eyes as she watched Goldhammer approach her. Jessie was glad to see that a few of the jurors looked nervous, too—their empathy with the girl was powerful enough to make them fear Goldhammer's cross-examination as if it were a personal attack. Others on the jury crossed their arms and leaned forward with serious expressions, determined to hear both sides of the case before reaching conclusions.

At the prosecution table, Jessie could see Elliot's back and shoulders tense up. She could imagine the cheat sheet on the table in front of him—a list of objections. They were the only weapons available to him, his only means of defending his witness from Goldhammer's attack. As pissed off at him as she was right now for telling Warren about Jack Ackerman at such a critical moment of the trial, she prayed he would do his job well.

"Ms. Dillard, you've been through a horrific ordeal," Goldhammer said. "You have my utmost sympathy."

Kristen did not shy away from him. She returned his gaze, her eyes clear. "I don't want your sympathy, or anything else from you."

"I understand. I have a few questions. I'll try to keep them brief."

Kristen's eyes tracked him as he stepped closer to the jury box. It was instantly clear to Jessie that he intended his questions, rather than her answers, to make an impact on the jurors.

"You testified that the man who attacked you did not remove his mask until after the attack, just before leaving the bedroom. Is that correct?"

"Yes."

"So it would be accurate to say that you only saw the man's face for one second, five seconds at most, right?"

"I don't know how many seconds it was, but I saw his face clearly."

"But you agree that you only saw his face for a matter of seconds, isn't that true?"

"Objection." Elliot stood up. When Spatt glared at him, he said, "Uh, asked and answered, Your Honor."

"Overruled. Ms. Dillard, please answer the question."

"I didn't have a stopwatch on me."

One of the jurors, a young woman named Joyce Brodie, smiled at the girl's retort.

"I understand," Goldhammer said. "Would you agree that less than ten seconds is a fair estimate?"

"I guess so."

Jessie bit her lip. She knew Goldhammer's reason for belaboring this point—"exposure duration" was one of the factors that Kate Moscow would later testify affected the identification.

"And Ramsey was facing away from you, wasn't he? He was moving toward the door?"

"Yes."

"So you saw the back of his head?"

"And the side of his face."

"You saw both the back of his head and the side of his face?" Goldhammer's voice rose on the word "and" as if the conjunction of the two visuals was preposterous.

"Yes." Kristen's voice did not waver.

"Interesting perspective." He turned to the jury with a doubtful expression, then faced Kristen again. "I only have a few other questions."

Kristen's eyes remained cautious. Jessie had warned her that Goldhammer would continually suggest that he was nearing the end of his cross-examination in an attempt to coax her into letting down her guard. It was an old lawyer trick. Kristen didn't fall for it.

"You testified that the murder weapon was a knife. Would you describe the knife for the jury?"

Kristen shrugged. "It was long and sharp."

"Can you be more specific? Can you recall details?"

Jessie chewed her lip. Again, she knew what Goldhammer was up to. Another of Kate Moscow's factors was known as "weapons focus." The more details Kristen provided, the easier it would be for Goldhammer to later argue that Kristen's attention had been fixed on the weapon instead of on Ramsey's face.

"I'm not a knife expert. It hurt when he stabbed me with it. What more do you need to know?"

"I'd like to know the knife's approximate length, what its handle looked like, the shape of its serrations, how much blood was on it—"

"Objection." This time Elliot rose with more confidence. "Mr. Goldhammer is assuming facts not in evidence."

"I agree," Spatt said. "The witness testified that the knife was long and sharp. Let's move on."

Although Goldhammer might use this exchange to argue that Kristen's inability to describe the knife in precise details indicated holes in her memory, he would not be able to use it in conjunction with Kate Moscow's expert testimony. For that reason, Jessie counted it a victory—small, but possibly crucial—for the prosecution. Elliot was doing well.

"We're almost done," Goldhammer assured her. "But first I need to ask you about the first time you identified Mr. Ramsey to the police. You testified that you picked Mr. Ramsey out of a lineup, is that correct?"

"Yes."

"Isn't it true that the day before the lineup, a homicide detective named Mark Leary showed you a photo array?"

"Yes, he did."

"There were six photographs in that array, correct?"

"Yes."

"And you were not able to identify your attacker as any of the men in those photographs, correct?"

Kristen squirmed in her chair. "Correct."

Goldhammer lifted a glossy sheet from the defense table and offered it into evidence. "Do you recognize this sheet of paper?"

"Yes."

"Would you tell Judge Spatt and the jury what it is?"

"It's the photo array that Detective Leary showed me while I was in the hospital after Frank Ramsey attacked me."

Goldhammer pointed to one of the photos. "Who is this?"

Kristen's jaw flexed. "Frank Ramsey."

"But when Detective Leary showed you this photo array, you did not identify that photo as the man who attacked your family, did you?"

"No." Kristen's voice was tight.

"You did not identify Mr. Ramsey until later, when you saw him in a lineup at the police station, right?"

She nodded. "Yes."

"*After* you had already seen this photo array."

She nodded again. "Yes."

Jessie tasted blood and realized she had bitten through the skin of her lower lip. Although Goldhammer did not offer any commentary to the jury—yet—he had just scored a point for the defense. Kate Moscow's data formed compelling evidence that a lineup identification can be easily compromised when the witness has been exposed to the suspect's face in a prior photo array. The witness's memory is, in effect, tricked. The witness, believing her identification is based on her memory of the crime itself, actually bases her identification on her exposure to the suspect's face in the photo array.

"Thank you," Goldhammer said. "Let me again say that I appreciate how difficult it must be for you to testify before us today. You are a very brave young woman. I admire you."

Spatt said, "Let's take a short recess. It's been an intense few hours. I think we could all use a breath of fresh air."

35.

Jessie hurried to the elevator, then outside into a blast of wind. She had pursued Elliot out of the courthouse, and now—her hair whipping around her head—it took her a moment to spot him. Across the street, he hugged and kissed a woman whose own hair—long and blonde—was also flying in the wind. Under her coat, a tight red sweater stretched across impressively large breasts, and when Elliot detached his lips from hers, Jessie saw that she was young and pretty. Was this the woman he had mentioned the day he'd talked her into showing him the draft of her opening statement?

The unexpected sight of Elliot publicly enjoying a romantic embrace was disorienting. She had planned to chase him down and use the brief recess to share an idea she'd formed during Goldhammer's cross-examination of Kristen. But now, standing in the wind, her mind fixated on that moment last week when she had printed the half-finished opening statement for him.

She regretted that kindness now. She had allowed Elliot to get his foot in the door, and now he'd pried the door wide open, forced his way inside, and shoved her out. Jessie disliked watching other lawyers try cases. It always made her feel frustrated, useless, to watch from the sidelines, unable to participate. But watching Elliot try Frank Ramsey's case was a whole new kind of torture.

And now he was out here kissing some woman instead of praising Kristen for her testimony and preparing her for redirect?

Get yourself under control.

Elliot's eyes wandered and he saw her. Hurriedly, he kissed the blonde on the lips, squeezed her hand, and darted across the street to stand with Jessie near the door of the CJC.

"I don't know if I should call you Judas or Casanova," she said.

"Listen, I'm sorry. I didn't want to, but I had to tell Warren about you and Ackerman. Ethically, dating a lawyer that—"

"I didn't chase you out here for an apology, especially an insincere one."

He shrugged. "Payback's a bitch, right? But you have to admit I did good in there."

Payback? So that was why he went to Warren? As revenge for her taking over the PCRA hearing? "Where's Kristen?" she said, feeling her patience slipping.

"Kristen?" He shrugged. "I think she's with a psychiatrist from the institution, the guy who brought her here this morning."

"Did you tell her she did a good job?"

His grin collapsed and he looked away, squinting against the wind. "This isn't kindergarten. You want me to give her a sticker, a gold star or a Care Bear?"

"Rookie to know-it-all in one day. That must be a new record."

"I'm not a know-it-all." He frowned. "Why don't you relax? We both want the same thing."

"No, I want Ramsey to pay for his crimes. You want to further your career and impress a girl. And apparently you're not above backstabbing your own colleagues to do it."

"I thought you didn't want an apology. So what do you want?"

She watched her breaths plume in the air for a moment, then said, "You're planning to close the prosecution's case after Kristen's redirect, right?"

He nodded.

"I have a better idea. The Dillard home is still vacant. No one's lining up to live in a murder house. Ask Judge Spatt to organize a jury visit to the crime scene."

"Are you kidding? On what grounds? A trip like that would be way too prejudicial. Spatt would never go for it."

He really had become a know-it-all. "Wrong. During his opening statement and his cross-examination of Kristen, Goldhammer made an issue of the fact that Ramsey's back was turned for most of the time that his mask was removed. If he's going to argue that the position of Ramsey's head affected Kristen's ability to identify him, then the jury is entitled to see the layout of the crime scene."

Elliot stood in silence, absorbing her argument. "And then the jury will see the house." He nodded his head as the idea began to appeal to him. "A typical suburban house any one of them might live in."

"Exactly."

Before the jurors were brought back to the courtroom,

Elliot requested a few moments to make a request outside their hearing. Spatt's eyes narrowed as Elliot explained the prosecution's intention of taking the jury to visit the crime scene.

Goldhammer jumped from his chair. "You can't be serious. Your Honor, the only reason that Mr. Williams wants to expose the jury to the crime scene is to prejudice them against my client. This is outrageous. I would expect more from the District Attorney's office of Philadelphia."

Spatt rolled his eyes. "My advice is to lower your expectations."

"Under the rules of evidence," Goldhammer went on, "if the relevance of evidence is outweighed by its tendency to unfairly prejudice the jury, the evidence must be precluded."

"You might want to start arguing now," Spatt prompted Elliot.

"Your Honor, uh, Mr. Goldhammer has raised the issue of whether Kristen Dillard and Mr. Ramsey were positioned in a way that made her identification possible." He glanced back into the gallery, where Jessie willed him to continue. Watching him struggle, her frustration mounted. "Mr. Goldhammer suggested to the jury that Kristen Dillard could not have seen both the back and the side of the defendant's head, as she testified she did. So it's only, um, fair that the jury have the chance to evaluate for themselves the likelihood of such a line of sight."

Goldhammer shook his head. "They can study a diagram of the crime scene. They can look at a blueprint. Photos."

The judge ran a weary hand down his face, from his white eyebrows to his creased chin. "It's been almost two years since the murders. I assume the place is cleaned up?"

"Yes, Your Honor," Elliot said. "The house has been on the market. But the layout of the master bedroom is the same. The carpet was cleaned and the bloody mattress, sheets, and bedspread were replaced, but the bed is the same and the rest of the furniture is the same."

Goldhammer continued to shake his head. "Cleanliness is not the issue. The jury doesn't need to see the place strewn with blood and guts to imagine it."

"You want me to instruct the jury not to imagine?" Spatt said. "Young Mr. Williams is correct that you made a stink about the back of the head and the side of the face. You made some people—including me—curious about where Mr. Ramsey was standing and where Ms. Dillard was seeing him from."

When Goldhammer, sullen and glowering, made no further argument, Jessie knew that they had won.

"I am inclined to schedule a visit to the crime scene," Spatt said. "You will show the jury the bedroom, let them see the layout. Then, back in the courtroom, you can redirect Ms. Dillard about the specific locations of the people involved."

"Thank you, Your Honor."

"No need to thank me. I love field trips."

36.

The Dillard house was located in Andorra, a section of the Philadelphia neighborhood of Roxborough in the northwest part of the city. Although only eight miles from Center City, Andorra was suburban, a bedroom community nestled near the border of Montgomery County. Riding through it in the back seat of a limousine, Elliot felt a strange pang of envy. The houses, with their driveway basketball hoops and personalized mailboxes, suddenly seemed infinitely more appealing than the posh interior of the limo. He caught himself entertaining absurd domestic fantasies as he watched the houses through tinted glass—he and Amber owning one of these homes, their son and daughter building a snow man together in the front yard. A minivan in the garage.

"I grew up in a town like this," Goldhammer said. Nostalgia had diminished the defense lawyer's characteristic swagger. For a moment, sitting beside Elliot on the long leather seat, he seemed like a normal guy. That moment ended when he puffed out his chest and said, "I've come a long way since then."

The judge said, "I grew up in a town like this, too." When Goldhammer looked surprised, Spatt's eyes narrowed. "You expected me to come from the ghetto?"

"No, I— I'm from Illinois," he said. "How about you?"

Spatt fiddled with the knot of his tie. He wore a nondescript suit, and Elliot could see scuffs on his shoes. Without his black robe, the judge looked more human, but no less mean. He scrutinized Goldhammer for a few seconds before answering. "Washington State."

"I grew up in South Jersey," Elliot said.

The conversation died. Through the limo's tinted windows, Elliot could see the bus leading this parade. Inside it, the jury rode like a group of schoolchildren. Meanwhile, in an unmarked police car behind the limo, Frank Ramsey sat handcuffed and flanked by sheriff's deputies.

For Elliot, this experience was surreal, like something out of a dream. Spatt and Goldhammer, on the other hand, seemed bored, as if they did this sort of thing all the time.

"One of my ex-wives was from New Jersey," Goldhammer said. His attempt to resurrect the conversation hung in the air. No one responded.

A few minutes later, the bus in front of them pulled to the curb. Situated on a short lane, the Dillard house was practically indistinguishable from its neighbors except for the *For Sale* sign jutting from the crust of snow covering the front yard. The limo passed the bus and turned into the narrow driveway. The car holding Ramsey followed and parked behind it.

"Looks like we're here," Elliot said. He patted his hair and checked his reflection in the window.

A line of jurors disembarked from the bus, chatting with each other, looking excited. "Where do they think they are," Spatt said, "Disney World?"

BURNOUT

"I guess it's a nice change of pace from the courtroom." Goldhammer shrugged.

Spatt continued to stare. "Idiots."

The real estate agent had assured Elliot that they would have the house to themselves. He was sure she would honor this promise—if for no other reason than that a reminder that the house was a murder scene is not usually good marketing for residential real estate—but just in case, he entered the house first and made sure it was empty. The last thing he wanted was an unexpected surprise—like a gaggle of anti-death penalty protesters, for example—that Goldhammer could manipulate to get his client another retrial.

He checked the house, then returned to the front door. Judge Spatt, Goldhammer, Ramsey, three sheriff's deputies, twelve jurors, and two alternate jurors waited on the front lawn. Standing in a half-inch of snow, they resembled a strange troupe of Christmas carolers. Elliot held the door open as they filed into the house.

One of the jurors, a forty-three-year-old mother of four named Katherine Baldini, shivered as she passed across the threshold. Her trepidation spread to the rest of the jurors. They stopped talking, cast wary glances at the shadows, stuck close to one another. Before he could suppress it, a shiver ran up Elliot's spine as well. Even in broad daylight, the Dillard house felt haunted.

Ramsey wore no handcuffs or other restraints—that might prejudice the jurors' opinions of him—but the two sheriff's deputies flanking him kept their hands near their holsters. Besides, Ramsey seemed docile enough. He held his large, calloused hands together at his waist and stood apart from the jurors, under the arch where the entryway met the dining room. He studied the rooms as if he had never seen them before. If it was an act intended to persuade the jury of his innocence, Elliot doubted it was working. Most of them didn't dare look his way.

Jenna Gottlieb, the twenty-year-old nursing student whom Jessie had identified as a potential problem juror, said, "This place is giving me the willies."

Spatt faced his uncomfortable charges with a smile pasted on his face. "Folks, I promise we won't keep you here any longer than necessary. Remember, the crimes that allegedly occurred here happened almost two years ago. We are accompanied by three of the sheriff's finest deputies. We're perfectly safe."

The judge's assurances did not appear to console the jurors, most of whom were visibly shying away from Ramsey. *Good.* Elliot searched for the spot on the stairway carpet where Officer Motes, one of the cops who had come to the house the night of the murder in response to a noise complaint by one of the Dillards' neighbors, had spotted a dark red stain through the window. He could find no trace of it. Too bad. Had the house not been so thoroughly cleaned before being placed on the market, Elliot would have had some potent evidence to show the already spooked jury.

"Mr. Williams, why don't you lead us to the primary crime scene?" Spatt said.

The primary crime scene—the location where the murders and rapes had occurred—was the master bedroom on the second floor. Elliot mounted the stairs. The others followed.

From the crime scene photographs he had studied, Elliot

knew that the Dillards had decorated the upstairs hallway with framed photographs—family portraits, photos of Kristen, even a picture of the white mouse Dr. Dillard had brought home from one of his labs as a pet for Kristen when she was nine or ten. The real estate agent had removed these memorials to a destroyed family and replaced them with innocuous art prints.

The jurors' attention focused on the open door at the end of the hallway. Sunlight spilled into the hall from the large windows in the bedroom but failed to brighten the mood. The jurors approached the room with dread, as if stepping so close to another person's tragedy invited their own.

Inside, the room looked almost the same as it must have looked on the night of the murders—an absence of gore was the primary difference Elliot could see between the room as it was now and the room as it had been captured by the crime scene photographer. The reading lamp, alarm clock, and phone—from which Ramsey had ripped the electrical cords with which he had bound the wrists of his victims—had also been replaced. And, of course, there were none of the personal possessions that gave a space life. But overall, the layout of the room and its furniture was unchanged.

Trent Slaney, the construction worker, another of Jessie's potential problem jurors, surveyed the room. His lips were pressed so tightly together that the lower half of his face was turning a pale shade of white.

"This is the room that the prosecution's witnesses have testified about," Judge Spatt said. "Bearing in mind the testimony you have heard, take a look around. Remember, it will be your job to decide whether Kristen Dillard's testimony—including her identification of the defendant—is credible."

A few of the jurors glanced in Ramsey's direction, giving Elliot an idea. "Could we speak privately for a second?" The jury remained in the bedroom as Elliot led Spatt, Goldhammer, Ramsey, and Ramsey's guards into the hallway. He closed the door, removing them from the jury's hearing.

"I think it would be helpful if Mr. Ramsey stood where Kristen Dillard testified she saw his face on the night of the attack. That way, the jury could judge the angle of her viewpoint."

"Why don't you just ask him to rape a few of the jurors, too?" Goldhammer said.

"Relax," Spatt said. He turned to Elliot. "Mr. Goldhammer is right. You can't ask the defendant to place himself in a position that will suggest his guilt to the jury, any more than you can force him to testify. If you want to demonstrate Mr. Ramsey's alleged position in the bedroom, you'll have to do it with your own body."

Elliot nodded. That could work. "I can do that."

"Good. Now let's go back inside. I don't like leaving them alone in there. One of them's liable to see a ghost, and then they'll all start panicking, jumping out the windows. We'll be digging their bodies out of the snow."

Elliot struggled for an intelligent response. He settled for, "We wouldn't want that."

"Certainly not," Goldhammer agreed.

Elliot stood near the bedroom door, his back to the king-sized bed. After several minutes of arguing, he and Goldhammer had agreed that this position approximated that described by Kristen Dillard in her testimony.

BURNOUT

One by one, the jurors took turns lying on the bed in the position where Kristen had testified Ramsey had left her for dead.

Judge Spatt had instructed them not to share their conclusions with one another. It would be improper if they influenced each other's factual findings. Each was supposed to judge for him or herself whether, from the vantage point of the bed, Elliot's face was visible.

It was only when he was enduring the silent, appraising stares of the jurors that he realized the foolishness of agreeing to Spatt's offer—he had no idea if he was helping his own case or that of the defense.

37.

"How did it go?" Jessie said, when Elliot and the jurors returned from their trip.

Elliot seemed to hesitate. "I'm not sure."

"What's that supposed to mean?" They stood in the back of the courtroom. Spectators were taking seats in the gallery. Goldhammer was waiting at the defense table for his client to be brought in. The jury box was vacant, as was the judge's bench. "Did the house make an impression?"

"Definitely."

"So what are you unsure about?"

Again, he hesitated. "In the house, I had an idea. I set up a demonstration so the jurors could see for themselves if Ramsey's face would have been visible to Kristen."

Jessie looked away from him, annoyed. He'd broken the cardinal rule of litigation. Never ask a question unless you already know the answer. "And?"

"I don't know. Spatt instructed them not to share their conclusions."

"Great. So for all you know, the trip to the murder house helped the murderer."

Elliot's face reddened. "I guess that's possible."

"This is exactly why only experienced prosecutors are assigned to homicide trials," she said. The benches in the gallery were filling up. Unless she wanted to stand, she needed to claim a seat now. "But don't let it distract you. Keep going. You have a strong case." She didn't know if she meant it, or if she was blowing smoke, but she knew that she needed Elliot to be confident if they were to have a chance of winning.

Elliot nodded, but he didn't look any less worried.

Called back to the stand for redirect, Kristen sat with her back straight and her hands folded in front of her, breathing evenly as Elliot approached. Apparently, the distress caused by reliving her experience for the jury earlier that day had faded.

Elliot, shooting anxious glances at the jurors and the defense table, appeared more nervous than she did.

"You've already told the jury about the defendant's attack on your family," he said, warming up. She nodded. "I have a few follow-up questions. First, would you describe in detail the view you had of Mr. Ramsey when he removed his ski mask?"

"I saw him from behind and to the side," she answered firmly, without hesitation. "I saw his hair, his right ear, both of his eyes. I got a very good look at him."

"How confident are you that Mr. Ramsey was the man who attacked you?"

"One-hundred percent."

"You don't have even the slightest sliver of doubt?"

"None," she said, with a brisk shake of her head. "It was

him."

Kristen was the Commonwealth's final witness. After she left the stand, Elliot announced to the courtroom, "The prosecution rests."

As expected, Goldhammer then moved for judgment. He argued that the prosecution had failed to prove its case and that, as a matter of law, no jury could convict the defendant based on the evidence presented. This motion was routine; every defense attorney made it in every case. Judge Spatt denied the motion without pausing to consider it.

"It's lunch time," the judge said. "Let's take a recess. When we reconvene, the defense will call its first witness."

As soon as Spatt finished his announcement, Jessie squeezed out of her pew and hurried down the hallway, avoiding the press. She planned to grab a quick lunch and then spend the remainder of the recess working on her notes for Kate Moscow's cross-examination. She knew Elliot would balk at the idea of using her work, but she also knew he wanted to win. Effectively crossing Moscow was crucial.

Outside the courthouse, Jessie almost collided with a woman walking toward her. She apologized before her mind identified the statuesque blonde as the person whom she'd just been thinking about.

"Dr. Moscow."

"Ms. Black." The woman's smile was cold, superior—the smile of an expert witness who had bested innumerable prosecutors and made bushels of money doing it. "I'm told you're no longer trying the Ramsey case."

"My colleague, Elliot Williams, has taken over for me."

BURNOUT

"That's too bad."

Jessie shrugged, tried to appear nonchalant. "Elliot is more than capable."

"Still, it must be frustrating for you to turn over control of the case to someone else. I know how close you are to the victim." Jessie felt a pang of uneasiness. Had she run into Moscow by accident, or had the woman deliberately started this confrontation? "Will Kristen be present when I testify, do you think? It would be enlightening for her, a nice educational experience. So few people really understand the limitations of their memories."

The psychologist seemed to be baiting her, but Jessie could not imagine a reason. What could be gained by antagonizing a lawyer who was no longer trying the case? Whatever Moscow's motives, Jessie did not intend to be riled. Keeping her own voice as dispassionate as Moscow's, she said, "Kristen won't be in attendance."

"But you'll be there, won't you?"

"Taking notes." Jessie squared her shoulders.

"Like the notes you took about me, when you visited my campus and questioned my students and colleagues?"

Ah, so that was it.

"Yes," Jessie said. "Like those notes."

"I suppose that's all you *can* do. Now that you've been caught with your pants down." Jessie felt her cheeks redden. Moscow smiled pleasantly, as if they were still making small talk. "Or panties, as the case may be."

The psychologist's eyes flicked over Jessie's body in a contemptuous perusal. *How the hell did she know about Jack?* There was no way Warren would have told anyone—he was too concerned about the DA's liability to engage in courthouse gossip—and even Jack wasn't reckless enough to make their relationship public. That left Elliot.

"Do you honestly believe that Frank Ramsey is innocent?" Jessie said. She didn't really care about the answer. She just wanted to change the subject, snap that look of disdain from Moscow's face.

But Moscow wasn't finished. "Men are expected to think with their genitals, but we women have to hold ourselves to a higher standard. I was looking forward to facing you from the stand. You let me down."

"You didn't answer my question, Doctor."

"You can call me Kate. We have a lot in common, you know. We're both headstrong. We're both misunderstood—and underestimated—by our peers. Neither of us plays well with others. Under different circumstances, I suppose we might have been friends."

Jessie remembered when Jack had said something similar to her: We're both very committed people. You're committed to your work, and I was committed to a mental hospital.

Gritting her teeth, Jessie repeated herself. "You didn't answer my question."

"Ramsey? Well, ninety-nine percent of criminal defendants are guilty, so he probably is, too. But that's not my concern. I'm not a juror."

"It doesn't bother you that victims like Kristen Dillard have already been violated once? That your testimony is another violation they have to endure?"

"Listen to you. Jessica Black, the champion of the wounded. Defender of the meek." Moscow laughed. "I'd say you need a good fuck, but we both know that's not your problem. Maybe you just need to get over yourself."

Without further comment, Moscow stepped past her, leaving her alone on the street. Jessie listened to her heels click on the sidewalk until the sound faded behind her.

Woody finished his meatball sub, pulled a small napkin from the paper bag, and wiped marinara sauce from his chin. Across the street, the Ice Princess left Jessie Black standing on the sidewalk. From here, she looked like she'd just been gut-punched.

What the hell did Moscow say? When the Ice Princess had boasted that rattling Jessie Black would be no problem, Woody had scoffed at her. He was usually a good judge of character, and in his view, the prosecutor had her shit together.

Apparently, he had been mistaken.

Leave it to a shrink to know exactly how to fuck with someone's head.

He couldn't wait to tell his brother about their progress. With the District Attorney's star prosecutor relegated to the sidelines and distracted by Moscow, her replacement hopelessly outclassed by Goldhammer, and Detective Leary chasing phantom leads to a contract killing that never happened, the trial would be over before the dust settled.

Then it would be time for Frank Ramsey to pay the piper.

38.

"You leaving us to go to accounting school, Leary?"

Two shadows fell across the financial records on his desk. Leary looked up. It took his eyes a moment to adjust after staring at pages of 10-point print. Detectives Nick Jameson and Robin Scerbak grinned at him.

"You're standing in my light," Leary said.

Jameson reached over the desk, flipped on Leary's lamp. "Wouldn't want you to strain your peepers." Other cops in the crowded room chuckled. "Say, when you're done solving the Family Man case again, could you double-solve some of my old cases?"

Leary leaned his chair back as far as his limited workspace allowed. "Don't get ahead of yourself, Jameson. I can't double-solve your cases because most of them were never solved the first time."

"Funny." Jameson brought his hands together. The joints popped like gunshots. Cracking his knuckles was only one of his many annoying habits. Next to him, Scerbak stopped grinning and took an interest in the financial statements.

Scerbak's gut mashed against the edge of Leary's desk as

he leaned forward to read the spreadsheets and tables. "Who's Rushford?"

"Michael Rushford. I think he may have been involved in the Dillard murders."

Jameson's eyes widened and he laughed. "Jesus, Leary, who needs defense attorneys when we have you trying to disprove your own cases?"

"I'm just being thorough." Leary rubbed his face. He certainly was not *trying* to disprove his own case. He believed Ramsey was guilty. He'd been there when Kristen Dillard had burst into tears the moment she'd seen his face at the lineup. But if evidence existed that exonerated Ramsey and implicated someone else, it was Leary's responsibility to find it. If he shirked that duty and Ramsey was wrongfully executed, then the man's blood would be on Leary's hands.

"Why don't you give me some space to work?"

Jameson and Scerbak exchanged a glance. Neither of them was a bad guy—Leary had enjoyed beers with both of them on occasion, and had even joined Scerbak's family for dinner once—but they were both uncannily skilled at making pests of themselves.

Jameson took one of the spreadsheets from Leary's desk and squinted at it. "Looks boring. You want some help?"

Leary looked up. "Yeah, if you have time to spare. Some help would be great."

Jameson dragged a chair to Leary's desk. Scerbak did the same. It didn't take long for both men to fall silent as they squinted at the papers. Leary wasn't surprised. The documents were confusing, with a lot of information jammed into tables with little context. It took all of Leary's concentration just to get a general sense of their meaning. He was parsing the entries on one spreadsheet when his phone rang. The noise jarred him backward and he almost knocked Scerbak off the chair beside him.

Leary picked up the receiver and heard the voice of a young woman. "Are you the detective in charge of the Dillard killings?"

"Why don't you tell me who you are first?" Wary of the press, Leary half-expected his caller to identify herself as an aspiring journalist, or worse, a blogger.

"Rachel Pugh."

His eyes turned to the next document in his pile. It was a bank statement from fourteen months ago. "And why are you calling, Ms. Pugh?"

"I saw him."

Leary ran his finger down the lists of deductions and deposits, trying to maintain his focus. "Who did you see?"

"Frank Ramsey."

Nothing on the statement looked suspicious, so he put it on the pile of reviewed documents and pulled the next sheet in front of him. "Ms. Pugh, I'm kind of busy—"

"I saw him run out of their house. It was the night of the murders. A lot of times I jog after dark. I don't like to—but by the time I'm finished with school and work, it's usually dark out. I saw him come out from behind the Dillard house and run onto the street. He ran under a street-lamp. He was pulling off his gloves with his teeth."

Leary shoved the financial records out of his way and found a blank sheet of paper. "Where are you?"

"Right now I'm at work. Starbucks."

Jameson and Scerbak stopped reading and watched him

scrawl an address. "When can we meet?"

"Whenever you have time, I guess."

Leary looked at his watch. "How about in ten minutes?"

Leary found the Starbucks and asked for Rachel Pugh. A girl who looked about seventeen untied her apron and walked around the counter. She pointed to a cluster of tables—mostly vacant at 4:07 PM—and they sat down.

"Why didn't you come forward with this information two years ago?"

Leary studied the girl's face as she looked at her hands. She wore very little makeup, kept her hair in a ponytail. After a few seconds, she said, "My father told me I should stay out of it."

"He was afraid for you?"

Rachel nodded. "I was scared, too."

Leary touched his chin, thinking fast. A second eyewitness, corroborating Kristen Dillard's testimony, would practically guarantee a conviction. But he had to make sure she was for real and not a pretender. There were always people—even innocent-looking teenagers like Rachel—who sought attention by going to the police with invented stories.

"You look about the same age as Kristen Dillard. Did you know her?"

"We weren't close." She looked up from her hands and met Leary's eyes. "We had some classes together, friends in common."

Listening to her now for inconsistencies in the story she'd told him over the phone, and watching her body language for signs of deception, he said, "Tell me again about what you saw."

"I was jogging."

"What was the date?"

She gave him the date of the murders.

"What was the time?"

"I got home from work at seven, said hi to my parents, did homework for an hour. So it was around eight."

"You didn't eat dinner?"

She shook her head. "I like to jog first, eat after. It's better for my stomach and my parents don't mind."

"What did you see?"

"I was running along Overlook Lane—that's what Kristen's street is called, even though it doesn't overlook anything—and before I passed her house, a man ran out from behind it. At first I thought it might be Kristen's father, but I knew he was a scientist and even in the dark this guy didn't look like a scientist. I could see he was big and muscular, like he worked out a lot. I slowed down because I always try to avoid strangers when I'm jogging alone."

"Did he see you?"

"I don't think so. If he did, he didn't try to talk to me or anything. He ran to the street, then started running up the street. When he ran underneath a street-lamp, I saw his face. He had short black hair, a square jaw. He put one of his hands near his mouth and used his teeth to pull off his glove as he ran."

"Which glove? His right or left?"

"He used his teeth to pull off his right glove, then he pulled off his left glove with his right hand."

"Did you see what he did with his gloves?"

"He stuffed them in the pockets of his jacket."

"Did you see any blood?"

Rachel shook her head. "But it was dark, like I said."

"How do you know the man you saw was Frank Ramsey?"

"I saw his picture on the Internet after he was arrested. It was him."

Leary watched cars pass outside. Through the window, he could hear the faint hum of their engines. He wanted to believe her story, but he knew that she could have learned all of her details from TV reports and news articles.

"You don't believe me." She looked frustrated, but also relieved.

"Do me a favor, Rachel. Close your eyes." Smiling sheepishly, she did as he asked. "Good. Now think back to that moment when the man passed underneath the streetlamp. Can you see him in your mind's eye?"

"Yes."

"You see his black hair? His square jaw?"

She nodded. "Yes."

"Now this is very important. I want you to look at the man's right hand."

"He's pulling his glove off with his teeth."

"That's right. But I want you to look at his wrist. Is he wearing a watch on his right wrist?"

She nodded. Even with her eyes closed, she looked excited. "Yes. There's a watch."

"And is that watch silver in color, with a metal band? A

Swiss watch made specifically for firefighters?"

The corners of Rachel's mouth turned downward in a frown. She was quiet for a moment. "No, I don't remember it looking like that. I think—what I think I saw was one of those ugly, clunky rubber watches."

"You can open your eyes now."

He looked away from her, at the other employees behind the counter. Kristen Dillard had described to him in detail the watch worn by her assailant. Her eyes had fixed on it while the man was raping her mother, and—as some kind of defense mechanism, Leary assumed—her mind had studied the watch as if every detail of its manufacture were crucial.

The watch Kristen had seen was a black Chase-Durer Blackhawk Mach 3 Alarm Chronograph. Designed for pilots. Sturdy, coated in rubber, ugly.

Leary had withheld information about the watch from the media.

"You haven't talked to Kristen Dillard about the attack, have you?"

The suggestion surprised her. "No. I haven't even seen Kristen since it happened. I mean, I've seen her on TV, but not in person. I didn't want to see her. I felt guilty, like because I had seen him and kept quiet I was part of it."

He believed her. "I'd like you to take a ride with me."

"Where?"

"Police Headquarters."

"I don't get off work for another three hours." Chewing her lip, she turned to look at a balding man eying them from behind the counter.

"I'll talk to your manager."

BURNOUT

"I ... I don't know."

Leary put his elbows on the table and leaned toward her. "Rachel, you called me because you want to do the right thing. Don't change your mind now."

She looked down at her hands again, but only for a moment. Then her eyes met his. "Let's go."

39.

Jessie received Leary's call on her way into the courthouse lobby. "I hope you're calling with good news," she said, clamping the phone between her ear and shoulder as she approached security.

"As a matter of fact, I am."

He sounded unusually happy, not the Mark Leary she'd become accustomed to. For some reason, that made her nervous. "Well?"

"I've got a new witness for you. A new *eyewitness*."

"You're kidding." She stopped walking and leaned close to the wall as Goldhammer and some of his underlings hurried past her. She watched them walk through the metal detector leading to the elevator bank. "But the prosecution has already rested its case."

"Can't you un-rest it?"

It was possible, but it wouldn't be easy. She—or, more accurately, Elliot—would need to make some pretty compelling arguments to Judge Spatt. "Who's the witness?"

"Her name is Rachel Pugh. She can put Ramsey at the scene on the night of the murder."

Jessie felt her heart rate increase. "Are you sure?"

"She's for real, Jessie. I just took her statement. I haven't done anything official yet—I thought it would be safer to keep her a secret for the moment. She's a little shaken up by the whole interview process, but her statement is solid. I'm about to drive her home. Then I'll call you back."

"Wait. Where was this Rachel Pugh the first time we tried this case?"

"She was afraid. She's a kid—the jury will understand. What matters is she knows details about the crime that were never released to the media. You need to get her on the stand."

"That won't be easy."

Leary laughed. "Am I speaking to Jessie Black? Maybe I called the wrong number."

"Maybe you haven't heard, but I'm no longer prosecuting the case. Warren's nephew has taken over."

Leary continued to laugh. She waited for him to realize she was serious. "What?"

A new witness, she thought. A chance to put this case to rest, finally, forever. "Don't worry about it," she said. "I'll get her on the stand."

Jessie ended the call and stood frozen for a moment, staring at her phone. A second witness. After all this time. It was just the break they needed.

"Something wrong?"

She jumped and turned to find Jack Ackerman standing behind her. "How long have you been standing there?"

He made a show of looking at her ass. "Not long enough."

"This is not the time, Jack."

"When would be the time? You haven't returned my calls in days."

It took her brain a moment to let go of Leary's phone call and focus on Jack. "I can't do this right now. I'm sorry."

"Listen, I have this dinner thing I need to go to on Friday night, for one of my clients. I don't want to go alone. Will you come with me?"

She shook her head, exasperated. "Jack, in case you haven't noticed, this thing we have between us? It blew up in my face, big time. I am in full damage control mode right now, trying to save this case, Kristen, my career, everything. So, no, I do not want to go to a dinner function with you on Friday night. Okay? I need to find Elliot. I'll call you when I can."

"What about us? You said you're trying to save everything. Does that include us?"

It wasn't easy turning her back on him, but she did. She walked away, leaving him standing alone in the courthouse lobby.

Judge Spatt's courtroom thrummed with anticipation, but not because anyone in it had forewarning about the bomb the prosecution was about to drop about its surprise witness. It was the presence of Dr. Katherine Moscow—seated in the first row of the gallery and clearly intended by Goldhammer to be the first witness for the defense—that had created the stir of excitement. In the world of criminal law, at least, Moscow had become a celebrity. In the last few years, her name had appeared in the news with more frequency than Goldhammer's. While he was merely a defense lawyer that liked to get his picture in the paper, she was real news—a rogue psychologist whose theories threatened to upset people's most basic beliefs about the reliability of memory.

Her beauty didn't hurt either. Every eye in the courtroom seemed drawn to her. She pretended not to notice the attention—or maybe, after being stared at for her whole life, she really didn't notice it anymore. Even Judge Spatt, whose range of facial expression had always seemed to Jessie to be limited to varying degrees of boredom and annoyance, looked at her with his lips slightly parted, as if he might at any moment begin to drool. The perfect witness.

Jessie chewed her lip. She knew they could beat Moscow, but it wouldn't be easy.

Spatt tapped his gavel, silencing the room. "Mr. Goldhammer, is the defense ready to proceed with its first witness?"

Goldhammer stood up. He glanced at Moscow, then turned to the judge. "We are, Your Honor."

"All right. Let's bring the jury in."

"Excuse me." Elliot stood up. His nervousness was evident—Jessie could see it from her seat near the back of the gallery—but his voice carried clearly. "Your Honor, the Commonwealth requests permission to reopen its case."

"For what reason?"

Elliot fired an uneasy glance at the gallery. "Sidebar, Your Honor?"

The judge beckoned Elliot and Goldhammer to approach him. Jessie hesitated for a moment, then breached protocol and crossed the courtroom to join them. No one objected. Elliot and Goldhammer were already huddled over the judge's podium, speaking softly to avoid being heard by the gallery.

"The Commonwealth wishes to call an additional witness to introduce direct evidence on the issue of the defendant's whereabouts on the night of the crimes," Elliot was saying.

"Who is this witness?" Spatt said.

Elliot pitched his voice lower. "The witness is a minor and we would like to keep the witness's identity confidential for the moment. The information will be made available to the defense once an appropriate protective order is in place."

"This is offensive!" Goldhammer sputtered. "Offensive! Your Honor, Mr. Ramsey is entitled to a fair trial. There are rules that must be followed."

"Yes, and as I've told you before, I am familiar with them." The judge's voice was like ice, and Goldhammer retreated slightly.

Elliot said, "Under Pennsylvania law, a trial court has the discretion to reopen a case for either side prior to the entry of final judgment." He paused, probably trying to remember case names. "Your Honor, please."

"Please what?" Spatt's face snapped in Elliot's direction. "Am I here to do you favors?"

Elliot's face flushed. "Your Honor—"

"My answer is no," Spatt said. "You may not call your magical mystery witness."

"Your Honor?" Jessie said. The three men seemed to notice her presence for the first time. Spatt's eyes widened. "May I speak?" she said.

"Absolutely not!"

"Your Honor, if you will not permit us to reopen our case-in-chief, please allow us to present a rebuttal witness after the defense has rested its case."

"Mr. Williams already told the court that this witness—whoever it is—would introduce *direct* evidence," Goldhammer said. "That's not proper testimony for rebuttal."

"It is if the testimony was not available during the prosecution's case-in-chief," Jessie said. She held her breath. No judge had ever held her in contempt of court, but if any was likely to be the first, it was Spatt.

Instead of berating her, he stared into space, thoughtful. He looked at Goldhammer, then at Elliot. "The parties will brief these issues—*in writing*, please—and I will decide whether or not the testimony of this minor is proper. Fair?"

"Yes, Your Honor." Goldhammer's voice was a grumble.

Elliot thanked him and looked relieved to back away from the bench, another battle behind him.

Jessie crept backward, past the bar of the court, and reentered the gallery where she hoped to disappear. Before she could sit, Spatt's eyes caught her.

"Are you sure you wouldn't be more comfortable at the prosecution table, Ms. Black?"

"Yes, Your Honor." Several people in the gallery—including Kate Moscow—turned to stare at her.

"Maybe you'd prefer *my* seat?" Spatt said.

A murmur of laughter moved through the gallery. Jessie felt her cheeks redden. "No thank you, Your Honor. I'm fine back here."

"Well, that's a relief."

40.

The courtroom hushed as Kate Moscow took the stand. She settled into the wooden seat and leaned back, looking as comfortable in front of the packed courtroom as she would in her own office. Before she even spoke, the jurors leaned toward her, mesmerized. Her posture—spine as straight as a ruler, shoulders rolled back—might have made a different witness look arrogant or prissy, but it made Kate Moscow look regal. For the first time, Jessie became conscious of the purpose behind the traditional design of the courtroom. Without the added effect of his higher altitude—the judge's bench rose a foot higher than any other seat in the room—Spatt would have looked small and insignificant next to her.

"Stand and place your right hand on the Bible."

Moscow pressed her hand to the book and tilted her chin up.

"Do you swear to tell the truth, the whole truth, and nothing but the truth, so help you God?"

She looked toward the jurors, already establishing a bond with them, when she answered. "I do."

Goldhammer began his direct examination by establishing Moscow's credentials for the benefit of the jury. He asked her about her education, beginning with her prestigious private high school—she graduated as valedictorian—and ending with her doctorate from Columbia University in New York. Next he elicited testimony about her experience as a professor and researcher, the journal articles and textbook she had authored, her memberships in professional organizations, and the awards she had received. By the time he had finished laying the foundation for her expert testimony, everyone in the courtroom was suitably impressed.

Elliot would need to hammer home during cross that she was a hired gun, doing this not for justice, but for a sizable paycheck.

"You said your specialty is memory," Goldhammer said. "Seems like a simple thing. You see something, you remember it. How does one devote a whole career to its study?"

She addressed her answer not to him, but to the jury. "First of all, memory is far from simple. No one knows for certain how it works, but scientists generally agree that memories are created by neurons forming connections in the brain. Long-term memories, which range from incidents that occurred as recently as a few minutes ago to experiences that happened fifty, sixty years in the past, are stored in these connections. In a lifetime, the brain can accumulate as many as a quadrillion—that's one million billion—separate memory impressions. So no, I would not call memory a simple concept. One could devote several lifetimes to its study and only begin to understand it."

Goldhammer laughed sheepishly, playing the layman to Moscow's expert, standing in for the jurors as the regular guy trying to understand the science. "Okay. But you claim to understand it."

"I have conducted research that has illuminated certain aspects of memory. Long-term memory as it relates to eyewitness identification, for example, is an aspect of memory that I understand very well. The point I was making is that many common assumptions about memory are based on oversimplifications and lack of knowledge."

"So let me ask you a hypothetical question. Assume a young woman watched a masked man stab her father to death. She then watched him rape and kill her mother. Finally, the man raped and stabbed the young woman, but she survived. During this ordeal, she had one small window of opportunity to see the man's face. Perhaps ten seconds, perhaps as long as a minute. In your expert opinion, is it possible that this young woman could later identify the wrong man as her attacker?"

"Not only possible," Moscow said. "Likely."

"How can that be?" Goldhammer made a face at the jury. "We see someone, we remember. Especially someone hurting us."

Moscow shook her head. "That's simply not the case. Contrary to popular belief, violent events actually decrease, rather than increase, memory accuracy. The relationship between stress and memory is known as the Yerkes-Dodson law. When a person is terrified, her ability to form memories stutters. It hiccups."

Several of the jurors were nodding, although Jessie suspected that more than a few of them were completely baffled by the testimony. The danger was that because Moscow was such an impressive figure, the jurors might simply let her do their thinking for them—a possibility Goldhammer was no doubt counting on.

"Well," he said, "if it's so hard for people to form

accurate memories in moments of trauma, why are some eyewitness-victims so confident about their identifications? Isn't confidence a sign of accuracy?"

"Absolutely not. My studies have proven that confidence has surprisingly little correlation with accuracy. People get attached to their memories, even when those memories are distorted or invented."

"Distorted or invented? Does that happen?"

Moscow smiled patiently. "More often than you would think, Mr. Goldhammer. For example, in the case of an eyewitness-victim of a violent crime, a false identification may be caused by unconscious transference."

Goldhammer's face scrunched as if he were hearing all of this information for the first time and struggling to comprehend it, just like the jurors were. Of course, this was an act—an attorney of Goldhammer's caliber would not only have rehearsed this testimony with Moscow several times, but would also have acquainted himself with the studies of other leaders in her field, reading their papers, maybe even attending a lecture. Jessie had no doubt that by this point, Goldhammer could offer his own lecture on the subject. "Could you explain what you mean by that term?" he said.

"Certainly." Again, Moscow addressed the jury. Her tone was friendly but authoritative. "Unconscious transference describes an inaccurate identification caused when the brain substitutes one person—a person the witness saw in situation A—with a different person—seen in situation B. This phenomenon is commonly manifested in the form of photo-biased lineups."

"And what are those, Dr. Moscow?"

"As part of the usual procedure followed by police

investigating crimes involving an eyewitness, the first thing the police will do is show the witness a photo array," she said. "Next, they take the witness to an in-person lineup. In almost every case, the photo array and the lineup have one man in common—the man whom the police suspect of the crime and hope the witness will identify. The problem is that, during the in-person lineup, the opportunity for unconscious transference is enormous. The witness recognizes one of the men and identifies him. But where does she recognize him from? The crime or the photo array? The problem is exacerbated by the fact that most people assume, when they are shown a lineup, that one of the men in the lineup must be guilty."

"Why would a victim assume that?"

"Think about it. Why would the police show her these people if they did not believe one of them was her attacker? Instead of asking herself the proper question, which is *Was one of these men my attacker?*, the victim asks herself, *Which one of these men was my attacker?* And because she already assumes that one of the men is her attacker, she picks the one who most closely resembles him in her memory."

Goldhammer next lead Moscow through a series of questions concerning other factors that negatively affect eyewitness identifications. Moscow described an experiment on weapon focus conducted at Oklahoma State University. Forty-nine percent of the test subjects correctly identified a person who held a harmless object in his hand. When that object was replaced with a weapon, the number of correct identifications plummeted to only thirty-three percent.

"Would a large knife have this effect?"

"Definitely."

"Let's return to my hypothetical." He took a breath—a

pause that alerted the jury that something important was about to happen. "Dr. Moscow, in your opinion, how reliable is the eyewitness identification that I described to you?"

"The situation you described is fraught with factors negatively affecting memory. I would approach the identification as extremely dubious."

Goldhammer smiled.

Elliot rose from his chair to begin his cross-examination, but Judge Spatt waved his hand. "I think I've had enough for one day. We'll pick up again tomorrow morning with the Commonwealth's cross-examination."

Jessie cursed silently. Now was the worst time to stop for the day, as the break would give the jurors a whole night to think about Moscow's testimony before hearing the other side. But there was nothing she could do. The jurors were already filing out of their box, and Spatt was collecting his things.

But there was a silver lining. The early break would give Elliot more time to write his brief, and it would give Jessie a chance to meet Leary's surprise witness before the girl spoke to anyone else in the DA's office.

41.

Woody parked the Lexus in front of a convenience store. He was tempted to enter the store and buy a soda, but his better judgment cautioned against making an appearance on the store's security camera, however innocent. So far he had remained in the background, practically invisible, and he preferred to keep it that way.

He climbed out of the car, closed the door, locked it and engaged the alarm. The Pugh house was eleven blocks away, a long, cold walk. A wicked breeze slashed through his clothing, made his legs burn inside his jeans and chafed his ears. He wrapped a scarf around his neck and buttoned his coat up to his chin. By the time he reached the house, he was freezing and questioning whether parking his car so far from the house had really been a necessary precaution.

It was, he decided. This was a lucky break—learning about Rachel Pugh before she'd even been officially processed by the police department—but luck could be fickle. His brother's life was proof of that. Woody expected to find the Pugh family alone, with no police protection, but he couldn't be sure that Detective Leary had not sent an off-duty friend to the house as an off-the-books safety measure while the DA's office decided how to handle her. He also couldn't be sure that Jessie Black had not taken her own actions to ensure the girl's security—though how she would have had time, he couldn't imagine. When Woody had raced here from the courthouse, the Ice Princess had still been on the stand, and all of Jessie's attention had been on her.

All the same, he would have liked to peek through the windows to make sure no guards were in the house, and to see if either of the girl's parents was home. But Andorra seemed like the kind of place that might have a neighborhood watch, and the chance that a nosy neighbor might witness him snooping made him sacrifice any extra information he might glean. If the girl's parents were home, he would deal with them. Cops too, if it came to that. He hoped it wouldn't.

He rang the bell. After several seconds of silence, he heard footsteps pound down a staircase inside the house. He felt himself studied through the peephole and forced a friendly smile. He lifted a police detective ID—counterfeit but of high quality—and held it near his face. The badge reflected the late afternoon sunlight.

The door opened.

"Rachel Pugh?" he asked the girl in the doorway.

She nodded but continued to block the entrance.

"My name is Detective Butler. You can call me Woody."

"Where's Detective Leary?"

"He's discussing your statement with the DA. He sent me here to ask you some follow-up questions." Woody showed her his phone. "I'm going to call him in a few minutes. You can talk to him, if you'd like."

She tucked her long, brown hair behind her left shoulder, then stepped backward, inviting him into the house. He entered quickly and closed the door behind him. He did not hear anyone else in the house. Certainly if anyone from the DA's office or police department were here, he would have been confronted by now. His luck was holding.

"Are your parents home?"

"Just my brother."

He nodded. That seemed strange—what kind of parents would leave their daughter home alone when they'd just learned she'd been a witness in a murder investigation?—but he didn't have precious seconds to waste contemplating typical middle class stupidity.

"Is there somewhere we can sit down?" As he followed her deeper into the house, he looked for signs of the brother. He had not had any time to get information on her family and had no idea if there was a harmless four-year-old or a hulking high school football player in the house. The latter could be a problem.

He kept his eyes open for toys or trophies. "What's your brother's name?"

"Tim." She led him to the kitchen, gestured to a seat at the table. "You want anything? A soda?"

"No thanks." He could not afford to leave his fingerprints or saliva behind. "Where is Tim?"

"In his crib upstairs. Sleeping for once, thank God."

An infant? Good, except that it meant the mother couldn't be far. "I thought your mom would be home," he said, trying to sound casual.

Rachel Pugh shrugged. "She had a thing, won't be home from work for another few hours. I have to stay here. I can't go to the police station, because of Tim. I hope that's okay."

BURNOUT

"Sure, that's fine. I just have a few questions."

She sat down across from him with a can of Diet Coke. She popped the tab, took a sip. "Wouldn't it have been easier for you to call instead of driving all the way over here?"

"You told Detective Leary that you saw Frank Ramsey near the Dillard house on the night of the murders, correct?"

"Yeah, didn't you read my statement? I saw him run out from behind the house. I saw his face when he ran under a street-lamp."

"I read the statement." Woody nodded, giving this information a chance to settle in his mind. He had hoped to hear something different—something less incriminating—but in his gut he had known the moment he'd learned about her that killing her would probably be necessary. "What made you decide to come forward now?"

For a moment, staring at her can of soda, she looked like she wished she hadn't. "I guess I couldn't live with the secret any longer."

Living with secrets was a survival skill. Too bad this girl would not survive long enough to learn that lesson.

Upstairs, Tim began to cry.

Rachel Pugh groaned. "Ugh. Do you mind waiting down here a second?" She pushed her chair back from the table and headed for the entryway, where stairs led to the second floor of the house. Woody waited at the table until he heard a stair creak under her weight. Then he stood up.

The upper hallway was dark. Halfway between the landing and the room at the end of the hall, sunlight shone into the hallway through an open doorway, casting a happy glow against the otherwise gloomy carpet and wallpaper.

Woody could hear the girl cooing to her brother, trying to calm him down. The baby had stopped crying and was now giggling and shrieking with delight.

Could a child that young see and remember his face? He'd have to ask the Ice Princess when he got the chance. For now, he'd err on the safe side, and take care of the kid's sister in a different room.

"Shhhhh. Shhhhh. Go back to sleep, Timmy. Shhhhh."

Woody crept from the landing to the hallway. He retrieved a razor from his inside coat pocket. Pressing his back to the wall outside Tim's bedroom, he waited, motionless, controlling his breathing.

Finally, the kid shut up.

He heard Rachel Pugh's footsteps as the girl backed quietly out of the bedroom. When she entered the hallway, she was still walking backwards. Their eyes met immediately. A half-second later, her gaze shifted to the razor.

"Don't scream. You'll wake up Timmy."

Because she looked inclined to scream anyway, he grabbed her with his free hand and rushed her down the hallway to the room at the end, closing the door behind them with the heel of his shoe. The door rattled in its frame. Tim started crying again.

Woody grabbed the girl's right hand and placed the razor, handle first, on her palm. She stared at it. The blade trembled.

"Sit on the bed. Slit your wrists."

Her eyes, not comprehending, returned to his. "What?"

"Sit on the bed. Slit your wrists."

"You're not a cop." She glanced at the door behind him as if she might try to get past him. Before she could do anything that would make his chore more difficult, he shoved her with his open hand. She stumbled backward. The backs of her legs touched the mattress and she sat down hard on the edge of the queen-size bed. He began to notice the rest of the room. Posters of male teens had been taped to the walls. Photos of groups of smiling girls had been tacked to a cork board over a small white desk. Makeup and cheap jewelry lay strewn across the top of a dresser. This was her room. Perfect.

"I'll tell them I didn't see anything."

"Too late."

"Please, I swear. I won't testify. I'll tell them I made a mistake."

He glanced at the Hello Kitty clock on her nightstand. Her mother would be returning soon. "Deep, across the veins. Do it right the first time."

She was crying now. Her hands were shaking. Behind him, Tim was wailing. He realized his idea was not going to work. The girl was not going to do his job for him. He was going to have to do it himself.

Woody had never killed a person before.

Once, as a C.O. at Huntington, he had slammed a rowdy inmate's head against a wall and cracked the man's skull, causing a hemorrhage that resulted in his death an hour later, but that had been an accident.

He did not want to kill her. He despised murderers.

But he had no choice. He needed to do this. For Michael.

She held the razor in front of her, trying to wield it in her own defense. Woody disarmed her. He replaced the razor in his coat pocket.

"I swear to God!" She scrambled backward onto the bed, pressed herself against the headboard. "I'll tell them I lied, for Kristen. I'll explain!"

Through the door, he heard Tim bawling.

"It's too late."

"No!"

She jumped from the bed and tried to rush past him, but she was clumsy and her direction was predictable. He yanked her close to him, wrapped one arm around her torso, clamped the other around her head. Her ear dug into his biceps through the material of his coat sleeve.

With a grunt, he wrenched her head to one side. Her neck made a cracking sound.

42.

Jessie watched anxiously as the shadows of the houses and trees lengthened. By the time Leary turned the unmarked police car onto Ginger Drive in Andorra, it was already 5:00 PM. Snow had begun to fall around four and now—only an hour later—blanketed the street, gleaming white under the street-lamps. The car's tires crunched through it.

"I still don't understand why you want to do this now," Leary said. "I can pick her up tomorrow morning, and we can all talk at the Roundhouse or the DA's office."

"She could be the key to the whole trial," Jessie said. "I want to talk to her first, before anyone else has a chance to influence what she says."

The truth was Jessie would have come sooner, but she had not dared to miss Dr. Moscow's testimony. She watched snowflakes twirl to the windshield. Each melted the moment it touched the glass. The wipers slashed away the tiny wet drops. Leary was leaning forward over the wheel, squinting at the numbers on the houses. She realized he didn't know where he was going.

She said, "Didn't you drive her home this afternoon after you took her statement at the Roundhouse?"

"No. She asked me to drop her at the Starbucks where she works after school. Uh oh."

"What?" But one second later, an explanation was unnecessary as she saw the red and white light strobe behind a copse of trees at the edge of a property midway down the street. The pulse was distinctive, and when Leary inched the car closer, neither of them was surprised to see an ambulance idling in the driveway. Smoke rolled from its exhaust, billowing in the cold air.

"Oh shit," she said.

Jessie waited while Leary showed his identification; then they both stepped inside. The man who'd opened the door made no attempt to stop them, nor did he close the door behind them. Jessie did it for him, sealing the cold and the snow outside.

Leary said, "What's going on—" His voice broke off.

Rachel Pugh lay at the bottom of the staircase. Two paramedics were kneeling over her, but their hands were still. Beyond the entryway, in the kitchen, a woman rocked a toddler in her arms. Both she and the toddler were sobbing.

"Oh my God," Jessie said.

The man who had opened the door turned to face them. The curls of his hair were in disarray. "She's—" His breath hitched in his throat. "When Peggy got home, she found Rachel here, on the floor. She's—" Again, he had to stop. He rubbed his forehead. "She fell and broke her neck."

Leary glanced at Jessie, then back at the man. "Slow down. Tell me your name."

"Fred," he said. "Fred Pugh."

"Fred, I'm Mark Leary. We spoke by phone earlier today."

"What?"

One of the paramedics stepped closer and said to Leary, "ME's on his way." As if on cue, Jessie heard sirens, then car doors opening outside, people approaching the house.

"Let's talk somewhere more quiet," Leary said to Fred Pugh. "Your wife, too." Leary guided them toward the family room. Jessie followed, hearing the deputy ME enter the house behind her.

Once they had some privacy, Leary said, "Mr. Pugh, did your daughter tell anyone about what we discussed earlier today?"

Peggy Pugh stared at her husband, confused. "What you discussed? What is he talking about?"

Fred Pugh shook his head. "I have no idea."

Leary blinked. "Rachel and I called you from Police Headquarters."

"I haven't heard from Rachel since I left for work this morning," Fred Pugh said. "And I think I would remember a call from the police."

Jessie felt a tightening in her gut. It was becoming increasingly clear that whatever Leary thought had happened earlier in the day had not been what it had seemed. Judging by the panic creeping into Leary's face, his thoughts were heading in the same direction. Jessie decided to be direct. "Rachel came forward today with information about the Frank Ramsey trial," she told the girl's parents.

"Ramsey?" Peggy Pugh said. "Isn't he the man who attacked the Dillards?"

"Yes," Leary said. Then, to Fred Pugh, he said, "This is not the time to keep secrets."

"I'm not keeping any secrets!"

Leary turned away and rubbed his face. Jessie could feel his frustration. He turned and in a calmer voice, said, "I don't know if I really spoke to you today, or if Rachel called someone else who pretended to be you. Maybe she was afraid you would try to dissuade her from coming forward, like you did two years ago. But she did come forward and we know that Rachel was out jogging the night the Dillard family was attacked. We know she saw a man run from the house. She saw his face."

"Rachel's never jogged in her life," Peggy Pugh said.

"Does this have something to do with Rachel's visits with Kristen Dillard? I knew that wasn't a good idea," Fred Pugh said, turning on his wife.

"They're friends, Fred!"

"Rachel and Kristen are friends?" The feeling in Jessie's gut worsened. As a prosecutor, she'd dealt with her fair share of deceitful witnesses. People who lied for attention, or for other motives based on agendas that had nothing to do with justice. Jessie turned to Leary. "She didn't tell you that?"

"She said they used to be friends, but had grown apart," Leary said.

Jessie crossed her arms over her chest. Aware that the Pughs, devastated and confused, were staring at her, she chose her words carefully. "I think we need to consider that Rachel may have been trying to help her friend."

Leary was speechless, but she could tell by his expression that he understood what she was suggesting. Eventually, he nodded. "It's possible."

"You said you confirmed her story by asking her about a detail only you knew about," Jessie said. "But Kristen would have known that detail too, right?"

Leary nodded.

Anger swelled in her. Rachel had been killed because someone had believed she would offer testimony that would incriminate Frank Ramsey. But that had been the very reason they had delayed officially processing her. Rachel's name had not been spoken in open court, and the only people who knew her identity were Jessie, Leary, and Elliot.

"What are you saying?" Fred Pugh said, still staring at them. "None of this makes any sense. My daughter fell down the stairs. Didn't she?" His voice cracked on the last word, and Peggy Pugh gripped her son tighter and pressed her other hand against her face.

"Please try to stay calm," Leary told them. "The deputy medical examiner will look at your daughter's injuries. He'll determine the cause of death. If ... foul play was involved—"

"Oh God," Peggy Pugh said.

A uniformed officer poked his head into the room and asked if everything was okay.

Fred Pugh rounded on the uniform. "Nothing is okay. I demand an explanation. What is going on? What does this have to do with the Dillards? *What happened to my daughter?*"

The uniform, startled, backed away. "Uh, sir—"

Jessie closed her eyes, trying to mentally separate herself from the chaos. Leary and the Pughs might be confused, but she thought she understood what had happened here today. Kristen had convinced her friend to lie for her, and someone who wanted Ramsey to be free had killed her before she could testify. The key to finding the killer was to find out how the killer had learned about Kristen's friend. Jessie had told no one. She was pretty sure Leary wouldn't have told anyone. That left one person. Opening her eyes, she took Leary's arm and gently tugged him to a corner of the room, where they could whisper out of earshot of the Pughs.

"I think this might be Elliot's fault. Elliot Williams. He must have opened his big mouth, told the wrong person. Or—"

He watched her. "What's wrong?"

She remembered how eager he had been to get his hands on a copy of her opening statement. How he had asked to assist her with the case. How quickly he had seized the opportunity to take over.

"What if Elliot's helping Ramsey?"

"That's ridiculous. Jessie, a young girl is dead. You're understandably upset—"

"Don't patronize me."

Leary sputtered. "I'm sorry. I—"

She looked at her watch. Almost six o'clock. Elliot was probably still at the office. "I need to find him. Now."

"I'm not telling you what to do, Jessie, but I think you should take a moment to think about what you're saying," Leary said. "Elliot Williams has no reason to help Frank Ramsey. He has every reason to want to win this case. To further his own career, make a name for himself in the DA's office."

"Someone with deep pockets is paying Ramsey's legal bills. Maybe that person is also paying Elliot."

Leary shook his head. "I don't think you're right." But he rubbed his chin, as if struck by something that she'd said. "I assumed Goldhammer was representing Ramsey *pro bono*."

"No. He told me he was being paid his regular fee. Why? What are you thinking?"

"It's too early to say."

His vagueness was maddening. "Leary—"

He looked at his watch. "I have to go. I'll let you know when I hear from the ME's office about Rachel Pugh."

"There's no way she fell down those stairs," Jessie said. "Someone killed her. Someone wants Ramsey to be free."

Leary nodded. "If that's true, then we need to find out who that someone is. And we need to figure it out *now*."

She had the strange feeling, looking at his face, that he already thought he knew.

43.

After 8:00 PM, the DA's office was quiet—most of the prosecutors had gone home for the evening—but the guards downstairs were not surprised to see Jessie enter the building, accustomed to her schedule after several years of admitting her at all hours of the night. Upstairs, Elliot's office light was shining. She took a deep breath, summoning her strength for this encounter.

She found him hunched over his desk. In the light from his monitor, his skin looked sallow. He was poring over a transcript and didn't notice her standing in his doorway.

His office was even smaller than hers. If she leaned forward, she could touch his shoulder from the hallway. She did and he jumped, almost falling out of his chair.

"Jesus Christ! You scared the crap out of me." His breathing sounded uneven.

Jessie stood over his desk. She crossed her arms. "She's dead."

Elliot stared up at her, looking as disoriented as if she'd just woken him from a dream. "Who is?"

"Rachel Pugh."

That seemed to penetrate. He leaned back in his chair

BURNOUT

and shook his head. "Holy shit."

"Yeah, holy shit. Who have you been talking to?"

"What? You think.... *You're blaming me?*"

Leary's words of doubt were fresh in her mind, and the wide-eyed, baffled innocence on Elliot's face looked too genuine to be a ruse. "You must have given her name to someone. I'm going to give you the benefit of the doubt, for now, and assume it was unintentional."

"Jessie, I didn't tell anyone. As soon as Judge Spatt sent the jury home for the day I came straight back to the office to work on Moscow's cross."

She leaned over his desk. The transcript in front of him was a record of the testimony Moscow had given earlier that day. It was covered in handwritten notes. Other documents—cases, photocopied pages of legal treatises, pages printed from the Web—were strewn across his desk and on every other surface in his office. A book on expert witnesses sat open on the floor near the legs of his chair.

"Ask security downstairs," he said. "I've been here."

"You could have made a phone call. Sent an e-mail." But her voice had already lost its conviction. Leary had been right—Elliot's interest was in winning the trial, not losing it. She leaned against his wall, closed her eyes. When she opened them, he was staring at her, watching her with a wary expression.

"What happened?" he said in a quiet voice.

"She was found at the bottom of a staircase. Her neck was broken."

"And you think Ramsey had something to do with it?"

"I don't believe in coincidences."

"Well, I promise you that I didn't tell anyone anything. To be honest, I haven't thought about her at all. I haven't even had time to start drafting the brief Spatt demanded on the appropriate use of rebuttal testimony."

"You've been concentrating on Moscow?"

He waved a hand over the papers on his desk. "So far. The jury seemed to buy her routine. I'm not sure of the best way to undo that."

"As long as I'm here, I may as well lend a hand." Jessie removed some documents from his other chair and sat down, then took the transcript of Moscow's testimony from his desk. "You marked this up pretty good."

"Trying to find holes. Inconsistencies between what she said today and what she's published in the journals."

"Did you find anything?"

He shook his head. "For a scientist, she's led a remarkably consistent career. All of her research points in the same direction. She's never contradicted herself."

"No, she wouldn't have." Jessie sat back in the chair, crossed her legs. "Because she's not a scientist. Scientists are open-minded, willing to test their theories and adapt to new discoveries. Katherine Moscow isn't interested in that. She's interested in testifying, writing books and journal articles, attending exotic conferences, appearing on television, and getting paid."

"I get the sense you don't like her."

Jessie smirked, thinking of their encounter outside the courthouse. "She's not my favorite person."

"How do we make the jury feel that way?"

She sat back, the chair squeaking. "You can draw

attention to the number of lawsuits in which she's participated, the amount of money she's made. But I'm not sure how much that will sway the jury about the soundness of her theories."

After a moment, he said, "You should cross-examine her."

"Warren removed me from the case. I would think that *you* of all people would remember that."

He lowered his head, chastised. "Sorry about that."

Jessie stared at the snowflakes falling in the darkness beyond his window. "Don't be. You did the right thing." Elliot looked up. His shocked expression would have amused her under different circumstances. "By dating Jack, I was creating a perfect vehicle for Ramsey's next appeal. I was jeopardizing the whole case. Even though Jack never violated his duty to maintain Ramsey's confidences, the Court of Appeals could have reversed based on the appearance of impropriety." She shook her head, disgusted with herself. "I was an idiot."

"Technically, that's not true."

"Sure it is."

"No." Elliot stood and reached for a stack of papers piled on top of a cardboard box in the corner of his office. "I felt guilty about telling Warren, so I did some research, just to satisfy my own conscience." He looked at her. "Turned out *I* was wrong, not you."

"What?"

"It's true that normally, your relationship with Jack would be highly improper. But in this case, it was fine. Because of the PCRA hearing."

"The PCRA—" Then she realized what he meant.

"Ramsey testified against Jack."

"Exactly. And when a client voluntarily testifies against his lawyer, the attorney-client privilege is destroyed. Jack couldn't have violated his duty because he no longer has one."

Jessie took the printed cases from him. "You did this research weeks ago. Why didn't you tell me? Why didn't you explain it to Warren?"

Elliot shrugged. "I wanted the case for myself. It's a career-maker."

"So why tell me now? The case is still a career-maker."

"Not if I lose." Elliot took the documents back and returned them to their place on the cardboard box. They dropped there with a thump. "So, will you cross-examine the bitch, or what?"

"With pleasure."

44.

PCIT—the Philadelphia Center for Inclusive Treatment—occupied a stark tower near Fairmont Park. The gray stones and barred windows comprising its edifice looked more like an insane asylum than the building's carefully selected name implied, and made a chill run through Leary's body that had nothing to do with the freezing weather. He crunched up the snow-covered steps to the lobby doors. They were locked, but he could see a guard at a desk inside.

He knocked and held his badge up to the glass.

A moment later he was inside. He followed the guard across a threadbare brown carpet to the desk, where he signed in. The air in the lobby was tropical compared to the falling temperature outside. He loosened his tie. Snow in his hair melted and ran down his collar. "Warm in here."

The guard shrugged, examined his entry in the log. "Too late to visit a patient."

"I need to see her. Police business."

He leveled a put-upon stare at Leary, then said, "Hang on." He picked up a battered black phone, jabbed a button, spoke quietly into the receiver. After a few minutes, they were joined by a middle-aged woman in a white nurse's uniform.

She walked like a man. Leary wasn't sure if the smudge above her lip was a shadow or a mustache.

"I'm sorry, Detective, but you'll have to come back in the morning."

Leary looked at his watch. It was only 8:00 PM. "I need to speak to Ms. Dillard immediately."

"Visiting hours are over."

"He says it's police business," the guard said.

"I'm sure it is. But you'll have to come back tomorrow."

"No."

The nurse's nostrils flared. "George, please escort this man off the premises."

George began to rise from his chair behind the desk. Before he could, a man emerged from a door behind him. He wore a white coat. Leary recognized him as Brian Schafer, Kristen's doctor.

"Doctor, I need to see Kristen Dillard. Please take me to her."

George and the nurse turned to Schafer with expressions of frustration. He waved a hand at them. "It's okay. I'll take care of this."

"Fine with me." The nurse stalked off. George went back to his newspaper.

The doctor led Leary through the door behind George's desk. The brown carpet of the lobby continued down a dimly lit hallway. The doctor opened a door on their right.

"Dr. Schafer—" Leary's frustration mounted as Schafer took a seat behind his desk and gestured for Leary to sit as well. The office had no windows and smelled like old books. Cheap fluorescent lights hummed from the ceiling. "I really need to talk to Kristen Dillard now."

"You can't."

"Why not?"

Schafer hesitated, then said, "She was medicated. She had to be subdued."

"What?"

He fiddled with a ballpoint pen on his ink blotter. "Kristen is not supposed to have access to the news, but there is a TV room she is allowed to use during certain times. Sometimes a show she is permitted to watch will be preempted by a news event. It's difficult to control—"

"What happened?"

"I wasn't present, but I'm told she saw a report of a young woman's death—"

Leary cursed under his breath. "And?"

"She became upset," Schafer said. "That can happen sometimes. She threw things, disturbed the other patients."

"So you decided to drug her? There wasn't a less extreme solution?"

The doctor shrugged. "Kristen has had violent episodes in the past, as you know. Usually directed toward herself. I believe these episodes are motivated by survivor's guilt—subconsciously, she hates herself for not dying when—"

"I'm not interested in psychiatric diagnoses. She's completely unconscious?"

"Dead to the world. If you return in the morning—"

Leary ran a hand through his damp hair. "Do you keep records of her phone calls? Her visitors?"

"Of course."

"May I see them?"

Schafer sighed, walked to a file cabinet against the wall to his left, and opened one of the drawers. He removed a file, opened it on his desk. "May I ask what you're looking for?"

"Contact with a person named Rachel Pugh."

"Doesn't sound familiar." He flipped through pages in the file, many of which consisted of handwritten notes. "No Pugh in her visitor log." He flipped more pages, leaned closer to study another list. "Do you know the phone number this Pugh person would have called from?"

Leary pulled a pad from the pocket of his suit jacket, found Pugh's number, and read it to him. "Check this one, too." He read the doctor Rachel's work number, the number she'd originally contacted him from.

"Nope. Neither one. What is this about, Detective? Perhaps if you were less cryptic, I could be of more assistance."

"Is there any other way—" An idea struck him. "Kristen spent time at the DA's office, preparing to take the stand. And then she went to the courthouse to offer her testimony."

"Well, yes."

"Does someone accompany her on these outings?"

"Of course. One of my interns, Susan McDavid."

"Is she here now?"

Schafer frowned. He picked up his phone, dialed a number, and hung up. "I just paged her."

Seconds later, there was a knock at the door. A young woman stepped into the room, looking nervous.

"Susan, this is Mark Leary of the Philadelphia Police Department."

She smiled awkwardly. "Hi."

Leary stood up, shook her hand. "You went with Kristen Dillard to the DA's office and the courthouse?"

Susan nodded. "I drove her. I sat in the gallery when she took the stand." The woman shuddered. "What a terrible story."

"Did she ever leave your sight?"

"No. Not really."

"What do you mean, not really?" Seeing the woman's back straighten, Leary softened his tone. "I just need to know if it's possible she met with someone during one of her trips."

Susan's eyes shifted to Schafer and she swallowed. "A few times, she asked for a moment alone. Outside."

"*You agreed?*" Schafer's face turned red.

"She was never out of my sight for more than five minutes. She always came right back."

"Did you ever see her talking to another girl of about her age, with brown hair?"

Susan nodded. "Once. When I asked her about it, she told me they were childhood friends."

Leary shook his head and laughed grimly.

Jessie was right. He'd been conned by a couple of teenage girls.

45.

Kate Moscow returned to her seat behind the witness stand. If she felt any nervousness about her imminent cross-examination, she hid it completely behind her usual icy facade. When Elliot informed Judge Spatt that Jessie would question the witness, a bemused smile touched Moscow's lips, as if she welcomed the news. Jessie suspected that she did. Although she had not mentioned it to Elliot the night before, Jessie believed that Moscow's egotism included an overdeveloped competitiveness—directed especially toward other professional women. Their exchange outside had been Moscow's attempt to intimidate her, to establish her superiority. This morning was a chance to do it again, but only if Jessie let her.

As Jessie rose from her seat at the prosecution table, she intended to make sure that did not happen.

Crossing an expert witness was not rocket science. There were traditional points of attack—bias, lack of qualifications, inadequate preparation, contradiction by other authorities. But knowing the strategies and employing them were two different skills. Francis Wellman had named his famous book *The Art of Cross-Examination* for a reason. Anyone could ask a witness questions. The artistry was in turning those questions into weapons.

"Good morning, Dr. Moscow."

Moscow crossed her arms across her chest and presented a guarded smile. "Good morning."

"In how many trials have you testified on the subject of memory?"

"This trial makes ninety-six."

"Are you paid to testify?"

"Of course." Moscow didn't blink, though she surely knew where this line of questioning would lead. "My time is valuable. I'm compensated for my preparation, my travel expenses—"

"And your testimony."

"Yes." Her voice was confident and she sounded utterly sure of herself.

"How much are you being paid for your appearance at this trial?"

"Total? About thirty thousand dollars."

Jessie tried not to let her surprise show, but the truth was most experts hemmed and hawed at this point, unwilling to give a direct answer to the question. Moscow was so arrogant she actually smiled at the jury when she said the number. But Jessie did not see any of them smile back. "Thirty thousand dollars for two days of testimony," she said. "That's a lot of money." Several jurors nodded. Good.

Moscow's gaze was on the jury as well. Her poise did not slip, but she said, "As I mentioned, that number includes travel—"

"You traveled from Manhattan, correct?" Jessie cut off her retreat.

"Yes. I am a professor at NYU—"

"How did you travel here? By car?"

"I took the train."

"Amtrak?"

"Yes."

"How much did the train tickets cost?"

Goldhammer rose from his chair. "Is this relevant, Your Honor?"

"Goes to bias," Jessie said.

Spatt twirled his hand, urging Moscow to answer the question.

"A round trip fare on the Acela is about two-hundred dollars," Moscow said.

"And you're staying at a hotel?"

"Yes."

"Is that part of your travel expenses?"

Annoyance flashed in her eyes, but still she maintained her composure. "I understand where you're going with this, so I'll save us all some time. My travel expenses are not a significant portion of my overall fees."

"So the cost of your preparation and testimony is about thirty thousand, give or take a thousand or so in expenses."

"Yes."

"You have expensive opinions, Dr. Moscow."

"I'm the best in my field."

"That field is the science of memory?"

"Yes."

"In your ninety-six trials, did you ever testify for the prosecution?"

"No."

"So you are always hired by the defense?"

"Yes."

"Did you always charge the same amount for your testimony?"

"No. The amount has varied."

"It's increased, correct?"

Moscow paused. Her eyes narrowed. "Yes."

"In fact, every time your testimony results in a criminal defendant's acquittal, your services become more valuable, wouldn't you agree?"

"Objection!"

"Sustained," Spatt said. "You're straying a little far from the path, aren't you, Ms. Black?"

"I withdraw the question, Your Honor. Dr. Moscow, would you agree that psychology is an inexact science about which reasonable professionals might disagree?"

Her pleasant expression broke. "Psychology is no less exact than any other science." Finally, it seemed that Jessie had hit a nerve.

"So you do not agree?"

"No."

Jessie walked to the prosecution table, retrieved a thick, leather bound book, and placed it on the witness stand in front of Moscow. Moscow's eyes narrowed as she studied the cover. "You do not agree with Alan Wahl, M.D., PhD, who calls psychology a science of fraud, a fusion of manipulation and imagination, and identifies it as one of the most dangerous developments of the twentieth century?"

"Wahl was writing about psychotherapy, not psychology in general."

"Shall I read you the exact quote?"

Moscow answered her through gritted teeth, knowing the distinction would be meaningless to the jury. "No."

"In your opinion, psychology is as exact a science as, say, chemistry, correct?"

"Mine is."

"Because you're the best in your field."

"Yes."

Jessie took Wahl's book and returned it to the table. With his hand near the edge of the table, Elliot flashed her a surreptitious thumbs-up. She couldn't risk smiling with the jury's eyes on her. She picked up some papers—the transcript of Moscow's direct testimony—and returned to the center of the courtroom. A glance at the jurors confirmed what she had guessed. She had their full attention.

"Dr. Moscow, yesterday, when you explained the concept of memory to the jury, you spoke about neurons and connections in the brain. Is it accurate to say that in the field of psychology there is general agreement about that theory?"

Moscow shifted in her chair. "There are multiple theories, actually."

"So the experts in your field don't agree about how memory works?"

"As I said—"

"Are there psychologists who disagree with your explanation of memory?"

"It's not *my* explanation—"

"Yes or no?"

"Yes."

"In fact, there are some psychologists who disagree with other parts of your testimony as well, aren't there? Psychologists who do not subscribe to your negative opinion of eyewitness identification?"

"There are some. Not many."

"Is Daniel Erlinger one of them?"

"Daniel has criticized my work, yes, but—"

"Isn't Dr. Erlinger a professor of psychology at Harvard University?"

"Yes, but—"

"Well-respected in his field?"

"I suppose—"

"You suppose? I was under the impression that Daniel Erlinger was considered one of the foremost experts on repressed memory in the world."

"*Some* consider him that."

"Do you?"

"Daniel and I have our differences of opinion."

"And your opinion is all that you offered during your testimony, correct? Not an unbiased, objective overview of the multiple theories that you now admit exist?"

"I shared with the jury what I believe is the correct theory."

Jessie returned again to the prosecution table. This time she exchanged the transcript of Moscow's testimony for the transcript of the testimony of Kristen Dillard.

"Dr. Moscow, during your direct testimony, you

described in some detail your theory of unconscious transference. Can you tell the jury, as you sit there, exactly what parts of Kristen Dillard's testimony described real memories, and what parts were, as you said, distorted or invented memories?"

"I—"

Jessie dropped the transcript in front of her. "Feel free to look over the transcript. I'll give you a few minutes, if you'd like."

"Ms. Dillard's memory of her attacker's face may have been altered during her encounters with the police—"

"Yes, I understand what *may* have happened, Doctor. I'm asking if you can point out to me, in your capacity as an expert, exactly which parts of Kristen's memory are distorted or invented?"

Moscow flipped through the transcript. Jessie had intentionally printed the pages in a shrunken font. Before Moscow could focus on any one line, Jessie said, "I'm asking you a yes or no question. Can you tell me which parts are real and which are not?"

Moscow held up the transcript. "Based on this?"

"Well, have you ever met with Kristen Dillard in person?"

"No."

"You've never talked to her, questioned her on her memories, explored the night of the attack with her?"

"No."

Jessie took the transcript from her. Instead of marking it, she had memorized the locations of the passages she needed. Now, speaking clearly and loudly for the jury, she read one. "*He threw me on the bed. He yanked my pants down and turned me on my stomach.* Is that memory real, distorted, or invented?"

Moscow shook her head. Jessie was fairly sure, based on her reading of past trial transcripts, that no one had taken this tact with her before. It was risky—there was a chance that she could answer that the memory was distorted—but Jessie felt she could take the risk here. She believed that Kristen's testimony had been so compelling that the jurors would reject a direct assault on her specific words. Moscow seemed to sense this, too. For once, the expert did not have an answer prepared. "You can't just read random—"

"Real, distorted, or invented?"

"I don't know."

"I saw him from behind and to the side. I saw his hair, his right ear, both of his eyes. I got a very good look at him. Real, distorted, or invented?"

"That memory may have been distorted."

"I know that it *may* have been. I'm asking if you can tell me whether or not it was?"

"No, I can't tell you for certain."

"In other words, you are in no stronger a position than the jury to assess the credibility of Kristen Dillard's testimony, are you?"

Kate Moscow opened her mouth to answer. No words came out. Apparently, she no longer knew what to say.

Goldhammer jumped up in her defense. "Objection!" He spread his hands, pasted an incredulous look on his puffy face. "This line of questioning is argumentative, it's badgering, it calls for a legal conclusion, it's improper impeachment, it's inflammatory—"

Spatt began to laugh. He covered his mouth. "I'm sorry.

Excuse me."

"Your Honor—"

"That's alright," Jessie said. "I'm finished." She smiled at Moscow, who glared back at her with barely concealed rage. "Thank you for your time, Dr. Moscow."

Goldhammer shuffled through papers at the defense table. Ramsey leaned over and whispered something in his ear. Goldhammer shook his head, patted his client's arm. He looked calm, but Jessie could read the defense attorney well enough by now to see some panic under the surface.

"That," Elliot whispered when she sat down, "was awesome."

46.

The deputy medical examiner lifted the sheet from the girl's body, and then paused, noticing Leary's discomfort. "Sorry, Detective."

"No." Leary pulled the sheet back, forced himself to look. The refrigerated body barely resembled the girl he had met at Starbucks the day before. He covered his mouth with his hand, not remembering that he was wearing gloves. The smell of the Latex surprised him and he gagged. Dr. Martin put a hand on his arm, concerned. Leary shrugged him off. "I'm okay, Tim."

"This isn't the first body you and I have looked at together. What's wrong?"

Leary grimaced. It was true that he and Martin had spent countless hours together staring at bodies in this morgue, but Leary had never gotten used to the odors, the chill. Tiles covered the floor and ran halfway up the walls to facilitate the cleaning of various bodily fluids. Stainless steel tables and operating room sinks gleamed under the overhead lights. There were no windows—the morgue and adjacent autopsy room were located in the basement, ignored by the patients, doctors, and most of the staff of the hospital above them. The room reeked of chemicals and human remains, and made him uneasy.

"Just tell me if I was right."

Martin clucked, an annoying habit he had, and traced Rachel Pugh's bruised throat with a gloved finger. "You were. Manner of death was definitely homicide."

Leary felt his guts twist.

"Cause of death was a transected spinal cord," Martin said. "The killer broke her neck."

"I thought she was thrown down the stairs."

"She was, post-mortem. Nice way to treat a body, huh? I imagine the stairs were supposed to make us think it was an accident. You're dealing with a real gentleman."

"The killer was a man?"

Martin clucked again. "Well, I was speaking broadly. But yes, the person who did this was almost certainly a man. A large one. He held her body with one arm." Martin showed him a bruise along her chest. "And then he grabbed her chin with his other hand and jerked her head. That's what caused the contusions you see here." He pointed to parallel stripes of bruises in the shape of fingers that curved around Rachel's lower jaw.

Leary looked closer at the gray skin of her face. "Any abrasions?" He was looking for marks where the killer's fingernails may have broken her skin. He saw none.

"He wore gloves."

That meant they would find no trace evidence left by the killer's hands. "What was the mechanism of death?" Leary said, adopting the ME's jargon.

Martin hung an X-ray and flipped on the light. The image showed a skull and spinal column. Martin pointed to the bones near the top of the spinal column. "These are the cervical vertebrae—her neck bones—the top eight bones in the spinal column. They protect the spinal cord from injury. Usually, death results from a broken neck because the cord is injured at or above the fifth cervical vertebra, here." Martin pointed to one of the bones. "Injuring the cord here can affect breathing and cause asphyxiation."

Leary stared at the image. "But that's not where Rachel's spinal cord was injured." The break was clearly visible, lower than the spot where Martin pointed.

"No. Her injury is below the sixth cervical vertebra. Generally, an injury to this area of the spinal cord will not cause death because the victim's ability to breathe remains intact. Paralysis may result, but not death."

"So why did Rachel die?"

"Severity of the injury. The killer used a great deal of force. I found bleeding in the neck muscles, and the X-ray shows the extent of the violence to the bones. As I said, the spinal cord was transected—*actually torn in half*. That created a sudden loss of nerve supply to the entire body, including the heart, which caused a sharp drop in blood pressure. The medical term is *spinal shock*. This young woman died almost instantly."

Leary looked from the X-ray to the body. "Jesus." He felt sick.

"Why does this one bother you so much?" Martin was studying him, another of his irritating habits. He pushed his glasses higher on his nose. "Mark?"

Leary sighed, leaned against the cold tiled wall. "She tricked me. Pretended to be a witness to a crime. Instead of checking her story more thoroughly, I jumped the gun and called the DA's office. Somehow her name and address reached the wrong people. The irony is that she never witnessed anything. She died for nothing."

Martin's eyes widened, but he quickly regained his composure and turned back to the X-ray, yanking it down. "You shouldn't beat yourself up about it. She made a choice. It was her mistake, not yours."

"She was just a kid."

"You called the DA's office because you were doing your job. If they have some kind of leak, that's they're fault, not yours." He slid the tray back into the refrigerator and locked Rachel Pugh's body behind an anonymous stainless steel door. "Don't waste energy blaming yourself. Find the killer."

"Don't worry. I plan to."

Outside the hospital, Leary braced himself against the cold wind and pulled out his phone. He called Jessie Black.

"Hello?" she said. Despite his mood, hearing her voice lifted his spirits.

"I just met with Tim Martin."

"And?"

An ambulance roared up the street. Leary turned in the other direction, pressed the phone harder against his ear. "Murder. No question. Ramsey has a friend on the outside." After a stretch of silence, he took the phone from his ear and looked at the screen to make sure the connection had not been broken. "Jessie?"

"I'm here. I'm thinking." Another moment of silence. "Ramsey has no family, no close friends. I don't ... I don't know of any person—"

"But he exists. There's no question about that. And whoever he is, he's willing to kill to help Ramsey. When I find his motive, I'll find him. Have you learned anything about how the information leaked in the first place?"

The phone crackled. "I confronted Elliot. I don't think he was the source."

"So who else knew?"

"That's the problem. No one. You called me and—" Her voice stopped with a sharp intake of breath.

"Jessie? Are you there?"

"I'll call you back."

The call ended. Leary looked at his phone, concerned. He didn't like the tone of her voice at the end of the call. He hoped she wasn't about to do something reckless.

47.

Elliot showed his identification to the woman at the front desk of the Sporting Club at the Bellevue. He explained that a woman he needed to speak to immediately—a witness in an important trial—was inside.

"I need to talk to her now," he said, and then waited while the woman studied his ID.

Located inside the Bellevue Hotel, the Sporting Club was considered one of the nicest gyms in Philadelphia—and one of the priciest. In addition to the usual aerobic machines, classes, weight-training gear, courts, and swimming pool, the gym boasted steam rooms, saunas, whirlpools, massages, a tanning salon, and its own full-sized indoor track. Elliot had taken advantage of a free trial period while in law school, but on his government salary, he could never afford a membership. Which begged the question—how could Amber?

Just what did Amber *do*, anyway?

She kept her professional life—assuming she had one—a secret from him. She did not seem to work during the day, but he had noticed that she disappeared approximately three nights a week. He would try to call her to get together for a late dinner and her phone would forward him directly to voice mail.

Was she a hooker? She had the body for it, the tattoos. The thought made him uneasy. They always used a condom, but still—having sex with a hooker, even with protection, was like playing a game of Russian Roulette. And he and Amber had been having *a lot* of sex.

He had toyed with the idea of paying someone to follow her, but in the end, his own lack of funds had defeated that idea. He had considered asking a vice detective to look into the matter, but he didn't know any vice detectives—in the Appeals Unit, interaction with the police was minimal. Besides, he liked her. It was even possible that he loved her. He didn't want to screw things up by acting like a possessive, paranoid ass.

Then Jessie Black had accused him of sharing information with Ramsey's legal team and an even more horrible suspicion had gripped him.

What if she was a spy?

The idea seemed ludicrous, like something out of an espionage thriller. And egotistical, too—why should anyone find *him* important enough to seduce? But the more he thought about it, the more it made sense. From the first night they'd met, Amber had questioned him about his job in general and about the Ramsey case in particular.

Granted, it was his most interesting case, but still....

She had pushed him to ask Jessie for a draft of her opening argument. She had suggested that he try to get involved in the case when it went back to the trial court. She had seized on Jessie's relationship with Jack Ackerman as an opportunity for Elliot to wrest control of the case. And, when he'd told her about the new witness Leary had discovered, she had pumped him for all the information he had about Rachel Pugh.

Ridiculous. Impossible.

But he had waited outside her apartment building, shivering in the cold. He had followed her on foot to Broad and Walnut, where she had entered the Bellevue through the elevator in the parking garage. He had followed her to the gym.

The woman at the desk finished examining his identification. "I'll give you a temporary pass."

He found her in the gym, where machines and workout gear gleamed under bright lights. The first thing he noticed were the women. Almost all of them were beautiful. They could be models, but he suspected most of them were the trophy wives of the city's wealthy lawyers and businessmen. And working out on an elliptical trainer near the center of the room was *his* girlfriend, as beautiful as any of them, blonde hair pulled back in a ponytail, headphones in her ears. She wore a tank top and yoga pants that accentuated her lithe, muscular figure. The bob of her breasts was hypnotic.

Absorbed in her exercise, she did not notice him. He considered turning around, leaving. He felt ridiculous in his suit and overcoat, and he had already begun to sweat.

Rachel Pugh. He forced himself to listen to the sound of her name in his head. Her name was all he had—he had never seen her face, never heard her voice.

He crossed the room. Men and women looked up from their magazines and TV screens to stare at him. He ignored them. When he was five feet from Amber, she looked up from the readout on the elliptical trainer and saw him. Her soft lips parted as her face registered surprise. With one fluid movement, she removed her headphones and slowed the machine.

"What are you doing here?" She had to gasp to catch her breath. "What's wrong?"

"She's dead, you know."

Amber stared at him, uncomprehending.

"Rachel Pugh," he said, trying to control his rising voice. "The witness I told you about. She's dead."

"That's terrible."

Elliot reached for the control panel and stopped the machine. Her eyes flashed with annoyance.

"She was murdered, Amber. Someone attacked her in her house, broke her neck."

Other people had stopped exercising to stare at them. A couple of muscle-bound giants put down their weights, eager for the chance to step in and rescue the beautiful damsel from the weasel in the coat.

Amber lowered her voice. "Why are you telling me this?"

"Have you been sharing our conversations with other people?"

Her laugh sounded nervous to him, cornered. "What are you saying?"

"Did you tell someone about Rachel Pugh?"

"Who would I tell?"

Two men wearing Polo-style shirts bearing the Sporting Club logo appeared at the doorway. The woman from the desk was with them. She pointed at him.

The two men headed toward him.

"Amber, tell me the truth—"

"Sir, I'm going to have to ask you to leave the gym." A hand clamped onto his right shoulder. The grip was like a vise. He felt himself being tugged backward.

"He's with me," Amber said.

The second man looked at her, then at Elliot. "You didn't fill out a guest pass for him."

"I forgot."

"I'm leaving in a moment," Elliot said. The hand released his shoulder. The two men hesitated for a moment, then shuffled back toward the door. He said to Amber, "Thanks."

"Why are you here? What do you think I did?"

"Why do you ask me so many questions about the Ramsey case?"

"Because it's interesting. It's always on the news. It's cool to know someone who's part of it."

He supposed that made sense. "But have you ever repeated things I've said to other people?"

"No. I swear. You told me how confidential the information is. You think I would betray that? Don't you trust me?"

Her eyes drew together in a look of hurt that made his heart clench. "Okay. I'm sorry I barged in here." He ran a hand through his hair, pacing in front of her machine. "Rachel Pugh was killed and I thought, because of my blabbermouth, I might have had something to do with it. I was upset. But I had no right. I'll see you later." He turned, averting his gaze from hers, and started to walk away.

"Wait." She stepped down from the machine. "Aren't you going to kiss me goodbye?"

BURNOUT

"You're not mad?"

"No." She pulled him close to her. "Are you okay?"

He nodded. "Yeah. I'm just ... an asshole, I guess. Sorry."

She pressed her lips to his and he felt her tongue slide into his mouth. She smiled as she kissed him and he smiled back, all of his troubles melting. Across the room, the weight lifters returned to their workouts. Their hard expressions, Elliot thought, looked suspiciously similar to envy.

48.

Jessie used her key to open the door to Jack's apartment. She felt guilty, but determined. Talking to Leary, she had remembered something. When Leary had first discovered Rachel Pugh, he had called her, and she had answered the call in the lobby of the CJC. Right as she ended the call, Jack had surprised her. How long had he been standing behind her? Long enough to overhear the conversation? Had she spoken the girl's name?

She hated herself for thinking it, but once the idea occurred to her, she could not get it out of her head.

What if Jack was the mole?

Like his clothes, Jack's home was significantly more lavish than that of the average public defender, most of whom drew even smaller salaries than assistant DAs. He lived in what was known in Philly as a "trinity house" on a cobblestone street near Seventh and Lombard, minutes from Society Hill and Washington Square. Trinity houses consisted of one room on each of three floors joined by a small, winding staircase. Old buildings, the trinities were once the residences of the craftspeople and servants who maintained the mansions on the larger streets. Many were historical buildings, now expensive to own.

BURNOUT

She had to push hard to force her key into the lock on the front door. It felt stiff, but it turned. She glanced up and down the quiet street. There was no traffic, only the sound of the wind blowing past the brick buildings and over the cobblestones.

She glanced at her watch. 8:30 PM. Jack had invited her to a client dinner function tonight, but he had not told her the time. She hoped it would run late.

The first floor consisted of a living room and a kitchenette. The furnishings were modest. A ratty recliner with a pile of books next to it. A small TV with dust on its screen. A couch that didn't match the recliner. A coffee table. Off to the right, the kitchenette's appliances looked a hundred years old.

She climbed the tight, metal staircase to the second floor. It was his bedroom. A queen-size bed occupied most of the space. There were two mismatched dressers, a nightstand with a phone charger and an alarm clock on it. Framed art prints decorated the wall above the bed. Through an open door, she could see his bathroom.

She climbed the stairs to the top floor. This floor was more impressive, with a cathedral ceiling, bookshelves built into one wall, and a large wooden desk and swivel chair. A laptop sat closed on the desk. There was a laser printer on top of a file cabinet that matched the desk. Jessie walked to the bookshelves, looked at the spines. Legal treatises on criminal law, criminal procedure, witness impeachment, appellate advocacy. Biographies of famous lawyers—Clarence Darrow, William Cullen Bryant, Oliver Wendell Holmes, Louis Brandeis. Memoirs by F. Lee Bailey, Alan Dershowitz, Johnnie Cochran.

Jack always seemed so laid-back, like everything was a joke to him, nothing serious. It was hard to imagine him sitting here, studying Darrow and Holmes. *Calvin and Hobbes* seemed more in line with his sensibilities.

But maybe these books were from his old life. Before the brief reactive psychosis, or whatever it was that had put him in a mental hospital.

She returned to the desk, sat in the swivel chair. She stared at the computer and hesitated. What she had done already seemed terrible enough—violated his privacy, completely abused his trust—and exploring his hard drive seemed even more invasive. And what did she want to look at, anyway?

E-mails.

She heard a car rumble over the cobblestones outside and brake. She froze, poised at the edge of the chair, straining to hear a lock turn downstairs. There was no sound. A moment later, she heard the car move on.

Her heart was racing. She couldn't imagine how some of the men she'd prosecuted—burglars who'd broken into dozens, often hundreds of homes—had handled the stress. She felt on the verge of a heart attack.

Get it over with, Jess.

She opened the laptop, turned it on, and waited as the Windows screen welcomed her. Then she clicked on his e-mail program and scrolled through his recent correspondence.

Nothing related to the Ramsey trial.

An unpleasant feeling began to creep over her. The feeling was guilt.

"What am I doing?" She shook her head, disgusted with

herself.

Another car bumped along the cobblestones. She shut down the laptop, closed it. Her instinct to come here today had been as misguided as her instinct to interrogate Elliot had been. Rachel Pugh's murder was eroding her judgment. Hell, the whole Ramsey situation was messing with her head.

She descended the narrow metal staircase. All Jack had ever done was shower her with affection, and she had been too wrapped up in the Ramsey trial to return it. And look at her now—she'd broken into his home, searched it for evidence. Incredible!

"Why am I such a—"

The front door opened downstairs and heavy footsteps clomped into the house. She heard two voices—men continuing a conversation as they shrugged out of their coats. She heard snippets—"cold as hell"—"nearing the end"—"glad when it's over." One of the voices was Jack's. The other sounded familiar, but she couldn't place it.

She crept off of the staircase, careful to make as little noise as possible on the metal steps and railing. The conversation continued below her. She heard the word *Ramsey*, heard the word *Dillard*. Then she heard her own name.

Her heart seemed to freeze in her chest.

That's when she placed the second voice. Gil Goldhammer.

Dinner function, my ass. Son of a bitch!

She crouched near the stairwell, listening. Judging by the sounds, Goldhammer was standing in the living room. Jack had walked to the kitchenette and was pouring drinks. She could hear the ice crackle in the glasses.

Goldhammer's voice sounded anxious, nothing like his courtroom bravado. "Did you have anything to do with that death? No. Wait. It's better if you don't tell me."

Footsteps. Ice and liquid swishing in glasses. She imagined Jack passing one to the puffy-faced defense attorney. "Of course I had nothing to do with it." His voice was low, tight. She had to strain to hear him. "Did you?"

"Don't be asinine."

"Then don't accuse me."

"I'm very uncomfortable with this whole situation," Goldhammer said. She heard ice cubes clink as the men sipped from their drinks.

"You're *uncomfortable*? A girl is dead, Gil. An innocent girl!"

"I never thought anything like this would happen," Goldhammer said. "The risks are getting too high."

"The risks? What exactly are the risks for you? Last I checked, I'm the one who had to pretend to be insane, watch my career go down the toilet."

"Come on, Jack. Pretend? Who do you think you're kidding? I've met Snickers bars less nutty than you."

"Well, uncomfortable or not, there's no backing out now," Jack said.

"I can't believe I allowed you to get me involved in this," Goldhammer said.

A silence followed. Quietly, Jack said, "We both know who was responsible for that girl's death."

"Bullshit. You have proof? No? Then relax. No one else does, either."

"I just want this to end," Jack said.

"We're almost there."

"Thank God."

Another quiet moment as they drank.

"What about Jessie cross-examining Kate?" Goldhammer said. She heard a hint of laughter in his voice, then a creak of springs as he sat on a couch. "Hell of a show."

"She was something, wasn't she?"

"You said there wouldn't be any surprises."

"I said I'd try to minimize them," Jack said.

Goldhammer sighed. "Hopefully she didn't hurt our case too much. I'm going back to the hotel. I need some sleep. I'm writing my closing this weekend." There was another creak of springs, and a quiet grunt, as he stood up again.

"You're not going to call Ramsey to the stand?" Jack said.

Goldhammer barked a laugh. "After watching your girlfriend savage my expert witness? Are you kidding? And Kate is a pro. If I put Ramsey up there, I don't even want to think what Black would do to him."

"I think he should have the opportunity to tell his own story," Jack said.

"Well, Jack, that's why I get paid the big bucks and you get psychotherapy. I'll see you on Monday."

"Alright. I'll see you."

Jessie heard a soft thump—she imagined Jack giving Goldhammer a friendly pat on the back as he took the empty glass from the lawyer's hand. The front door opened with a creak. Wind whistled into the house. A moment later, the door closed.

Jack cursed under his breath. Footsteps moved past the staircase. Two glasses clinked in the basin of the sink. Water surged briefly. Then the footsteps moved close to the stairs again.

Jessie heard the metal step at the bottom of the staircase clang beneath Jack's foot. He was coming upstairs.

She turned, scanned the bedroom. *Don't panic.* There were a few places to hide—the closet, the bathroom—but if he'd just come home from a meeting, either of those places might be his first destination. That left the bed. Moving with as little noise as possible, she crawled underneath it.

The space between the hardwood floor and the box spring was tight. She lay on her back, her nose inches from the dark cloth covering the bottom of the bed frame. Jack's footsteps seemed impossibly loud as he climbed the stairs, the metal squealing at every step. He stepped from the stairs to the floor and flicked a light switch. The room brightened and she saw his shadow on the hardwood floor near the bed. She held her breath.

Two feet, wearing socks, stopped near her shoulder at the edge of the bed. She twisted her neck until she could see them—black and thick, pointed away from the bed. He sighed and the dark cloth above her lurched downward until it brushed her face. The rows of coil springs inside the frame pressed against her cheek.

It's okay. Breathe. You can breathe.

During her rush to slide beneath the bed, the strap of her purse had slid off her shoulder. Carefully turning her head, she saw the black leather bag peeking out from under the bed, no more than six inches from his left foot. She hooked two fingers under the strap and yanked the purse out of sight.

If Jack noticed, he gave no indication. He continued to sit, his body still, his sock-clad feet unmoving.

He sighed again. The springs shifted under his weight, extending and recoiling as he squirmed on the mattress. Jessie realized a moment later that he had reached for something in his pocket—his phone—when he sat still again and tapped the screen.

"Come on, Jessie."

She froze. Waited for his face to appear in the space between the bed and the floor, a cold smile on his face and a gun or a knife in his hand. But all he did was say her name again, his voice sounding irritated this time. "Jessie, pick up the phone."

He was calling her.

Her mouth opened in silent panic. Dust from the cloth of the box spring drifted onto her tongue.

Her phone was in her purse.

She still had two fingers of her right hand hooked around the strap. Frantic, she tugged the purse toward her, reeled in the strap like a fishing line until the leather corner of the purse bounced against her hand.

With her left hand, she groped for the zipper. She could see nothing except Jack's sock-clad feet and the hardwood floor leading to the staircase. Slowly, cringing at the noise it made, she slid the zipper along its track.

It stopped halfway. She tugged harder, but it would not budge. She must have trapped some of the lining in the zipper's teeth.

She yanked at the zipper. It was stuck. Above her, Jack drew one leg up onto the mattress. More dust dropped from the bottom of the box spring into her mouth.

Breathe.

Her hands scurried over the purse, examined it. She had zipped open a hole of no more than three inches. Not enough room for her hand. She thrust three fingers inside. The teeth of the zipper raked her skin. Her knuckles burned. She wriggled the fingers inside the bag. Fished past tissues and a pen and a pack of gum and a box of Altoids. The pad of her index finger brushed the edge of the phone, then slipped away.

From the tiny speaker of the phone pressed to Jack's ear, she heard a ring.

In seconds, her own phone would ring in response.

Her index finger found the phone again. This time, she clamped the phone between her index and middle fingers and pulled. When the top of the phone cleared the zipper, she grabbed it, and yanked it out of the bag. She thumbed the power button, holding it until the phone silently shut down.

Barely audible, the speaker of Jack's phone rang again. After a few more rings, she heard—faintly—her own voice mail greeting.

Jack leaned forward.

"Hey, Jess. It's me. Again. Please call me back." He paused, then added, "I really miss you."

Bastard.

He ended the call. The dark cloth lifted away from Jessie's face as he stood up.

From her narrow vantage point, she watched him undress. He danced out of his khakis like a boy, undid the top button of his shirt and pulled it over his head. The T-shirt next, the boxer shorts, the socks. Naked, he padded toward the bathroom.

The door closed. Beyond it, she heard water pound into the bathtub. Now was her chance.

Jessie slid out of her hiding place, careful not to disturb the clothing he had tossed around the room. Steam escaped from under the door of the bathroom, warming the air. She resisted the urge to bash the door open, grab him by the throat, and drown him in his own tub.

She shoved her phone past the stuck zipper of her purse and hurried down the stairs. She had come here looking for a traitor, and she had found one. It was time to leave.

Jessie had parked her Accord a block away from Jack's cobblestone lane. She dug the keys out of her purse through the three-inch opening of her stuck zipper, raking fresh scratches into her fingers. That pain was nothing next to the thought that Jack had been playing her for a fool for months.

Sliding behind the wheel, she replayed the last ten minutes in her mind. Unless she had left something behind or out of place—and she was almost positive she hadn't—Jack would never know she had been there.

She suppressed the urge to punch the steering wheel. It wasn't so much his betrayal that infuriated her as her own gullibility. She had thought she was smart, but all it had taken was a charming smile and a few corny compliments to turn her into a sucker.

She twisted the key in the ignition, got the heater going. Warm air puffed against her open palms as she held them up to the vents. The engine thrummed.

She did not want to go home. Not yet. She needed to

talk. She needed to be with someone who would listen, and care.

Only half-surprised by the person who came to mind, she shifted the car into drive.

49.

"Jack Ackerman? Are you kidding?" Leary paced in front of the bookcase in his one-bedroom apartment.

Her mouth and throat felt dry. She swallowed. Finally, she said, "I'm sorry. I didn't know where else to go, and I need your help."

Tears were gathering in her eyes and she wasn't sure why—whether they were tears of anger, despair, or relief. Because she was feeling all of those emotions right now.

"Okay," Leary said. He stopped pacing, ran a hand through his hair, and sighed. "Tell me what happened."

She took a deep breath. "I don't know. I thought there was something between us. Apparently it was all bullshit and he's been manipulating me, spying on me, God knows what else."

"You slept with him?"

She looked up sharply. "What does that have to do with anything?"

Leary turned away. For a brief moment, she saw his eyes squint shut, his jaw bunch. He rubbed his face with his hand and the expression vanished. "Okay, so why would he want to help Goldhammer and Ramsey? What's his motive?"

Like most cops, Leary had a tendency to retreat into procedure and jargon. Jessie sighed. "Not everything has a rational motive."

"Do you think Ackerman is financing Ramsey's defense? Paying Goldhammer's bills?"

"I don't know. I hadn't thought of that." It seemed plausible. He'd managed to buy a nice house, and his stint at Wooded Hill Hospital could not have been cheap. He had money, probably from his family.

"I'll tail him this weekend, see where he goes, who he talks to. Okay?"

She nodded. "Thanks." She tried to open her purse for a tissue, then remembered the stuck zipper and cursed.

"What's wrong?" Leary took the bag and held it under the light. He peered at the zipper's teeth. Calmly, with one thumb, he tugged the interior fabric, stretching it away from the metal. With the thumb and index finger of his other hand, he yanked the zipper. It popped forward, moving smoothly across its track. He handed it back to her.

"They teach you that at the police academy?" she said.

For the first time since she'd arrived at his door, he smiled. "It's my solemn duty as a member of the Philadelphia Police Department to serve, protect, and fix women's handbags." His face became serious again. "I'll call you in a few days and let you know what I find. For now, you need to play along, or we'll lose whatever advantage we have. Can you do that?"

Jessie felt a flash of rage. "I can do whatever's necessary to nail that prick."

Leary nodded approvingly. "Then let's get him."

50.

The Lexus idled in Woody's brother's driveway, but despite the heat blowing against her face, Amber felt a chill. Michael's lawn was layered in a thin crust of snow, through which dead, brown blades of grass poked. Amber, in the passenger seat, crossed her arms over her chest. Woody was talking to her—yelling at her—but she refused to look at him until he grabbed her roughly by the chin and forced her to face him.

"Don't you ever, *ever* ignore me when I'm talking to you."

She thrust her chin in the air. She was sick of his bullshit. His interrogations, his bullying. "Fuck you."

He slapped her, hard, before the word was fully out of her mouth. Her face stung and tears jumped to her eyes. She could feel her lower lip begin to swell where his index and middle fingers had struck it. She raised a hand to touch her face.

"How did he find out?" The question boomed inside the Lexus. "What did you do that tipped him off, you stupid cunt?"

She should have known better than to tell Woody about her confrontation with Elliot at the gym. But during the drive to his brother's house, when he'd asked her all the usual questions about Elliot and the trial, she had been unable to conceal it from him.

No, that's a load of shit. You told him because you knew it would mean the end of your little mission, the end of your usefulness as a whore.

He was staring at her. His eyes were feral. Something in her stomach did a somersault as the certainty overcame her that he had read her thoughts. "I swear to God, I didn't say anything. I didn't do anything." She blurted the words, sputtering, her eyes unable to resist glancing at his right hand. "He figured it out himself. He figured it out when Rachel Pugh—"

The hand moved. There was no room in the car to dodge the blow, but she jerked her head away from him, lessening its impact. Not that it mattered much. Her face still throbbed from his first slap. She barely registered the new pain.

"Don't say that name. Forget you ever heard it."

"Did you—" She was surprised by the steadiness of her own voice. She wasn't crying, wasn't sobbing, wasn't begging him not to hurt her. She met Woody's eyes and said, "You killed her, didn't you?"

He raised his hand again, but this time she blocked him. Their wrists collided with a *smack* that sent waves of pain reverberating down her arm, but she kept her eyes locked with his.

He didn't need to answer her question. His confession was written all over his face. In the guilty way he averted his eyes. In the rabbit-quick jerks of his fingernails as he scratched his goatee.

"If you keep staring at me like that I'm going to hit you

again." The roar had faded from his voice. His threat sounded hollow. For the moment, at least, she had beaten him back.

But she wouldn't be able to beat him back forever.

She had loved him. As recently as one month ago, she had loved him so much that the only thing in the world she had wanted for Christmas was an engagement ring.

He reached for her chin, cupped it in his hand, gently this time, and studied her face. He pulled his wallet from the back pocket of his jeans. "Your face is going to bruise. You might have to skip a few nights at the club." He handed her a wad of cash. She took it. "When he asks, tell Elliot you slipped on an icy sidewalk and smacked your face against the ground."

"Wait. You mean ... you're sending me back?"

"The trial's not over yet. I still need your help." After a moment, he added, "I'm sorry."

"But he knows."

"You said he believed you when you denied it."

"I said I *thought* he believed me. And even if he did, he's still going to be suspicious if I start asking questions about the trial again."

"But he won't be suspicious if you suddenly dump him?"

He cut the engine. Apparently the conversation was over. She had been given her marching orders and he expected her to obey them like a good little soldier.

"Woody."

The truth, although she would never confess it to the monster in the seat beside her, was that she had actually started to like Elliot Williams. Not in a sexual way—fucking him was a chore—but she had begun to see him as a person, a goodhearted nerd whose biggest faults were arrogance and gullibility, faults dwarfed by those of most of the men she'd encountered over the years. She didn't like scamming him.

Woody opened the door, slid halfway out of the Lexus. "Michael's waiting."

"I'll stay in the car."

"No you won't. He wants to have a look at you."

The story of her life. She stared at him for a moment, then opened the passenger-side door and followed him to the house.

Amber once resented Michael's nurse, Natalie Baron, who couldn't seem to help mooning over Woody with the eyes of a lovesick twelve-year-old girl. Today she didn't mind at all. She wished Natalie all the luck in the world with her conquest of the psycho's heart.

"How is he?" Woody's whole body seemed to stiffen the moment he and Amber met Natalie in the foyer. He licked his lips.

"Not great." Natalie followed his gaze as it slipped toward the dark staircase "He seems comfortable, though. He hasn't been in a lot of pain."

"Good." He started up the stairs. Natalie followed closely behind. Alone in the foyer, Amber considered running. But where would she go? It wasn't like she had a secret identity, or the knowledge and resources to acquire one. Wherever she went, she would have to use an ATM or a credit card. She would have to get a job and give her employer her social security number. Tracking her down would pose no problem for a guy like Woody. And once he did, what would stop him from killing her, breaking her neck like he broke Rachel Pugh's?

His voice boomed down from the upstairs hallway. "Amber, come on."

She walked up the steps.

The first thing she noticed when she entered Michael's bedroom was not the medical equipment surrounding the bed. It was not the jug of urine on the nightstand. Nor was it the laptop computer tethered to the wall by an Ethernet cable that eerily mimicked the tube tethering Michael's emaciated right arm to an IV drip. All of these things she noticed, but only after her eyes had zeroed in on the chessboard. It was one of those nice sets made of marble, with beautifully carved pieces. The board had been placed on the seat of a chair near the bed, the pieces arranged in an unfinished game. Propped on one of the chair's armrests, dog-eared and worn, was the beginner's guide to chess that Amber had given Woody for Christmas.

"You read it," she said.

Both Woody and Natalie turned to her, confused. Then Woody followed her gaze to the book. He frowned. "I learned the rules, but he still beats me every time."

Michael smiled with effort, his gaze seeming to float toward but not focus on Amber's face. "I ... always beaten him. Sports, school...." A dry laugh sifted from his parted lips.

Amber had never liked Michael. The strange hold he had on his younger brother was creepy. Had anyone else called Woody a loser, Woody would never have stood for it. But his only response to Michael was a loving smile. He leaned over the bed, gently touched one bony shoulder, and kissed his brother's cheek. His lips made a scratchy sound, as if he'd kissed paper.

Amber shuddered. She couldn't help it. A tremble began at the base of her spine—near the tattoo at the small of her back—and shot upward to the cleft between her shoulder blades.

Natalie caught the movement in the corner of her eyes and frowned with disapproval. Amber ignored her. At this point, the nurse's opinion of her was just about her lowest possible concern on a very long list.

"Woody." Michael's voice had decayed to such a low rasp that his brother had to practically touch his ear to the man's mouth to hear him. Natalie disappeared into the hallway, leaving Amber to stand alone and watch the discussion like a scene on a muted TV.

In the months before Christmas, observing Michael's condition had always filled her with sorrow and fear about the fragility of the human body. Now she wondered if the man really lacked the strength to speak—or if he and Woody were simply being secretive.

Was Michael involved in the seventeen-year-old girl's murder?

Of course he was. Michael's in charge. Has been from the start. Woody's nothing but his stooge.

She watched them whisper to each other. In her line of work, Amber met plenty of assholes—met them on a nightly basis. But these two, Woody Butler and his bedridden brother, they took the prize. The longer she watched them, the stronger her intuition became that she was in trouble. Real, major, life-threatening, up shit creek without a paddle trouble. If she didn't do something soon, she was going to end up as dead as Rachel Pugh.

And no one will care when your body turns up. A dead stripper. Good riddance.

Elliot. Elliot would care.

Her fingers itched to call him right now. Tell him everything. He worked at the DA's office. He knew other prosecutors, cops—people who could protect her. People who could stop Woody and Michael.

As if he had somehow sensed her betrayal, Michael's eyes—yellow instead of white around the irises—shifted from his brother to her. "Come here." The rasp had gained volume, and with the volume, authority.

She stepped closer to the bed, Woody moving clumsily out of her way. Michael raised a bony arm toward her. His hand trembled at the end of it. Reluctantly, she placed hers within its grasp. It felt powdery, like the old men at the club whose fingers brushed her skin when they pushed dollar bills into her garter.

Michael squeezed her fingers with surprising strength. "I appreciate what you're doing for me, Amber."

She swallowed. "You're welcome." She knew her voice sounded nervous, scared. Both Michael and Woody studied her more closely.

"Rachel ... Pugh was a liar. Did you know that?"

She shook her head. Michael had not released her fingers, but his grip slackened. Slowly, careful not to offend him, she withdrew them from his grasp.

Woody said, "Michael," but the sick man silenced him with a glare.

"Rachel intended ... to perjure herself. That's what the police learned after she died. It's ... sad, what happened to her.

But ... it's justice, too. Every person is entitled to a fair trial."

"Elliot says Ramsey's definitely guilty."

Michael looked up at Woody, questioning.

"Elliot Williams. The assistant DA prosecuting the case. The guy Amber's been ... watching for us."

Michael nodded, and a small smile played across his lips. He grunted and leaned toward her, as if he wanted to share a secret. Then he stopped himself. To Woody, he said, "Can I trust her?"

"No."

Disappointed, Michael relaxed back against his pillow. "Maybe some other time ... I'll tell you more."

"I think it's time we left," Woody said. "I have a meeting to get to."

Michael's eyes swam in his direction. "Remember what ... I told you."

"I will. And you stay healthy."

In response to that sentiment, Michael coughed out a grim laugh.

51.

There were a lot of things Leary would rather do on a Sunday evening than tail a jackass public defender—or ex-public defender, as the case may be—all over Philadelphia. As he sat in an unmarked car, watching Ackerman withdraw cash from an ATM at a TD Bank on 19th and Market, a whole list of fun activities occurred to him. A beer with the guys. A movie rental and a pizza. Even a phone call to his mother would be better than this.

But who was he kidding? He had a thing for Jessie, and had ever since that damn night they'd slipped out of a bar together and into his unmarked cruiser. It had been dumb, casual sex. He had wanted more. She hadn't. He just wasn't her type.

And apparently, Jack Ackerman was.

The thought made him want to puke. He shifted the car out of park when Ackerman emerged from the bank. The lawyer didn't even glance at the street as he walked up the sidewalk toward Chestnut. Leary drove past him in traffic, then circled around and picked up his trail again walking east.

When Ackerman met another man at the entrance to a bar between Chestnut and 15th, Leary's work suddenly got interesting. At first he could not remember where he had seen the tall, broad-shouldered man with the goatee before, but a moment later his brain placed him as the guy Leary had seen visiting Dr. Eduard Urlyapov at the hospital. The man whose tightly coiled, malevolent energy had been palpable to Leary as they stood side by side at the nurse's station.

Leary found a parking space and debated following the pair into the bar. The man with the goatee might not recognize him, but Ackerman certainly would. If Ackerman spotted him, he would know that Jessie was on to him.

But if he didn't follow them inside, he'd have no chance of eavesdropping on their conversation.

He popped the glove compartment and grabbed the baseball cap he kept there—an unremarkable Phillies cap. Fitting this onto his head, he rooted around for the other half of his makeshift disguise, a cheap pair of reading glasses. The lenses had a limited magnification which would give him a headache if he wore them for too long, but the frames were effective at changing his appearance. Not a foolproof disguise—not even close—but if Ackerman and his friend weren't looking for a tail, they were unlikely to pick him out of a crowd.

Assuming the bar was crowded.

Let's hope.

He reached under his jacket and withdrew his 9-mm pistol, popped the cartridge to make sure it was fully loaded, then rammed it home. He did not expect violence, but he left the safety off. There was something about the man from the hospital—Mr. Goatee—that made this feel like a rational precaution.

* * *

BURNOUT

Blake's Tavern was not exactly crowded, but it was dark, smoky, and there was a free stool at the bar that would conceal Leary behind a fat trucker type. Ackerman and Mr. Goatee sat together at a small table, the one farthest from the windows. A waitress took their orders. She put one hand on her hip and laughed. Ackerman was flirting with her.

The icy stare Mr. Goatee turned on Ackerman seemed to remind him that they weren't here to pick up chicks. The lawyer's smile faltered and the waitress moved on to another table, where a gaggle of middle-aged women were talking excitedly.

"What can I get you, bud?"

A shadow fell over him. Leary turned away from his quarry and looked up at a hulking bartender. If he had noticed Leary spying on his clientele, he didn't seem to give a shit. The smile on his ruddy face looked friendly.

Leary smiled back. "Just a Coke, please."

"Coming right up."

Ackerman and Mr. Goatee were leaning close to each other over the table. If they were trying to be discreet, they were failing; their body language screamed *secret meeting*. Whatever they were discussing, the conversation looked unpleasant. Ackerman was practically spitting his words through gritted teeth. Mr. Goatee, listening in silence, looked ready to wring the lawyer's neck.

Or break it.

Unconsciously, Leary's hand brushed the butt of his pistol through his jacket. He needed to know who Mr. Goatee was. When the waitress returned to their table with two beer bottles, a plan began to form in his mind.

Mr. Goatee tilted his bottle—Yeungling Lager—to his lips. His thumb pressed against the glass just above the label, leaving—Leary hoped—a pristine fingerprint.

The bartender returned with Leary's Coke. "You sure you don't want some Jack along with this?"

"I've already got more Jack than I can stomach."

"Huh?"

"I'm all set, thanks."

"If you change your mind—"

"You'll be the first to know." The bartender shrugged and headed for the other end of the bar where two new patrons had just seated themselves.

Now Mr. Goatee was doing the talking and Ackerman was the one who looked ready to wring necks. Half-standing, his ass in the air, Mr. Goatee thrust his index finger in Ackerman's face. The women from the next table turned to look at them. When he realized he was drawing attention, Mr. Goatee settled down. Ackerman shook his head, looking disgusted.

Leary felt disgusted himself. He took a swig of Coke. He could accept the fact that Jessie had rejected him. He could even accept that she might find other men more appealing. But Ackerman was going to pay for messing with her heart, not to mention her body. And if he found out that these jerks were responsible for Rachel Pugh's death, he would hound them to their dying fucking breaths.

He waited. Drank his Coke as the argument at the table died down. A few minutes later, Ackerman put some money on the table and stood up. Leary turned his face in the opposite direction as Ackerman walked past the bar on his way to the door.

Apparently Mr. Goatee did not mind drinking alone. He finished his beer slowly, a thoughtful expression on his face. Then he added more money to the bills Ackerman had left and stood to leave.

Leary waited as long as he dared after the door closed behind Mr. Goatee. A busboy emerged from the kitchen. Leary slipped off his stool, walked to the table, pulled a baggie from his jacket, and, as nonchalantly as possible, took the Yeungling bottle before the busboy was halfway across the room.

Five minutes later, he was back in the unmarked car studying his prize under the dome light. His satisfaction dimmed as he carefully turned the bottle under the light.

No prints.

Leary was sure he had not been spotted. That meant that Mr. Goatee wiped his prints habitually, probably with a shirt sleeve. And that meant he had something to hide.

Leary peered through the windshield at the dark city street. Focused on the bottle, he had not followed the man out of Blake's Tavern, had not even looked out the window to see his general direction. He had no idea who he was or where to find him.

Damn it. He'd fucked up.

52.

Jessie arrived at a courthouse packed with reporters. The mob lent the corridors of the CJC an excited buzz. The media knew that today might well be the climax of the Ramsey trial—the defense might rest, the trial might end, the jury might even reach a verdict—but that it was equally possible that Goldhammer might draw things out for another week, eliciting tedious testimony from character witnesses or, even worse from a news standpoint, more experts. The best case scenario for them, of course, would be if Ramsey took center stage and testified in his own defense. That would give the talking heads enough content for days. Jessie did not share their uncertainty. She strode through the media throng with the confidence that there would be no surprises for her. She had inside information, straight from the horse's—or jackass's—mouth. Jack and Goldhammer had clearly indicated that Ramsey was not going to testify. That meant the trial would end today.

She joined Elliot at the prosecution table. "How are you holding up?"

"Not bad, considering." His body seemed to vibrate as he arranged and then rearranged his files. Both his exhaustion and his excitement were evident in every move. They had worked from dawn to dusk the day before, crafting a closing argument that would hammer the nails into Ramsey's coffin. "I guess my moment in the spotlight is finally here."

The thought of Elliot delivering the closing argument instead of her made her nervous, but she'd seen his abilities improve over the course of the trial, and knew he could handle it. He turned in his chair as the courtroom door opened. "Here comes Goldhammer," he said.

The defense attorney strutted toward them, his entourage of lawyers and assistants trailing behind him. His suit looked expensive—even more so than the others he'd worn during the trial—and the expression on his puffy face was smug.

"He looks pretty confident." Elliot's voice barely rose above a breath.

Goldhammer stopped in the aisle between the tables, smiling cheerfully. "Jessie. Elliot, good morning."

"You look pleased with yourself," Jessie said.

"I'm pleased that this trial is almost finished. And that, with this victory, you'll be seeing a lot more of me in the Philadelphia courts." He winked at her, no doubt anticipating a victory that would serve as a prime advertisement for the city's drug kingpins and gang leaders.

"You haven't won yet, Gil."

"Not yet, no."

"Are you planning to rest your case today?" Jessie strained to sound innocent.

"Yes. After I've called my final witness."

"What final wit—"

As if on cue, the side door opened and two sheriff's deputies escorted Ramsey into the courtroom. His entrance was accompanied by the usual murmur in the gallery, but he did not look in that direction. He walked straight to his lawyer.

"Are you ready?" Goldhammer asked him.

"I hope so," Ramsey said with uncharacteristic nervousness. The sudden vulnerability that flooded his features almost made Jessie sympathize with him. Almost.

"Wait a second. He's testifying?" Jessie said.

"You look surprised." Goldhammer adjusted Ramsey's tie. His voice was casual. "Were you expecting something different?"

Elliot's earlier excitement had turned into something more alarming—panic. He leaned close to her ear. "I thought you said there was no way he would take the stand—"

"I was wrong."

She ruffled some papers, tried to ignore Goldhammer's knowing smirk. She rearranged the documents on the table, for no reason other than to look busy. To look prepared.

"I'll cross," she said.

"No, I'll do it."

"Elliot, we didn't prepare for this." She had been so damn sure, after overhearing Jack and Goldhammer, that Ramsey would not take the stand, that she had focused all of her energy—and Elliot's—on the closing argument.

"No, listen. I know you said he wouldn't testify, but I worried he might surprise us, so after I got home last night I studied his statement to the police. I reread the transcripts of his trial and the PCRA hearing. I'm prepared to cross him."

Jessie was stunned. She knew Elliot had come a long way as a trial lawyer since she'd first met him, but she was still impressed by his initiative. "Are you sure?"

BURNOUT

He nodded. "I can do it."

She took a deep breath and nodded. "Okay. I trust you."

The packed courtroom was absolutely silent as Frank Ramsey took the stand. Even Judge Spatt leaned forward to peer more closely at the defendant. The man accused of being the infamous Family Man, the man who, when he'd first been arrested over a year ago, had been a gruff and physically imposing fireman, still retained much of his physique. But even though his muscular frame filled his designer suit, his face showed the effects of his time served in prison. Two haunted brown eyes glared from sockets in cadaverous gray flesh. No fancy suit could disguise the fact that Frank Ramsey had been to death row and back, and bore the scars of his journey.

"Do you swear to tell the truth, the whole truth, and nothing but the truth, so help you God?"

Without hesitation, he said, "I do."

53.

"Mr. Ramsey, I know it's been difficult for you to sit here in court with us," Goldhammer said, "remaining silent as the prosecutors accused you of unthinkable crimes. Now you will have the opportunity to tell the jury your side of the story."

Ramsey leaned forward, looked at the jurors. From her seat at the prosecution table, Jessie could see their faces. Some looked angry and judgmental, some skeptical, some unreadable—but none friendly. Goldhammer's tricks had failed. Kate Moscow had failed. Certainly Ramsey, whom she knew to be a less than articulate speaker, would fail as well. He had lost his first trial and he would lose this one, too, for one reason.

He was guilty.

"Mr. Ramsey, did you kill Robert Dillard?" Goldhammer stepped closer to the jury, his body language implying that he was on their side, an aid in their quest for truth.

Ramsey inclined his body toward the jurors. When he spoke, his voice was strong and sure. "No, I did not."

Goldhammer glanced at the jury, then asked Ramsey, "Did you rape and kill Erin Dillard?"

"No."

"Did you rape and attempt to kill Kristen Dillard?"

"I never even saw her before my arrest."

"Who arrested you?"

Ramsey's face seemed to darken as he recalled the experience. "A homicide detective named Mark Leary. He and a bunch of cops showed up at my apartment early in the morning. Around six in the morning."

"On the day after the murders were committed, correct?"

Ramsey shrugged. "That's what I'm told."

"But you don't know?"

"I don't know anything about those crimes except what I've been told by the cops and lawyers, and what I read."

Elliot pushed his legal pad in front of her. Scrawled on the first line was a thought that had occurred to her seconds before: *Scripted.* Goldhammer's direct examination felt rehearsed. Judging by the dubious looks of several of the jurors, the canned nature of Ramsey's testimony had not escaped their notice either.

"What happened?" Goldhammer said.

"There was a knock on my door. I opened it. Leary and some cops were standing in the hallway with my landlord, Mrs. Samsel. She and I had always gotten along—she thought I was a hero ever since learning what I did for a living—but now she was looking at me like I was some kind of monster. That's what scared me, more than the cops at my door. The look on Mrs. Samsel's face."

"What happened next?"

"They put me in a car, no handcuffs or anything, and took me to the police station. Said they needed to ask me some questions. I agreed. Then they took me to an interrogation room. Put me in a metal chair. And the detective, Leary, reads me my rights."

"Did you invoke your right to an attorney?"

Ramsey shook his head. "I didn't think I needed one. I hadn't done anything."

"What happened next?"

"Leary wanted to know where I was the night before."

"And by the way, Mr. Ramsey, where were you during the time the crimes were committed?"

"I was at home in my apartment watching TV."

"Not a very good alibi."

Ramsey nodded grimly. "If I could go back in time, I would try to get a better social life."

A few of the jurors smiled at this, giving Jessie a moment of unease. She had been fighting him in the legal system for almost two years, and in that time she had never known Frank Ramsey to be charming. Had Goldhammer scripted his jokes, too? No, more likely that had been Jack's touch—he was the master of the self-deprecating one-liner.

"I worked a day shift at the fire station. Then I went home. I microwaved a Swanson Hungry-Man sirloin steak dinner and ate it out of the tray while I watched basketball. Then I went to sleep."

"And yet, you were sitting right there next to me"—Goldhammer pointed to the vacant defense table—"when Kristen Dillard identified you to the jury as the man who terrorized her family. Can you explain that?"

Ramsey shook his head. If the look of misery on his face was phony, it was certainly convincing. "I can't explain it, other than maybe Dr. Moscow's theories. All I know is I never saw Kristen Dillard or her parents before the morning I was arrested. I did not rape or kill anybody."

"What was your job, before your arrest?"

"I was a firefighter."

Jessie rose. "Objection. Relevance."

Judge Spatt shook his head. "I'm going to allow Mr. Ramsey some leeway, considering the stakes."

"That's a very noble profession," Goldhammer said. "Very brave. You must have faced some dangerous situations."

Ramsey nodded. "I did."

"Did you save any lives as a firefighter?"

"I rescued seven women in a nursing home fire once. I pulled twin six-year-old girls from a fire in an apartment building just a few months before my arrest. I've saved lots of lives."

"Before your arrest, had you ever had any trouble with the police?"

"No."

"Not even as a kid?"

"No. I've always respected the law."

"After what you've been through for the last two years, it must be getting pretty hard to do that."

Ramsey shook his head. "I have faith that the system will work and I will be acquitted."

Jessie wanted to groan. If Ramsey's testimony continued in this melodramatic vein she could sell the transcript as a movie-of-the-week. But a few of the jurors were watching Ramsey with less antagonistic expressions. Elliot would have his work cut out for him.

54.

Goldhammer took his seat, and Elliot rose to face Ramsey. As he strode to the center of the courtroom, the jurors watched him with expectant gazes. Jessie pulled her legal pad close to her and gripped her pen.

"Hello, Mr. Ramsey." Elliot's words, loud and clear, flowed without the "ums" and "ahs" that had plagued it during his previous bouts of lawyering. His eyes maintained contact with the killer's, devoid of fear. Jessie relaxed, her hand unclenching from around her pen, the tension flowing out of her shoulders. She allowed herself a quiet sigh.

Ramsey must have heard her. His eyes flicked in her direction. The hatred she saw in them was nothing new, no different than the hundreds of other angry glares launched at her from defendants and witnesses throughout her career. She didn't let it faze her. Seconds later, jolted by Elliot's first question, his eyes snapped away.

"Mr. Ramsey, you have not produced one single witness to corroborate your alibi. I suppose you expect the jury to take your word for it?" Elliot said.

"You never watched TV alone? It's a crime to be single? To not have a lot of friends?"

"I'll ask the questions, if you don't mind."

"Yes, I hope the jury will take my word for it." Ramsey looked at the jury box. "I was home, alone, all night during—"

"You mentioned that you're single, Mr. Ramsey?"

"You know I am."

"But you were married once, weren't you?"

Ramsey's jaw twitched. "Yes."

"You were married to Coral Anne Ramsey?"

"Lennon. She remarried."

"I see. And did she leave you? Or did you leave her?"

Goldhammer lunged from his seat. "Mr. Ramsey has been divorced for ten years. How is this relevant, Your Honor?"

"It's not," Spatt said. "The jury will please disregard the line of questioning—"

"She left me," Ramsey said.

Spatt's mouth clamped shut. He turned to Ramsey, looked as if he might chastise him, then seemed to think better of it. Apparently his scorn was reserved for members of the bar.

"Why?" Elliot said.

"Sidebar, Your Honor!" Goldhammer said.

Jessie had to suppress a grin watching the defense attorney's puffy face redden. She understood his dilemma. By prying into the details of Ramsey's marriage, Elliot was attempting to introduce damning character evidence that would put Ramsey in a bad light.

Trusting Elliot, she did not attempt to join the lawyers at

Judge Spatt's podium. She could easily imagine the exchange anyway. Goldhammer would argue that Elliot's questions were improper and would unfairly bias the jury. Elliot would respond that Goldhammer had opened the door to such evidence by introducing evidence of Ramsey's *good* character when he'd explored Ramsey's heroic actions as a firefighter. Unless Spatt was in a particularly sour mood, Elliot would prevail.

She watched the lawyers huddle in front of the judge. The court reporter leaned toward them, straining to hear so she could record their whispered colloquy in the transcript. After less than a minute, Goldhammer thanked the judge in a gruff tone, but Elliot was the one smiling.

Elliot faced the witness again. "Why did your wife leave you, Mr. Ramsey?"

Ramsey shook his head, the pride in his eyes fading. "She said I didn't show her enough affection."

Elliot nodded. Jessie might have used the opportunity to make a comment about sociopaths having difficulty feeling emotion—a comment that would have earned an objection but might have sparked the jurors imaginations—but Elliot simply moved on.

"You testified that you were friendly with your landlady, correct?"

Ramsey looked almost relieved by the change of topic. "Mrs. Samsel. Yes."

"In addition to owning it, Mrs. Samsel lived in the building, correct?"

"Yes."

"On the first floor?"

"Yes."

"With a view of the entrance?"

"Through her living room window, yes."

"Would you call Mrs. Samsel nosy?"

"Nosy?"

"A busybody? A woman who liked to keep tabs on her tenants' whereabouts?"

"I don't know if I'd call her a busy—"

Ramsey's words died as Elliot walked to the prosecution table and retrieved a sheet of paper from a folder. Leaning forward, Elliot's face came close to Jessie's. He winked at her.

"Don't get cocky," she whispered. But she did not feel worried. His newfound confidence was infectious.

He took his time returning to his place in front of Ramsey. Ramsey had no more hateful stares to spare on Jessie. All of his attention was now riveted to Elliot.

"At the time of your arrest, when you gave your statement to Detective Leary, did you argue to him that you couldn't have left your apartment that night because Mrs. Samsel would have seen you leave the building?"

"I might have."

"Did you, in fact, urge him to question her on the subject?"

"It's possible."

Elliot placed the sheet of paper in front of him. "You *did*. But by your own logic, shouldn't Mrs. Samsel have seen you when, as you testified, you returned home from work several hours before the killings? And shouldn't she have observed that you did not leave the building after that?"

"Objection," Goldhammer said. "How would my client know what Mrs. Samsel should or shouldn't have seen?"

"I'll withdraw the question. Mr. Ramsey, don't you think that Mrs. Samsel is a witness who should have been able to corroborate your alibi?"

"Objection! Any defense strategy regarding the selection of witnesses is privileged attorney-client communication and work product!"

"I agree," Spatt said. "Move on, Mr. Williams."

Elliot, looking bemused, turned from the judge to the flustered defense attorney to the defendant. "Just a few more questions, Mr. Ramsey, and then I'll be finished. Do you ski?"

"What?"

"Do you ski?"

"I used to. Before all this ... trouble."

Elliot returned to the prosecution table, grabbed another sheet of paper. "When the police searched your apartment, they found a pair of skis. Does that surprise you?"

"No. I just told you I used to ski."

"They also found a pair of ski poles. Does that surprise you?"

"No."

Elliot looked at the document in his hands. "They found a Gore-Tex ski jacket. Snow pants. Boots. Gloves. A hat. But they didn't find a ski mask. Does that surprise you?"

"No."

"Because you didn't use a ski mask when you used to ski?"

Ramsey shifted awkwardly in his chair. "I.... No, I didn't

ski with a mask. Just a hat."

"Really?" Elliot returned to the prosecution table again, opened the file, and withdrew a stack of photographs. Jessie recognized them as the photos the police had taken at the crime scene, but before anyone else could see them, Elliot turned them over so that the pictures were hidden. He approached the witness stand with the blank sides facing Ramsey. "Mr. Ramsey, are you sure you never skied with a mask?"

Ramsey's face paled. "I might have worn a ski mask sometimes."

"You might have?"

"I did. Sometimes."

"You owned a ski mask?"

"Yes."

"Why didn't the police find it in your apartment?"

"I ... I don't know."

"Did you dispose of it when you disposed of the other evidence of your attack on the Dillard family?"

"Objection!" Goldhammer said. "Compound question!"

"Did you dispose of the ski mask?"

"I don't remember. I—"

"Why wasn't it in your apartment with your other ski equipment?"

"Objection! Asked and answered! Badgering!"

"I have no more questions, Your Honor."

Judge Spatt watched Elliot return to his seat. The judge's customary scorn had momentarily been displaced by an expression that looked almost approving—but it vanished before it could fully settle into the grooves of his face. "Mr. Goldhammer, I assume you'd like to redirect?"

Goldhammer ran a hand through his thinning hair. His enthusiasm for practicing law in Philadelphia, Jessie suspected, had just diminished considerably.

55.

Jessie tried not to get too confident as she watched Goldhammer attempt some damage control during his brief redirect of Ramsey. She knew they could still lose this trial. Goldhammer knew it, too, and seemed to hurry through his redirect to get closer to the end of the trial, when he would have the opportunity to deliver a closing argument, one of his specialties.

"Let's talk about ski masks, since the prosecution seems so interested in your winter sports attire." Goldhammer showed the jury a smirk, as if to suggest that he found the topic ridiculous. "When was the last time you wore one?"

Ramsey shook his head. "I don't know. A long time ago."

"Within the last five years?"

"No."

"Do you keep ski masks in your home even though you haven't worn one in five years or more?"

"No."

"Thank you. I have no further questions."

Judge Spatt leaned forward. "Let's take a break."

BURNOUT

After a ten minute recess, the court reconvened. Judge Spatt offered the jurors his most encouraging smile and promised them that their valued contribution to the criminal justice system was at its end. "It's been a long, grueling process, I know."

Several of the jurors nodded in agreement.

"The good news for you is that it's almost over. Consider yourselves lucky. After you reach your verdict—or fail to, as the case may be—you will be free. Your state-imposed participation in this process will be over. I, on the other hand, will have to start it all over again the next day, bright-eyed and bushy-tailed."

The idea of a bright-eyed or bushy-tailed Judge Spatt exceeded the bounds of Jessie's imagination. Elliot shot her an incredulous sidelong glance, apparently sharing her view. Across the aisle, Goldhammer chuckled under his breath as his client silently brooded.

"You've heard the parties' opening statements. You've seen the evidence, heard the testimony of the witnesses. Now comes the part where the lawyers do what lawyers do best—repeat themselves."

Polite laughter rippled through the spectators in the gallery. A few of the jurors joined in. Jessie, Elliot, and Goldhammer sat stone-faced.

Spatt leaned over his podium to look down at the court reporter. "You getting all this?"

"Sure am, Your Honor."

"All right then. I'd like to remind you folks that nothing the lawyers say constitutes evidence in this case. Evidence consists of witnesses like Ms. Dillard and things like the crime scene photographs and your tour of the Dillard house. You've already seen and heard all the evidence in this case. What the lawyers are going to do now, in their closing arguments, is to try to influence your interpretation of that evidence before you go to the jury room to deliberate. And I expect," he said, turning his attention to the defense and prosecution tables, "that they will keep courtroom theatrics to a minimum."

It didn't take the sharpest legal mind to anticipate Judge Spatt's stance on courtroom theatrics. Jessie and Elliot had taken pains to draft a straightforward, concise closing argument. Jessie assumed that Goldhammer, no fool, had done the same.

"Mr. Goldhammer, are you ready to present your closing argument to the jury?"

"Yes, Your Honor."

"Well then." Spatt waved a hand, gesturing for him to get on with it.

Goldhammer squeezed his client's arm and patted his hand before standing up. It was an old defense lawyer routine, one Jessie had seen many times from lawyers who barely gave their clients the time of day until the final moments of the trial, when they wanted to signal to the jurors that *this* client was different, that *this* client was innocent, that *this* client mattered.

"Ladies and gentlemen of the jury," Goldhammer said as he approached the jury box, "the Commonwealth has proven nothing. Absolutely nothing." He spread his arms, as if to demonstrate the enormity of the nothingness.

Jessie and Elliot exchanged another glance. On his legal pad, Elliot wrote: *So much for no courtroom theatrics.*

"Before you go back to the jury room to make your decision, Judge Spatt is going to remind you of your burden of reasonable doubt. You've heard the phrase before, in movies, on TV, in novels. It means that unless you are one-hundred percent certain that Frank Ramsey committed the crimes of which he has been accused, you must acquit him.

"And surely, *surely*, you have doubts. Do you really believe that Frank Ramsey—a firefighter who risked his life to rescue old women from a burning nursing home, a man who carried twin girls out of the mouth of a fiery high-rise, a man with absolutely no history of criminal activity, not even a traffic ticket—do you really believe Frank Ramsey is capable of these horrific crimes? Stabbing a man? Raping a mother and stabbing her over and over again, viciously, with a knife, in front of her terrified daughter? And then raping and stabbing the daughter, too? Do those sound like the actions of the man you listened to on the witness stand this morning? What possible motive could Frank Ramsey have had? None!"

He had the jurors' complete attention. Several of them—and not just the ones Jessie had identified as tough sells—looked convinced. She ground her teeth.

"The Commonwealth's entire case is built around one eyewitness identification. They have presented no other evidence. No murder weapon. No DNA. No fingerprints. Certainly no confession. Just one single eyewitness identification. And this identification—made by a terrified teenager who saw her attacker's face for a total of five, maybe ten seconds—has been analyzed by Dr. Katherine Moscow, the foremost expert in the field of memory, who concluded that it was very likely tainted by distorting factors such as weapon focus, stress, and unconscious transference caused by exposure to Mr. Ramsey's photograph prior to the lineup. On the basis of this flawed identification alone, the Commonwealth wants you to convict Frank Ramsey of the most heinous crimes known to man.

"But you don't have to. It's not your job to do what the prosecutors tell you to do, even if they do represent the state of Pennsylvania. In the final analysis, the state is powerless. You, ladies and gentlemen, a jury of Frank Ramsey's peers, are the ones with the power here. And no matter what you might hear from a certain curmudgeonly trial judge, that's what makes our criminal justice system the best in the world."

Words overheard days ago—it seemed like an eternity—echoed now in Jessie's mind. *Well, Jack, that's why I get paid the big bucks.* Indeed.

Judge Spatt, probably as surprised as anyone by his own reaction, was smiling.

"As Judge Spatt told you, nothing I say is evidence. I could stand here and tell you a hundred times in a hundred different ways that I believe my client is innocent, but in the end, I'm just a lawyer advocating for a client. But don't forget that there is another person who told you that Frank Ramsey is innocent. That person is Frank Ramsey. And what he says, testifying under oath, *is* evidence. He told you he was at home on the night of the crimes, watching basketball and eating a microwave dinner. In order to convict him, you must be certain, beyond a reasonable doubt, that he lied to you. Are you?

"Ladies and gentlemen, very soon the time will come for you to decide. Personally, I don't think the decision will be all that difficult."

He returned to his seat and patted Ramsey on the back again. This time, even knowing she was watching a professional manipulator, Jessie found it significantly more difficult to dismiss the gesture as mere showmanship. She could only imagine what the jurors were thinking.

BURNOUT

Luckily for her, the prosecution would have the final word.

56.

Cross-examining Ramsey had been thrilling, but it was not until he stood before the jury box, facing the twelve jurors and two alternates who looked to him for the final word in the trial, that, for the first time, Elliot actually liked his job.

Right now, he was the pivotal figure in the biggest criminal trial in the city. Reporters were poised over their notepads, ready to copy down as many of his words as they could for their blogs and the evening news and the next morning's papers. Others had shown up just to observe his work. There were a few politicians. A handful of cops. Kristen Dillard sat with a nurse and a doctor near the rear of the room—now that she had given her testimony, there was no legal reason to exclude her from the courtroom. And sitting in the front row of the gallery, just behind the prosecution table, were his uncle Warren and the District Attorney himself, Jesus Rivera.

Now he understood why a showboat like Gil Goldhammer would gravitate to this field, why a disillusioned judge like Martin Spatt would remain on the bench rather than retire, and why Jessie Black would invest herself so personally in these proceedings.

Here, like nowhere else, Elliot would be *listened to.*

BURNOUT

"Mr. Goldhammer was very eloquent, I think we would all agree," he said to the jurors. "But, as Judge Spatt reminded us earlier, this is a courtroom, not a theater. Within these walls, facts and law are all that matter. And the facts prove, beyond a reasonable doubt, that Frank Ramsey violated the law in the most despicable ways possible.

"Mr. Goldhammer spent a lot of time during the course of this trial trying to focus your attention on the quantity of the Commonwealth's evidence. Well, I won't deny that the quantity is low. We're dealing with a very smart, calculated, and careful killer. He left no fingerprints at the scene. He disposed of the murder weapon before the police could recover and analyze it. Likewise, he disposed of the costume he wore during the attack—including his ski mask—before it could be examined for trace evidence. And, of course, he killed most of the people who could have identified him.

"But he didn't kill all of them, did he? He tried to. But he screwed up. This smart, calculated, careful killer made one mistake. He assumed that the multiple stab wounds he inflicted upon her killed Kristen Dillard. But Kristen Dillard was alive. She saw him when he took off his mask. She saw his face. She identified him to the police. And that's why we are here today.

"So when Mr. Goldhammer tells you that the Commonwealth has built its case on only one piece of evidence, he's right. But as all of you know, quantity is less important than quality. One good steak is worth a hundred hotdogs. And what better evidence could you possibly ask for than the eyewitness testimony of one of Mr. Ramsey's victims?

"She was there. She felt that knife punch through her ribcage. She felt his penis thrust into her body. And she saw his face."

In the corner of his eye, he saw a group rise from the gallery. Kristen, crying, was rushed out the door by her minders. Elliot paused, gave the jurors time to notice the condition Ramsey's attack had left her in, and what simply the recollection of that attack could do to her, even now.

"You listened to the testimony of Dr. Moscow, a hired gun paid by Ramsey's defense counsel to tell you, basically, that memory is too complicated for you to understand. That everything you think you know about memory is wrong and that you should therefore put no weight in the things Kristen Dillard claims to remember. But Dr. Moscow's opinions represent a handful of recent and relatively untested theories, not facts. You don't have to listen to her. You can rely on your own common sense instead.

"Put yourself in Kristen Dillard's place. You are lying on that bed, bleeding next to your murdered mother, and looking up at the killer's face. Even if you see that face for only five seconds, will you forget it?"

The jurors stared at him with a mixture of horror and ... reverence. There was no other word for it. He was no longer just a lawyer to them—certainly not a government flunky. He had become the voice of the state.

"There are many crimes that are typically proved by the testimony of one eyewitness. Child abuse, for example. Should we impose Mr. Goldhammer's heightened standards of evidence on those crimes as well?

"Our justice system is not based on numbers. One piece of evidence, if sufficiently compelling, is enough. In this case, ladies and gentlemen, one is more than enough."

Outside in the hallway, acquaintances from law school

pushed through the crowd to shake his hand. Reporters asked him to gauge his likelihood of success (which he declined to do) and how it felt to be part of such a major trial at his age and level of experience.

"Well, I have an excellent mentor."

"Are you referring to Jessica Black?" one of the reporters asked.

"Yes. She was instrumental—" Before he could finish, he was grabbed and thrust forward. By Warren on his right, Jessie on his left. He knew that Jesus Rivera was behind him only because of the storm of questions the DA's presence evoked from the crowd.

They escaped the Criminal Justice Center intact. A private car waited for them outside, a black Lincoln limousine with tinted windows.

In the limo—Elliot's second during this trial—Rivera clapped him on the shoulder. "You did good. But you've got a lot to learn."

Elliot buzzed with the compliment. Jessie must have noticed, because she turned toward the window, stifling a laugh. Warren, too, looked amused.

Rivera wasn't laughing. "For one thing, never, *ever*, speak to the media before you know the outcome of the trial."

"But you think we're going to win, don't you?" Elliot still could not quite believe this conversation was taking place—that he, less than one year out of law school, was sitting in the back of a limo with the District Attorney of the fifth largest city in the United States discussing a murder trial *he* had prosecuted.

"We'll know soon enough. Why guess?" Rivera looked

out the window as the limo cruised through an intersection toward the DA's office. The building loomed above them a moment later. His eyes moved to Warren. "Have you prepared my statements?"

"They're on your desk."

Rivera opened the door and climbed out of the car. They watched him disappear inside the building.

Elliot, at a loss for words, settled for, "That was so cool."

Warren smiled. "Well, like the man said, you did good. You'll have some fond memories to keep your spirits up back in the Appeals Unit."

Even this news couldn't dissipate his buzz. "Fair enough. So what were those statements Rivera asked you about?"

Warren and Jessie exchanged a bemused glance that made him feel as naïve as a law student attending his first class. In some ways, he supposed, that was exactly what he was.

"Two statements for the press," Jessie explained. "One for if we win. One for if we lose."

57.

"You got swept away in that limo so fast, I didn't get a chance to say hi."

Jessie stared at the smiling man sitting in the chair behind her desk.

"You do understand that this is *my* office, right?" Her eyes moved automatically to her computer screen. A screen-saver program obscured whatever Jack might have been looking at—although, now that the trial was over, further spying seemed unnecessary. "What's up?"

He laughed. "Fantastic closing argument. I'm guessing you wrote it."

"Not really. I mean, I helped...."

He nodded, but the mischievous glint in his eyes made it clear that he did not believe her. The smug bastard thought he had her all figured out. "Well, it was excellent," he said. "You're going to win for sure."

She leaned her hip against the door frame. "Is that what you want, Jack?"

"Of course. I know how hard you've worked on this case."

"Uh-huh."

"Jessie, what's wrong? You should be ecstatic. Ramsey's cross-examination, the closing argument—you couldn't ask to be in a better position at the end of a trial."

"I don't like to count my chickens before they hatch."

"You're conservative by nature." He leaned back in her chair, the smile still on his face. "One of your many endearing qualities."

The fact that the trial was out of her hands and he was still playing games infuriated her. "If you don't mind, Jack, I'd like to work on some other cases while I wait for the jury to finish its deliberation."

"And afterward, may I take you somewhere nice for a celebratory dinner? You can celebrate your victory, and I can celebrate the end of the only obstacle to our relationship."

"Tell you what, Jack. I'll answer that question *after* the verdict. Deal?"

His smile widened. "Deal."

Returning to the courthouse, she thought about her encounter with Jack. She had assumed that once the trial was over, he would drop his act and quickly fade out of her life. Instead, he had invited her to dinner. He wasn't done with her yet, apparently. Why?

It was only when she was back in Judge Spatt's courtroom, trying to ignore Elliot's trembling body as they waited for the jurors to enter with their verdict, that she thought she'd figured it out.

The prick wanted to remain close to her even if Ramsey was found guilty, so he could spy on her during the appeals.

She turned, spotted him seated in the gallery.

"If we win this," she said to Elliot, "I want you to do some research into the criminal penalties for tampering with a criminal prosecution."

"I thought I was going straight back to the Appeals Unit."

She smiled. "I'll talk to Warren about extending your reprieve. I need your research skills."

His face lit up. "Sounds good."

A moment later, everyone rose as Judge Spatt entered the courtroom. Sheriff's deputies escorted Ramsey to his seat next to Goldhammer. The lawyer patted his shoulder and said something Jessie could not hear in a low, encouraging voice. The jurors filed in last. The foreperson, a small-business owner named Nancy Luman, held a folded sheet of paper in her hand.

The judge summoned a dignified tone for this ceremony. In a bellowing voice, he said, "Madam foreperson, has the jury reached a verdict?"

"We have, Your Honor." The charge slip was passed to Spatt, who glanced at it before passing it along to his clerk. His face revealed nothing, even as his eyes settled on Ramsey.

The clerk read, "In the case of the Commonwealth of Pennsylvania versus Francis Ramsey for the unlawful death of Robert Dillard in violation of Penal Code Section 2502, we, the jury, find the defendant not guilty."

Elliot gasped. Across the aisle, Ramsey looked like he was just as stunned as Jessie felt. She gripped the edge of the table and let herself hope that this part of the verdict had been a fluke, that Ramsey would still be convicted of his other crimes.

"In the case of the Commonwealth of Pennsylvania

versus Francis Ramsey for the unlawful death of Erin Dillard in violation of Penal Code Section 2502, we, the jury, find the defendant not guilty."

Elliot leaned close to her ear. "What the fuck is wrong with these people?"

"I don't know. They must have believed Kate Moscow's testimony about the fallibility of memory."

The clerk continued. "In the case of the Commonwealth of Pennsylvania versus Francis Ramsey for the rape of Erin Dillard in violation of Penal Code Section 3121, we, the jury, find the defendant not guilty."

Ramsey's body had begun to vibrate. Jessie turned to glare at him, no longer concerned with her deportment in front of the jury. The beginnings of a smile tugged at the corners of his mouth.

"In the case of the Commonwealth of Pennsylvania versus Francis Ramsey for the attempted murder of Kristen Dillard in violation of Penal Code Sections 901 and 2502, we, the jury, find the defendant not guilty."

Jessie closed her eyes as the clerk continued to the final jury finding, the one she most dreaded—and the one she had never really believed she would ever have to hear.

"In the case of the Commonwealth of Pennsylvania versus Francis Ramsey for the rape of Kristen Dillard in violation of Penal Code Section 3121, we, the jury, find the defendant not guilty."

The court erupted. Politicians, armed with a new scandal, leaped from their seats in the gallery to run to the nearest media outlets. Reporters scurried to gather comments from anyone with anything to say. Lawyers speculated loudly with one another about the verdict. Despite Judge Spatt's gavel

BURNOUT

hammering, no one shut up.

The jurors, watching this scene with the naïve expressions of surprised sheep, were the only people in the courtroom with nothing to say.

"You did it!" Ramsey was hugging Goldhammer, dragging the lawyer halfway out of his chair in his enthusiasm. "I never thought ... I never thought—"

Jessie turned to Elliot. "I need to go."

"What?"

"Finish up here. There's someone I need to talk to."

"Jack?" He gaped at her, incredulous.

She shook her head. The thought of ever again speaking to the man nauseated her. "Kristen. I made—" Elliot watched her sympathetically as she struggled to get the words out. "I made her a promise I couldn't keep."

"Jessie, this is not your fault. Remember what Rivera said? It happens."

She knew he meant well, but she didn't stick around to hear the rest. She had spotted Kristen running out the door, leaving her doctors behind. Jessie ran after her.

She crashed through a mob of reporters in the hallway, tripped, regained her balance, and lurched after the seventeen-year-old girl. The reporters called questions after her, but she barely heard them. Two words rang loudly and clearly in her mind, forming a clarion call only she could hear.

Suicide watch.

58.

Jessie caught up with Kristen at the elevator bank. A small host of media people pursued her, but the elevator doors opened—one tiny bit of good luck in an otherwise luckless day—and she pushed Kristen inside with her and got the doors closed before the reporters could catch up.

"I know you're upset," Jessie said. "I am, too."

Kristen did not look at her. Tears sparkled in her eyes. Her lips were pressed together. She pushed the button for the ground floor.

"Kristen?"

The girl refused to face her. Before the elevator could complete its descent, Jessie pushed the red emergency button. The car lurched to a halt, suspended between floors.

"Look at me, damn it."

The tone of her voice seemed to snap Kristen back to the moment. The tears gathering in her eyes spilled down her cheeks. She turned and fixed Jessie with her watery gaze.

"This isn't the end," Jessie said.

"He's free. He ... he can't be tried twice. You told me that. He's free. It's the end."

BURNOUT

"The end of the trial. Not the end of you."

She was shaking her head. Her blonde hair looked stringy, dirty. Her eyes had returned to the blank and distant gaze Jessie had seen when they'd first entered the elevator.

"Kristen, listen to me. You've got your whole life to live. And you will live it. You will finish high school, go to college, find a rewarding job, marry a wonderful man, and raise a family. And Frank Ramsey—Frank Ramsey will die all alone, despised."

Kristen rounded on her. "You can't understand." The expression on her face twisted from agony to anger. She stamped her foot and the elevator car shook around them. "You have a home. A family!" She brought her foot down again with a strength her body did not look capable of. Jessie pressed a hand to the wall to steady herself. She imagined the elevator car dangling from its cable in the dark shaft.

"Kristen—"

"Shut up! I'm sick of you. You're no better than the doctors. You don't know me. You don't know shit."

"It's okay to be angry, Kristen. You can hate your doctors. You can hate me. Just don't hate yourself—"

The girl's eyes flashed. "Is that why you chased me into the elevator? You're afraid I'm going to kill myself?"

Jessie nodded. Under the circumstances, honesty seemed like her only alternative. "I am afraid. Yes."

"Well, don't be." Kristen slid down the wall until she was sitting on the floor in the corner of the elevator. Jessie, not wanting to look down at her, crouched until their eyes met at the same level. Kristen's had dried. The tear tracks were fading against her red cheeks. "I'm done hurting myself."

Jessie released a sigh of relief. "I'm glad."

"The only person I want to hurt is Frank Ramsey."

"Kristen—"

Her jaw set. "I'm going to kill him."

The words stung. Jessie assumed that given Ramsey's acquittal, Kristen's doctors would be sure to watch her extra closely, and she could not imagine it would be easy for her to break out of the institution, arm herself, and hunt down Ramsey. And maybe the revenge fantasy itself was therapeutic, a step toward recovery. But it still hurt to see this innocent teenager's face twist with hatred and rage. She touched the girl's shoulder gently. "That's not the answer, Kristen."

"Wouldn't you do the same, if you were in my place?" the girl spat out.

Jessie closed her eyes, shook her head. "No. I would learn to accept it, move on with my life."

Kristen laughed. "I don't believe you."

Jessie was not sure if she believed herself.

59.

Elliot could not go back to the office. He walked home in a daze, barely feeling the wind that bit him through his coat and scarf. He did not notice a homeless man warming himself over a steam grate until the man shouted at him for almost stepping on his hand. He walked past a convenience store, and came close to colliding with two men stepping out of the exit. He felt like a ghost.

Mere hours ago, he had felt like the reincarnation of Clarence Darrow. His job, which for a few hours had seemed like the greatest job a man could ever hope for, now seemed hopeless in every way. Money, job satisfaction—these things seemed as far from his reach as ever.

Part of him wanted to quit. Walk home and never show up at the DA's office again. Apply for a job in some other industry. Investment banking, maybe. Move to New York City, start over. He had not yet completely morphed into a clone of Uncle Warren. He still had time. He was young.

My God. I'm a bigger burnout than Jack Ackerman.

Fuck that.

He'd lost a case. Big deal. Considering his level of experience, it was amazing he'd done as well as he had. And there was no denying that he had enjoyed the feeling that consumed him when he faced the jurors and delivered his closing, a feeling that he not only *could* do this job, but that he had been *born* to do it.

He was walking faster now, weaving between groups of pedestrians, skirting food trucks and bus stops. A sudden impulse stopped him in his tracks. He felt an urge to turn around, return to the DA's office. Spend the remainder of the day among the only other people in Philadelphia who could understand how he felt right now. Jessie Black, Warren Williams, Jesus Rivera.

Prosecutors.

But he was only a few blocks from home. His body's complaints about the cold finally penetrated the din in his mind. He wore no hat, and his ears and nose burned. Tugging his scarf higher to protect his face, he hurried onward. He could commiserate with Jessie and Warren—and maybe even Rivera—another day. They weren't going anywhere. Today, he would spend a quiet afternoon and evening at home. Turn up the heat. Make himself a mug of hot chocolate. Read a novel. Call Amber.

He did not need to call her. She was waiting for him in his studio apartment when he unlocked the door. She looked as beautiful as always, but she also looked unhappy, maybe even frightened. Seeing her that way momentarily shocked him out of his own self-pitying funk.

"Are you alright, honey?"

She looked at him and shook her head. He saw that her mascara had smeared. Had she been crying? He dropped his briefcase and crossed the room. Hugged her without taking off his coat. After a few seconds, she pulled out of his embrace, shivering. "You're cold."

He shrugged out of his coat, tossed it on the bedspread. "Sorry. I came home early because—"

"I know." She pointed at the TV in the corner of the room. "It was on the news. I'm really sorry, Elliot."

"That's not why you're crying, is it?" He smiled. "It's just a trial." Despite his earlier depression, he realized with some surprise that he actually felt this way. "There will be others."

"That's not why I'm upset." She sniffled. The way she rubbed her nose was almost childlike. "There's something I need to tell you."

A pit opened in his stomach. He was suddenly sure she was going to dump him. In a moment of vertigo, he practically dropped into a sitting position on the edge of the bed. She was the best girlfriend he'd ever had—the only girlfriend he'd had since his sophomore year in college. If she ended their relationship, he'd be drinking whiskey instead of hot chocolate tonight. That was one thing he knew for certain.

Then he saw the suitcase.

It was on the floor next to the bed. He had not noticed it before because his attention had been riveted to Amber. The suitcase was his.

"What's going on?"

"We need to get out of here. Now. Stay at a hotel, somewhere safe until—"

"Amber, what are you talking about?" His eyes shifted to the TV and he tried to make a connection between the trial and her sudden panic. "If you're worried that Frank Ramsey is going to come after me, you can relax. That only happens in the movies."

She picked up his phone and started dialing. He listened to her request a taxi. Barely had time to hop off the bed, grab the phone from her, and cancel the request.

"What the hell are you doing?" She snatched the phone from him and began to punch in the number again.

"Amber, wait. Talk to me."

Reluctantly, she put down the phone. "I'd rather explain later, when we're safe."

"We *are* safe."

"I'm an exotic dancer."

After the way this conversation had begun, he had not thought she could say anything that would surprise him. "Wait a second. What?"

"A stripper, Elliot. I dance at Heartbreakers, a club on—"

He shook his head. He knew what Heartbreakers was. Although he had never patronized the establishment himself, several of his law school friends had celebrated there after exams. It was a full-nudity strip bar in a seedy neighborhood. "I thought you were a model."

Looking exasperated, she cast her eyes about the room as if for help. "I lied to you, okay?"

"You didn't need to. I wouldn't have held it against you."

"I lied to you about other things, too. Remember when you barged in on me at the gym and accused me of being a spy for Ramsey's lawyers?"

The pit in his stomach yawned wider. "Amber—"

BURNOUT

"I had no choice. There are bad people involved in this, Elliot. Killers. And now that Ramsey's been acquitted, they might come here. They'll probably come here. To tie up loose ends."

He felt like his brain was overdosing on new information. "Killers? Besides Ramsey?"

"Who do you think killed Rachel Pugh?"

"I don't know. Are you telling me that *you* do?" Now he was the one who took the phone and began pushing the buttons.

"Who are you calling?"

"Jessie." He turned his back to her, punching in the rest of Jessie's mobile number. "She'll know what to do."

"Call her later, Elliot. We need to get out of here."

The doorknob rattled. Before he could finish dialing, Elliot's hands went numb and he fumbled the phone. It hit the carpet and rolled under the bed.

"Shit." Amber walked aimlessly around the tiny apartment, looking around, eyes wide. "Shit. Shit."

Keep your head. Ridiculous as her story seemed, her panic was infectious. And if they both panicked now, and there really was a killer in the hallway outside, they were dead for sure. He took a breath, scanned the room. There was nowhere to hide. His studio apartment consisted of one room, a kitchenette, and a bathroom.

He hurried to the window and grabbed the string that raised the mini-blinds. He yanked it and the blinds zipped upward. The window was old, the glass slightly warped, set in a chipped wooden frame. A latch on top locked the window. Through the glass, he could see a metal fire escape. He'd never bothered opening the window before, and now, after twisting the latch and trying to slide the window up, he realized that even unlocked, it would not budge.

"Open it!" Amber was right behind him. Her rapid breaths stirred the hairs on the back of his neck.

He hushed her. Across the room, the doorknob stopped rattling. Now he heard a soft, metallic clicking. He had seen enough heist movies and TV shows to imagine the lock picks being inserted into the lock.

He pushed hard against the window. His breath caught in his lungs. His biceps bulged and burned. The window did not move. "I'm not strong enough."

She put her hands beside his and added her own strength. After a moment of strained effort, there was a soft *crack* and he felt the window give slightly before jamming again. "Keep ... pushing." Even in this situation, the press of her body against his—and the puff of air as she spoke in his ear—made him tingle. He renewed his effort.

Behind them, the apartment's door swung open. Amber struggled even harder against the window, but Elliot released his grip and turned to face the intruder.

A tall, broad-shouldered man stepped inside the apartment and closed the door behind him. He had short-cropped hair and a goatee. The expression on his face was grim but determined.

"What are you staring at?" the man said.

Elliot blinked, looked away. Staring at the floor, he said, "What do you want?" He was willing to do just about anything, at that moment, if it would keep Amber and him alive.

BURNOUT

He kept his gaze on the floor as the man came closer. Although he had only looked at the man's face for a matter of seconds, Elliot found that he could remember every detail vividly. He wondered what Kate Moscow would say if presented with the results of *this* experiment.

Amber stopped struggling with the window. Elliot felt her presence at his side. Somehow he knew that, unlike him, she was staring the intruder in the face.

Then she stepped in front of him, shielding him from the intruder.

"Get out of the way, Amber." The man's tone was exasperated but familiar, like a man irritated by his wife. A ridiculous flush of jealousy brought a blush to Elliot's cheeks.

"Let him go," she said. "He doesn't know anything."

The man laughed. "I think he knows enough now."

"Woody—"

He slapped her. The sound echoed in the silent apartment like a plank of wood cracked in half. Amber stumbled backward. Her heels crushed Elliot's toes and her hair—smelling faintly of coconut—brushed against his face.

Tears slid from her face but she maintained eye contact with the intruder—*Woody*. "I hope your brother dies and rots in hell."

Woody raised his hand to strike her again. Elliot pushed her out of the way. He watched his own hand as if it were a stranger's. His fist connected with Woody's nose. He felt bones shatter against his knuckles.

"Fuck!" Woody danced backward, clutching his nose. Blood gleamed in his goatee as it gushed down his face. The top of his shirt turned dark red. He let go of his nose with one hand and tried to stop the blood from pattering on the carpet. He seemed more horrified by the red spots appearing near his shoes than by the pain. "Shit! No!"

Elliot looked at Amber. "Run."

She sprinted for the door. Woody was faster. He grabbed her hair as she passed him, yanked her backward. She lost her balance and fell. After a sickening ripping sound, a handful of blonde strands dangled from his fist.

Lying on the ground, Amber began to scream.

Woody did not hesitate for a second. He kicked her in the head. Her face pivoted violently to the side. Then he brought his heel down hard on her neck and Elliot heard a *crack*. After that, she was silent.

"You made this harder for yourself, lawyer." His broken nose muffled his voice, forcing Elliot to strain to understand the garbled words. He looked down at Amber. She no longer appeared to be breathing, but blood leaked from her left ear. Dead people didn't bleed, so she must still be alive. He stared at the growing stain on the carpet, anchored his hope to it. Woody followed his gaze, but this mess did not seem to concern him.

Of course not. *Only his own blood concerns him. The bastard's worried about DNA evidence.*

"Don't worry, lawyer. I'll finish her when I'm done with you."

Then he came at Elliot.

60.

Even though a backlog of new cases required Jessie's attention, Warren had not protested when she left work early. He knew how much the Ramsey case meant to her—knew how much Kristen Dillard meant to her—and, Jessie supposed, he also knew she would be back soon enough. When it came to her job, Jessie was predictable.

It was dark by the time she walked into her apartment and tossed her keys on the table by the door. She went to the bedroom, changed into flannel pajamas, and then walked back to the kitchen. Memories of Jack's attempt to cook her dinner threatened to rise to the surface of her mind. She turned on the TV in the living room to drown out the rogue thoughts. The TV would stay on until she fell asleep on the couch. She knew from bitter experience that if she attempted to fall asleep in bed like a normal person, her mind would ambush her in the silence of her apartment, replaying moments from the trial until she screamed for mercy.

She dug a Domino's menu from a drawer in the kitchen and ordered a large pepperoni pizza, then settled onto the couch. A comedy quickly lured her attention from the failures of the day.

Then her cell phone rang.

She looked at the display and was surprised to see Jack's name. She had assumed that Ramsey's acquittal would have spelled the end of his charade. She put the phone to her ear. "Jack."

"Jessie." He sounded happy, the bastard. "I thought you might need some cheering up."

"And you're just the man to do it, right?"

"It's sort of one of my specialties."

She couldn't believe his nerve. She reached for the remote and muted the TV. Silent images of shenanigans in a Vegas casino continued to play on the screen, casting light and shadow against the walls of the apartment. "Jack, why don't you go fuck yourself?"

She heard his sharp intake of breath, then a few seconds of silence. "I know you're upset, Jess, but you don't have to take out your anger on me."

"Sorry." Any effort to temper the vitriol in her voice would have been hopeless. "It's sort of one of my specialties."

"Jessie—"

"Don't you have a party to attend, Jack?"

"A party?"

"In Goldhammer's hotel suite. I'm sure the fat bastard's ordered a whole case of champagne for the occasion. You can all toast to Frank Ramsey's future victims."

"Jessie, whatever you think you know, you don't." The humor had left his voice. Somehow hearing him speak this way—earnest and intense—stung her more than all of his fake joviality. This was the Jack Ackerman she had really fallen for, the man behind the comedian's mask. "Don't leave your apartment. I'm coming over now."

BURNOUT

According to her watch, it was only six o'clock. She usually did not leave her office until eight at the earliest. "How do you know I'm in my apartment, Jack?"

He started to say something before his voice faltered. "Jessie, just sit tight, okay? I'm coming over. I need to do this in person."

He ended the call, but not before she heard another voice, faint but audible, on his side of the line. It was a voice, up until now, that she had only heard in two places—the courtroom, and her nightmares.

She turned away from the TV, to the window next to the couch. Outside, the street looked empty and peaceful. She stared at the cars parked bumper-to-bumper along the curbs, glowing under the street-lamps. She peered at the shadowed doorways of the neighboring buildings. The fact that she did not see anyone brought her little comfort.

The voice she had heard on the phone had been Ramsey's.

She closed the curtains and turned off the lights in the living room and kitchenette on her way to the bedroom. All thoughts of TV and pizza had fled her mind. She wasn't sure how much time she had. For all she knew, Jack and Ramsey had made their call from the hallway right outside her door. She changed out of her pajamas and into a pair of jeans and a blue University of Pennsylvania sweatshirt, then shoved her feet into a pair of sneakers without bothering to untie the laces first. Standing on her tiptoes, she reached the shelf at the top of the closet and carefully brought down a shoe box.

The box's contents shifted heavily as she carried it to the bed. Inside, wrapped in a handkerchief, was her Glock 9-mm.

She lifted the pistol out of the box, ejected its empty magazine and quickly loaded it with bullets from the shoe box. She cursed as one of the bullets slipped from her fingers—she had begun to sweat—but with renewed concentration she managed to finish loading the magazine without fumbling any more. When it was full, she rammed the magazine into place.

Back in the living room, she stood to one side of her door and held the gun in a two-handed grip, arms extended in front of her. At this range, even without aiming, she'd have a better than average shot at killing anyone coming through the door.

The gun trembled at the end of her outstretched arms. She took a couple of deep breaths, but lost the rhythm a moment later when someone knocked loudly on the door.

Was it Jack, here already? There was no way he could have traveled from his house to her apartment in that time, but then, he'd known she was home, which meant he'd probably been watching her. From where? Down the street? In her hallway?

With her left hand, she grasped the Glock's slide, pulled it back, released it. The slide rushed forward and she heard the first bullet pop from the magazine into the chamber, ready to fire.

"Who is it?" Her voice, aimed at the door, came out louder than she'd expected. A shout.

"Domino's."

Shit. She had forgotten about the pizza. The voice did not sound like Jack's or Ramsey's, but she was in no mood to take chances. "Tell me what I ordered."

"Large pepperoni pizza."

She hesitated. Her door was not equipped with a chain,

and an irrational fear kept her from using the peephole.

"Come on, lady. I got other deliveries to make."

She let out her breath. Placed the Glock on the kitchen counter, where it would be out of sight from the doorway but within easy reach. Then, slowly, she opened the door.

A pimply kid stood alone in the hallway, a pizza box balanced on one hand. But there was someone else nearby. She could sense it. She looked past the kid at the shadowy hallway, and Jack stepped into view.

"Hey, honey!" Before she could slam the door, his arm shot forward. His hand caught the door and forced it inward. Jessie was pushed backward into her apartment. Away from the kitchenette. Away from her gun. "Perfect timing on the pizza." He pushed a twenty into the delivery boy's free hand, took the pizza, and closed the door.

Jessie thought about running after the kid, or screaming, but Jack had brought the box to the coffee table in front of Jessie's couch. Her path to the kitchenette—and the gun—was clear. *And what are you going to do with the gun?* She wasn't sure.

"I love pepperoni." He opened the pizza box. Steam rose and the aroma of fresh pizza filled the room. He pulled a slice from the pie and tried to hand it to her.

"It's messy," she said. "I'll get some plates." She took a step toward the kitchenette.

For a moment, Jack looked like he might object. Then he said, "Good idea. We should eat like civilized people."

She smiled. The wall of the kitchenette shielded her from view as she scooped the Glock off the counter. After a moment of nervous fumbling, she folded her hands around the grip.

Jack did not notice her as she stepped quietly into the living room. He remained on her couch, eating. Tomato sauce spotted his chin. "You might want to grab some napkins, too, Jess—"

His eyes glanced up and the slice of pizza dropped from his hands, splattering face-down on her carpet. Slowly, he stood from the couch. "Jessie, put down the gun."

She jerked the Glock in his direction, aligning the sites with his chest. "Take another step and I swear to God I will kill you."

He raised his hands. "I came here because I need help."

"That's an understatement."

"Frank's innocent. He did not torture and kill Kristen Dillard's family."

"That may be the jury's opinion, but it's not mine."

"It's the truth." That earnestness she found so appealing had returned to his voice. She fought her inclination to listen to him. If she let him wrest control of this situation, he'd turn the tables on her, get her gun, and do whatever it was he'd come here to do.

What had he said to her over the phone? *I need to do this in person.* She shuddered. "I'm calling the police."

"Please let me explain. Then, if you still want to call the cops, I won't stop you."

His arrogance galled her. "You *can't* stop me, Jack. I'm the one holding the semi-automatic. You're the one with your hands in the air."

Carefully, she took one hand off the Glock. Aiming one-handed was more difficult, but she kept the sights lined up on Jack's heart—or the place where his heart would be, if he had one. With her other hand, she fished her phone from the pocket of her jeans.

"Ninety-nine percent of my clients are guilty," he said. "I'm not naïve enough to think otherwise. I defend them because I know that without a healthy defense bar to keep it honest, even with good intentions, the state would trample citizens' rights."

"Spare me the lecture. You defend scumbags because you think it's fun. Law to you is nothing but a game you need to win. The only thing that's changed since your breakdown is the way you play it."

Her thumb pressed *Nine*. *One*. Hovered over the *One* button.

"Maybe that's true. I won't deny that taking on a tough case and winning gives me a kind of high. You, of all people, know what I'm talking about. But Frank is innocent. If he had been executed, it would have been the grossest miscarriage of justice imaginable."

She laughed. "You're a real piece of work. Where did you get that speech, one of the books in your library?"

"Don't you get it, Jessie? Frank was my first client that was actually innocent, and I couldn't help him. That's why I burned out. After his sentencing, I couldn't sleep. Every time I closed my eyes I saw the sheriff's deputies dragging him out of the courtroom to be put on a bus for SCI Greene. For death row."

"You told Goldhammer you faked the breakdown."

His eyes widened. "You spied on me?"

"I conducted some surveillance."

Despite the gun pointed at his chest, he laughed. "I

should have known you'd suspect me. I thought I was smarter than you."

"I guess you were wrong."

"The breakdown was real, at first. But it gave me an idea and I ran with it. I acted nutty in court, committed myself to a hospital for six months. I had already scoured the trial transcript for reversible error, but there was nothing to base an appeal on. I knew my breakdown, in the hands of a good lawyer, could form the basis for an ineffective assistance of counsel claim."

"You called Goldhammer? You've been paying his bills?"

"No. Woody Butler has."

That threw her. "Who?"

"Near the end of the trial, I was approached by a man looking for one of the souvenirs the Family Man had taken from his victims. Butler wanted Bob Dillard's briefcase. He made it clear to me that I could name my price. After I returned home from the mental hospital, I called him and told him that if he got Frank out of prison, Frank would give him the briefcase."

"I thought you said Frank was innocent."

"He is. But I told him to pretend he was guilty, for Butler's benefit. With Butler's money, he could afford a legal team with the resources to win at trial."

"Jack, how fucking gullible do you think I am?"

Her phone, forgotten in her left hand, began to ring.

"Jessie, please. I am telling you the truth. Frank is in my house now. When he fails to deliver the briefcase, Woody Butler—or whoever Butler works for—is going to come after him."

Her phone continued to ring. She put it to her ear. "Hello?"

"I have some bad news." It was Leary.

"Listen to me," Jack said. "I'm—"

"Elliot Williams is dead," Leary said.

Her gun hand wavered, but Jack made no attempt to take it from her. He kept his hands in the air and studied her face. She swallowed. Her throat felt thick. "What?"

Leary's voice sounded strained. "His neighbor heard a struggle and called the police. Two uniforms responded. They found Elliot and a woman named Amber Gibbons on the floor. They were both murdered." After a moment, he added, "Jessie, their necks were broken."

"Oh God."

She could hear other voices behind Leary's. He was probably still at the crime scene. "You were right. Jack Ackerman is definitely involved. If you see him, do not—"

"He's here with me now."

"What?"

"Don't worry. I've got a gun aimed at his chest as we speak." Now Leary was the one at a loss for words. After a moment of silence, she said, "You're the cop. Tell me what we do now."

"I'm thinking," Leary said.

On the couch, Jack cleared his throat. "If you're taking suggestions, I propose that we all go to my house. You, me, Leary, and as many cops as he can round up."

Jessie lowered the phone with a sigh. "Why would we do that?"

"To trap a killer."

61.

Ten minutes later, Jessie heard an engine outside. Keeping her Glock trained on Jack, she peeked out the window and saw a car double-park outside the building. She recognized the vehicle as an unmarked police car, but still felt relieved when Leary emerged from it.

"Time to go," she said to Jack.

Jack rose slowly from the couch, keeping his hands raised. "You don't need to force me at gunpoint. This was my idea, remember?"

She edged across the room and unlocked the door. A moment later, Leary knocked and entered. His gaze went from her gun to the man standing in her living room and back to the gun. He scowled.

"We should get moving," Leary said to Jack. "We don't want to miss the party at your house."

Jack didn't respond to Leary. His attention seemed fixed on her. "You're coming, right?"

"Chasing killers isn't her job," Leary said. He shot her a reassuring look, then reached for her gun and took it gently from her hands. She let him take it. "Don't worry, though, you'll see Jessie soon enough when she prosecutes you and your buddies for first degree murder."

"I'm coming," Jessie said.

Leary looked at her sharply, but did not argue the point. If her insistence on tagging along annoyed him, he took out his frustration on Jack, grabbing the man and shoving him toward the door. "Let's go."

Outside, after depositing Jack roughly in the back seat of the unmarked car, he turned to Jessie. "I won't stop you, but I don't think you should come with us. We're dealing with dangerous people, Jack included."

"Then why did you leave my gun in the apartment?"

"That's my point. I don't want you running around with a gun. And I don't want you to have to participate in the circus show Jack's been planning."

Jessie appreciated his concern. Jack's plan to "trap a killer" involved hanging out with another one. In addition to a specific list of cops, technicians, and specialists that Jack had requested Leary summon to his house, another man would also be present. Ramsey.

"Come on, Mark. I can't just go back into my apartment and watch TV. I need to see this through."

They stood in the cold for another moment as he looked at the ground, mulling her words. Finally, he nodded, and gestured for her to get in the car.

Entering Jack's trinity house, Jessie was surprised by the number of people. The house had appeared quiet on the outside—she supposed the police had kept their arrival low-profile, in case the house was being watched—but inside, cops and technicians crowded the living room. Their faces turned expectantly toward the new arrivals.

Leary took her by the arm, guided her to one of the chairs near the center of the room. "Try to stay away from the windows."

"I'm fine." She moved toward the chair but did not sit. On the couch, no more than four feet away, Frank Ramsay sat, watching her. No way in hell she would sit down with that man.

Leary cleared his throat and addressed the room. "Thank you all for coming on short notice. Just to recap, we are here because there may be an opportunity to get a bead on a man named Woody Rushford, who we believe to have murdered multiple people, including a witness in a homicide trial and the nephew of a prosecutor, among other innocents."

"Rushford?" Jack said. "You mean Butler."

"No, I don't. We recovered blood and one partial fingerprint from Elliot Williams's apartment," Leary said. "They were identified as belonging to Woody Rushford, a former corrections officer at the state prison in Huntington and the brother of Michael Rushford, creator of the Rushford Foundation, Bob Dillard's employer. Butler is an alias."

"Bob Dillard?" Jessie did not understand the connection. "Are you saying Rushford had something to do with the attack on the Dillards?"

"No. I think that much is clear. Whoever committed that crime"—Leary's gaze seemed to linger on Ramsey—"let's just call that person the Family Man, didn't seem to even know about Rushford when he chose the Dillards as victims. I think the attack on the Dillards, as well as the theft of Bob Dillard's briefcase as a trophy, were completely unrelated to Woody Rushford and his brother."

"Then how do you explain the connection?" another cop said.

Leary shrugged. "Bad luck? I know it sounds incredible."

"Not to me," Jack said.

Ramsey, nodding, had a faraway look in his eyes. "Woody thinks I did it. He couldn't have been directly involved, or he would know that's not true."

"And it means Woody will be in touch with Frank soon," Jack said. "Woody fulfilled his part of the bargain by getting Frank out of prison. Now he'll expect Frank to deliver the briefcase."

Leary must have sensed some confusion in the room. He said, "Rushford believes this briefcase holds information that can save his brother's life. Research into ALS, a disease Michael Rushford is dying from."

"So if I understand this," one of the cops said, "we need to catch this Rushford guy, and we're going to use the infamous Frank Ramsey as bait? I'm in!"

Ramsey turned away. He looked ready to bolt, and why not? For two years, most of the people in this room had worked overtime to ensure his execution. Now they were his only chance at staying alive.

They waited.

"Maybe we should order some Chinese food." Jack, pacing back and forth in his kitchenette, was holding a menu.

Jessie looked away from him, disgusted,

"Jessie, before this is all over, we need to talk. I need to—"

"Apologize?"

"Well, yeah. And explain—"

"Don't bother."

"I did what I thought I needed to do to keep an innocent man out of prison. But that's no excuse for using you the way I did. Although, I'm sure you'll admit that under different circumstances, you might have used me. To put a man in prison."

She laughed. "No, Jack. I wouldn't have."

"It was a matter of life and death."

She walked away from him. Arguing with him would be useless; she didn't know how to express her feelings anyway. To explain to him why some things should be out of bounds.

"How about that Chinese?" he said to her back.

Before she could answer, Jack's mobile phone began to ring.

They gathered around the desk in Jack's upstairs office. His mobile phone had been moved to the center of his desk and connected to a chunky police department laptop. Someone had pushed the swivel chair to a corner of the room. Jessie, Leary, Jack, Ramsey, and assorted cops and technicians crowded the small space.

When Leary gave him the signal, Jack leaned over the ringing phone. One of the techs triggered the laptop, and the phone line became audible. Jack directed his voice at the phone. "Hello?"

Jessie knew it would probably be Jack's mother, or an old fraternity buddy. But she leaned forward anyway, her body taut.

"It's me."

The voice coming from the speaker was gruff, but also strangely fuzzy, as if he had a broken nose. Jessie caught Ramsey and Jack exchanging an uncertain glance, as if they weren't sure it was Woody at the other end of the line. Jack seemed to forget that it was his turn to talk until Leary nudged him. He blurted, "How's it going, man?"

"How's it going? Where is he, you jackass?"

Leary made a twirling motion with his hand. *Spin this out. Keep him on the line.*

"Uh, where is who?"

A sigh crackled through the speaker. "If you're trying to hold me over a barrel, don't. I am not in the mood." The distortion in his voice seemed to increase as his anger simmered.

"Hard day?" Jack seemed to be warming up to his role. He glanced around at his audience, smiling. No one smiled back. Jessie willed him to take this seriously, to not fuck this up. *Do something right, you asshole.*

"I'm only asking one more time," the voice said. "Where is Ramsey?"

Jack looked to Leary, who nodded. "Where do you think? He's staying with me until he finds his own place."

"He's there now?" The caller's voice seemed to perk up.

"Eating me out of house and home." Jack laughed. Jessie had heard him laugh hundreds of times—and this was the first time it had ever sounded forced. "The man's ravenous. All that prison food, I guess. He hasn't tasted real food in—"

"Put him on."

Jack stepped backward, made room for Ramsey in front of the desk. Ramsey had abandoned the blank expression he'd worn in court, finally allowing his emotion to show. Anger. A wave of uneasiness rolled through Jessie as she watched him lean toward the phone.

"You want your fucking briefcase, Woody?"

"You got your freedom, didn't you?"

One of the techs pulled Leary aside. Jessie watched them whisper to each other near Jack's bookshelves. When they returned, Leary said into her ear, "We have a fix on his cell phone's GPS and two cars en route."

"Where?"

"Center City, moving down Chestnut. If we're lucky, we'll be able to grab him now."

Jessie shook her head and lowered her voice to a whisper. "Luck hasn't exactly been on our side."

Leary nodded grimly, his eyes glued to Ramsey. "Keep him occupied," he said quietly.

"If you want the briefcase, come here and pick it up," Ramsey said.

"You're going to drop it off."

Ramsey was either a much better actor than Jack, or he really had no fear of the man on the phone. "I'm not a delivery boy. I just got out of prison—"

"Because of me!"

"—and there are a few things I've been waiting to do." Leary signaled to him again—*keep it going*—but the gesture was unnecessary. Ramsey seemed to know exactly how to antagonize the man on the other end of the line. "I've got a whole list of things I've been missing. A good meal. A movie on a nice, big screen, maybe 3D. A drink at a bar. A girl."

"You listen to me, you murdering, rapist son of a bitch—" Now there was real rage in Woody's voice. "I don't want to hear about all the shit you're going to do. You deserve to be dead, and the only reason I can live with myself for helping you is that I know—*I know*—that eventually you'll burn in Hell."

"Then I guess you'll be there to keep me company."

"What's that supposed to mean?"

Leary shook his head and sliced his hand in front of his throat. Jessie felt his panic. The last thing they needed was for Ramsey to tip his hand. He was not supposed to know about the murders his benefactor had committed.

"Isn't that where assholes go?" Ramsey said, recovering.

"You're calling *me* an asshole? That's a laugh. You know how many years I spent keeping animals like you in line? You're going to bring the briefcase to me."

"Where?"

"There's a house—"

"Streets change. I've been in prison, remember? I may not know my way around as well as I used to."

"You won't have a problem finding *this* house."

Ramsey glanced at Leary. Apparently he'd run out of ways to stall. "What's the address?"

"The Dillard house. I'm sure you remember it. Leave the briefcase in the master bedroom. You know, the room where you raped and stabbed a happy family to death? Leave it on the floor. Do that, and we'll go our separate ways. Think you can manage, killer?"

"Won't the house be locked?"

BURNOUT

"You're a fireman. Knock the fucking door down."

Leary was gesturing again, more fiercely now. *Keep him on the phone.* Already Jessie could hear, faintly, the sound of police sirens coming through the speaker, from Woody's end of the line.

"When?" Ramsey said.

"Now. Tonight, you—" Woody must have heard the sirens, too. The call ended abruptly.

Leary jerked toward the tech, but the man, holding a cell phone to his ear, was already shaking his head. "Our guys just found his phone discarded on the street. He's gone."

Ramsey looked at Leary. "Now what?"

"Now we set the trap." Leary turned to Jack. "Can you spare a briefcase?"

"Uh, yeah. Sure."

"Hold on." Ramsey held up his hands. "What if Woody knows what Dillard's briefcase looks like? He'll know right away it's a trap."

Leary didn't look concerned. "By the time he gets close enough to see the one you're carrying, it will be too late. We'll have him."

"Sounds like a pretty big risk," Ramsey grumbled.

Leary nodded. "It's one you're going to have to take."

62.

They drove to the Andorra section of Roxborough, in the northwest part of the city, where the Dillard house waited. Leary rolled past the house without stopping, but took a good look. While warm light glowed in the windows of its neighbors, the windows of the Dillard house were dark. No TV screen flickered in the living room downstairs. No reading lamps glowed in the upstairs bedrooms. Even the roof, blanketed in a thicker layer of snow than its neighbors because the house was infrequently heated, had become a reminder of the tragedy that had occurred here.

In the passenger seat, Jessie said, "No footprints on the lawn."

Leary had noticed that, too. But it was unrealistic to think that Woody had not been here. "He must have approached the house through the backyard." At the end of the street, he turned right.

"Where are we going?"

"We're setting up a command center in a house on a street that runs parallel to this one. I'm told that from the second-story window, we have an unobstructed view of the back of the Dillard house, and a few sightlines to this street."

BURNOUT

He glanced at her. The look on her face—one of trust—brought a smile to his face. It had been a long time since either one of them had been anything but awkward in the other's presence. Tonight he felt comfortable, and he suspected that she did, too. He did not want to think about it too much—over-thinking was one of his problems—but maybe one positive result of this Ramsey debacle was the reopening of communications between them. Maybe she was even ready to give him a shot at being more than a colleague or a one-night-stand.

"What are you smiling about?" she said.

"Oh." He looked away from her, focused on the road. "Nothing."

She turned in her seat, looked through the rear windshield as if she would be able to see the car that had been following them, a yellow taxi. But the taxi had stopped in front of the Dillard house.

"I hope he doesn't get himself killed."

Leary looked at her. "Ramsey? Yesterday, you practically wanted to kill him yourself."

"I'm still pretty sure he's guilty. But...."

"But you're not sure beyond a reasonable doubt?"

"I've been thinking about Kate Moscow's testimony. During the trial, I didn't really consider any of her theories. They were just verbal artillery, you know? Testimony that I needed to undermine. But now that the trial's over—" She sighed. "Kristen failed to identify Ramsey's photo in the photo array. It wasn't until she saw him in the lineup, *after* being exposed to the photos, that she recognized him. Isn't it possible, what Moscow said about unconscious transference?"

Leary shrugged. He had read some of Katherine Moscow's journal articles, and they were pretty convincing on paper, but he'd been a detective too long to dismiss the value of eyewitness evidence. Still, he planned to bring Moscow's research to the attention of the department brass, so they could use her research to improve the identification process. If nothing else, it would have the benefit of cutting off another defense attorney tactic.

"We can't worry about any of that now," he said. "Whether Ramsey's guilty or not, he was acquitted, right? He's innocent in the eyes of the law. His case is over. Woody Rushford, on the other hand, has murdered three people that we know of—Rachel Pugh, Elliot Williams, and Amber Gibbons. As far as I'm concerned, nailing Woody is our sole priority now."

He turned the unmarked car into a driveway and cut the power. The blue house that loomed above them looked like a typical suburban family home. And it was, its occupants temporarily relocated to a hotel room on the government's dollar.

The garage door opened and Leary drove inside. Even though it was unmarked, and even though they were a block away from the Dillard house, he did not want to leave the car in plain sight. He was taking no chances tonight.

The door connecting the garage to the house opened and Nick Jameson walked across the oil-stained floor to the car. Leary lowered his window.

"Ramsey's in, and waiting," Jameson said. "Hurry up."

The window that afforded the best view of the Dillard house was located in a child's room midway down the upstairs hall. Leary stepped carefully around toys strewn across the carpet. They were mostly action figures. Monsters, soldiers, athletes, policemen. He wondered if the kid's imagination had ever produced a scene as tense as the one taking place now.

The presence of his fellow homicide detectives Jameson and Scerbak was reassuring. Scerbak handed him a pair of binoculars. Leary fumbled with them for a moment, and then the branches of a tree, heavy with snow, filled his vision. He adjusted downward and saw, in the space between the Dillard house and its neighbor, the plowed blacktop of Overlook Lane. Turning carefully to the right, he centered the taxi in his view. Smoke chugged from the exhaust pipe as the car idled.

Leary touched his index finger to a wheel on the binoculars, zooming in until he could see two shapes inside the car. Jack Ackerman, leaning forward in the backseat, was making conversation with the driver. Leary would owe Earl—who was a cop, not a cabbie—at least one beer for trapping him in a car with that bozo.

"Do you see him?" Jessie's voice came to him from his right.

"Not yet."

He zoomed out and scanned the binoculars sideways until the back of the Dillard house filled his view. Snow blanketed the back yard. It also covered the planks of the wooden deck built against the back wall of the house. There was a gas grill at one end of the deck, and Leary felt the hairs on the back of his neck rise as his imagination conjured a summer barbecue—Bob Dillard flipping burgers in the sun while his family drank iced tea.

All of the downstairs windows remained dark, but upstairs, a beam of light flicked from the windows of the master bedroom. As instructed, Ramsey had raised the blinds and motioned with a flashlight, signaling that he had placed the briefcase on the floor. Then the light went out.

"He left the briefcase. Should be walking downstairs now."

"May I?" His view jumped as Jessie's hand clasped the binoculars. He pulled his face from the lenses and watched her raise them to her eyes. "I don't see— Wait. Ramsey's out front. Walking to the taxi now."

Leary looked at her, then out the window. Without the binoculars, all he could see was darkness punctuated by moonlit snow.

"He's in the cab," she said.

Tension drained from Leary's shoulders. They had executed the first stage of the plan without complication. The trap had been set. He hoped the next stage—springing it—would go as smoothly.

He wondered how long they would have to wait.

"Leary." Jessie's voice was strained, almost a whisper. "A man just walked up the steps to the deck. He's opening the back door."

63.

The yard was ice-cold after the warmth of the house. Leary's shoes crunched snow as he jogged into the neighboring property. His earpiece crackled with Scerbak's voice. "I think I just saw movement in the bedroom. Hard to tell with no light."

Leary leaned against the vinyl siding of the Dillard house. In the darkness, he could just make out Jameson bounding from the trees at the back of the yard, his heels kicking up puffs of snow as he ran toward the stairs leading to the deck.

The earpiece crackled again. "Nick just left his footprints all over the back lawn. If this guy looks out the window, you're busted."

"Fuck." Leary drew his 9-mm, flicked the safety and racked the slide.

Keeping his back to the wall, he sidled around the corner of the house. Light from the street-lamps reached him as he stepped out from the gloom, making him feel too exposed. He darted along the front. Ramsey had broken the deadbolt on the door.

"Going silent." He stepped through the doorway. Jameson should be entering through the back door around the same time, into the kitchen.

At the sound of a slamming door somewhere above him, Leary aimed his gun up the stairs. Then, silence.

He climbed, treading the steps carefully to minimize creaks. Below, he could hear Jameson sweeping the first-floor rooms. *Hurry.*

His heart raced. Sweat broke out on his palms, making the grip of the pistol feel clammy. He moderated his breathing as best he could, kept the gun extended in front of him.

He did not want to enter the master bedroom without backup. He peeked into the hallway. The door at the end of it was closed. No light showed through the crack at the bottom.

Shit. Now Woody had set a trap. If Leary burst through that door, he would be an easy target.

At a sound behind him, he swung the pistol around. Jameson, standing a foot away from him on the top step of the staircase, froze. Leary turned the gun back in the direction of the closed bedroom door.

Moving in a crouch, he hurried down the darkened hallway. His pulse thundered in his temples. Jameson followed, ready to provide cover. Leary put one hand on the doorknob and looked at him.

Jameson nodded.

Leary opened the door and darted inside, aiming at the shadows. "Don't move! Drop your—"

The moonlight that entered through the windows illuminated his surroundings enough to show him that he was yelling at an empty room.

His mouth felt dry.

He crossed quickly to the master bathroom, kicked the

thin door open. Empty.

Carefully, he checked the walk-in closet. Empty.

"What the fuck?" Jameson said from the hallway. The detective gestured with his gun at the briefcase in the middle of the room. Apparently it had not fooled Woody.

To hell with radio silence. Leary touched his earpiece. "Scerbak? Talk to me."

"I can't see shit."

"Well he's not in the bedroom anymore," Leary said.

Jameson snorted. "He got past us? Classic." He shook his head and leaned against the bedroom doorframe, reached into his jacket to holster his gun.

Leary said, "No, don't—"

A hatch opened in the hallway ceiling behind and above Jameson. A man dropped from the attic, and landed in a crouch. A gunshot cracked. The noise was stunning in the enclosed space, the flash of light blinding.

Jameson stumbled toward Leary and landed on his knees. He dropped his gun and clawed frantically at his back like a man with a hard-to-reach itch.

Leary rushed past him.

He heard the man's footsteps charge down the stairs. He started to follow. Another bang, a hundred times louder than the gunshot, sounded behind him. Heat seared his back and punched him off his feet.

He threw his arms out, tried to stop or at least slow his fall, but it was no use. He banged his way down the steps. Pain flared in his leg as it twisted, his chin as it collided with carpet-covered wood, his elbow as it struck the wall. All he could do was clutch the pistol in his right hand and hope it wouldn't go off in his face. His shoulder slammed hard against the marble floor and his body slid to a stop.

He rolled over. The front door was open, but seemed a million miles away. Wind whooshed past his face, the air being sucked upward. From his position on the floor, he could see smoke curling around the bend in the staircase above him. He smelled the noxious odor of synthetic fabrics burning.

A fire. Woody had set off some kind of bomb.

He tried to move. Pain coursed through him. Reaching for his earpiece, he realized it was no longer there.

"Nick!"

No response, just the sounds of the fire spreading—crackling, blowing, breaking its way across the upper level of the house.

He tried to raise himself to a sitting position, but pain flashed through his left leg, roiling his gut with nausea. He cried out. Reaching down, he carefully touched his leg. His fingers traced the jagged edges of a broken bone just beneath his skin. *Oh, no.*

A shadow fell over him, and with a struggle, he raised his gun. But it was only Jessie, standing in the doorway with Scerbak. Both of them were panting from their run from the other house.

He winced as Scerbak grabbed his shoulders and started to lift him. "No!" His leg screamed with pain. "My leg ... broken."

"We need to get out of here," Jessie said. The light of the spreading flames reflected from her skin.

"Where's Woody?" Leary said.

"The explosion threw us off," Scerbak said. His eyes

slipped away from Leary's. "I dropped the binoculars."

"Jesus, Scerbak."

"What about Jameson?" Jessie said, looking back at the staircase.

Leary shook his head. The air felt like it was full of tiny stinging insects. They bit at his eyebrows, raked his throat, burrowed into his lungs. "No way he survived that. Leave me here. You need to find Woody. He couldn't have gotten far."

Scerbak barked out a laugh. "Leave you here? Are you kidding? You'll be cooked alive."

Leary knew he was right. Black ribbons had already appeared in the wallpaper behind Scerbak. The stink of burning glue made it hard to breathe. Looking up, he saw flames writhing on the walls and dripping toward them like liquid. Black smoke already obscured the ceiling. He heard a groaning sound, coming from the house itself. Another groan followed, louder. "Run!"

But his warning came too late. The ceiling buckled, cracked and poured plaster, wood, and fire down on top of them.

64.

Several blocks away from the Dillard house, Earl, the cop who was their escort and pretend taxi driver, popped open the driver's side door. "I'm gonna have a smoke." He didn't wait for either of his passengers to comment before he closed the door behind him, leaving them alone in the car.

Jack turned to Ramsey, who was staring out the window. Judging by the distant expression on his face, it wasn't this snowy suburban street that was on his mind.

"Not exactly what you dreamed about in prison, huh?"

Ramsey looked at him. "What?"

"Your first night of freedom. Not what you expected, right?"

Ramsey snorted. Instead of relaxing, the grim clench of his jaw seemed only to tighten as the night dragged on. "I've wanted to ask you something, but I had to wait till the trial was over. In case someone was listening."

"Good thinking," Jack said. If only all of his clients had been as wary as Ramsey, he might have won even more trials. All of the phone lines in prisons were monitored, and all letters were read. A prisoner of the state had no privacy, even when meeting with his lawyer.

BURNOUT

"Why did you believe me?" Ramsey said. "No one else did. Why did you believe I was innocent?"

If only he had an impressive answer. If, like Sherlock Holmes, he had picked up on some detail overlooked by the police. But it wasn't anything as cool as that.

"A gut feeling, I guess." He shrugged. "I've met a lot of guilty people. Something inside me told me you weren't one of them. I can't really explain it any better than that."

Ramsey nodded slowly. His gaze became distant again. "A lot to risk on a gut feeling. Even that cop outside, Earl, thinks I'm guilty. Can't stand to be in the car with us."

"You want to get out of the car, stretch your legs?" Jack said. "Make him feel even more uncomfortable?" He looked out his window at the cop, and something else caught his eye. Beyond Earl, the sky looked strange, as if a bright light were shining beyond the roofs of the houses on this street. He turned to ask Ramsey if he saw it, when the sudden appearance of a face in the window of Ramsey's door made him jump. The door was yanked open.

"Get out of the cab."

Ramsey tried to turn, but stopped when a gun—a big revolver that looked like something out of the Wild West—pressed against his temple. Kristen Dillard leaned into the car.

"Out, you son of a bitch."

The sight of the revolver made sweat break out on Jack's face and hands. But Ramsey didn't look frightened. He slid out of the car. Kristen, keeping the gun trained on his head, stepped back. Her sneakers crunched in the brittle clumps of snow along the curb.

Jack scrambled out of the car after them.

"The hell do you think you're doing?" Earl stared at them over the roof of the taxi. His cigarette hung limp from the corner of his mouth. His right hand moved toward his waist, then hesitated. "Put that gun down, kid."

Kristen held the barrel against Ramsey's head. He didn't flinch or try to defend himself. Her gaze darted from Ramsey to Earl. "Get in your cab and drive away."

Jack weighed his options. Should he rush her, and try to wrestle the gun from her hand before she could pull the trigger? There was no way Earl could do it, with the taxi sitting between him and Kristen. The houses on this quiet street were dark. Five blocks away, Leary and the other cops were preoccupied with Woody. No one was going to appear to rescue them.

"Drive away!" Kristen said.

"I'm asking you nicely," Earl said. "You look like a nice kid. You don't really want to hurt anyone, do you? Put down the gun."

"Kristen, listen to the—" Earl's eyes snapped to Jack's and he shook his head. It took Jack a moment to realize Kristen did not know he was a cop. As far as Kristen knew, he was a harmless taxi driver. If only that harmless taxi driver could maneuver closer to her....

Jack said, "We haven't ... uh ... paid him yet."

Kristen's eyes found Jack's and he almost recoiled from her hateful stare.

"Pay him and tell him to drive away."

Jack reached slowly into his back pocket, withdrew his wallet. He held it up where Kristen could see it.

"How much do we owe you?"

BURNOUT

Earl didn't miss a beat. "Eleven ninety-five."

Kristen watched warily as Earl began to walk around the taxi.

"Where did you get that gun?" Jack said. Her gaze snapped back to him.

"From a friend," she said. "You meet a lot of interesting people in a mental hospital. You should know that."

Ramsey sniffed. "Do you smell something?"

"Shut up." Kristen jabbed the gun harder against his temple.

Earl cleared the side of the taxi. Something in his walk must have triggered an alarm, because the girl said, "Stop there."

Still too far away to rush her. Earl gave Jack a look, and he cursed silently. This was about to get messy.

"Kristen," Jack said, "please put the gun down while you still can."

"Or what?"

In a smooth, rapid motion, Earl drew his gun from its concealed holster. "Drop your weapon now!"

Kristen's eyes popped wide with surprise, but she kept the revolver against Ramsey's head. "Do you even know who this is? He killed my parents!" She looked from Earl to Ramsey and her face twisted. "Admit it. *Admit it!*"

Ramsey pressed his lips together.

She cocked the revolver.

"Drop the weapon *now!*" Earl said.

"There's a fire." Ramsey spoke as if oblivious to his peril. His nostrils twitched.

Kristen snarled at him, looked like she might actually pull the trigger, but before she could, Ramsey brought his elbow up and slammed it into her stomach, driving the wind out of her. Then his hand flew up, slapped the gun from her grasp. It landed in the snow with a soft *thump*.

Earl charged forward and kicked her gun further along the curb, then—keeping his own gun aimed at her—opened the passenger-side door and leaned into the taxi. He popped the glove compartment, and retrieved a pair of handcuffs.

"You're in a lot of trouble, girl."

Ramsey looked at Jack. "I need to go."

"What? Go where?"

He didn't answer. He ran.

"Christ Jesus." Earl fastened the handcuffs to Kristen's wrists. "Normally I would secure your hands behind your back, but given the circumstances"—he shot Jack a reproachful look—"I think cuffing you in the front will be good enough."

Kristen's eyes locked on Jack. "How can you live with yourself?"

"No matter what you think, Frank Ramsey is an innocent man. If you're lucky, he won't press charges against you. It would certainly be within his rights to—"

Earl turned on him. "Shut up or I'll cuff you, too."

"But—"

"I said shut up." He leaned into the car and withdrew a walkie-talkie. "Guess I can turn this on now, since I don't need to play taxi driver no more." Clicking a button, he said, "Earl here. No sense staying silent—"

The noise that burst from the walkie-talkie sounded like

BURNOUT

pure pandemonium.

Jack saw his own fear mirrored in Earl's face.

Something had gone wrong.

65.

Frank Ramsey realized, as he pounded over the snow-crusted street, that he had not run—really run—in over a year. He had learned to live in boxes. His cell, the exercise cage, the stall in which he learned to shower handcuffed. He had forgotten what a pleasure it was to stretch every muscle and *fly*. Even on this slushy surface. Legs pumping. Arms pistoning. Lungs burning as he sucked the frigid air down his throat.

Free.

How easy it would be to just keep running. Run until he reached the grid of the city and then disappear. No one could stop him. The jury had found him innocent. And the cops? The lawyers? He owed these people nothing—these people who had stomped his life to dust. Fuck them.

Midway through a quiet intersection, the blazing house appeared on his right.

He staggered to a halt, his breathing ragged. It was the Dillard house. He could see that plain enough. And he was running again—running up Overlook Lane, toward the house—even before he realized what he was doing.

The fire drew his eyes until he was running almost blindly, his field of vision narrowed to the flames poking through the windows, the smoke billowing into the night. The fire had begun upstairs—he could see that right away. It was a bad one, too. No carelessly forgotten cigarette had caused this one. Some sort of explosive.

Cops swarmed the lawn, but no firefighters had arrived yet. Ramsey grabbed the closest man. "Anyone inside?"

The man nodded, his face sweaty and frantic. "Three people in the foyer. One upstairs. The one upstairs is dead, we think, but—"

Ramsey pushed past him, and the familiar crush of heat engulfed him. It was only going to get worse when he went inside.

And he was going to go inside.

You don't owe them anything!

Someone had left the front door open. Before he reached it, he dropped to the ground and rolled. The snow soaked his hair, his khaki pants and wool coat, but he knew the sogginess would not last long.

The moment he charged inside, a mist surrounded him as his clothes steamed. He covered his face. Flames seared his knuckles and the backs of his hands. Through the spaces between his fingers he saw three people on the floor, half buried in rubble that had come down from the upper story.

One was a man he didn't recognize. His head was caved in, and blood and brains steamed on his corpse. The other two were still alive. Jessica Black and Mark Leary.

He stopped, but only for a second.

"Come on!" He grabbed the prosecutor's arm, but she resisted him.

"We're stuck, and Leary's leg is broken!"

Ramsey cursed. If he had his gear—fire retardant, a suit, an axe—digging them free would take only minutes. But with his bare hands?

Forget them.

How many nights had he fantasized about killing these two people? The man who had arrested him for a crime he didn't commit and the woman who had prosecuted him for it and recommended the death penalty.

Let them die.

He dropped to his knees. Thrust his hands into the pile of rubble.

"Can you get us out?" Jessie said. A coughing fit doubled her over.

He put a hand on her back, pushed her down. "Keep your face near the floor. More air."

The pile consisted mostly of plaster chunks from the ceiling, but a few wooden beams had fallen as well. These had landed on Black's legs. The jagged edges had jammed into her calves. Trying to yank her out would shred her legs to bloody ribbons. Next to her, Leary looked like he'd gone into shock. Ramsey had seen it before. Loss of fluids caused the blood pressure to drop, not enough blood reached the brain, and the victim fainted. Ramsey leaned over him, studied the blue tinge of his lips, the moist gleam of his skin. *Fuck.* "How long has he been out?"

"A couple minutes."

"Brace yourself. This is probably going to hurt." He pushed his hands into the pile again and gripped one of the larger beams. Sharp spears of broken wood popped free of the meat of Black's calf. She screamed. He grabbed another beam, pulling until his arms throbbed.

Outside, the wail of sirens approached.

"Thank God," she said.

He ignored her. The second beam had stabbed deeper into her leg. He grunted, pulled, but the other end of the beam had jammed into the pile of plaster and would not budge. He turned to that side of the pile, grabbed chunks of the crumbling white plaster, threw handfuls of it across the room. The beam slid half an inch out of her leg. Ramsey grabbed it and yanked it the rest of the way out. She screamed again.

He ran back to the door and sucked in a lungful of air. Two fire engines and a police car swerved to a stop in front of the house. He held up his arm, two fingers extended, until he'd caught their attention, then he returned to the lawyer and the cop on the floor.

He pulled Jessie Black free of the debris, the ability to lift an injured person returning to him as if he'd never had a break from his profession, and carried her.

"Frank Ramsey—is that you?" Bryan Tomko leaned over him, wiped his face with a wet cloth. "Holy shit."

Ramsey realized he was lying on his back on a gurney. "How've you been, Tomko?" His lips were cracked, his tongue blistered. Speaking was painful.

"What are you doing here?"

"You know ... fighting fires." He reached for Tomko's arm and leveraged himself off of the gurney. The Dillard house still smoldered, but it looked like the fire was defeated.

Tomko laughed, at first uneasily, then with what looked

like genuine happiness. He embraced Ramsey, squeezed him. "The Frank-Man's back!"

Ramsey coughed and patted his shoulder. The year the police had arrested Ramsey, Tomko had been a nervous rookie. The intervening time had made a man of him—his hug was as strong as a grizzly's. "Yeah, I'm back."

Tomko let him go, and turned to another firefighter coming around the front of one of the trucks. "Yo, Donny, you're never gonna believe who's here!"

Tomko took a step toward his friend, and Ramsey was able to see past him. His eyes met those of a man watching him from across the street.

Woody Butler. Or whatever the hell his real name was.

Then Woody turned, and lumbered into the gloom between the houses. Ramsey bolted after him.

66.

Woody watched the scene, trying to gauge the effect of the bomb he'd placed in the Dillard bedroom. Paramedics tended to two people on stretchers—he thought they were Jessica Black and Mark Leary, though he couldn't be sure—and loaded two more, their faces covered by sheets, into an ambulance. One of these was almost certainly the cop he'd shot in the back. Incapacitated in the bedroom, he would have taken the full force of the explosion. The other dead one was probably the cop who'd come running with Black when the shit hit the fan. They would all have died if not for Ramsey's intervention, which made no sense to Woody. In his experience, psychotic murderers rarely experienced the urge to risk their own lives to rescue their enemies.

The idea that Ramsey was not a killer, that he was actually innocent—that was ridiculous.

Then Ramsey spotted him.

Fuck.

Woody turned and ran in the opposite direction of the smoldering house, through a suburban yard, past a swing-set. He could hear Ramsey pursuing him, could hear the *clomps* of his shoes striking the snow. Woody plunged into the woods at the back of the yard. Branches raked at his arms and face. Roots rose from the snowy floor to trip him. His fingers itched to grab the revolver from his belt, pivot, and blow Ramsey's head off. But the man was too close, too big. What if Ramsey launched himself at him, drove Woody to the ground before he could get a shot off? He didn't dare stop running, even to look over his shoulder. He crashed through the last of the trees and emerged in someone's backyard.

Close behind him, he could hear Ramsey tearing his way through the trees like an enraged gorilla.

Then he heard other noises, ahead of him.

"We need to take her back to the hospital." A familiar male voice.

"What hospital?" Gruff, the voice of a corrections officer. Or a cop.

"Kristen's a patient at the Philadelphia Center for Inclusive Treatment."

"You mean the nuthouse?"

"I'm not going back there!" A girl's voice, shrill.

Woody threw his remaining energy into his legs. A car came into view—a yellow taxi—and standing beside it, three people. Jack Ackerman was looking at his watch, his expression as shifty as ever. Kristen Dillard, her hands handcuffed in front of her, scowled at the ground. And a man holding a gun watched both of them—definitely a cop.

They turned as one to stare at him. Woody did not waste time. Panting, he yanked his own gun from his belt, aimed it at the cop, and fired. The cop's head jerked backward and he dropped.

"Jesus!"

BURNOUT

Ackerman jumped in front of Kristen. As if Woody had any intention of shooting her. As far as he was concerned, she was the only innocent party in this fiasco.

Ackerman, on the other hand, was far from innocent. Rachel Pugh, Elliot Williams, Amber—Woody had killed all of them because of a promise made by Ackerman. And then Ackerman had turned around and set him up.

He raised the gun to fire.

The roar behind him made him lower the gun and run. Ramsey barreled toward him, hands bunched into fists. Woody barely had time to race past Ackerman, sliding in the snowy grass, and grab Kristen Dillard's arm. He shoved the barrel of his gun against her ear.

"Try that again and I'll kill this bitch!" Even as he spoke the words, he knew it wasn't a bluff. Innocent or not, he'd shoot her if that's what it took.

Ramsey skidded to a stop next to Ackerman. His face looked like it had been smeared with charcoal. The ends of his hairs were singed. His clothing was burned, slashed, ragged. His chest heaved with labored breathing.

"Let her go," Ramsey said.

Ackerman, looking from one man to the other, nodded. "Come on, Woody. She's been through enough."

Woody jabbed the gun harder into her ear. She let out a little whine. "Where is the fucking briefcase?"

"I don't know," Ramsey said. "I never did. I'm not the man who took it."

Standing here in the cold, a seventeen-year-old girl in one hand and a gun in the other, he knew Ramsey was telling the truth. But part of him wouldn't accept it—*couldn't accept it*—

because that meant that Bob Dillard's research was just as lost now as it had been two years ago. That meant that everything he had done for Michael, he had done for nothing.

"Let her go," Ramsey said.

Ackerman, no doubt thinking himself sly, was moving slowly closer to them. Woody would have laughed if he hadn't been so damn pissed off.

He took the gun from Kristen's ear and aimed it at the lawyer. "You think you can lie to me, manipulate me?" He put both hands on the gun and cocked the hammer. Ackerman's face paled to a shade slightly whiter than the snow.

Woody's feet slid out from under him. It was the girl—Kristen Dillard. The bitch shoved him. One of his hands released the gun to break his fall, and before he hit the ground she'd wrenched the revolver from his other hand. He squeezed his eyes closed, one cheek buried in the icy snow, and waited for her to pull the trigger.

He opened his eyes. Turned his head. She wasn't pointing the gun at him.

"Don't do it, Kristen." Ackerman looked like he wanted to move, but didn't dare.

The revolver trembled in her hands. The chain linking the handcuffs rattled between her wrists. She aimed the cocked revolver at Ramsey.

"You killed my mother."

"No." He had his hands in the air. "I didn't. I swear to God. I—"

"Shut up!"

Woody's finger touched something warm and slick in the

snow. He recoiled, then realized he had landed only about a foot from the body of the cop he'd shot. And that cop had been holding a gun.

"I don't know why you think I'm the man who did those awful things, but I'm not. I don't know how I can possibly prove it to you. It's the truth."

"Shut the fuck up!"

Woody spotted the gun near the hand of the dead cop. He moved his arm slowly, pushing his hand toward the gun. One finger, two touched the cold, textured grip. He tugged the gun into his grasp.

Ackerman saw him. "Look out!"

Woody brought his arm up, aimed at Ramsey—

He heard the blast of his own revolver and felt the bullet punch through his chest. The girl—the fucking girl had shot him. She stood above him, aiming his own gun at him. He could tell from her eyes—empty, like those of the more hardened inmates at Huntington—that she would not hesitate to shoot him again.

He dropped the cop's gun. Ackerman darted forward, grabbed it off the ground. At the same time, the look in the girl's eyes—the jailhouse look—drowned in a well of tears.

"It's okay, Kristen," the lawyer said. "Everything's going to be okay."

Shoot him, you fucking spineless bitch. Shoot them both!

She handed Ackerman the revolver without a word. Then she sank to her knees, crying. Ackerman crouched beside her, placed his hand on her shoulder.

Ramsey approached, shoes crunching through ice. Woody stared up at him and coughed.

Blood splashed the snow, steamed there. Ramsey leaned forward and stared at the dark patch. His expression was maddeningly blank, unreadable.

"What are you— What are you staring at, you son of a—" Woody coughed again. More blood blasted past his teeth into the snow. The black pool actually hissed as it melted the snow beneath it.

Then he understood. She'd punctured his lung. The goddamn weepy bitch had shot him in his chest and punctured one of his fucking lungs.

Ramsey was staring at a dead man.

67.

Jessie pulled a black suit from her closet and laid it across her bed. Her doctor had urged her to remain at home for a few weeks, to fully recover from the fire and the wounds in her calf, but Dr. Friedman would not be the first doctor whose advice she had chosen to disregard. She shook two Tylenol capsules from the container and downed them with a glass of water on her dresser, then began the process of redressing her wounds.

She started with her left arm, peeling the bandages off with a wince. Most of the blisters had opened, but her skin was still red and swollen. Second-degree burns, according to Dr. Friedman. She was lucky. She cleaned the area of the burn, then applied the antibiotic ointment he had prescribed. If Ramsey had not come when he had, she might have needed skin grafts. Or a tombstone.

Next she tended to the gashes in her leg. The skin was purple and swollen around the stitches. Every time she looked at it, she was reminded of Kristen Dillard's stab wounds. She supposed that was appropriate—as it turned out, none of them had escaped the Dillard attack unharmed.

The thought made her hurry. She patted a fresh bandage over the stitches. Her eyes glanced at the digital clock next to her bed. She did not want to rush, but the minutes were speeding by. Elliot's funeral would begin at 3:00. She was supposed to pick up Leary in twenty minutes.

One of her fingernails caught the ridge of a broken blister and she cried out. God, she was a mess.

But she was not going to miss the funeral.

Leary was ready and, thankfully, not in any more mood to talk than she was. They made it to the service just in time, even with Leary fumbling with a crutch.

She had to square her shoulders and force herself to enter the funeral home. Funerals had always been difficult for her. Leary saw her hesitate and gently took her hand—careful not to squeeze the red skin—and walked her inside.

Elliot had drawn a sizable crowd. His funeral would lack the grandeur of Jameson's and Scerbak's—a prosecutor killed in the line of duty did not receive the same honors as a cop; no bagpipes, no twenty-one gun salute, no folded American flag—but the assembled mourners included several faces Elliot would likely have been proud to see.

Leary nudged her. "Look out."

For a second she failed to recognize the man striding toward them. Without his black robe and frowning countenance, he looked like a different person. But it was Judge Martin Spatt, dressed in a plain black suit, a sad smile on his craggy face.

"I heard about the explosion. Are you two recovering well?"

Jessie shook his hand carefully. "My doctor says I should heal in another week or so, no permanent scarring."

Spatt nodded. "Good. Detective Leary." He shook

Leary's hand just as carefully. "Nice to see you out and about. Your leg is mending, I see."

Leary nodded. "How's the courtroom treating you?"

Spatt's brow furrowed. "Let's not speak of unpleasant things. We're here to remember Elliot Williams. You know," he leaned toward them, conspiratorially, "usually when a lawyer kicks off, I consider it one less cockroach in my kitchen. But Elliot's death saddens me. He had potential to be one of the good ones. And they are few, believe me."

Jessie suppressed the temptation to ask where on this scale he ranked her.

"I heard through the judicial grapevine that our friends Jack Ackerman and Gil Goldhammer are knee deep in ethical violations," Spatt continued, "and may face criminal charges. And they had such promising careers. Such a shame."

Jessie sensed a distinct absence of sympathy in the man's voice.

"You taking some time off, Detective?" Spatt said.

"A month, Your Honor."

"Good. Fewer arrests, fewer trials. We can all breathe easier. Well, I better move along. I'm expected to mingle, you know." He gave Jessie a wink. "See you in court, counselor."

As soon as Spatt's back disappeared into the crowd, Leary turned to Jessie and laughed. She laughed, too, and leaned against him.

That's when his phone began to vibrate.

They walked outside together. A cold wind whipped Jessie's hair, which had been unruly since the fire. Leary leaned on his crutch, put his phone to one ear and covered his other ear with his hand. "Mark Leary," he said. Jessie saw his eyes widen. "What?" he said. "When?" He listened for a moment. The seconds seemed to spin out in cruel slow motion as she waited to hear what had turned his face ashy pale. Finally, the call ended and he put away his phone.

She raised her eyebrows.

"That was the Camden County Police Department, in New Jersey. They claim they've arrested the Family Man. The real one this time."

68.

At a police station in Camden, New Jersey, a Camden homicide detective named John Costa led Leary to the evidence room. The man was a bear, at least six feet, six inches tall, but he seemed mellow and eager to help. More importantly, he was kind enough not to look impatient as Leary limped his slow way forward on his crutch, or to make any jokes about Camden succeeding where Philly had failed. At the desk, Leary scrawled his name, the date, and the time into the evidence log.

"What are you looking for, exactly?" Costa said. Leary did not answer his question. The truth was, he didn't know exactly what he was looking for. Wouldn't know even if he saw it.

The evidence clerk placed the briefcase on the counter in front of them.

"Oh, we opened that already," Costa said.

"I see that."

The broken locks reflected the overhead light in weird patterns where the metal twisted away from the side of the briefcase.

"We took photographs before we broke the locks," Costa

said. "You can look at those if you want."

Leary shook his head. He pulled a pair of latex gloves over his hands and popped the case open.

Leary removed two thick notebooks from the case. He opened the first, flipped through the pages. Bob Dillard's neat handwriting covered every one. Here and there, a computer printout had been pasted into the book—a graph, a spreadsheet. Leary did not bother trying to make sense of it. He placed the notebooks to one side.

Under the notebooks was a collection of glass tubes. Fluid swished inside them. Leary held one close to his face and read the label wrapped around its neck. Dillard must have used some sort of code—the sequence of letters and numbers seemed arbitrary.

The briefcase also contained a rubber-banded stack of Petri dishes. Leary removed the rubber band and examined each dish. Again, the labels told him nothing.

"You didn't send these to a lab for analysis?" Leary said.

"Why bother?" Costa said. "They're not relevant to the murders."

"They may be relevant to a case I was working in Philly."

"Yeah?" Costa looked interested. "We can release the briefcase into your custody. I'll get someone started on the paperwork."

"Thanks." Leary closed the briefcase, snapped the gloves off of his hands. He would learn more about the contents of Bob Dillard's briefcase after the lab in Philly analyzed them.

Maybe they revealed a breakthrough treatment for ALS.

Maybe they revealed *dick squat*.

For one person, the answer no longer mattered. Early

that morning, in the bedroom of his home in Chestnut Hill, Michael Rushford had quietly passed away.

"Anything else I can help you with?" Costa said.

Leary nodded. "There is one other thing."

69.

Jessie and Leary stood to either side of Kristen Dillard. They had agreed to remain quiet, give her time. She stared through the one-way glass into an interrogation room where a man named Todd Wilson sat in a battered metal chair. He resembled Frank Ramsey in general shape only—both were big, broad-shouldered men, with square jaws and black hair—but the resemblance ended there.

"That's not him," Kristen said.

Jessie's eyes shifted focus from Wilson to Kristen's reflection in the glass. "He was caught in the act, Kristen," she said. "The police pulled him off of a woman named Rebecca Purcell. He had a butcher knife in his hand."

"He was wearing a ski mask," Leary said. "Gloves, a watch like the one you described."

"When they searched his house, they found your father's briefcase, among other souvenirs."

Kristen shook her head. Tears spilled from her eyes and trailed down her cheeks. "That's not him. Ramsey set him up somehow."

Leary said, "One of the souvenirs found in his house was an antique compact mirror belonging to a woman named Irene

Barker. She and her family were murdered in their home during Ramsey's second trial, while he was in custody. Until now, the police assumed it was the work of a copycat."

"I don't care. That's not him."

Jessie tried to take her hand, but she yanked it away. She turned from the window, stalked out of the observation room and into the gloomy hallway. Leary sighed, looked at Jessie with a defeated expression.

She said, "I thought this would ... help her."

"I know. Come on. Let's take her back to the institution."

They found her on a bench in the hallway. She was bent over, her head in her hands. Watching her body shudder as she sobbed opened a pit in Jessie's stomach. She went to the bench, sat down beside her. "I'm sorry, Kristen. We shouldn't have brought you here."

"I'll give you some space," Leary said. "Need to use the bathroom anyway." Before she could stop him, he crutched his way down the hallway.

"Kristen?" Jessie found a clean tissue in her bag and tried to give it to her, but the girl would not take it.

"Come on, Wilson. Move it."

Her back stiffened. Two officers had taken Wilson from the interrogation room and were leading him down the hallway. In this direction. She looked at Kristen, looked down the hall to the cops.

There was no time to stop them. They marched Wilson right past the bench on which they sat. Kristen looked up as the man trundled by.

"That smell...."

Jessie looked at her, concerned. Wilson was past them now. The officers pushed him through a door at the end of the hall, and he was gone.

Kristen continued to sniff the air. "That ... oh God. That smell."

Fresh tears burst from her eyes.

Jessie sniffed the air. A faint trace of the man's odor lingered. She remembered, suddenly, her meeting with Monica Chan at NYU. Kate Moscow's former graduate student. The one conducting research on the relationship between scent and memory.

Did you know that odors are the strongest memory triggers experienced by humans?

"Oh God." Kristen repeated the phrase as she pressed her hands against her face. "Oh God. Oh God."

Jessie hesitated only for a moment, then pulled the girl to her. Kristen pushed her face into Jessie's shoulder. Warm tears dampened Jessie's blouse as the girl shuddered in her arms. Her keening sobs echoed down the hallway. Jessie held her shaking body and rubbed her back, the motion reminding her of the way her own mother used to soothe her, so many years ago. Her own tears filled her eyes, blurring the hallway.

"It's okay," Jessie said. "It's over now. It's finally over."

Thank You

Thank you for reading **Burnout**! I really appreciate it.

If you liked the book, please consider posting a review online and telling your friends. Books succeed or fail by word of mouth. Your help will make a difference.

Want more? I'm writing new Jessie Black Legal Thrillers as we speak, and they are coming soon! Be the first to know by signing up for my newsletter. You can do that at the following Web page: http://larryawinters.com/newsletter/ (newsletter subscribers also learn about special promotions and are eligible for free goodies, contests, and other cool stuff). I promise to never share your information or send you spam, and you can always unsubscribe.

Can't wait for more Jessie? Try my other book, **Hardcore**, a shocking mystery that explores the dark side of the multibillion-dollar porn industry. Critics love Hardcore, describing it as "a sexy, exciting mystery that's definitely worth a read" (kacunnin, Amazon Top 500 Reviewer), "a darn good well-written mystery" (Cheryl Stout, Amazon Top 1000

Reviewer), and a book with "everything that a reader could want - shady characters, murder, lies, sex and even some romance!" (L. Storey, StoreyBook Reviews). Here's the premise:

Ashley Hale was a rising star in the adult entertainment world before she abruptly moved to the other side of the country, leaving behind money, fame, and excitement for a nine-to-five bank job and a sensible apartment. But there was one tie to the industry she could not sever. Her sister, Tara, was also a porn star. Two years later, when Tara supposedly commits suicide, Ashley must return to the San Fernando Valley and the life she thought she'd left behind. Now she's not sure who she can trust—especially the handsome new video editor who seems intent on helping her. But she won't leave Los Angeles until she's proven Tara's death was a murder. And until she's faced the killer.

Pick up **Hardcore** at your bookseller of choice.

Want to talk? I respond to all reader e-mails. Drop me a line at larry@larryawinters.com.

About the Author

Larry A. Winters's stories feature a rogue's gallery of conniving lawyers, avenging porn stars, determined cops, undercover FBI agents, and vicious bad guys of all sorts. When not writing, he can be found living a life of excitement. Not really, but he does know a good time when he sees one: reading a book by the fireplace on a cold evening, catching a rare movie night with his wife (when a friend or family member can be coerced into babysitting duty), smart TV dramas (and dumb TV comedies), vacations (those that involve reading on the beach, a lot of eating, and not a lot else), cardio on an elliptical trainer (generally beginning upon his return from said vacations, and quickly tapering off), video games (even though he stinks at them), and stockpiling gadgets (with a particular weakness for tablets and ereaders). He also has a healthy obsession with Star Wars.

You can reach Larry at larry@larryawinters.com. He loves chatting with readers and responds to all e-mails. You can also follow Larry at his blog and website (www.larryawinters.com) and Twitter (@larryawinters).

The best way to stay current on Larry's books, learn about special promotions, and be eligible for free goodies, contests, and other cool stuff, is to sign up for Larry's newsletter. You can do that at the following Web page: http://larryawinters.com/newsletter/ (newsletter subscribers also learn about special promotions and are eligible for free goodies, contests, and other cool stuff). I promise to never share your information or send you spam, and you can always unsubscribe.

Made in the USA
Middletown, DE
30 October 2020